W9-AYZ-828

UNDER
A
GILDED
MOON

UNDER
A
GILDED
MOON

A NOVEL

JOY JORDAN-LAKE

LAKE UNION
PUBLISHING

Published by Lake Union Publishing, Seattle

www.apub.com

Amazon, the Amazon logo, and Lake Union Publishing are trademarks of Amazon.com, Inc., or its affiliates.

ISBN-13: 9781542019415 (hardcover)
ISBN-10: 1542019419 (hardcover)

ISBN-13: 9781542090032 (paperback)
ISBN-10: 1542090032 (paperback)

Cover design by Rex Bonomelli

Printed in the United States of America

First edition

This book is dedicated to my mother,
Diane Owen Jordan,
who loves people so well,
and to the memory of my grandmother,
Evelyn Hopson Wood Owen,
who passed on her love for the mountains and
art and words,
and to all my family and friends,
who teach me about kindness and courage,
and, finally, to everyone working to make our world
more compassionate, peaceful, and just.

Chapter 1

October 1895

Through clouds of steam that swirled around smokestacks and train tracks and billowing skirts, a whistle sounded from Grand Central Depot's farthest platform: time to face a past she thought she'd outsmarted, outrun, left safely behind. Top hats and bowlers and swooping feathers bobbed as other passengers hurried toward the platform—toward adventures and escapes and secret intrigues. But Kerry MacGregor stood still in this moment she'd dreaded.

For her, the whistle was the sound of a summons to a trip she'd give half of Manhattan not to make. Her head, her whole body throbbed with resentment.

"*There* you are," said a voice from behind. The older woman came to stand at Kerry's shoulder. "I hoped I might find you still here."

Kerry met Miss Hopson's gaze, her old teacher's eyes lined at the corners these days but still full of a steady strength, like an oak you could lean into when you couldn't walk another step. Kerry tried to muster up something to make them both laugh—her old way of handling crises. But her mind, swirling like the smoke, would not focus.

Outside, it was still the pitch black of predawn, but gas lanterns lit the depot's platforms in a hazy gold. She looked far down the parallel lines of steel, as if she could make out the silhouette of her future—about to be crushed on the tracks. "Thank you for coming."

"You know I understand, Kerry. Why you feel you've no choice but to go back. And—forgive me, but it has to be said—how much it could cost you."

They let the words hang between them a moment along with the steam and the train station scents of hot steel and wet concrete and roasted chestnuts. Kerry's stomach churned. She'd eaten almost nothing since the telegram came three days ago. That was part of the churning. But also, chestnuts smelled to her of troubles.

She'd gathered them in milk pails back home to help pay the bills. Even after two years away, she still felt bile rise in her throat when she caught the scent of them roasting. Taxes unpaid. Collectors at the cabin door. Her daddy cocking his Remington.

"Kerry, you'll recall that I know as few others do how far the tentacles of poverty reach. How that world can suck you back in."

Kerry heard the whish of releasing steam and wondered if she was also hearing her lungs giving up the last of their air.

"You've worked hard to get to this place. I so hate to see you . . ."

"Toss my life away?"

"You only have one, you know."

"Once I've squared things away back home, I could come back."

A pause. "We haven't much power over Columbia's board, not with so many other worthy young women clamoring for scholarship places at Barnard, but you know we would try. So long, that is, as you manage to keep yourself clear of . . . entanglements."

"Entanglements." Kerry did not need to ask for specifics. Miss Hopson had been there years ago in the one-room schoolhouse as those attachments had first taken root.

The older woman sighed. "My dear, I applaud your sense of duty. Particularly in the face of, let us say, a less than easy upbringing."

Kerry flinched. It was true—and a gross understatement. But painful to hear it spoken out loud.

At the far end of the depot came the clanging of a streetcar's bell and the strains of a violinist playing for passersby's change. Closing her eyes, Kerry could hear her little sister on the cowbell, her brother with the banjo made from a gourd and squirrel hide, and their father pulling a slow, mournful ballad from his fiddle.

Their father. Who could make you weep with the raw beauty, the open-wound pain of one of his songs. When he was sober.

Their father, who, when he was not, could make you weep for any number of other reasons.

Miss Hopson sorted her words with care. "I worry for your future back"—she paused, as if the North Carolina mountains were too remote from New York to be real—"there."

A conductor on the far platform checked his pocket watch against the depot's clock on its elaborate iron stand near Kerry. She tried not to feel it ticking against the inside of her skull.

"I understand," Kerry said. And she did.

Which was why she'd not already clambered onto the train and settled herself by a window so she could watch the land hurtle by in cities and flat, unremarkable farms before at last beginning to buck and plunge and turn misty blue. She understood this could be a decision that sent her life in a U-turn off the tracks. A complete derailing.

Miss Hopson cleared her throat. "In the interest of time, allow me to be blunt: How will you handle Dearg Tate?"

"With any luck, he'll be married by now with triplets." Kerry smiled. "Which would solve any *mis*handling I'd be likely to manage."

"In other words, you're as worried about it as you ought to be. You know, Kerry, I may look to outsiders now like a spinster Barnard professor who knows little of these things, but I can assure you, there are forces beyond the"—she rearranged her skirts—"fully rational that can knock a woman completely off course."

A few yards away, a gentleman in a top hat halted near the depot clock. A youngish face, but with shadows of something flitting over it, like a gathering storm. Anger, perhaps. Or sadness. Kerry followed the man's gaze toward a child limping past the clock—and crying. The gentleman in the top hat stepped forward as if he would reach for the child. But then another man was running, sliding to his knees. The kneeling man threw his arms around the boy.

"Nico!" The second man, a tweed cap flopped at an angle on his black hair, held the boy close. "*Ero cosi spaventato!* You cannot wander away when I turn the back for even the moment." He held the boy's face in his hands. "I won't let them take you from me again."

Kerry crossed her arms to close up the hole, the ache she felt in the absence of her own brother and sister. Which gave the telegram its pull.

"What on earth," she murmured to her old teacher, "have those two been through?"

A movement from the gentleman near the clock made her glance back at him. He was bringing two fingers from his right hand to his left lapel—like some sort of reflex or sign. Holding them there.

Turning, he met her gaze. A shock of dark-blond hair dropped across his forehead. Stiffening, he dropped his hand from the lapel.

A contradiction, she thought: the elegance of the top hat, the arrogant set of the shoulders—against the something else in his face she couldn't quite read.

"So, then," Miss Hopson was saying, "I gather your father's illness is serious."

"The fact that they sent a telegram . . . No one has cash money for that. And Western Union tends to frown on bleached apples as payment." Kerry held up the rectangular paper.

YOUR DADDY GONE SICK. ME & TWINS WISHING WE COULD CARRY YOU HOME.

"*Gone sick* means *dying*, since it's a cable they can't afford. The *me &* *twins* means my aunt Rema's counting on my missing my brother and sister something terrible fierce—which I do. Counting on that winning out over the terrible fierce that brought me up here. The *carry* isn't just slang for *bring* but also her saying I might need help going back to what, whether I like it or not, still is *home*."

Miss Hopson nodded. "When you told me of the cable, I knew you'd feel you should go. So I took the liberty of trying to help—by sending a telegram of my own. A surprise, which I hope will be a welcome one, is waiting for you in the foremost car."

Kerry looked to the farthest platform and back. "Whatever you've done, thank you."

The train's whistle sounded again. Another release of steam. Kerry felt her lungs contract.

"All aboard!" the conductor bellowed. "Royal Blue express to Washington!"

Kerry lifted a small leather-bound trunk, borrowed from Miss Hopson, and her own brown bag. Together, not speaking, they moved toward the train. Then suddenly, eyes wide, Miss Hopson gestured toward the end of the train. "My heavens . . . look."

"They've hitched on a private car?"

"Not just anyone's car. That's the Swannanoa. George Vanderbilt's, hooked to your train."

Kerry tipped her head. "I'd say it's more his train than mine. Since his family probably owns the tracks."

A woman in mauve was waddling past, her several chins layered above a lace collar. "They say it's elegant as a Fifth Avenue parlor, his train car is. But I don't see Mr. Vanderbilt himself, do you?"

Miss Hopson flushed. "I'm not certain I'd know his face."

"Oh, but from the society pages, surely! They say he's built himself a new estate somewhere down . . . there." She waddled on.

Kerry shot a wink at her old teacher. "'Somewhere down there.' Because like every New Yorker, her geography of the South includes some cotton fields, some tobacco farms, and one town that perhaps isn't quite a city, Atlanta."

Ladies in tight-waisted tan or gray or dark-blue traveling jackets and matching skirts swept toward Kerry's train, their sleeves tight on the forearms but puffed so voluminously from the elbows to the shoulders that they walked well apart. The feathers and flowers of their millinery bobbed as they chatted. In the next wave of passengers boarding, two gentlemen in top hats meandered past.

"There," said the taller of the two, shoving a shock of dark-blond hair back from his eyes—the gentleman from earlier. "That's George's car at the end."

The other dusted a coat sleeve. "He couldn't have picked a more unlikely spot for this latest venture. I understand the mountain people in the environs are rather a challenge. Ferociously independent, for one thing."

"So I've read." A stride in front of Kerry, the taller one turned back to check the time on the depot clock. "And tragically illiterate."

Kerry fisted her right hand on her smaller brown bag, a flour sack she'd dyed with pokeweed and chicory. The effect was supposed to blend in with the rest of the traveling world's leather, though the taller gentleman glancing down at it now cocked his head at it as if it were a museum piece from a primitive culture.

Heat flooded her face, her neck, her chest. She returned the man's stare. "Ferocious," she told him, "would not be the half of it."

He blinked, startled.

But the train whistled again, and this time the sound spun Kerry back to her old teacher for a hurried hug. Somehow the gentlemen's words, superior and detached, had launched her past a final gut-wrenching goodbye and straight, square-shouldered into what had to be done.

Miss Hopson placed a gloved hand on her arm. "Godspeed. And one final word." Her eyes sparkled above her lined cheeks. "Just remember, 'Have more than thou showest.'"

"'Speak less than thou knowest.'" Kerry walked backward as she lifted the hand holding her sack.

"'Lend less than thou owest.'" Miss Hopson ended the volley as she always did, with a blown kiss.

"Wait." The waddling lady in mauve turned. "I know that quote. Is it the King James?"

But now Kerry was struggling to run with her flour sack luggage and the borrowed trunk toward a porter. She headed not toward the end of the train, where passengers in their feathered hats and satin lapels were boarding the ladies' cars and the Swannanoa, but toward the first car. Where the smoke and the sparks drifted in—where the immigrants and the less moneyed sat.

She'd made her choice.

Which would likely, she knew even now as she ran, whipsaw her future into something far from what she'd worked for. Far from what she'd dreamed.

But so be it.

She'd heed her old teacher's warning. She'd keep herself clear of entanglements, whatever power remained of the old currents and pull.

And she'd keep the resentment that burned in her bones toward her father in check. She'd have to—if she didn't want to explode.

The porter took her trunk with a small bow. The flour sack luggage she pulled back from his reach. "This I'll keep with me. But thank you. It has my"—she turned her head toward the blond gentleman, who'd paused a few feet away—"valuables."

His eyebrow arched. Pausing, then touching the brim of his hat, he strode with his companion toward the Swannanoa.

Ferocious, she wanted to shout after him. *And stubborn. Beyond anything you and Vanderbilt and your millionaire friends could imagine.*

7

Chapter 2

Trailing behind the lady in mauve, who hauled herself up with the help of a porter, Kerry mounted the steps. As she made her way down the aisle, her eyes were still adjusting to the train's blazing electric light, its royal-blue ceilings and mahogany walls and two rows of gleaming, front-facing wooden benches, and the cigar smoke that hazed around a man in a brown bowler. She had only an instant to brace for impact as two passengers toward the front of the car rose from their seats and threw themselves at her.

"Tully!" Kerry wrapped first her sister then her brother in a hug. "Jursey! How on earth?"

Squeezing them close, Kerry felt their hearts beating up against hers. Her own thudded louder, like it had only been just keeping time—a weak, grudging beat—these past two years so far away.

Tully flipped back a braid. "It was Miss Hopson did it, paid the tickets for us to come up. Said it'd do us a world of good getting to travel all snug together."

Jursey said nothing but shyly held on to Kerry's arm as if she might disappear again into the steam of the station.

Beaming, Rema looked up from her knitting. "Well now, here's a sight for sore eyes. My Lord, how we've missed you, sugar."

"And I've missed all of you." Kerry surprised herself with how true this felt. How prophetic her old schoolteacher had been in arranging the family's tickets—a gift of mooring lines to bring Kerry back home.

She lifted her head from the twins but kept an arm over both sets of shoulders even as the three of them huddled their way to the front of the car. "So, Aunt Rema." Here was a woman who'd shot her share of black bears and mountain lions and the leg of one tomcatting husband, but who appeared to be cowed by New York. "What do you think of the city?"

Rema shrugged, sparing only a glance out the window. "Bunch a buildings that outgrowed the sky."

Chuckling as she settled herself between Tully and Jursey on a bench toward the front, Kerry listened to both twins talking at once. News of the village schoolhouse—without a teacher again, four of them having left since Miss Hopson, who'd stayed there so long. Romeo, their daddy's bloodhound, kept everyone awake with his snoring. The air smelled of apples back home, and apples were the only thing still growing strong on the farm.

Nobody mentioned the reason for this whole journey: their daddy himself.

As the train clattered out of the station and began gaining speed, Rema's needles clacked in time with its crankshafts and wheels. Her dress, made of yellow homespun, hung crookedly from her shoulders, like from a broken clothes hanger. She'd insisted on taking the twins so Kerry could go up to Barnard. But maybe Kerry shouldn't have let her.

By Pennsylvania, the twins had sprawled over the bench and were sleeping, Tully's head and Jursey's feet in Kerry's lap. They were thirteen this fall and both growing lanky, their bodies often shifting at the same moment, as if nudged by the same dream. But their faces, Kerry noticed, lay serene—unusually so for both of them. As if now that their older sister was back with them, all was bound to be well.

Which Kerry knew could not be true.

Having left well before dawn, the Royal Blue, an express, reached speeds of ninety miles an hour and covered the distance to Washington in an impressive five hours. But after they changed there to the Southern

Railway, the stops were slowing their speed. The four of them settled back in for the rolling Virginia farmland. And now, after a longer stop and a train change in Salisbury, North Carolina, where George Vanderbilt's car was decoupled from their previous train and attached to the new one, the land was buckling still more from hills to low mountains.

Outside the train windows, open a crack, the earth smelled of rain and pine and decaying leaves. A flood of longing and then of dread washed over Kerry, currents of emotion so powerful and so contradictory that only a journey home could stir.

The locomotive's headlight cut through the mist, illuminating hillsides in patches of autumn red and yellow and green, like fold upon fold of bright quilts.

Kerry and the twins shared a bench again, this time at the back right of the first car. Rema knitted on the bench just ahead, alongside a young man with curly black hair beneath a yarmulke. He'd been in their car since the journey's first leg from New York, Kerry recalled.

Turning, he smiled. "On holiday?"

Kerry forced a smile back. "Headed back home." She smoothed Tully's hair and Jursey's trouser leg. "These are my sister and brother. And my aunt just beside you."

He extended his hand. "Aaron Berkowitz. On assignment."

Shaking his hand, Kerry took in his face, eager and wide-eyed, a small pad of paper and a fountain pen protruding from the outside pocket of his jacket, its tweed a bit frayed. "You're a journalist, then."

"Investigative reporter." He craned his neck back toward her. Waiting, it seemed.

"Let me guess. For the *Herald*. Or perhaps *Harper's*."

He turned around on his bench to face her more fully. "*The New York Times*."

"Ah. I am impressed. And this is your first big assignment?"

Blinking. "How did you know?"

She laughed. "You're bursting with it. Your eyes. Your whole face."

He deflated just slightly. "I promised myself I'd appear more jaded, like the veteran writers. But it's what I've wanted to do since college. Or before: since coming to this country as a kid. The power of a free press. Guarding the integrity of a democracy. You must think I'm a little ridiculous."

"On the contrary, I think everyone should love a job as you do. Where are you being sent?"

He hesitated. "I believe I can trust you, Miss . . ."

It was more forward than New York manners generally allowed, but they weren't in a drawing room, after all. And Kerry couldn't help but like him. "MacGregor."

"I'm being sent"—he glanced both ways—"to Asheville."

"Good heavens. Is there really anything glamorous enough—or diabolical enough—in Asheville for the *New York Times* to notice?"

"It's more the people drawn there, you might say. People with secrets they'd like to keep covered up."

"Don't we all have things we'd like to keep secret, Mr. Berkowitz?"

"Sure. But you and me, we have our embarrassments, our peccadilloes. The secrets I'm referring to cost a whole bunch of lives and mountains of money." He leaned toward her. "And now . . . now we've got new information to go on. And a surprise attack, so to speak. The key player who thinks he's gotten away with it all will be caught off guard. *Now* the truth will finally come out."

"That's quite dramatic. And how do you plan to pry out the truth?"

He patted his pad and pen. "I know how to ask questions. How to observe."

"Oh, Lord," came Rema's voice from next to the reporter. "*How to observe.* If that don't sound like our Kerry."

Kerry shook her head at her aunt. But Rema, her needles still clacking in time with the train, glanced back only once and pressed on.

"Lord, she's always noticed the teeny details. And witched out the story behind. Her *noticings*, we called 'em. Got herself a gift, that's what."

"Is that right?"

"*Not* a gift," Kerry said, more bluntly than she'd intended.

She knew what it was, this not-gift of hers: just a learned skill. Her fight to survive. To protect the twins. Only the art of paying attention, to glances and tones, to footsteps off rhythm.

The journalist nodded at her companionably. "What do you notice right now?"

"Only what everyone else would."

"Such as?"

Kerry's gaze wandered across the aisle to the bench that Tully's feet bumped up against. A dark-haired man—the one in the tweed cap who'd chased after the boy in the depot—was turned slightly away, his body hunched protectively over the child asleep at his left and a tube of rolled paper in the crook of his right arm. Evidently feeling her eyes on him, he glanced toward Kerry and the reporter, then quickly looked away. His left hand dropped to the boy's chest, as if just feeling the child breathe were a comfort.

"Like . . ." Kerry leaned forward and lowered her voice. "Why is the skin at the back of our fellow passenger's neck and on his upper lip so pale? Everywhere else, his skin is tanned—fairly dark. He must have cut his hair and shaved off a mustache recently. His suit looks hardly worn, yet its shoulder seams are about to split and the cuffs fall well above his wrists, as if he's wearing the clothes of a smaller, more sedentary man."

"Ah." The reporter raised an eyebrow. Then whipped out his pad with a playful flourish and whispered, "Now, Miss MacGregor, the question is *why*."

As if on cue, the man glanced again, wary, unsure, across the aisle.

Lifting her head groggily, Tully sat up. Followed her sister's glance. "Kerry, this here's our friend. Showed me and Jursey the prettiest sketch of Mr. Vanderbilt's house just before you boarded back in New York."

The man's face paled. He'd clearly not meant for others to know about this.

Kerry held out her hand—proper manners be hanged. "Kerry MacGregor."

He extended his and they shook. "Marco Bergamini," he said. His lips formed the sounds deliberately, taking great care with each syllable—an odd way to pronounce one's own name. "This"—he gestured toward a sleeping child of about eight—"is Carlo. My brother."

Again, the deliberate care with the name. And the boy's name was different from the one the man had called out in the depot.

Kerry cocked her head at the man and smiled. "New names for a new place?"

Aunt Rema turned her head slightly and rolled her eyes. "There's times when a gift can come off as just a big pain in the donkey's shank."

No, Kerry wanted to argue. *Never a gift.*

There'd been her poor momma, always in bed and often too sad to move from a string of babies born smaller than cornhusk dolls, and just as still. And her daddy: not a bad man when he was sober. But so very different when he was not.

Like the whiskey seeped into his brain and relit every glowing coal of betrayal—every collapse of grain prices, every humiliation when a merchant demanded cash instead of barter. All that scorched through his blood and settled, so far as Kerry could tell, in his right arm.

Kerry learned young to hear when her father's stride was hitching—a stumble or slide. The faintest blur of a word.

To know when to snatch up the twins and run.

So, no. Not a gift. Just a survival skill she'd never asked to learn.

13

The not–Marco Bergamini opened his mouth as if he'd defend himself—and his name, which she'd challenged. But then he touched the brim of his cap. "It is the pleasure."

"The pleasure's mine," Kerry returned as he swiveled away.

She leaned up close to her aunt's ear. "Rema, why would that man have a sketch of the Biltmore?"

"Mighta told you his ownself if you hadn't just shy of accused him of making up his own name." Rema dropped her yarn. "Near up to home, and I plum forgot what I brung."

She unwrapped a red cloth, the aroma of fried ham and cinnamon wafting throughout the coach. From her feet, she lifted a large Mason jar and unscrewed its metal lid.

"The sweet milk's not been cold for some time, but I don't reckon it's gone blinked, chilly as my feet tell me they been on this floor." She plunged a broad knife into a smaller jar filled with fried apples. After slipping a slice of salt pork and a knife blade of apples inside two biscuits, she handed one to each of the twins. Then one to the reporter and three to Kerry, who passed two to the not–Marco Bergamini and his brother, just rousing.

Rema nodded toward the child. "Poor little thing's got to have the mulligrubs by now, long as he's traveled."

"So hungry that he's despondent," Kerry translated. And the two Italians looked relieved.

"How very kind," said the reporter. But he offered his back.

Rema frowned. "Well, son, it was a hog who'd got some real age on him and not much lust left for the living, if that helps your squeamish."

Kerry opened her mouth to explain to her aunt, but the reporter gave Rema a smile that mollified her. "Thank you, madam, for wanting to share."

Kerry bit down on the apples and salt pork and the biscuit that melted away in her mouth. Then squeezed Rema's shoulder.

"Don't have none of these," Rema said, "up there in that briggity city."

The older of the Italians, having propped Carlo up to eat a biscuit, now bit into his own. "Oh," he said, more groan than word. *"Mio dio."*

Looking pleased, Rema picked up her knitting. "Well, *mio dio* yourself, hon."

Her needles clicked. Outside the colors were dimming to gray, but inside the car, hanging bulbs swung, yellow and warm. The train clacked and clattered, all of them in the first car lulled into silence. Fingers of late-afternoon sun reached through the windows as they hurtled along.

Kerry tried to make herself plan what she'd be needing to say. *How're you feeling today, Daddy?*

So far so good.

I hear you've quit drinking. All these years after driving Momma into her grave. You selfish bastard.

She sighed. Not good opening lines after two years away.

She'd like to see him grovel for mercy. Beg for forgiveness.

Which Johnny MacGregor, come hell or high water—and then a heap more of hell—would never do.

Kerry felt the rock and the rattle of the train beneath her, its comforting sway on the wide bends as they climbed higher into the Blue Ridge Mountains. To her left, the man with his little brother and the rolled paper tube clutched to his chest slumped lower into his seat. Head drooping, he fell asleep.

Out the window, blurred bands of green formed themselves into trees as the train began slowing. A passenger shambled into the aisle. Kerry felt her body relax for the first time since the cable arrived.

Then, suddenly, a screech of the train's brakes, its whistle blasting. A lurch.

To her left, the Italian cried out in his sleep and grabbed for his little brother.

"No!" He lurched to his feet. *"No!"*

15

Chapter 3

The shriek of a steam whistle cut through the dark. A ship, it must be. Just approaching the wharves.

Or . . . no. Not a ship this time.

He couldn't think. Couldn't make his mind clear. Sparks swirled, singeing his arms.

They had him trapped. Just a matter of moments now before their faces appeared, torchlit and raging.

"Nico," he murmured. "Stay close to me."

The very ground under him vibrated, another wave of men swelling behind the first, all of them livid.

Even through the cloud of his fear, he could smell the tar and pitch, the brine and sweat.

"Mafia rats," one of them sneered. *"Goddamn lying garlic eaters."*

"Who killa the chief," another mocked. *"Filthy dagos."*

Alone, he might have escaped. But he'd made a promise.

Behind the shipping crates where they crouched, he pulled his brother closer.

More shrieks, more quaking beneath him.

It all happened at once: the whistle, the rumblings. Grabbing for Nico, he leaped to his feet. His body ramming now into something ahead, he tumbled backward.

And jolted awake.

It was no longer dark but twilight, as if time had spun backward to wrest the sun up from where he'd watched it sink into the bay. There were no longer torches blazing. Only a weak wash of gold over some bright-colored trees and a glowing glass bulb swinging from the ceiling a few feet away.

He'd fallen back onto a bench. Not on a ship this time, but a train. Not crossing an ocean, but careening through mountains.

Half standing, his weight balanced on one leg, little Nico opened one eye from sleep. Seeing Sal there, he squeezed his eyes shut again and slumped back.

Nico was used to these outbursts.

But the same couldn't be said for these strangers.

Every passenger in the railcar had turned to stare—from beneath hat brims and behind black-and-white newsprint barricades. The slick, colored magazine pages of *Godey's Lady's Book* flickered as a heavyset woman in mauve stole frightened peeks around its sides.

He'd lit a fear in them, he knew. Not only with his lunge just now but also before that. Just by his presence, even when he said and did nothing at all.

Behind them, the door whacked open, and Sal jumped. But it was only the conductor stalking up the aisle.

"All off here for Old Fort! Black Mountain next stop!" He stopped to scrutinize Sal. "Tickets?"

The conductor had already checked everyone's ticket. Hesitating, Sal reached again for his. Arguing was not an option for people like Nico and him.

The conductor examined it—and him. "Hey. *Yous.* That little scene just now . . ."

"A dream only."

"Yeah, well, I don't allow no dreams that scare the holy crap out of my passengers. *Yous got that*, guinea?"

17

Yous. These Americans in their separate parts of their country; they seemed not to be using the same language.

Spinning on one heel, the conductor stomped toward the door. Behind it was the vestibule, the new accordion-sided connector between cars, which, for most passengers, probably beat being thrown off on a sharp curve. But for Sal it meant one fewer place to escape.

Like every time, his nightmare was slow to loosen its grip. He was still sweating, pulse racing, as if he and Nico had been running for their lives all over again.

Directly across the aisle from him sat the young woman Kerry, who'd challenged his name. Reason enough to speak little to her.

And there sat the reporter. He and Sal both being careful not to acknowledge each other. There'd be time for that later. If all went as planned.

His chest tightening with the old spasms of worry, Sal focused on the young woman, Kerry. Her face had beauty in it, but also—what was it?—*risentimento.*

She and her brother and sister all had hair the color of Palermo roofs, with their dark-red tile. And so did the graying older woman who stole looks at Nico and him over her knitting. Wiry hair prickling out from her bun, the elbows of her blouse worn to threads, and her toes poking through the ends of her shoes, she was giving Nico and him looks of pity. Well, fair enough.

"Aunt Rema," the boy Jursey said now, glancing toward Sal, "has that man yonder gone loose to the head?"

The old woman held a finger to her lips.

"All their kind is," a man in front of the old woman offered—loudly, as if addressing the whole car. Flicking his bowler back from his face, he snapped the pages of his *Baltimore Sun.* "Paper's full with them extorting from their own kind. Murder, too."

Murder.

Hundreds of miles from the wharves of New Orleans, yet the word had followed them here. Like it was scrawled in blood across Sal's face.

Maybe the man in the bowler had recognized him. Alongside pictures in the newspaper of a police chief, gunned down, who'd lived long enough to name his killers.

Glancing to the other side of the car and also forward, Sal could watch his fellow passengers in the windows' reflections now as twilight began to settle outside. Across the aisle, the girl Tully tugged at her braid, a shredded strip of burlap tied at its end.

The woman Rema addressed the boy. "Hush, Jursey. Ain't neighborly to point. And I'll thank you to recollect the Lord also loves them that's done lost their minds." She lowered her voice—though not enough that Sal couldn't still hear. "Just stay a piece clear of the poor soul, in case he pitches to muzzied again."

Sal pulled his cap's brim lower over his face.

More scenes like the one he'd just caused would alert anyone paying attention—not to mention hunting for him—that he and Nico were here. Here and alive, when they shouldn't have been either of those.

Winching his brother closer, Sal breathed in the mountain air, brisk and full of scents he couldn't name. A world apart from the sultry swelter of four years ago.

Although that other world could come raging back any moment. With one particular man bursting into the car, his fury having festered and swelled in four years.

Bastard got away with murder, he'd say. If he spoke before he shot.

Sal reached for the oilskin tube that poked out from the mouth of his rucksack. Slipping loose the twine that held it, he unrolled it onto his lap. Its edges had become a stained fringe. Creases cobwebbed the image. Still, after all these years and all these miles traveled, the ink lines of the sketch popped out nearly as clearly as when he'd seen it drawn in Florence—and added his own strokes.

Running a finger over the lines, Sal marveled: the soaring rooflines, the intricate detail. And there, the sketch's one word scrawled at the bottom: *Biltmore*.

Tully leaned close, peppermint on her breath, stick candy clutched in one fist. "Mighty pretty—even seeing it a second time." She gave a low whistle, then stopped. "Aunt Rema says I shouldn't ought to whistle like I was some sort of randy sailor. Only she won't tell what *randy'*d be."

The boy nodded. "It's awful nice, sure enough. Where'd you get it from, mister?"

"Firenze," Sal said. But maybe that was saying too much. "Much far away."

The girl whistled again while the boy offered a low "Ah."

Both nodded, as if the simple, literal truth somehow explained a story of years and oceans, of a millionaire and a peasant whose paths should never have crossed.

Hurriedly, Sal rolled the sketch up again.

Jursey, who had risen from his seat, tapped Sal on the shoulder. "You'uns sure did rile things up back yonder."

Sal glanced away. "Is nothing."

Tully tossed back her braid by its burlap-sack bow. "Had to be *something*, way you reared up like a horse with his hay on fire."

Far, she pronounced it. It took Sal a moment to sift out the sounds.

The girl leaned toward the boy. "Me 'n Jursey'd be twins, though we don't favor at all." The boy squeezed in closer. "That's our aunt Rema ahead with the knitting. And you met Kerry. She only looks to be not paying attention."

Kerry's eyes flicked to Sal, then back out the window.

Tully cocked her head. "You don't much favor the type that comes here from the outside for the breathing porches. They got a look to them, all gussied."

Jursey leaned in to stage whisper. "Rich as Jesus."

"Croesus," Rema corrected without looking up from her needles. "Jesus hadn't got one flea-bitten donkey to be calling his own, which is an especial hard thing if you're God."

Jursey said, conspiratorially, "You friendly up close with Mr. George Vanderbilt?"

Sal paused. "From a long time ago."

At the rear of the car, the vestibule suddenly flew open again, its door smacking the wainscoting. Heart slamming his ribs, Sal watched the reflection in the window.

But it was only two gentlemen in top hats who'd entered. Sal knew their kind from when he'd hauled luggage for tourists back in Italy: Baedeker-toting Brits and Americans, looking down on all they surveyed. These two must have strolled up from one of the luxury cars at the far end of the train—curiosity, maybe, to view the commoners' car, which was missing the plush, upholstered chairs and crystal chandeliers and filigreed mirrors of their own. He'd seen this before: rich people who liked to peek at the lower classes—like royalty surveying the peasants. As if the great width of the gap made them feel richer still.

Standing just feet away at the back, the gentlemen peered alternately at the passengers and at what was still visible through the dusk of the landscape. Berkowitz, Sal noticed, glanced behind at the two men, then stiffened in his seat. The color drained from his face.

The shorter one stroked a thick, brown mustache, waxed on its ends. "The cuisine in the dining car was surprisingly adequate, wouldn't you say, Cabot? Rather good oysters, really. Not a bad choice of pairing with the Château d'Yquem Sauternes—though I might have chosen a different white." He glanced toward the view. "Extraordinary."

The taller, clean-shaven one, Cabot, ducked his head to see out better, a shock of light hair flopping into one eye. "Yes. Extraordinarily beautiful."

The young woman Kerry was watching them in the reflection of her own window.

"Actually"—the shorter man stroked his mustache—"I meant how extraordinary that Vanderbilt would build this grand château of his down *here*."

The taller one, Cabot, kept his eyes on the landscape rushing past. "Then I wonder, Grant, what you're seeing."

"Isn't it obvious? Log cabins tucked into the land with a trickle of stream running past. Whole mountainsides timbered down to stumps. Ribs on four legs—one presumes they are cattle—roaming loose through the forests. Have these people not been apprised of the invention of fences?"

"Yet it's also breathtaking."

"Smitten by fog, are you? And by land that buckles up as if it's been left out too long in the rain?"

Both, Sal thought. *Both of these men are right.*

These mountains did look, in places, like they were sorrowing. Depleted. Like they were haunted, even. Yet also . . . *incredibilmente belle.*

"I will say this," Grant added, "my efforts with wildlife preservation might very well be needed here. No bison remain in this region, of course, but undoubtedly other species may be endangered."

As they rounded the next bend, up ahead to the right on a dirt road crossing the tracks, a farmer was hauling back on the reins of his buckboard. The ears of his mules flattened on their heads as they ignored the farmer's commands and plunged forward.

The train's whistle blasted again.

Sal held his breath.

Grant stepped toward the closest window. "One wonders what size impediment we might encounter without deterring our progress. A buck, certainly."

Sal pictured a buck rotating high above a smokestack, then falling, lifeless, back to earth.

Not but a few yards away from the tracks now, the mules, crazed by the train whistle, were bolting ahead. The passengers in the first car gripped their seats.

Grant's voice, unperturbed, came from behind. "I suspect we'd leave little but a flotsam of horseflesh and hickory boards and farmer."

Cabot's voice followed, louder and strained. "My *God*, Grant. Is this really nothing more than an intellectual question to you?"

But Grant, bending lower to watch, looked unfazed.

Standing, the farmer threw his whole weight against the reins. Just as the train thundered even with them, both mules reared back. The farmer collapsed onto the buckboard's floor.

Silence as the passengers in the first car let out their breath.

"Perhaps," Cabot said finally, "we should head back to the Swannanoa."

Grant lowered his voice a notch. "Perhaps also, we should speak less freely. There are those in this country these days who wish to harm its leaders, and any allusion to a Vanderbilt . . ."

Cabot's tone was dry. "An anarchist lurking behind every tree, is that it?"

With effort, Sal did not react.

"The threat is quite real," Grant insisted. "The bomb at Chicago's Haymarket. Or the Café Terminus in Paris. Anarchy. Damned foreigners. Scowl if you like. But the Vanderbilt men—with the exception of George—have cut more than their share of corporate throats. Biltmore will be hosting guests of influence and power . . ." Grant swept an arm, including Cabot and himself in those realms.

The bastard's caution about anarchists, Sal thought, *just got outweighed by his need to be recognized—even by strangers in the third-class railcar—for what he thinks is his importance.*

The other passengers had gone eerily quiet. Grant's eyes rested again on Sal. Then on Berkowitz.

23

At the rear of the car, the door flew open again. Instinctively, Sal slumped lower still in his seat. Reached for Nico. He had to protect Nico.

Above the passengers and their newspapers, a flat-topped circle of braided hat appeared. Sal released his breath. But kept his hand protectively on his brother's shoulder.

"This stop Biltmore Junction! Formerly known as"—smirking, the conductor glanced out at the village—"Best!"

Through the glow of the village's handful of gaslights on their stands and a few lanterns, Sal could make out mud like a rusty chain of linked brown lakes from the station's platform to a stand of scraggly pines. Swaddled in fog, the train station and its timbered gables were fuzzy, along with the hint of town beyond it—mostly a tumble of log cabins and farmhouses, with a few newer structures mostly obscured by the mist.

Looking at Sal, the woman Rema gathered her things and nodded toward the village as the train slowed. "There's folks hadn't much favored the new name, Biltmore Junction, that Mr. Vanderbilt give it. And that's puttin' it nice."

Tully MacGregor leaned across the aisle to him. "Mister, if it's Biltmore you're wanting, you'd best hop off here."

Sal thanked her, distractedly. In the reflection in the window, Grant was still staring alternately at Sal, then Berkowitz, then back at Sal. Grant smoothed the tips of his mustache. Then turned away toward his companion.

Berkowitz spun around in his seat toward Sal. *Watch out,* he mouthed, jerking his head toward the backs of the two gentlemen, *for that one.*

Sal gave a quick nod. He assumed he knew which of the two men Berkowitz meant, but would check later to be sure—when there was also time to ask why.

Kerry MacGregor may have caught their exchange, though she'd turned her face back toward the window. At the very least, she might've seen something pass between them—as if they weren't entirely strangers.

"Perhaps, Cabot," said Grant, "we should indeed return to the Swannanoa. I understand our party will soon include guests of the fairer sex who've already arrived."

In the reflection, Cabot appeared to be gazing out at the village—or possibly at the young woman Kerry. "Vanderbilt's niece, I believe," he said without enthusiasm. "A Miss Sloane."

"Yes, and a friend of hers, lately of New Orleans. A Miss Barthélemy."

Barthélemy.

A vise closed around Sal's chest. Even having known he'd hear the name if he came to North Carolina, it was a jolt.

Vaguely, he realized Berkowitz was scribbling something onto his pad.

Sal's head throbbed with the screech of the train's brakes and its whistle, which rolled out over the hollows and peaks.

But still louder was the name echoing now in his head after four years of hiding. Four years of hoping to outlive its reach.

Barthélemy.

Chapter 4

Lillian Barthélemy never allowed herself any regrets, so this was not one. Nor did she allow herself any doubts.

But the train's whistle came from not far away, and it chilled her blood. Because it meant the time had come.

A spasm gripped her middle—and it wasn't the grind of the corset stays or the too-tiny waist of the riding habit. Perhaps she'd acted a trifle rashly in what she'd arranged. But her family's name was at stake.

Shifting forward, she let out the reins. Despite the wet leaves underfoot, despite the darkening woods, she urged the horse to a gallop.

Her friend Emily was somewhere behind. But as her father liked to say, "Slowing down has never been in our Lilli's nature."

Was there a time, she wondered now, *that he'd said it proudly?*

"Lillian has far too much of you in her, Maurice," Lilli's mother always made clear. "Too much of the mad, headlong drive. It'll be the death of us all."

By the time Lilli and her mother had left for New York last summer, Maurice Barthélemy may also have seen too much of himself in his daughter.

"Consider the lilies, *ma chère*," he'd called after her.

One foot already on the ramp to the ship, she'd turned. Startled. *"Excusez-moi?"*

"The lilies. You know. Of the field. They neither sow nor do they reap. And you, daughter, needn't rush at life so."

It sounded ludicrously like something the priests of Our Lady of Guadalupe might drone into a homily. From Maurice Barthélemy, titan of the waterfront, though, it sounded more like a jest. A wink. A good cynical joke.

"Not how you built your empire, though, was it, *mon père?*" She'd patted her father's cheek. And noticed how gaunt he'd become.

"I worry that I have set an example for you of—"

She'd not let him finish. Because of course he'd set the example for her. Of course she'd become her father's child. Even when he disappointed and hurt her as he'd done just this week yet again, she understood him. Because she was like him.

Even now at a full gallop, her pulse did the opposite of what it should have done. Her heart rate decreased, settled to a slower thud—almost suspended in time.

Danger had always done that for her, calmed her in a strange way. Which she suspected might not be normal.

Men of her class were searching for a wife who was docile. Angelic. Prone to fainting. And capable of finding all the ecstasy she required in a Trollope novel.

Lilli, on the other hand, when trapped in a drawing room full of women, paced near the windows. When the conversations trenched, as they always did, on how much their children had grown—*Don't all children grow? What's noteworthy about that?*—she fashioned elaborate excuses to leave.

Society women tittered over the latest soirees—the cigarettes rolled from hundred-dollar bills and handed out as party favors. Or at Newport, a game of digging in sand for diamonds the hosts had strewn there for guests.

Lilli found the women unspeakable bores.

Gentlemen of her class were no better, none of them looking for a wife who craved speed and courted risk and preferred the outdoors to in. And none of them looking for a woman at the center of a storm of scandal.

She bent lower over her horse's neck, her cheek brushed by the flying mane. The thrill of an unknown road, the rhythm of the strides over the wet gold and burgundy leaves: *this* was what she needed to pound away the worry—the panic.

She and Emily had rented from the stables at Battery Park Inn, but this was no barn-sour nag. Over the stone bridge he charged now, left front leg on the lead, reaching farther each time.

Gripping the uppermost pommel on the sidesaddle's left with her right leg, she relaxed into the gallop. Around her, the ring of mountains rose above the forest and fields in a great blue bowl with fog rising like steam from its sides.

Slowing her mount at last, she scanned the roadside: birches and rhododendrons and ferns. Stone bridges and streams.

A few moments alone to think, to try and sort out her father's most recent behavior. She and Emily had traveled down here from New York a week early in order to meet him.

Asheville, the Land of the Sky, he'd cabled from New Orleans. All the rage, the papers say. Since you and your friend are going, your last letter says, what if I met you there? A spontaneous visit with my beloved daughter.

He hadn't cabled since she and her mother had moved to New York, and on this one, he'd not economized on his words—instead he let them flow as if he'd been in a rush or wanted her to be sure of his warmth, or both. In the past months, he'd dashed off the rare letter from time to time, but they were a businessman's notes, full of labor strike threats and import disputes. *Beloved daughter* was not his typical language. Warmth and spontaneity weren't really his style.

But she'd welcomed the chance to be with him, the elusive Napoleon of New Orleans whom she was like—and whom she barely knew. Lilli relished the four days she and her father and Emily had shared here. Until yesterday morning, when her father had been handed the telegram by the Battery Park Inn concierge.

His face had drained of all color. "Damn *New York Times*. Can't let a story die after all these years. *Bordel de merde.* Thought they'd outsmart me and send someone here, did they?"

"The timing," she said, as much to herself as to him, "couldn't be worse. If word got out there was any question at all—"

"Precisely, *ma chère. Ils sont cons*, the idiots. Will no one stop them from dogging my life?"

He'd packed his bags and left—for where, he'd not even said—within the hour. And forgotten to tell her goodbye.

From behind now came hoofbeats: Emily approaching at a sedate trot.

"I can tell, Lils, by the way you're sitting stock-still: you are amazed by the Approach Road. I'm so sorry your father couldn't stay to see it." She paused here, as if unsure whether to add how odd his sudden departure had been. But appearing to decide to steer clear of the subject, she only smiled. "George will be thrilled with your reaction."

"I imagine your uncle has more pressing concerns than the opinions of a lady he's never met."

"But wait till he meets you. *Then* we shall see how much he cares what you think of his project." Emily beamed at her friend. Which was her way: a childlike kind of warmth that, for all its naivete, was hard to dislike.

"Your uncle seems perfectly content as he is: traveling the world, collecting his art, reading his books, building this hidden estate . . ."

"He does, yes. But the right kind of woman can teach even a contented man just how miserable he really is."

Lilli laughed.

"Without her, I mean," Emily added.

"Let me make perfectly clear that I did not come south with you because I was desperately seeking a husband."

"No one, dear Lilli, suspects you of *desperately* seeking anything. You secure whatever you want with hardly seeming to try. Which reminds me to ask about what it was you were saying to that man this afternoon. By the station."

Lilli turned back to the Approach Road. "It's hard to imagine a structure at the end that would live up to the suspense of all these twists and turns."

Emily rearranged the drape of her riding skirt. "Change the subject if you like. I only hope that man from the station won't make a nuisance of himself. He looked to me like he might be the kind to . . . become too familiar."

Lilli felt her pulse drop again, and the words seemed to hang suspended there between them. No one was supposed to have seen her talking to the man at the train station. Lilli must have miscalculated how long it would take Emily to send her telegram. Perhaps Emily saw her approach the man. Who knew what she might have heard.

"He was only a local man. Asking for work. I sent him away, naturally."

She wheeled her horse as if she were admiring the mountains.

Approaching them at a canter was a broad-chested bay. The horse was a Hanoverian warmblood, Lillian guessed, his movements as elegant as they were powerful.

The rider's attire included high black boots that shone and a precisely tailored riding jacket with a stiffly starched winged collar and black cravat. Above that was skin as pale as she'd been expecting from a man known to be an inveterate bookworm. Still, his was a pleasant, intelligent face—a good deal better looking than the grainy pictures of him in the society pages.

His mouth, beneath a dark, neatly trimmed mustache, turned up only slightly. But his eyes, dark and soulful and creasing at the corners, were warm—even merry.

"Uncle George!" Emily flicked her crop to edge her horse close to his. "How wonderful to see you! And before you scold . . ." She held up her hand, palm flat. "I was just on the point of reminding Miss Barthélemy that I gave you my word we'd wait to see your new house together along with your other visitors tomorrow."

George Vanderbilt seemed in no hurry to scold, but Emily plunged on, defending herself. "I know your other guests are arriving soon—and, in fact, we considered waiting at the train station. But the daylight was nearly gone and the rain was approaching, and we were wanting to extend our ride. And there was your lovely winding drive into the estate. So we've only come to this point, no farther."

"We'll not count a view of the spires as breaking the promise." He gestured high to his left, where a break in the treetops showed a towering roof, two parallel spires catching the last of the waning light. And something—some creature—leered from one side farther down.

Lilli did not intend to gasp aloud. But a gargoyle dangling there in the distance, peeking through the forest of a Southern Appalachian valley, was not something she'd prepared for.

"Someday"—George Vanderbilt swiveled back in his saddle—"these trees will obscure all views of the house until the end of the third mile. But forgive me. I've not properly met our guest."

His tone was surprisingly tentative for a man with the world at his feet.

Unassuming. Even shy.

He had a slim frame, which underscored what the society columns said: that he was the kind of man, odd in their circles, who'd rather read than eat. Rather discuss philosophy late into the night with a single close friend than dine with a host of steel barons' daughters batting their eyelashes at him.

For a moment, his attention dropped from her. He seemed to be measuring the arch of the stone bridge at the next bend, the precise layering of greens and maroons and golds of the plantings.

In anyone else, Lilli might have thought this showed a man of too little action. But in George Vanderbilt, grandson of one of the most merciless titans of business ever to have drawn breath, she found it peculiarly appealing.

Squinting, she examined a spot on a ridge ahead where a spiral of smoke melted into the fog. In the air swirled the smell of fire and ash in the distance.

"One or two cabins remain," he offered, following her gaze. "Mountain families who've yet to sell to me—or my agent, McNamee."

"And in your experience, Mr. Vanderbilt, do people always eventually sell what they love for enough money?"

Lilli could see the horrified expression Emily turned on her. But it was too late for a softer rewording.

As if mesmerized by the spiraling smoke, he nodded. "Yes. They do." And he seemed almost sad with his own answer. "The last family here will, too, one day."

Then, as if suddenly remembering his manners, he jolted forward, extending his hand to Lilli. "Again, forgive me. George Vanderbilt."

Emily urged her horse forward.

"George, I'd like you to meet Miss Lillian Barthélemy, formerly of New Orleans. More recently of New York. I'm sorry to say her father, Maurice Barthélemy—I believe I wrote to tell you he was meeting us here—couldn't join us today after all since he was called away quite suddenly"—her eyes shot sympathetically to Lilli—"and unexpectedly on business. Lillian, may I introduce my uncle, Mr. George Washington Vanderbilt II. Formerly of New York. More recently—and I envy him this"—her gaze swung now toward the mountains—"more recently, of here."

George Vanderbilt took Lilli's hand gently, as if not quite sure what to do with it. And she felt that strange drop of her heart rate again.

"Miss Barthélemy, I'm honored to meet you. Your aunt, Mrs. Wharton, has been a dear friend for years. Our taste in books runs much the same."

"Ah, yes. Aunt Edith." Lilli invested the title with all the affection due it. "The Charge of the Light Brigade, my father calls her, in intimate family circles."

Vanderbilt smiled. "She is a woman who knows her own mind."

"I'm afraid he's accused me of being much like her."

Emily cut her eyes at Lilli. Gave a single shake of her head.

But their host's face did not change. "So much the better for you, then, Miss Barthélemy."

So, then: here was Mr. George Washington Vanderbilt II. Intellectual. Shy. And unafraid of strong women.

"Mr. Vanderbilt, may I compliment you on the gait and conformation of your horse? I'm partial to warmbloods myself."

"Ah." His eyes lit. "You have an interest in breeding, then?"

Emily erupted in giggles. Lilli might have laughed, too, if their host hadn't been so sweetly earnest. So apparently unaware what he'd asked.

"Oh, I think most of us do," Lilli returned. "Under the right circumstances."

Patting the neck of his warmblood, he turned in his saddle, and she saw she'd earned his approval. Not his affection, of course. Not yet. But his approval. And possibly interest. In so short a time.

Do ugly women, she wondered, *earn a man's trust so quickly?*

George Washington Vanderbilt II seemed likely to prove an enormously interesting challenge.

One well worth pursuing.

No more whistles echoed from the station back in the village. Which meant the train must have arrived. Must be sitting there, its steam releasing with a *shhhhh* into the fog, great clouds of white billowing over the platform and into the woods.

The billowing white and the dark that could cover what would happen now.

What didn't need to be seen.

Chapter 5

Kerry stared out at the billowing steam as if her future could be projected there, jerking and flashing onto the white, like moving kinetoscope pictures. All over the platform, ladies swished past in their tight satin waists and their swooping hats, gloved hands pointing out which leather-girded trunks were theirs. Gentlemen's black bowlers and top hats bobbed about in circles—*like a roiling kettle of pitch,* Kerry thought.

Jursey leaped around the foot of the train's stairs, his red froth of hair bouncing. "Them two top hatters back there," he announced, "were some kind of briggity proud. I liked them others, though." He looked from the reporter in one direction to both Bergaminis a few feet away.

Aaron Berkowitz offered his arm to Rema, just behind him. Leaning into him, she eased down to the platform. Even at her age, Aunt Rema was still as strong as an ox, Kerry knew—but she still liked the arm of a young man.

Tully was studying little Carlo Bergamini, dragging his left leg as he limped beside his brother. "How'd you go getting the gimpy leg?"

The child only turned large black eyes on her.

"A stumble," his brother said. "Down the stairs." He turned quickly away.

A lie, Kerry saw.

People only turn that swiftly away from their own words when it's a lie. As if they can't bear to face a mangled up truth of their own making.

"The porters," one passenger sniffed as she swept by, "certainly do take their time unloading here. Why, in Boston . . ."

Those who'd traveled in the ladies' car and the Swannanoa were overseeing the transfer of their luggage from railroad porters to stocky men calling out "Battery Park Inn!" and "Kenilworth!" Trunks swung up to balance on broad shoulders, then to the tops and backs of waiting carriages and hansom cabs. Horses nickered.

The Italian turned back to Rema. "If you would do the kindness, we ask only which is the way to the Biltmore."

"The nighway's what you'd be wanting, hon."

"Closest road," Kerry translated.

"Called the Approach Road—the give-out for why it got built. But it's a good three mile long. Near up to dark now and nobody living there yet, so you'd be making the trek for nary a thing."

He turned in the direction she'd pointed.

"But, sugar, if you's bound and determined to set eyes on Biltmore tonight, fog and all, then the big ole stone arch, that there's the gatehouse. Through it's the Approach Road, whole heap of showing-off switchbacks and winding around." She waved her arms in *S* patterns.

He gave a quick bow. Heaving his sack to one shoulder, he whipped the cap from his head and tossed it toward the twins. *"Per voi due."*

Jursey snared it, and the twins squealed in delight. Plucking it from her brother's grasp, Tully angled it on her head and tossed her braid back over her shoulder. Slumping, Jursey withdrew.

"Jesus," Rema told them, "would want y'all to share cheerful-like. And me, I'll snatch you bald-headed if you don't."

The not–Marco Bergamini lifted a hand to tip his cap—no longer there. Then he cupped his palm under Carlo's elbow and the two of them walked on.

Tully and Jursey went leapfrogging over steamer trunks and hatboxes. Kerry, with Rema at her elbow, began searching for the trunk she'd borrowed. Probably buried by now under mounds of luggage being loaded onto carriages bound for the area's largest inns.

Jostled from behind, Kerry stopped. The two gentlemen from the train were passing, the shorter one with the thick mustache, Grant, having turned to speak. He gave a deep bow, extending his top hat in a broad sweep. "Begging your pardon."

"It's quite all right. My siblings over"—she swallowed the *yonder*—"there. They've already stomped on half the crowd."

From a few yards away, the *Times* reporter was waving to her. "Hope to see you again while I'm here!"

"Good luck!" she called back. *With uncovering all those secrets,* she stopped herself from adding aloud.

He might be just the man for the job: the slight, unintimidating frame and the sweet, eager demeanor—and behind that, a hunter's nose for the story. If the meek could inherit the earth, maybe the kind could capture the truth.

The gentleman with the mustache stepped around in front of her now. "Do allow me to introduce myself. I am Madison Grant, of the New York Grants, and lately of Yale University. And this is John Quincy Cabot. Of Beacon Hill, Boston."

This was clearly meant to impress, which amused Kerry. Underneath the top hat, Grant's hair was thinning, but his face was unlined. Early thirties, perhaps.

The taller of the two, this John Cabot, the gentleman she'd seen at Grand Central Depot, lifted his own hat stiffly. He looked to be in his early twenties. Raking back the dark-blond shock of hair from his eyes, he nodded to her. "How do you do." His jaw squared.

He would've been strikingly handsome, Kerry thought, if his face hadn't been set so hard. Mean, almost. Like he was mountain stone and not a real man.

Cabot was already turning away. "Please excuse us. Grant, that must be Vanderbilt's man over there, talking with the fellow on the ancient horse."

Kerry followed his gaze. The *fellow on the ancient horse* referred to Robert Bratchett, who owned a farm high on a ridge up from the MacGregors. Or *had*, perhaps. Like everyone else, he might've sold out to Vanderbilt by now.

The skin of Bratchett's hands was nearly as dark as his bay horse. He gripped the reins in his one good arm, his maimed one hanging limp. His horse's hips jutted from behind the simple woven pad he sat on. The gelding *was* old, his front hooves pigeon-toed and gray brindling his coat.

Still, Kerry bristled for her neighbor at the word *ancient*. Especially from this outsider, Cabot, who'd know nothing of having no choice but to ride your one horse until he dropped, or you did—no choice but gratitude for every day you could both still walk to the field.

Kerry studied the rigidness of Cabot's profile. "So." She could hear chilliness steal into her tone. "You are guests of George Vanderbilt?"

John Cabot met her eye. "You know the gentleman, then?"

Surprise in his expression. As if she were clearly not the sort of person who would have crossed paths with the great George Washington Vanderbilt II.

She raised her chin. "We have had . . . dealings."

Rema let out a snort.

But Kerry only raised her chin a notch further. Stiffening, Cabot said nothing.

"In that case," Madison Grant offered, "I hope we shall see you again, Miss . . ."

"MacGregor." She dropped the hint of a curtsy and was turning away, but stopped.

John Cabot was scanning the village—what little of the farmhouses and privies and cabins could still be made out through the fog and the dim light. Now he was studying Rema, her back turned, and the twins—their old boots with broken squirrel-hide laces and holes at the toes—thudding over the station platform's pine boards as they chased each other around towers of trunks.

"On the outside of the station," Kerry offered pointedly, "you'll also want to take note of the tools hanging there—the axes, the rail dog, timber wedges, and hammers. For the men here who *repair* the railroad, not just *own* it."

His gaze swept to her. He must have heard the defiance in her tone. One of his eyebrows lifted. But still he said nothing.

Rema's hand dropped to her arm. "Back in my day," she murmured to her, "we gave the good looking-est of the roosters some smidginy benefit of the damn doubt."

But Kerry's hands had already gone to her hips. "We are *not* a National Geographic Society feature, you know."

He stared back at her.

"I've seen the magazine." She'd seen it a total of once was the truth, and that one was Miss Hopson's. "The photos of poor villagers somewhere in the world. Their quaint, primitive ways. To be gawked at by arrogant outsiders."

Ignoring her aunt's pats on her arm, Kerry stood her ground.

Locking eyes with her, John Cabot touched the brim of his top hat.

She must have looked like a crazy harridan to him. Red hair a mass of tangles from the wind through the train windows. Cheeks flushing— probably nearly matching her hair. She could be too impulsive, she knew, but she'd not allow him to scrutinize her and her people like dragonflies on a schoolboy's pin.

"I say." Madison Grant stepped forward. "Do let us assist you with your luggage, ladies."

With a glance of what looked like utter contempt at Grant, Cabot turned back to Kerry. "We'd be happy to help." He looked anything but.

And Kerry was in no mood to dispense mercy. "We are quite capable of taking care of ourselves, thank you."

Rema hoisted her own bag to her shoulder. "Lordy, that is real kind. But Kerry's trunk she borrowed hadn't yet got dug out from under that pile belonging to the breathing-porch folks, and this here's all I got. Kerry, she made it for me, but you can see for your ownselves you couldn't never tell it wasn't store-bought."

Kerry felt herself sinking into the silence, humiliating and deep, that followed. Grant managed something about the bag's loveliness.

But John Cabot kept his expression blank—except a flash of anger as it settled on Grant. Instead of praising the flour-sack bag, he merely turned away.

Giving a final bow, Grant followed. And perhaps he meant his voice to carry back to the women. "When Vanderbilt spoke of the beauty of these mountains, I see now he must also have meant its young ladies."

Rema nudged Kerry, which Kerry ignored. Even so, she couldn't miss Cabot's response.

"Is this a habit of yours, Mr. Grant, vying for the attention of the village milkmaid?"

Whipping around, Kerry faced the backs of the gentlemen walking away. *"Village milkmaid?"*

"You know, sugar, you may be just a tiny little bit on edge." Rema tapped on her arm to swing Kerry around. "Understandable, 'course, you having to face that daddy of you'rn. Wish I hadn't had to take the new job in the kitchens over to Biltm—" She caught Kerry's look. "Can't hardly say it around you, can I?"

Crossing her arms, Kerry made herself focus. "I'm sorry, Rema. Your new job. That's important. It's steady pay. I'm glad you took it. It's just not something I could ever do."

"I learned early in life, child: don't never say *never*."

"With all respect, *never's* exactly what I'm saying about Biltmore."

39

Rema drew the knot of her lips to one side. Then, evidently, passed the argument by. "Me taking the job means I'll be living there on the grounds."

Kerry tried not to feel the full weight of that all at once, her aunt's decision. A dying father. The growing twins. Saving the farm from being taken for unpaid taxes or gobbled up by George Vanderbilt. Now that they were here, the weight pressed heavier by the moment.

As more steamer trunks thudded to the top of hansom cabs and the inns' carriages, Kerry and Rema wound through what was left, looking for Kerry's luggage. At the office at the closer end of the station, the telegrapher, Farnsworth, glowered at the line that had formed at his window. "I don't have but the one messenger boy, and not but one set of hands."

Just behind him stood the person Kerry assumed to be that one "messenger boy." A man, stoical and silent, that Kerry had seen only fleetingly around town two years ago. The only man from China here—the only man from anywhere in Asia at all—Ling Yong had not been hard to spot the rare times he stepped out of his dry goods shop on Haywood Street. Now it appeared he'd taken on a second job—or perhaps the shop had gone under. Staring directly ahead, he merely listened as the telegrapher ticked off delivery instructions, then dismissed him.

Farnsworth yanked a cigarette from his vest pocket. As he tapped in the next customer's message, the cigarette dangled unlit from his mouth—like a promise to himself of a future smoke if he could keep his manners civil just a few moments more.

Ling Yong offered a piece of paper to Kerry. "A cable for you."

Then, placing a hand on the satchel as if to say he had others to deliver, he mounted his bicycle and rode into the mist.

Two telegrams in three days, after none my entire life. Kerry steadied herself as she tore it open.

It had been received and then typed a few hours ago—Farnsworth's initials, *EDF*, at the top—having come from a mill town at least a day's ride away.

REMA SAID YOU WAS COMING BACK. SORRY CAN'T BE AT STATION. STUCK IN WHITNEL. REAL GLAD YOU COME HOME. DEARG

For Dearg Tate, this was a torrent of words.

Real glad you come home. There was history behind that. And she would need to sort things out with him later. For now, her mind was already too full.

Several yards away, the two gentlemen in top hats were shaking hands with a man in a wool riding jacket and tall boots covered in leaves and muck.

"Gentlemen, I am Charles McNamee. Mr. Vanderbilt sends his welcome and hopes you will join him for a late dinner at the Battery Park Inn, where you'll be staying, along with two other guests—though we're delighted you can at least view Biltmore House in the final stages of construction. If you'll forgive me a moment, I need to conclude a business conversation." He gestured with his head toward Robert Bratchett.

John Cabot might have said something, but he was jostled from behind on the still-crowded platform. Aaron Berkowitz stood there, valise in one hand, his reporter's pad in the other.

The two men stared at each other as Kerry watched, riveted. Though about the same age, the two were a good head apart in height, and from their expressions, they must have recognized each other. Neither apologized for the jostling; neither greeted the other like an old friend. Both looked rattled—horrified, even—at having to face each other.

The reporter turned away first, clutching his valise closer to his side and striding off to the right.

Cabot watched him go.

"Kerry!" Jursey was calling from behind her. "Where's Tully gone to?"

Oddly, Tully had slipped out of sight. "She's probably helping look for my trunk—I described it to her. Come on, Jurs, we'll find her—and it—together."

Grant squinted into the dusk. "By the time we settle into the hotel, it'll be too dark to see George's estate today. What the devil is keeping McNamee?"

Grant strode ahead, enveloped by the mist at the far end of the station. Watching him, Cabot slipped toward its opposite end and disappeared.

With another release of steam and a long blast of its whistle, the train chugged back into motion. Its locomotive headlamp sent a javelin of light ahead into the churning white.

At the whistle, the voices on the platform fell quiet. Even Jursey, at a trot in his search for his twin sister, slid across the moss-slick boards to a halt.

But then, just as the whistle was fading to an echo, came a shout of surprise from out of the darkness at the station's far end.

Followed by a sharp cry of pain.

And then nothing at all.

Chapter 6

"Tully!" Kerry screamed, already running. *"Tully!"*

But only silence followed—too full of sounds cut short, and of the darkness that suddenly seemed to deepen around the tracks.

"Tully!"

Past huddles of skirts and luggage, Kerry bolted the length of the platform, its wet boards thundering under her. Fast as a colt, Jursey caught up, grabbed for her. As if whatever was waiting for them had to be faced holding hands.

At the far end of the station, Kerry could make out a circle of spectators looking down without speaking: the agent, McNamee, and other passengers. The scene was lit only by a scrim of moon, the one streetlamp on the opposite end of the platform, and the lantern swinging drunkenly now from the crook of the stationmaster's arm.

"What the hell hap—" Jackson, the stationmaster, began. But he never finished, the spill of his own light answering for him. He rasped a long breath.

A tremor shooting the length of her spine, Kerry leaped down off the platform's far end and burst into the center of the crowd's concentric circles. On the ground, sprawled facedown, lay a body, unmoving. And hunched beside it, a girl.

Tully.

With a cry, Kerry dropped down to the mud and threw both arms around her sister. "Are you all right?"

Tully swiped at her tears with the back of her hand. "Kerry, check. Please. Please say the man here's only knocked out terrible cold."

Jursey and Rema ran up close behind Kerry's back, Jursey taking his twin sister's hand.

John Cabot knelt beside Kerry. Together, they rolled the man on the ground to his back.

Kerry's hand went to her mouth. "Aaron Berkowitz! Oh dear God." Blood gushed from a wound over one eye.

She bent down, bringing her cheek beside the reporter's nose. "Breathing. Just barely."

Kerry jerked off her coat. With the flash of her right hand under her skirts, she whipped out the knife she kept always sheathed in one boot and slit the right shoulder seam of the coat. In her peripheral vision, she saw Cabot's eyes widen. Perhaps in Beacon Hill, Boston, ladies did not yank up their skirts for just-sharpened blades.

But there were days, Kerry knew, that called for keeping a knife in your boot.

Flipping the sleeve inside out, she wrapped the softer, cotton-lined side firmly around the wound. Felt for a pulse just below the reporter's jawline. "It's there. But shallow."

Still no movement.

Up on the platform, the woman in mauve from the train was swaying in place. The too-shiny silk of her dress glinted as her body teetered under the light.

McNamee knelt on the other side of the reporter and gently smacked Berkowitz's cheek. "You all right, mister?"

Footsteps, the suck and thump of boots on the leaves and mud, sounded in the dark. Faces of local villagers appeared from out of the mist like actors unsure if their roles were required on stage. All of them, staring down.

Madison Grant appeared from the shadows of the train station and came to stand beside Cabot.

Kerry scanned the scene, what little she could make out from the gas lamp on the platform and in the light from the stationmaster's lantern, spilling in dissipating pools to the edge of the trees. At the edge of the woods, nothing stirred in the ragged fringe of dark green.

Beside the body was a scuffle of footprints, Kerry saw—mostly the narrower, sharper prints of shoes such as Cabot and Grant wore, with harder heels, sharper lines, and the defined left and right slopes of shoes made to fit opposite feet. But there, too, approaching the body, were the wider, uniform prints of shoes with no left and right: homemade boots.

Now the villagers were closing in, obliterating any hope of distinguishing prints that had been there before from those made by the encroaching crowd.

Ling Yong approached, his knuckles white on his bicycle's handlebars. To his right stood Robert Bratchett, who'd dropped the reins of his horse. He removed his hat and held it over his heart.

"That'd be about far enough," the stationmaster said to the crowd. But his eyes rested on Bratchett.

Stepping back, Bratchett scanned the crowd warily now. As if at any moment it might turn on him. Start reaching for things: dogs or guns or ropes. His right hand went reflexively to his bad arm.

The telegrapher, Farnsworth, was calling across the crowd. "You. Ling. Make that contraption useful. Go find Dr. Randall!"

The stationmaster added his voice. "And for God's sake, somebody see if Wolfe's at home."

Ling threw a leg over the bicycle's seat and, with a small lantern swinging from its handlebars, rode back into the dark.

The stationmaster turned to Cabot, then Grant. "Don't got a doctor here in the village. Closest one's over to Asheville. 'Bout three miles away. Might be a good stretch of wait."

As if, Kerry fumed silently, *anyone owes an explanation to outsiders.*

Her head ticked back toward Rema. "This wound. It's—"

"Serious," Cabot put in. "We need a doctor. Quickly."

Rema leveled a look at him. "Ain't a mountain woman that's lived past her first bleeding that don't know a thing or two about healing arts."

Kerry cringed, mortified at the shock on Cabot's face from the word *bleeding*. Grant cleared his throat.

Rema, though, wasn't done. "Kerry here, she beat back death for her momma, poor frail little thing, for years."

Still kneeling but his back straightening, Cabot took in the crowd—and then Kerry herself. "Do you people here have a problem with thieves lurking around the train station?"

Kerry settled a look on him. *"We people,"* she said, "do not."

McNamee was shaking Berkowitz's shoulder now. "Can't get him to come to. Anybody want to fetch some cold water?"

Kerry focused on the reporter's face—its pallor. His lips. Now a tug on her sleeve.

"Is the nice reporter man all right?" Tully's voice had gone tight with panic.

Kerry reached for her sister, shivering in the cold. Lifting the remainder of her coat, Kerry draped it over Tully's blue homespun.

"But, Kerry, you—"

"Shhh. Don't fuss with me. You're cold and I'm not."

Tully opened her mouth to argue.

Kerry shook her head. "It's how everyone wears them in New York now, trust me—with only one sleeve." She drew a deep breath to hide a shiver.

McNamee lifted the reporter's wrist. "She's right. Awfully shallow."

Kerry bent again over the unmoving reporter, the kind face gone so still. The cold wet of the mud and the pine straw seeped through Kerry's skirt all the way to her skin.

Waiting there, listening, feeling, she could sense the crowd watching her. From up on the platform, the woman in mauve said, "Surely she doesn't have medical training."

Kerry lifted her head just long enough for their eyes to meet. Kerry would not list for this woman the bodies she'd bent over in her short life: the passed-out ones and the ones passing on. She and drunken stupors and death were none of them strangers.

She kept all this to herself. But let it show in the set of her jaw.

"Perhaps," the woman added more meekly, "with no doctor up in their hills, the natives here learn to cope. I wonder, couldn't this have been nothing but an unfortunate little accident? Perhaps the man slipped off the platform, maybe hit his head on a rock?"

The crowd silent, no one answered the woman. Kerry saw John Cabot, watching as she felt again for the reporter's pulse.

Her eyes moved to the north wall of the train station, where she'd pointed out to Cabot—meaning only to make a point about the softness of rich men like him who owned rather than worked on the rails—the line of tools that always hung there, always in the same order, when they weren't in use. Leaning against the wall, the stationmaster held his lantern high, casting light around the body—and back on the implements.

"The rail dog," she said.

The woman in mauve sniffed. "What breed is that? And what in heaven's name does any dog have to do with this?"

Ignoring the woman, Kerry scanned the wall again. "The rail dog is always there. But now it's gone."

Turning to count one by one the tools on the outer wall, the stationmaster grunted. "Well, I'll be damned." To Cabot and Grant, he added, "Rail dog's a big ole iron tool shaped like a *T* with a grip on one end for lifting up rails for repair. Takes two strong men to do it. Damned if it ain't missing."

Scanning the tatters of woods at the edge of the gaslight, Kerry kept her voice low. "Rema. That clump of boneset."

"Hon, you got to speak up. You're chirping faint as a one-legged cricket."

Kerry gestured toward a four-foot mound of wildflowers, the little white blooms in clusters that in the far edges of the stationmaster's light took on a faint glow. "Look where the line's broken."

Kerry walked to the edge of the woods, the stationmaster following behind her with his lantern. Sure enough, in the middle of the mound were broken and bent stalks, as if something had been hurled through them.

She pushed her way past. Bent down. Then straightened. With the rail dog in her hand.

Murmurs rippled through the crowd.

Madison Grant shook his head. "Intriguing. Although who's to say this was used in the attack and not merely slung to the side last time the rails needed repairing?"

"It was there," Kerry said. "The engine's headlamp shone on the wall as we were rounding the bend to come into the station. It was on the wall. Just before."

Grant smiled at her—doubtfully.

And she saw again that moment on the train when the reporter had gestured toward Grant and Cabot, then mouthed something to Marco Bergamini, words that looked like *Watch out.*

Rema turned to the gentleman, her voice slow as sorghum in winter. "Hon, I wouldn't pit my rememberings against Kerry's if I was you. Give you the allovers hearing what that girl can recall."

Kerry examined the bluing face of the reporter, who'd trusted her, a stranger, with a hint of why he'd been sent here to the mountains. The gentle brown eyes stared up unseeing into the mist and the pools of light from the lantern.

People with secrets, he'd said, *they'd like to keep covered up . . . And now we've got new information to go on.*

With a hollowing sorrow that she already knew what she'd find, Kerry leaned in to feel again at Berkowitz's neck for a pulse. Bent to feel for his breath.

It was Aunt Rema, not the strangers, whose eyes she met. Kerry spoke across the newcomers.

"He's been murdered," she said.

Chapter 7

Even as she said the word *murdered*, she realized she'd not used the more tame or politely vague *dead*.

The truth had simply slipped out before she could pad its sharp, cutting edges.

After the crowd stood a moment, stunned to silence, murmurs simmered and rose. Now came the recollections, the roiling of whispers and mutters, the remade rememberings of who had been where when the attack had occurred.

The woman in mauve suddenly wailed, "I *knew* this was a godforsaken backwater. I *told* Melvin, and did he listen?"

Rema rolled her eyes. "Lord, she's gone pale as death eatin' a cracker."

Kerry said nothing. But John Cabot was still watching her face.

John Cabot. Who must have known the reporter somehow. Who'd disappeared behind the building just before the attack—which could have given him time to slip to the far, unlit end of the station where they stood now.

The same, Kerry realized, was true for Grant, who'd ducked into the fog a different direction. He was someone Berkowitz had felt he needed to mouth a warning about—unless that warning referred to Cabot.

Arms crossed—partly from cold and partly from a sudden, ferocious need to guard the reporter's body—as if she could save him now from more harm—Kerry remained there by his side. Quietly, Tully slipped off Kerry's one-armed coat and laid it over the reporter's chest.

"We're so sorry," Tully said to him. "So sorry this happened here."

Kerry, Rema, and the twins circled there together, unspeaking, as they waited.

Careening suddenly into the crowd, Dr. Randall arrived with a clatter of metallic pedals and wheels. He tumbled from the bicycle.

Ripping his trouser leg as he dismounted, Randall cursed. Then bent over the reporter's body.

"I didn't see," Tully whispered. "Nary a thing. Will they be mad at me, Kerry? For not being able to give out what happened?"

Madison Grant lifted something round from the mud, shook it off. The reporter's yarmulke. "Ah. It would appear the man was a Jew."

Kerry turned. "More to the point, Mr. Grant, the man, who was a newspaper reporter on assignment, was killed."

"Yet another newspaper man"—Grant smiled at her evenly—"who is a Jew. Or *was*, in this case. Extraordinary. Wouldn't you say?"

Extraordinary? What exactly did he mean to imply? How could the fact that Berkowitz was Jewish have any possible bearing on . . . She gave her head a frustrated shake.

"My point," she said, turning back to the victim, "is that it seems a reporter, by profession, might well know things about people, secrets they'd like to keep hidden, that could motivate someone to kill him."

Silence. Only the suck and squish of mud as several villagers nervously shifted their feet.

John Cabot bent his head to say something to the doctor. Despite the cold mountain air, his face glowed with perspiration, and his hair, no longer covered by the top hat, flopped thick and damp on his forehead.

Randall held a fluted wooden tube to Berkowitz's chest, his ear to the other end of the tube. With a flourish, the doctor held up his free hand for silence.

Rema cleared her throat. "Charlie, you can stuff a tube up your durn ear if it makes you feel better. But Kerry here's already pronounced the poor blighter—"

"Dead." Randall employed a bass note to deliver the verdict.

"Murdered," Rema countered. "Have to side with my niece on that. Unless you'd rather be calling a spade just a club without the ruffling to it."

"Reckon we can wait a piece until we get the law here to be saying what's what. What might be called an accident and what might be called . . . something else. No point in rushing to judgment."

"Unless folks need to get judged." Rema planted her feet. "In which case putting some rush into it might just be a good thing."

Ignoring this, Randall stood to face Kerry. "You seem to have all the answers today, Miss MacGregor."

There was no admiration in the statement, and more than a hint of a warning. She'd overstepped—and into his territory.

But Kerry was in no mood to cede ground. "A hit to his head. And the rail dog was missing, then turned up just over there." She pointed toward the woods. "As for his having passed, my family, our neighbors, we've seen our share of death." She might have added that folks like her family, far back into the hollows, had no money to call for a doctor. And doctors, with their insistence on bleeding a patient who was already hanging to life by a thread, often seemed to snap the final fibers.

She did add, "And I've seen my share of head wounds."

John Cabot turned like she'd just admitted to being part of a marauding band of outlaws. She met his eye.

But Doc Randall probably knew enough about her father to guess what she meant. She owed this Cabot no explanation.

Struggling to her feet, the sodden drag of her skirts pulling at her, she stood beside Randall. "Even before the law arrives, I wonder if we shouldn't be thinking of who might have done this."

Now hoofbeats approached at a gallop.

"The law's here!" somebody called from the back of the crowd.

The rider, hatless and thick as an old stump through the middle, reined in a gray gelding.

Even before he'd begun to dismount, he was shooting questions into the crowd. More, Kerry suspected, to establish himself as in charge than because he knew what to ask.

Various spectators from the crowd began talking at once, volleys of information that sent his head whipping one direction, then the other. Spotting Kerry, the sheriff nodded in recognition.

Dr. Randall took him by the arm. "All right, Wolfe, let's get you caught up."

Listening as Randall summarized, the sheriff knelt to confirm the death.

Tilting his head toward Kerry, he added, "With all due respect to your past *noticings* . . ."

Rema patted Wolfe on the shoulder. "You say that like you was referring to cow turds, there, Donny. I know after all these years you'd want to be more respectful of my niece's gift."

"Even still, I know she'll want to let the menfolk handle this here thing."

Kerry continued studying the edge of the woods as Wolfe hauled the heft of himself back up to his feet. "So. Any of you folks see suspicious types lurking around?"

Kerry stroked her sister's hair.

Eyes welling, Tully shook her head. "It was me that got to him first. But he'd already been knocked out flat."

"You telling me you didn't see nothing at all?" He looked from Tully to the rail dog and back, as if judging whether a girl of her build could've swung such a weapon. "Not much more than a rag doll of a thing, are you?" he said, which seemed to be his conclusion.

Now Wolfe strutted through the crowd. "Before y'all leave to go on home to your hearth fires, let's hear did anyone know the victim personal-like."

Silence. Kerry watched John Cabot open his mouth. Take a step forward, even. For an instant, he met Kerry's eye. Then turned away.

Her gaze still on Cabot, Kerry raised her voice. "I spoke to him on the train, if that counts. About why he was coming to Asheville."

"Might be a piece of helpful." Wolfe looked doubtful, though. "Come see me after. Now, let's hear from you folks. Who else could've been acting a mite suspicious?"

The woman in mauve gave a small chirp of distress. "Do you mean, sir, including the passengers who disembarked? Because there was that man on the train. In my car. The man in the peculiar tweed cap." Suddenly spotting the offending item, she pointed. "That cap right there!"

Jursey, who'd just rescued the cap from a few feet away, where it must have fallen from Tully's head, shrank under the stares aimed at him now.

"This here," Rema began, "was a gift from the nice—" She stopped.

Kerry hurried to stand by her brother. "The cap wasn't originally his."

Jursey raised a hand protectively to it. "Wasn't the nice man from the train who done the attack."

But the woman in mauve wasn't finished. "Suspicious is what he was. The man in front of me observed as much while we were still on the train. 'All their kind is'—that's what he said. The kind that cause all the crime—that's what he meant."

They all turned to the woman, her voice climbing an octave, gathering speed.

"And he disembarked all in a hurry."

Wolfe gave her his full attention. "Where'd this fellow go? What'd he look like?"

"Foreign type. Shifty. Slinking away as fast as he could." She turned to the crowd for confirmation of this.

Without a coat, Kerry's arms caught the serrated edge of the mountain winds. She forced her shoulders still and wrapped an arm around Tully.

Wolfe sauntered to stand inches from her, his eyes nearly level with hers but his presence making him seem like he took up more space. Kerry had to force herself not to step back. She could smell the fish on his breath from his dinner. And wild onions, fried.

"Now, I'd hate to go assuming a man'd be guilty first thing out of the milking stall, but it sure 'nough sounds like we got us a likely suspect."

Rema pushed forward. "He didn't make a move for nothing out of my bag. And he had plenty of chance."

All eyes traveled downward to Rema's bag on the ground, the brown-and-blue satchel clearly handmade from a flour sack.

Kerry met Cabot's eye as he looked from the bag to her aunt, and back to her. She knew what he must be thinking, he and his sort: *What in God's name would any thief want to steal from that old hillbilly's sack?*

A silence followed, and Kerry felt the cut of it.

"All's I'm sayin' is he had the chance," Rema insisted. "I caught a few winks. The twins was entertaining theirselves. He didn't so much as make a jab at it."

The voice of the woman in mauve had gone shrill again. "Everyone in our car saw how he leaped to his feet and shouted like some sort of madman. The conductor had to threaten him. And the foreigner had something in his hand he was terribly protective of—and jumpy about. A weapon, for all we knew."

"No'm." Jursey spoke hoarsely.

All eyes turned on him again.

"It weren't any weapon. I can swear to that. It was a sketch drawn up by hand was all. Of Biltmore."

Madison Grant stepped forward. "A sketch? As in a kind of *layout of the house*?"

Eyes wide with confusion, Jursey shook his head. "A sort of layout, I reckon. I don't . . . it was just the house."

Wolfe's forehead rumpled. "Now why would any foreigner type cart around a drawing of somebody's house?"

"Unless," Grant suggested, "that person meant trouble to somebody inside. I hesitate to cast aspersions, but such things do happen these days: prominent persons like the Vanderbilt family in New York and Newport being intentionally targeted."

Tully smacked her brother's arm. "Judas," she hissed. "Judas Damn Traitor Iscariot."

"I didn't say he done it, Tuls. Only said he wasn't carrying a weapon."

Wolfe snapped his suspenders. "That's it, then. Good a place as any to start in the searching. What'd he look like, this fellow? Italian, somebody was mumbling just now? Which way'd he set off?"

Someone pointed toward the stand of balsams.

"Everyone knows," quavered the woman in mauve, "you can't trust Italians. Not south of Florence, you can't."

Stepping behind a balsam, Wolfe shook its branches as if the man himself might fall like a pine cone from among its needles. "Well, now. I reckon we can make out his prints in the mud setting out toward the lodge there."

Slowly, Jursey pulled the cap from his head. Then tossed it to the ground.

Kerry joined him. Rested a hand on his shoulder. "Nothing's been proved, Jurs. Far from it."

Jursey lifted his face, pale and drawn. "You don't reckon our friend really killed him?"

Kerry again pictured the Italian with his phony last name yanking the cap lower onto his head and slumping down in his seat each time the vestibule door opened.

"Sure wouldn't seem likely, Jurs, I'd agree. Sometimes people get blamed when they don't deserve it. But also, sometimes people we don't want to blame . . . sometimes they disappoint us."

Cocking back his foot, Jursey kicked the cap, sending it and a glob of mud into the balsams. He turned to Kerry like he might bury his face in her neck, but then he seemed to remember his age and the manhood he was supposed to uphold. He slumped. And looked as if he might cry. "I just wanna go home."

Kerry hugged her brother close. "I know."

Tully sniffled. "The man on the train made hisself out like he was nice."

Kerry bent to kiss the top of her sister's head. The stationmaster's lantern spilled yellow light toward the edge of the woods. Kerry's eyes followed the strand.

Now she sprang toward the shifting light.

From the mud, she lifted two small black wooden boxes, each with sodden black ribbons attached to its base. With one finger, she worked away the mud from one side of a box to reveal a gold symbol. "Phylacteries. With a Hebrew letter on the side. These must have been in his jacket pocket when he fell." Kerry held them up for her siblings to see. "I had a friend at Barnard whose father had boxes like these. Some people of the Jewish faith wear these on the arm and the forehead when they pray."

"So," Wolfe said, "the man who dropped these is Jewish."

"Which," Madison Grant pointed out, "we already knew."

Her eyes filling as she let her gaze shift back toward the reporter's unmoving form, Kerry turned to Wolfe. "We owe it to him to find out who did this, and why."

"Why the hell do you think I come here in the middle of good catfish and corn? Only you got to let the men handle it. You hear me, Kerry?" Wolfe's gaze swung over the crowd. "Somebody just said ole

Robert Bratchett mighta been here right before the attack, then all of a sudden"—he snapped his fingers—"clean out of sight."

"There were others who disappeared from the crowd just before the attack happened." Kerry's eyes shot toward John Cabot and Madison Grant a few feet away. "Shouldn't you be talking with them, as well?"

From a few yards away, Cabot's gaze swung to meet hers—as if he had heard.

"Men," she insisted to Wolfe, "that perhaps no one would ever suspect."

Chapter 8

With Nico clinging tight to his back, Sal struggled forward. He and Berkowitz weren't scheduled to meet until tomorrow, and meanwhile, Sal and Nico needed a place to sleep. More than that, they needed a future here in Asheville after he and the reporter cornered their man.

It had been Berkowitz who'd found him working in the quarries of Pennsylvania, where he'd been since leaving New Orleans. Berkowitz who'd shown up with questions based on another Italian who'd been arrested four years ago in New Orleans and who, like Sal, had escaped. That one had passed through the quarries, one of the few places hiring Southern Italians, and worked alongside Sal for a time, then ended up in Manhattan. He'd evidently decided this fall that four years was long enough to not tell what he knew—or guessed—about the forces behind all those deaths in New Orleans. He'd gone to the *Times*. Which had sent Berkowitz out on a fact-finding mission, including to the quarries to find—and then to recruit—Sal.

Sal hadn't been hard to convince. Four years in the cold of the quarries was hard on Nico, made his leg ache. It was time for a move. Sal had his own long-ago connection with this place that rich tourists flocked to in the Southern mountains.

And now, too, a chance at revenge.

He and Berkowitz would meet up tomorrow, and it all would begin.

Meanwhile, even before finding a small inn where he and Nico could stay, Sal had to see Biltmore. Had to see if the sketch from all those years ago had really risen up from the ink and taken on form.

His feet on the wet leaves slid and stumbled. Head pounding along with his heart, he doubled over to breathe.

Then suddenly, along with a stomping and snapping of branches, a horse plunged out of the fog. Its front hooves boxed the air as it reared, catching the light of the lantern its rider held. Sal leaped for the horse's bridle and hauled it back to all fours.

Standing up in the left stirrup and holding the lantern high in her opposite hand, its rider brought the shank of her crop down hard on Sal's head.

"*Che cavolo!*" he cried, letting go. Leaping out of reach of the crop, he swung Nico to the ground and slung an arm protectively over his shoulders. Angrily, he pointed to the crop she held cocked to bring down again on his head. "For what do I owe this?"

The rider backed her horse out of his reach. "How *dare* you grab my mount."

Sal lifted both arms, palms up. "A horse on the hind legs, it needs to be grabbed." He dropped one arm back onto Nico, who shrank in close.

"I can control my own mount quite well, thank you."

"I see a horse with two legs in the air: I see a rider with need of the help."

"I was *not* in need of help. And it was *you* who spooked my mount."

The rider kept the mare pawing several feet back, as if ready for any attempt on Sal's part to approach. As if saying she could run him and Nico over at an instant's notice.

"I'm only out in the dark because . . . ," she began, as if she'd rehearsed the line to herself. She stopped. "I've no reason to explain it to you. Although the rest of my group has just arrived at the station. I was hoping to welcome them there."

Sal didn't believe this for an instant—a fancy young woman like this out alone in the dark—but her motives for sneaking about in the fog were no interest of his. "You should not ride the horse so fast in this." He pointed to the mud. "The feet of the horse, they are not a goat. They have the good footing, but not the perfect, not in wet such as this. You could have broken the leg." He was not referring, he hoped she realized, to her leg but the mare's as the thing to be cared for.

"You ought to be told," she retorted, "that you're on private land."

"We are the travelers." He pulled both Nico and the tube of paper in tighter.

"Oh? And what brings you here, Mr.—?" She lifted the lantern in front of her to better see his face. She studied him for a moment.

It was odd that she asked, a rich lady like this. Running into a strange man in the dark. And looking at him with a spark in her eye. Ladies, he'd found, especially the beautiful ones who liked danger, could mean trouble for him.

He kept his answer guarded. "Bergamini."

The lady's gaze dropped to Nico. "Your son?"

"My brother."

She raised an eyebrow, assessing him. "So then, what precisely are you doing here, Mr. Bergamini? I assume you work for Mr. Vanderbilt if you are on his land." It was a challenge, he knew. Her saying he could not be here legitimately.

"I am hired in the stables of Mr. George Vanderbilt."

Nico's head jerked at the lie. But he said nothing.

Sal patted the tube of paper as if the stables could somehow be found inside.

"Well, then. I am a guest of Mr. Vanderbilt's. I assume you were hired in his stables because you are so very adept at controlling horses that others are riding."

Stupido, Sal berated himself. *Cosi dannatamente stupido. So stupid to lie to someone who could so easily prove it wrong.*

So now, even if he and Nico could find their way to whatever person made the decisions about hiring, what were his chances of being taken on? Even if he could hide all evidence of his past—with a dead chief of police at his feet.

Even if he could prove how George Vanderbilt had promised him a job long ago, he might be barred from employment if this guest of Biltmore talked to her host. Because no one hired a liar on purpose.

Not to mention a murderer.

With a nod, Sal enunciated the proper words: "I wish you the good evening."

Then he swung Nico up to his back and, not looking to see if the rider was watching, slogged on down the Approach Road.

A shiver shook Nico—perhaps from the cold. Perhaps also from fear.

Sal would not allow himself a shiver from the cold. From his time in the Pennsylvania quarries, he'd learned you could never allow yourself to admit just how dangerously cold you'd become.

"Grit-a the teeth against it," an older Italian advised. "And do not complain in the words. *Senza parole.* The cold, it'll hear you and come harder the more."

As he squished through the mud, Sal's back ached from the oak bench of the train and from carrying Nico. By what little moonlight glowed behind the scrim of fog that remained, he could find his way through the murky dark. His feet on the wet leaves, each step was a soft, sodden slap.

Moisture clung in elongated beads to the jagged tips of the maples—it must be close to freezing. Just as the Aunt Rema from the train had said, this Approach Road twisted back on itself. Over stone bridges. Under trees that did not grow in Palermo.

It made no sense to keep going into the dark. But after all these years, Sal had to see the house he'd watched being built with only a pen.

Had to see it, even here with little light but a veiled moon's and Nico clinging to his back like a barnacle on their steamship to this country.

"Biltmore," he said aloud. And then, for Nico's amusement, he added, "The place of work—and the home—of the gifted Salvatore Francis Catalfamo and Nicholas Peter Catalfamo. Sicilians. Poets. Horsemen. Gentlemen." He paused. *"E fuorilegge. Al tuo servizio."*

And outlaws. At your service.

How many times he'd said that each day at the *pensione*. Not the *outlaw* piece—that was before he'd become one. But the *At your service.*

Back when he'd had to leave his mother and Nico in Palermo to find work, he'd said it to the two American gentlemen who'd come to Florence for inspiration. All through the night, they'd bent over the large sheet of thick paper, its upper-right corner brindled in coffee rings.

The gray-bearded one of the two had kept his fountain pen poised over the paper and did not turn to make his request. "The best wine you have, *garçon*. Mr. Vanderbilt and I both prefer a good burgundy before dinner."

Garçon. Though they were in Florence, not Paris, and Sal spoke little French. He understood even less English, though he'd been studying with Father D'Eridita in case the chance arose someday to leave Italy.

The younger gentleman, his dark, serious eyes still narrowed in concentration above high cheekbones and a neatly trimmed mustache, glanced around. *"Merci."* Then flushing, he switched from French to a nearly flawless Italian: *"Perdonami. Sono appena arrivato in Francia. Grazie per aver portato il vino.* Thank you for bringing the wine."

Sal addressed the men in halting English. "We have only left today for the wine the best of the Chianti. But it is the most cost."

A flicker of amusement passed between the two men.

The older one chuckled. "If you mean it is expensive, that is no matter. By all means, bring us whichever wine is the house best." His eyes under shaggy gray brows twinkled. "Mr. Vanderbilt's tastes appreciate the *most cost.*"

The one with the dark mustache might've been even younger than Sal had initially guessed. When he bit a lower lip, it made him look more like an intelligent but unconfident boy than the man of great wealth he apparently was.

Since Sal had become one of the few able-bodied males working for the local *pensiones*, as so many of the others had already emigrated to America, he'd been saddling Mr. Vanderbilt's horse for him each morning. Already Sal had noticed the man knew how to pick the best horse in the stable. Of course cost would be of no consequence in his choice of wine.

The younger man, Vanderbilt, strained his neck toward the paper. "I don't quite see, though, Richard, what you mean by moving the grand stairwell to one side and having it appear more fully as a major feature of the front aspect."

The older man gripped the barrel of his pen over the paper. Then sent its nib back to the page.

Spires. And wings. And parapets.

Sal stood transfixed, mesmerized, longer than any good server should have.

Murmuring over the structure that was emerging on the piece of paper beneath the older man's pen, both gentlemen paused. Glanced up at Sal.

"Perdonami," Sal apologized. *"Chiedo scusa."* He hurried away for the Chianti.

The two men, Vanderbilt and the one with the pen, talked late into the night. Called for more Chianti. More pecorino cheese and a platter of red-globed grapes they popped by twos and threes into their mouths, often both talking at the same time. Then, around three in the morning, two espressos.

They had circled a spire here, drawn arrows there, added windows. As a rosy dawn nudged at the edge of the vineyards, they had risen and stretched.

The younger man, Vanderbilt, offered a tired smile. And again the flawless Italian. *"Grazie. Grazie mille. Non avresti dovuto rimanere sveglio con noi." You should not have stayed awake with us.*

Sal shook his head and risked a response in English. "At your service." That much he knew by heart. The next he cobbled together. "I am good . . . I am the happy to be awake as I . . . as you work."

Vanderbilt's mouth lifted again under the mustache. *"Bene.* Your English is coming along very nicely."

Bashfully, Sal took his risk then. Without stopping to think how presumptuous it was, he pointed to the oil painting in the front parlor over the fireplace, the landscape of Monte Bianco and its reflection in a shimmering lake, then bent to the table and sketched in more lines, the roofline higher—a fair match for the Alps—and reflecting in a fountain pool he drew in front.

The two Americans stared at the sketch, so rudely revised. Then at the upstart Sicilian boy.

"My God," the older man said at last. "I daresay he's right."

"I hesitated to say so and offend you, Richard. But our young friend here has an eye for proportion. And grandeur."

That next morning in Florence, the man Richard, whose last name turned out to be Hunt, and the younger man Vanderbilt checked out, and Sal helped them load their luggage into a hansom cab on its way to the pier where they would board their steamship for London. But just as the cab pulled away, Sal found in the *pensione*'s entryway the drawing the two Americans had labored on all night.

Far down the road, he ran after them calling, *"Aspetta! Wait!"*

He'd run for nearly a mile before Vanderbilt, apparently hearing his cries, finally poked his head out the hansom cab window. Seeing Sal, he shouted to the driver up high and behind them to stop.

"Good Lord!" Hunt said once Sal staggered up to the cab.

Those two words, at least, Sal understood, thanks to Father D'Eridita.

"He ran that entire way?" Vanderbilt asked his older companion, eyes tracing their path.

"It would appear so. I feel a bit winded merely contemplating the thing."

Catching only individual words—*he* and *ran* and *thing*—Sal tried to hand the two men the paper they'd left. "Is *importante*? Yes?"

Vanderbilt laughed—but not derisively. A gentle laugh, and quiet. "The truth is, we have far better renderings than this. And be assured we have already mentally included your revisions. You may throw this away."

He made a tossing away gesture with one hand. But then, perhaps struck—even troubled—by the look on Sal's face, he paused. "Or you may keep it." He pointed to Sal, then crossed his arms over his chest as if he were clutching something close. "*Lo tieni tu.* You keep it."

"*Grazie.*"

Vanderbilt inclined his head here. "I am hiring a great many of your people to build my house in America. A great many stonecutters." He paused, as if to gauge Sal's understanding. Then repeated himself in Italian.

Sal made himself nod gratefully.

He did not say—in halting English or in Italian—that "his people" were Sicilians, not these Northern Italians who looked down on him and his kind. Nor did he offer that stonecutting was the profession of Northern Italians, especially those close to the Alps, whose fathers instructed their sons in the ancient art. His own people grew lemons and oranges, and also grew sons into strong men who were drafted into the army, or taxed until death or emigration yanked them away.

"Yes," was what Sal said instead. "I like this. *Grazie.*"

Because someday—you never could tell—you might want to go to America.

Vanderbilt had drawn a small paper rectangle from his inside coat pocket. "Take my card. I realize the chances are remote, but I like a young man who would try and outrun a horse and cab in order to deliver a sketch that might have been lost. If ever you should come to America, you must come work for me." He'd smiled a shy, boyish smile. "That is, if you would like." Once again, he'd repeated himself in Italian.

That was some time ago now.

Back before Sal had realized he could not go home to Palermo to live after Florence as he'd planned, that all of Sicily had become so hungry, the entire weary-soiled island had already eaten up anything short of the thoroughly putrid or soured or stinking. And now was starving slowly to death.

That was back before Sal had realized his own future—and Nico's, once their mother died—would have to be scratched through and redrawn like the plans of the great house.

It had been six years at least since he'd taken the card from George Washington Vanderbilt II, Esquire, who could hardly be expected to recall the Sicilian who'd served him in Florence, or the boy's mad dash after the hansom cab.

Sal would have to make him remember, then. Because Salvatore Francis Catalfamo—with Nicholas Peter barnacled to his back—would need some sort of future after tomorrow. After justice. And maybe also revenge.

Sensing he must be approaching the end of the drive now, Sal slowed his pace. The road was giving way to a vast opening up ahead, as if to announce the view of the house itself. High up through the trees was a flicker of something—some dark outline of a steeply pitched roof with a blur of moon backlighting it.

Sal stepped out of the tunnel of trees and into a vast promenade. At the far end of the expanse of a level lawn and circled by deep purple mountains gone nearly black now was a structure utterly unlike anything he had ever seen.

Sal's jaw dropped, and he took a full step backward. Biltmore's rooflines, just as Sal had sketched them, were pitched as steeply as the Alps. A reflecting pool in front.

"Mio dio," he breathed into the silence. *"Magnifico."*

But that breath was cut short by the cocking of a gun just behind him. And the cold metal shock of a muzzle finding the back of his neck.

Nico whimpered in terror as they both froze.

The voice, like the gun's muzzle, was full of cold and of steel.

"Hands up," it said.

Chapter 9

After walking three miles by the faint glow of a moon shrouded in clouds and by the memory of every curve of the brook, Kerry and the twins and Rema arrived at the cabin long after dark. Smoke, which Kerry could smell more than see, curled from the chimney.

"Who on earth," she whispered to Rema behind the twins' heads, "agreed to stay here with him?"

Because it was hard—impossible, really—to imagine a neighbor who'd been willing to keep watch on Johnny MacGregor while Rema and the twins went to New York to fetch Kerry home. They had almost no neighbors left now. And Johnny Mac had long ago severed all barn-raising, crop-sharing community ties.

Until his recent supposed homecoming and repentance, at least. And Kerry had her doubts about that. The approach of death up the front path had a way of making even old knaves gentle up, just in case.

Kerry wanted none of a deathbed, blubbering plea for forgiveness.

Someone had propped the door open, as everyone did here with no windows in a one-room cabin. From the flickering light of the fire inside, Kerry could see a horse tied to the porch railing, the creature's silhouette badly swaybacked.

As Kerry stepped from the porch through the cabin's one door, the ladder-back chair by the hearth creaked, Ella Bratchett rising from it.

From the shadows at the foot of the cabin's one bed, Robert Bratchett crossed to them in three strides.

Kerry's jaw dropped. But before she had the chance to ask even one question, Ella had thrown her arms around Kerry's neck.

"Welcome back, hon. It's been an age. Dear God, I miss your momma bad when I see her in you."

"How kind that you would be here. With him. Ella, I—"

Ella squeezed her hand. "No, don't try to thank me for staying. I did it for you and Rema and for your momma, rest her soul. Can't stand the old bastard myself, God help me, Jesus. And Rema, don't go pushing on me all how he's changed. Good thing for him the doling out or the not of mercy wouldn't be up to me."

Ella patted Kerry's cheeks. "I told him you were coming, and that got him stirred up. Reckon he's got things he'd like to be saying to you. Tell you the truth, I got things I'd like to be saying to *him*, before it's all over. You rest now."

With that, she swept out the door, Robert Bratchett following silently behind her. Ella sprang from the porch up onto the ancient bay horse. Clucking to the animal, her husband walked beside them.

"There was some trouble," he was telling his wife as the horse moved away from the door. "Down to the station. Fella got murdered . . ."

Suddenly, the man in the bed clutched his bedclothes to his chest and cried out. As if he'd heard that final word, *murdered*. As if that word had some kind of dreaded connection with him.

No longer staring blankly upward, his eyes had gone crazed. Frantic. Kerry forced herself to reach for his hand. "What is it?"

At her feet, something moved. And then growled. Romeo, her father's old bloodhound. Kerry had named him as a pup, though he'd taken to no one in the family but Johnny Mac.

"Maybe," Rema whispered, "it's knowing you was headed home on a train that got Johnny Mac stirred."

Kerry watched her father's eyes drop closed again. *Seems like,* she thought, *his thrashing had more to do with hearing that word* murdered.

She lowered her voice so the twins, a few feet away by the glowing coals of the hearth, would not hear. "He looks . . ."

The wasted frame, the sunken eyes.

Rema nodded. "Like death plum on the doorstep."

For anyone else, Kerry would have bent then and kissed the gaunt figure on the forehead. Dropped her own tears onto his cheeks.

But for this man, who'd taught her to gauge exactly how much corn whiskey a man had downed by the sound of a fiddle—when the rills of music turned to long, mournful groans, or when the notes turned violent and reckless . . .

"Moves in and out of that fog, poor thing. Gets hisself clean wrung out. Give him castor oil packs and ratsbane tea all the day long for where he says it hurts, the liver complaint. But we all know what it is, all the years of the drink and more drink, and no undoing it now." Rema patted Kerry's arm. "He'll be real glad to know you're home, hon. Once he comes back to hisself."

Together, they made a pallet on the floor for Kerry so that Rema could share the straw tick, also on the floor, with the twins. Kerry bent to kiss her aunt good night.

"And thank you. A thousand thank-yous."

Rema patted her hand. "See you soon, sugar." She did not say what they both knew: that Rema would be up and gone in the morning before first light.

~

Kerry's sleep came tattered that night, disrupted by frayed images of a body sprawled on the ground. The people in the dream were mostly faceless, a blur of dark curly hair here and there—sometimes with a tweed cap or a top hat, sometimes with the long floppy ears of a bloodhound. A bicycle rolled through her dream, too, and Robert Bratchett's ancient horse hobbled in and out as, somewhere in the distance, a rooster crowed.

Kerry woke up in a sweat, despite the chill of the cabin. Blinking as her head cleared, she slid up on the floor to a sitting position, careful not to jostle Tully on Kerry's right. Or to wake her father a few feet away on the cabin's only real wooden bed.

The tent she'd made of three quilts and a broom handle thrust in the middle of the straw tick had at least kept the four of them on the floor warmer last night, and it had kept bits of rotted wood and tendrils of moss from the roof off them. It was caving in over their heads in several places. First thing today after sunup, she'd buttress the rafters as best she could and hew some shingles for patches.

The rain had been allowed to leak in for years, it appeared—whole beams rotted half through. Long term, whatever patches and propping up she could manage would do little good. But then, long term the bank would take the land if she couldn't pay the taxes. Thinking *long term* was like a bear rousing from a long winter's sleep—and there was no point inviting something ravenous in.

She'd take only this day that stretched out ahead.

Blessed are the poor—the peacemakers, too, her momma would have told Kerry now if she'd still been alive.

But her momma had died long before Kerry left for New York. Before Kerry's father despaired of making ends meet on the farm and left for the cotton mill. Back before every outbuilding and fence and the cabin itself had sunk well past a crying need for repair. Before he'd come back beaten and sick—and also changed for the better, Rema claimed.

Quietly laying the fire, Kerry set the water to boil in the cast-iron kettle. Coffee this morning would have to be made from grains of wheat and ground-up chicory plant since there was nothing else. Stepping outside onto the porch, she scanned the clearing, the farm's outbuildings taking shape in the pearl gray of early dawn.

A possum on his way to sleep was skulking at the base of the smoke-house. Snagging the breechloader from just inside the door, Kerry moved forward a few soundless steps, then fired without taking time to steady her aim. The shot nevertheless hit home—straight through the head. The gun, though, kicked with a vengeance, knocking Kerry hard in the jaw. The creature rolled to its back and lay still.

One hand touching the sore place on her jaw, Kerry plucked the possum up by its tail and swung it over her left shoulder. With her right hand, she peeled bark from a dogwood. Seeping that in boiling water would ease the pounding in her head—from the breechloader's kick and from the weight of what life was asking of her now. Armed with the possum and the bark, along with the blasted breechloader she'd always despised, Kerry crossed the clearing back to the cabin.

With the crackling of the fire—or, more likely, from the one blast of the gun—the twins were rising now, staggering to two pairs of gangly thirteen-year-old legs. Jursey buttoned his only other shirt on top of the one he'd slept in and snatched up the milk pail as he lumbered out the door. Eyes only half-open, Tully shrugged on their daddy's wool coat and stumbled out in the half dawn toward the chicken house.

Only three throbbed inside Kerry's head. Only three hens left, Rema had said on the train ride home. And the mule, Malvolio, already slumping in his traces two years ago, already at the porch stoop of death. And the cow, Ophelia, Rema had warned her, was now no more than a moving skeleton, her dirty brown hide stretched tight across jutting hip bones—though Rema had tried to make it sound more cheerful than that. "A mite too much lean" had been among Rema's carefully worded phrases, but Kerry knew what this meant.

A half hour later, Jursey stumbled into the cabin with a pail of fresh milk from Ophelia and with buttermilk chilled from the springhouse. Kerry stirred a splash of it into the biscuit batter, then spooned batter onto the griddle suspended above the flames. She turned her back to her brother as she cut two thin slices of the salt pork for the twins and none for herself. She would eat standing up so they couldn't see what her plate was missing.

Tully and Jursey huddled close by the fire, eating their biscuits and pork. Kerry spooned apple butter on both of their plates, and they beamed.

"I'll say this for Daddy's being sick," Jursey said.

Kerry braced herself. She'd tried to shield her brother and sister from the worst lightning strikes of his rages. But she couldn't know how much they recalled of the worse squalls.

"We finally got enough plates," he pronounced, "for all us to eat at the same time."

Tully and Kerry exchanged glances. Their brother was right, technically: down to three people, and only ever three plates. It was typical of Jursey: being able to ignore the wild boars of sickness and death and fear of the future there in the room and focus only on the thin gladness of enough plates.

Now there, thought Kerry, *is a gift.*

As the twins ate, she rose to attend to their father, whose eyes had fluttered open. Never once meeting his gaze, she changed his soiled bedclothes. Propped him up to feed him what pieces of biscuits and apple butter he would eat. Held a tin cup of sweet milk to his mouth for him to swallow.

"Kerry," he rasped.

"Anything you need?" She kept her tone matter-of-fact.

"I want . . . ," he managed. One of the slurry of words that followed might have been *sorry*.

Repulsed, she kept up her bustling.

Kerry called Jursey over to help their father use the chamber pot. Their momma had molded it from Carolina red clay, then painted it with dyes from wildflowers—bloodroot and coreopsis and sunflower—and fired it in a small kiln she'd constructed behind the barn.

How symbolic of what happened to Momma, Kerry thought with a rush of bitterness that left her queasy.

By the time they finished lifting his hips onto the chamber pot, Johnny Mac was too exhausted to do anything but sink back and close his eyes.

Just as well, Kerry thought. *I'd rather not see your eyes. All that sorry-so-sorry behind them, too late.*

At last she perched near the old fiddle to eat a biscuit herself.

"Who," Tully demanded suddenly, "really did the bad thing down to the station?" She pressed her lips tight, as if the word *murder* was forcing itself to her tongue.

Jursey mopped his biscuit through apple butter. "Likely still caviling over whether it was our Mr. Bergamini to blame. But it wasn't."

Tully was studying Kerry. "How come your face done gone all pinched up like a dried turnip just now?"

"Face *went*," Kerry corrected.

"You're bound to have noticed more'n other folks missed. Who swung the rail dog, you reckon? And why?"

"Could be someone they aren't even thinking about yet."

Tully frowned. "Some folks in the crowd, they vowed and declared Mr. Bratchett was likely to blame. Said colored men are like to get angry too easy and—"

"*Tully MacGregor.* The Bratchetts have been our neighbors from way back. Always kind, ready to help. You ignore that sort of talk, hear me? It's ignorant and mean, and I won't have any sister of mine repeat it."

Tully flinched at the slap of Kerry's tone. But Jursey only sopped up the rest of the milk in his cup with his biscuit.

Kerry scrubbed at the cast-iron griddle. "I've got to spend the day down to Asheville looking for work. With the crops not much tended all summer, I need to find a cash-paying job. Let you two do what trapping and gathering y'all can during the day while I'm gone, then I'll work alongside you as soon as I get back in the evenings."

Jursey jumped to his feet. "The chestnut grove's ankle deep with what's already felled."

"Fallen."

"Yep. We'll gather so much it'll make your head spin clear around."

~

Kerry and the twins spent the morning storing the last of the corn and turnips in the root cellar and bracing the roof with boards they broke out from the walls of the smokehouse.

Kerry tried to make a joke of it. "No point in protecting the smokehouse like it was some kind of sacred. Nothing left hanging for wolves to get to."

Tully and Jursey blinked at her sadly, like double vision of the same face.

Preparing for town, Kerry smoothed her hair into a loose braid slung to one side—no point in attempting the Gibson Girl styles she and her friends had worn in New York. It was far too humid here in the mountains, and the work was far too physically taxing for hair that had been twirled and puffed and pinned.

She smoothed her skirt, made of simple blue serge, and the white blouse handed down from her Barnard roommate when the styles had swelled toward more mutton-leg sleeves. It might not be satin, and it was not trimmed in Brussels lace, but it wasn't covered in roofing shingles and moss, which made it the best choice today.

After pouring ginger root tea with honey into her father's mouth, she slathered beeswax across his chapped lips. But with more business-like efficiency than tenderness.

"Killed," he wheezed with effort. "Somebody . . . killed . . . station."

Questions in his eyes. Jursey might have told him pieces of news while she was out banging boards off the smokehouse this morning. For a man so close to an end himself, his desperation to know more about the attack seemed odd.

"I'm walking to town to look for a job," she told him. "The twins'll be back in a short while if you need anything. I'll likely be back around nightfall."

Kerry kissed the twins on their foreheads—nearly at the same height as hers now. "If you two are taking that path anyhow for the chestnuts, I wouldn't object to company part of the way. I've missed you two urchins."

Flour sacks slung over their shoulders, the twins hung close—their way of saying they'd missed her, too. Instead of a sack, Kerry grabbed a book: the one book left from Miss Hopson's days here, a poetry collection of Wordsworth. Even just holding its frayed cover helped her recall lines. And that helped distract from the endless pictures sprocketing through her head: the attack at the station. Her father's reaction to Bratchett's word *murdered*. The collapsing roof.

It was good just to ramble through their mountains. For a few minutes, at least, to let loose the worry over how they would survive. And to push back resentment, clawing and fierce, over having to leave what she'd worked so hard for.

She breathed in the sun on the pines.

With one finger, Jursey twirled the tweed cap he and Tully had salvaged back out of the mud. "Powerful good thing Mr. Bergamini didn't get arrested."

"Yet." Kerry muttered it more loudly than she meant to.

The twins' heads came up.

"That is," she reassured them, "the whole truth will come out. Eventually."

Kerry pictured John Cabot and Madison Grant on the train, the way the reporter had stiffened when he saw them, mouthed a warning about one or both of them, and seemed to note when they'd mentioned the name of a guest toward the end. How he'd taken notes.

But there'd been no notepad on Berkowitz when he'd been killed. She shook her head. She wouldn't upset the twins with the jumble of her own suspicions. She'd report to Wolfe what the reporter had said to her on the train and the warning he'd seemed to mouth to the Italian, the *Watch out* about the two gentlemen who'd entered their car. She'd tell the sheriff what she'd seen and heard, then let him do his job. Incompetent as he might be.

"So maybe today's the day I get a position in town." It was the perkiest voice she could muster. But even she could hear the weariness underneath.

Walking ahead, Jursey emerged into a circle of morning sun. On a broad, steep-sloping hill of bright green. And a gazebo with a Greek statue just there up ahead.

"No." Kerry halted. "I didn't really just follow you two straight onto . . ."

Tully sniffed. "Aunt Rema said she'd be back around lots to help out caring for Daddy. But for now she's all moved in here to the castle."

Kerry stalked to catch up with them. "We do *not* need any castle!"

Like their heads could swivel on a single neck, Tully and Jursey both looked away.

Kerry reached for a softer tone. "Not when we have each other."

Biltmore House was going from lilac to a light pearly gray as the sun, sprawling low and golden over the tops of the mountains, began rising higher now in the sky. Encircling it were autumn patches of scarlet and ochre and topaz mixed with green bands of hemlock and balsam.

Kerry shook her head. "I'll look at the mountains. But I won't look at that house. Castle. Whatever it is." She faced sideways.

Tully was the first to speak again. "Looks honest to God like a quilt pattern. One of them Momma did most. Bear's Paw, maybe. Or Lost Children."

"Drunkard's Path, looks to me," Jursey said. "Or, no . . . Bachelor's Puzzle."

Kerry flopped down on the grass, knees and her book hugged to her chest. "Love in a Tangle. That's what it is."

Collapsing beside her, the twins gaped at the gray-violet sprawl of the house.

At least, Kerry thought, *they know better than to comment on it.*

"School," she said suddenly. "You two are supposed to be in school."

Jursey shrugged. "You got to find a job that pays during the day. Me and Tully, we got to take care of Daddy and things at the farm till you get back and take up the night caring. If a schoolteacher can learn us, we can learn our ownselves."

"*Teach.* We can *teach ourselves,*" Kerry corrected, sighing. "Between the last couple of schoolteachers who left midyear and . . ." She could not add *living with Aunt Rema.* "And how plenty of people speak here, you two could use some attention to your education, don't you think? I'm more to blame than anyone, my being so far away. Maybe I can get some schoolbooks sent down through Miss Hopson. For however long . . ."

When Tully spoke, her voice had gone boggy, wet and unsteady with tears that she rarely let herself cry. "Reckon Daddy won't ever recover?"

Rather than answer, Kerry leaned over to wipe away a single tear. Which was so like Tully. And mountain women. Controlled. Restrained. In grief and in hope. Because there was always more grief, and more hope, ahead.

Jursey, on the other hand, already had two streams of tears rivering down his cheeks. Just like he'd devoured his biscuits that morning in big desperate bites—with gusto. In case there were no more biscuits—or tears—to be had in this life.

The three of them stared down the long slope of green toward the house.

Dragging a heel that was coming unstitched from its sole across the grass, Jursey pondered. "Maybe you could check that inn where them people from the train station were staying—Battery Park. They might be needing extra help there."

"I don't . . . ," Kerry began. She pictured John Cabot and his stare that bored like a leather punch. Observing everything here like it was on display in a museum.

Primitive people of a primitive land and their pathetic attempts to survive now that their habitat had been threatened.

The village milkmaid.

She wanted to go nowhere near him or Madison Grant or their kind.

"I won't—" Kerry stopped. Sighed. Pulled the twins to her.

This much was clear: she'd have to march through the grand hotel doors. See the glint of the marble, the glow of the ladies' gowns, the stares of the gentlemen, pausing, brandy in hand. She'd hold her head high.

She glanced down. Her hands were blistered and stained a deep turnipy purple. Which no amount of holding one's head high could hide.

Kerry sighed. "For your sakes, I'll ask for a job at the Battery Park and any place this side of hell. Anywhere except Biltmore."

Chapter 10

By twilight, Kerry had covered all of the village of Best and much of Asheville. Still no offer of cash-paying work.

Alone, she tromped past the train station. In the telegraph office, Farnsworth sat quietly smoking, feet propped up on his desk where a framed crest sat, the crest's central shield surrounded by elaborate tendrils. Maybe, Kerry mused, workers all had to frame the Vanderbilt family crest when the village's name changed to Biltmore Junction—who knew?

He did not look up as she approached, which was just as well. She needed to send a telegram but had no money for payment. Mountain people asked for no favors.

Digging in her skirt pocket for a stamp—her last from her Barnard days, when she'd had a small stipend with her scholarship—Kerry stepped to the trash outside the telegraph office and, head high, sorted through clean, though used, slips of paper. One was a telegram to Madison Grant.

LNA GROWS IN INFLUENCE, PARTICULARLY AMONG ERUDITE.
GALLIC ROOSTER LIKE THE REICHSADLER AND BALD EAGLE GAINING
STRENGTH.
CONTINUE TO SPREAD MESSAGE: THE RACE WILL BE LOST IF WE CONTINUE
THIS WAY.

An odd message. Maybe about the wildlife preservation efforts Grant alluded to on the train? Kerry crossed out its handful of words and scrawled out what would no doubt sound like a desperate handful of her own, addressed to Miss Hopson:

> *In need of schoolbooks for the twins, now thirteen years old. Bright but . . .*

She hesitated here, then scratched out the last line, torn between the truth and loyalty to her siblings—to her mountains, as well. And to the one-room schoolhouse that educated its students well only with the rare kind of teacher she'd had herself, the twins having had Miss Hopson for just four years before she'd left for New York. After Miss Hopson, there had been a span of almost interchangeable teachers whose reformer's instincts and good hearts had not even remotely prepared them for so many students at so many levels with so much need. One after the next, they grew thin and sad, and then left.

> *<u>Very</u> bright, but in need of remedial grammar . . .*

She sighed.

> *Mathematics, science, geography. Anything helpful. Truly.*
> *Warmest regards,*
> *Kerry*

She refused to give in to the shame of how the letter would look— no proper stationery, not even a fresh page. Kerry folded the former telegram so that it was blank on its outer two sides, then added Miss Hopson's address at Barnard and the stamp. For its seal, she stepped to a pine tree that grew near the tracks, wiped a stick over nodules of sap, then knelt at the tracks for a sliver of charcoal spit from an engine's smokestack. The glue would have been better if she could have heated the sap and the charcoal together, but this would do.

Farnsworth had been watching her, evidently, as she'd scavenged and scrawled. He stroked his beard.

"I'd be grateful, Mr. Farnsworth," she said, handing the letter to him, "if you'd see this gets out with the next post." She'd walked on before he could ask questions.

Following the line of hemlocks, she rambled back past the gazebo with its marble goddess. The twins not here to witness her seeing Biltmore—*really* seeing it, for the first time in two years—Kerry stared down the long slope of grass.

She'd rarely in her life struggled with envy, not even as the scholarship student strolling with her Barnard peers up Fifth Avenue as the cabriolets and four-in-hand carriages of the merchant princes passed. But now, back in her own mountains . . .

She'd pictured nothing like this, not even reading to the twins from the old storybook, a brown tattered thing with only string and a piece of the name *Grimm* left for binding. These fairy-tale turrets. The glint of copper on gables and towers. The utter unlikelihood of the thing, a castle surrounded by forest and mostly abandoned cabins.

Mostly abandoned. Because they could not make her leave hers.

Yet here the castle stood in the dimming light: spires that seemed to snag at the clouds scudding by. A domed section of glass, reflecting—and becoming—the clouds. As if the laws of gravity or those that dictated where sky ended and castle began did not apply here.

Stopping at the stone railing, she was aware of the footsteps behind her. She knew the hurried snap of the twigs, the quick squinch of damp earth, the thunk at every other stride. And she knew Dearg Tate would not call out for her.

Mountain men were laconic. They answered the good and the bad with the same stoical silence. It was his running that spoke now: something throbbing in him.

She tensed. With the old gladness. The old draw toward the sheer physical force of him. The old friendship, too.

But also with dread pricking its way up her spine.

Climbing on top of the stone balustrade, she looked below, a double ramp zigzagging its way down the hill on both sides, with a brick terrace and fountains a good fifteen feet beneath where she stood, balanced, just barely. But she'd grown up rambling on cliffs, her balance as good as any goat's. And just now, she needed to feel taller.

She'd seen the castle in its earlier stages—its vast lawn swarming with workers and cluttered with sheds and lean-tos and crude wooden towers for viewing its progress. But today, she saw for the first time more than its grandness and size.

Today, for the first time, she understood what it meant.

The door that it opened to change—but didn't leave a way back.

Far off in the distance, she thought she could hear the train whistle. And then, swelling behind it, the imagined strains of her father's fiddle—from the nights back when his pupils were focused, his fingers true on the instrument's neck.

Now, from behind a bank of rhododendrons, the thunk as the butt of Dearg's gun landed alongside his foot with each stride. Reaching her, he pulled to a stop. Lifted his face to where she stood balanced up on the stone balustrade.

Without speaking, they both put out their hands, fingertips touching: the old current there. Then her hand pulling back—the current stronger than was safe.

He followed her gaze out toward the house and the blue wave upon wave of mountains that ringed it.

"We all missed you, Kerry. A hell of a lot."

"I missed all of you."

She dropped down. Let him wrap her in his arms, thick and heavily muscled. It was one of the things that kept her away, this pull toward him. Like the cords that bound them together might also someday cut off her breath.

"Sorry I couldn't meet your train," he said, "me getting stuck in Whitnel—problems at the mill. Saw Farnsworth at the station when I finally rolled in. Said he gave you the message."

Kerry's fingers went to the pocket of her skirt: the telegram from Dearg that was still there, a crackle of paper under her hand. With the attack, she'd not thought of it since. "Thank you for that. You heard what happened—before you got back to town?" Spooling images again now: the eager reporter, the kindness of him, facedown in mud.

"Damn shame. Whole station still talking about it when I come in." Dearg shook his head. "How's your daddy?"

"Bad. But I knew that before I came."

From his vest pocket, he pulled a watch, its brass gleaming.

"That'd be new." She leaned back to see that his hat was new, too: a light-gray felt that would show dirt after the first row of plowing. And his gun, she realized: not the old flintlock but a rifle, a new one. A Winchester. "I thought from your letters . . . ?"

Rather than answer, he propped his Winchester against a stone baluster. "Look at you, Kerry MacGregor. Nothing ever changes with you." He pointed to what she gripped at her side. "You with a book in one hand."

She'd forgotten for a moment she'd brought it. Though she'd read passages between job rejections all afternoon.

Books will remind you, Miss Hopson had said, *you can make of your life what you want it to be.*

Kerry winced now at the memory. Because it just wasn't true.

Dearg's mouth tilted. "It's how I pictured you while you was gone. Even with all them people to ask you to dances and parties and such— you with a book was what I pictured. When I went missing you hard."

This last admission, she knew, was a risk for him. Turning the *we* missed you to an *I*. Like a bobcat rolling onto its back, soft side exposed.

She gave him one of the old smiles—with all the sweet weight of their growing-up past: chalked messages on slates and forget-me-not crowns and bare feet in creeks.

But she wasn't the same person she'd been when she'd left.

She glanced down to the Wordsworth. Like some sort of shield against her father, so gaunt and so gray, against the collapse of the cabin roof, the coming of winter.

A book. Pitted against all that. Some sorry shield.

"It was one of Miss Hopson's," she said. But of course Dearg would know that.

"How is she?"

"She loves teaching at Barnard. Getting to live in New York. Worth it, I think she'd say, the extra years she had to put in to teach there."

"I recollect how she brung you things to be reading your momma all them times she was laid up. It was when you started talking like her. Thinking like her."

It was true. Miss Hopson had let Kerry start school at age four—since she'd sat pining every day on the schoolhouse stoop. Then for years after, Miss Hopson had sent her own books home with the little girl to hide from her daddy and read to her mostly bedridden momma. It became Kerry's—and her momma's—salvation.

Dearg's voice had a husky edge to it now. "She was a good one."

It was the huskiness there in his voice, the reminder again of how they shared a past—and these mountains—that made Kerry turn toward him.

The blue of his eyes above sunburned cheeks. The stiff coarseness of his shirt, homespun, hand-dyed and stiff, in the mountain tradition—things she'd missed the two years she'd been gone. Always the shadow of beard, a shade darker than his hair. Beaded sweat on a broad forehead. He'd have walked several miles to find her—probably starting at the cabin where the twins would've pointed him toward town. He'd likely tracked the prints of her store-bought boots.

He followed her gaze toward the castle. "You wishing you was one of them folks who'll come to stay there?"

"'Course not."

But she could picture it even now: women in glittering gowns and long strands of diamonds and rubies and pearls swooping down a long flight of stairs they would never be asked to mop. Women who'd not boiled turnips all morning, whose skirt hems were trimmed in lace, not bits of hay and manure.

And here came the men, their faces unlined by years in the sun and the frost, their spotless shirtsleeves not stinking of smokehouses and fermented corn mash and malted barley. Men who bowed low to the ladies.

Dearg scowled. "Looking down their damn noses. Like just because some bastard can buy up the land like some manor lord means the rest of us got to be peasants." Resentment was roiling off him. "You realize what's happened here, don't you? You and me, we went from folks with farms nearby the construction of the *great* Biltmore House to nothing but eyesores needing removing."

"We're *not*," she said, "eyesores. And we're not leaving."

She made herself focus on what had always been here—always been hers: the deep, layered green of the hemlocks, the endless sifting of light through birches that flickered and trembled and rarely hung still. The flame of the sugar maples. The rush and roar of the falls in the distance. The damp of the pine straw. The musky rot of the leaves.

She'd always loved autumn here. And no millionaire outsiders, no construction of castles, no sick father or failing farm or spasms of change could take that away.

Before she'd left for New York, she'd rarely stood still like this, not when there was creek water to haul and dough only half-kneaded and corkscrews of apple peel to boil over the fire. Even now she was seeing the faces of Tully and Jursey with round, hungry eyes and her father in bed. Kerry was all that stood in the path between her family and the ravenous stalking of winter ahead.

For only an instant, the last stretch of daylight reached its fingers across the tops of the mountains and turned Biltmore's limestone walls to a pale, almost translucent blue. The blue of ice on the falls near the cabin. Its towers cast long shadows across its sprawling lawn. Which meant it was time to go.

With sudden gentleness, Dearg plucked rotted wood from her hair. "Farm okay?"

"Roof needs new trusses." She forced a chuckle. "But then, everything on the place needs propping up, including me."

"All you got to do is ask." He fixed his eyes on hers, and looked as if he might like to say more.

"I know. Thank you."

He reached to touch her jaw. "Hell of a bruise."

"Wasn't him." But then, Dearg would have to know her father was too sick anymore to raise bruises. "But his breechloader always did kick worse'n a mule."

"Shoulda let me shoot it for you. Do a heap more'n that. If you'd let me."

The old question hung between them.

"I'm not selling the farm. Me and Daddy agreed on that much even back when. But I got to find a way forward."

"If you weren't so almighty stubborn . . ." His face was a good one, strong and square, like the rest of him. He smelled of wood chips and pine.

She lifted a palm to his arm. "Dearg. How've you been—*really* been?"

He looked away. But leaned in toward her palm. Like he needed to feel her close.

She studied his face. "There's something you're not saying."

Kerry saw the tightening between his eyes at her trying to force out his words. But you couldn't make a man speak, not when you've left your breechloader back home.

He pressed his hand over hers. "Here we are, you and me, still yet trying to grow food out of rock."

She glanced once more toward Biltmore, where she could now make out a man on a horse, the horse cantering slowly from the entrance gates across the wide lawn toward the house, like the man was reining in his mount so he could admire its full impact. The man and the horse melted into the fairy tale now. Like the candles were all about to be lit, the music for some royal ball about to commence playing—some kind of new story about to begin.

The man reined to a halt and scanned the blue crescent of the mountains. Turning, he spotted them. Lifted his hand in a wave. Then rode on.

Dearg spat again. "Don't nothing grow out of rock."

She would regret her next words before they were out: "Turns out castles do."

A beat of silence.

Then here it came.

"Two damn years I waited for you to come back from that city." His voice was thick. "Thought when you got back . . . thought we . . ."

"I know." She reached to touch his hand, the leathered coarseness of it. She'd cringed at the touch of nearly every man's hand in New York, how soft they all were at the dinners and balls, all those sons of bankers and lawyers who'd never held anything rougher than a tennis racket or polo mallet. She'd missed Dearg.

And yet, being back here, she missed the wider world she'd found in the city. The things people knew and read and thought.

"I got a right," Dearg said, his arm circling her waist, "to know what you're thinking."

A faraway whistle, low and long, echoed again. For several moments, it undulated toward and then through her, as if it had learned its up-and-down, short-and-long rhythms by following the never-straight line of the blue hills.

"I can't, Dearg. I can't give you an answer right now. I'm sorry."

"If you're waiting for Vanderbilt to gallop off into the sunset with you . . ."

"Don't be stupid, Dearg."

"So that's it. I'm too damn stupid."

"Don't be *ridiculous*, I meant. Right now, all I can let myself think about is how to survive—how to take care of a man I learned to hate as a kid. How to keep food on the table. The roof from crashing down on our heads. I'm sorry, Dearg. It's all I can focus on now."

Dropping her hand from his arm, she walked away. With dark falling fast now that the sun had slipped behind the mountains, she broke into a run, the pounding of her steps muffled by pine needles and the damp of bright leaves.

Hemlocks feathered past. Beside her, a stream wound through mountain laurel.

The train whistle sounded again. Its call hung over the hemlocks for several moments, drifted on through the valley. Still heard by the old-timers here as new and foreign and sad, it used to strike her as mournful, too.

But today it was like an announcement. Something coming. Something fearsome, perhaps. Something that rattled and roared, shook the earth like the train.

But change. A change she had to be ready for.

The train whistled again. She thought she could hear, too, as she ran, its churning axles and pistons and wheels: *Something coming, coming, coming. Something . . .*

Chapter 11

"So today," Lilli mused, "we finally see." Morning sun blazed through a Battery Park Inn window, white petals of light scattering on the marble floor.

Emily shuddered. "I'm thrilled for George to show us Biltmore, but I have to say, I'm still shaken by the thought of what happened at the train station. That poor reporter's . . ."

Death went unsaid.

Lilli wished she could shudder like Emily. Or weep—also as Emily had done—for poor Aaron Berkowitz. Instead, she felt paralyzed. Numb.

And rather frightened, which wasn't an emotion she often allowed.

She'd made arrangements, certainly. She'd taken a tremendous risk in trying to save the family name. She'd specified just how the thing should be approached. But *this . . .*

Emily straightened after hooking up the longer left side of her riding habit's skirt to allow for walking. "I assume you caught what Mr. Grant said last evening, that there are reasons to suspect several men—and even to investigate what Mr. Berkowitz might have been involved in that could have brought this on himself."

Lilli made herself nod. "I understand reporters sometimes push too far. The authorities probably know best."

Emily laughed weakly. "Honestly, Lils, I can't recall the last time you accepted any authority's opinion, ever."

Forcing her breathing to steady, Lilli tilted her hat more daringly to one side. What's done was done, and however badly askew it had gone, she could not panic. She would distance herself from it entirely, of course. But she would not run away. "Let's go see Biltmore, shall we?"

~

As they passed the clerk's desk, a young woman in a blue serge skirt and white blouse—not bad fitting, though a couple of years out of fashion—was saying, "Yes, I understand. You've no work to offer."

The creature marched away—head high. Lilli watched with approval. *Being* destitute couldn't always be helped; *looking* the part was inexcusable.

The young woman's hair had come loose from some sort of braid, and now it hung wild. She'd be pretty enough—with some smoothing and polish.

Madison Grant was also walking away from the clerk's desk.

"And so good to have you back again this season, Mr. Grant!" the clerk called.

Grant pitched his voice louder than necessary, as if he wanted the entire lobby—including the young mountain woman—to hear and take note. "Sadly, I wasn't able to persuade the manager to take on more staff."

Beside him, John Cabot frowned. "Always working toward your own ends," he murmured.

But if Grant heard—which he surely must have, standing so close—his smile did not fade.

"Mr. Grant," Emily gushed, "how gallant of you to offer assistance to the poor mountain girl."

Together, the four of them walked through the inn's front doors to find their horses waiting.

Grant eased himself up onto a lanky chestnut that Lilli disliked for the same reason she'd refused at least one offer of marriage: various body parts out of proportion. She was not shallow. She did, however, expect a husband of not only considerable means but also reasonable looks. Hardly too much to ask.

"I," Grant pronounced, "only did what any gentleman of *breeding* would have done." That one emphasized word he seemed to toss John Cabot's way like a challenge.

"We're meeting George at the gatehouse" was Cabot's only comment—his tone more terse, Lilli thought, by the moment.

She nodded to the groom approaching her with an animal far superior to Grant's. That, at least, was a relief. Lilli could not abide mediocrity in horses—or men.

Placing her foot in the groom's cupped hands and vaulting herself upward in one swift, graceful movement, she studied the two gentlemen from behind: Madison Grant with his breeding and perfect, cloying manners. He was beginning to get on her nerves. By contrast, there was John Quincy Cabot—she'd taken note of the pedigree right there in the name—with that unruly hair forever flopping into one eye and the newspaper always under one arm. Whenever the conversation lagged, he stole glances at it rather than engaging with others.

Apparently, he came from some blue-blooded Beacon Hill Bostonian stock—though he'd paled when she asked about his family. She'd thought him quite handsome at first. Until he seemed oddly indifferent to her. His looks had then dulled.

He glanced to the side of the road now as they passed the young woman in the blue skirt.

Lilli cocked her head. "Feeling pity for the damsel in distress, Mr. Cabot?"

Startled, he turned to her. "I . . . Pardon?"

"The young woman who was just turned away from employment. The interest, I believe Mr. Grant said you had, in the plight of the mountain people in their poverty, *oui?*"

Those hard, unreadable eyes met hers, and she saw anger there she'd not expected.

George Vanderbilt himself was just up ahead, arm raised in greeting. Relieved, Lilli was just raising her own in return when a figure stepped from the shadows. Her horse spooked, wheeling.

"I got to speak with you," came a low voice. "About the station."

Lilli spun her horse back to face him—then quickly away. "Do *not* approach me in public again. Or *ever. At all.* Do *not* stop me again."

She kicked the mare into springing ahead. One hand uncharacteristically shaking, she joined the others and did not look back.

~

Streams gurgled beside the road and beneath the stone bridges. Overhead, the gray skies of yesterday had subsided into a brilliant . . . *sapphire* was fair to say. Lilli was rarely histrionic. But she'd never seen sky quite that color.

At the gates just before what appeared to be a vast span of lawn ahead, George Vanderbilt reined in his horse. "Mr. Olmsted's hope in designing so long and winding a drive was to produce a kind of mounting anticipation, leading to"—he motioned the group forward to where they could now see the full house—"this."

Stunned silence.

Then: *"Je ne peux pas y croire,"* Lilli breathed. *I can't believe it.*

Here in this flea-bitten backwater of the Appalachian Mountains . . . a palace.

It wasn't that she hadn't seen splendor before. She'd toured estates in France's Rhône Valley and England's Derbyshire back when money flowed boundless into their family coffers. Back when her short-statured, hardheaded father had ruled the wharf district with, some said, an iron fist: the Napoleon of New Orleans.

But this . . . this was something altogether different.

At the far end of a green expanse rose four stories of palace. Deep-blue mountains rose around it like so many hulking watchmen.

All four guests of George Vanderbilt sat their horses in a stunned silence.

"Mon Dieu," Lilli murmured at last.

Emily nearly stood in her saddle. "It's three times the size of the White House. George isn't one to brag about it, but I feel perfectly free to do so as his niece. The estate has grown to more than a hundred thousand acres—is that right, George? Sixty-five fireplaces—"

"My architect," Vanderbilt broke in gently, deflecting, "has done all I asked and far more." He paused there, frowning. *"Did. Did* far more. It is the genius of our late Mr. Hunt, and the landscaping vision of Mr. Olmsted, that have made Biltmore."

Lilli maneuvered her horse alongside his. "My condolences, Mr. Vanderbilt, on the passing this summer of your chief architect. I read about it in the papers."

"Richard Hunt was like a father to me. And a mentor. No finer American architect ever lived. And this was his favorite of all his creations, I believe."

Madison Grant trotted abreast of them. "Simply splendid. Another example of what Western civilization has achieved through centuries of refinement."

John Cabot's gaze shot toward Grant. Their eyes engaged for an instant.

A sort of cocking of pistols, Lilli thought. *But over what, exactly?*

Emily beamed. "George, it's even more spectacular than when I last saw it."

They rode forward slowly, the four guests awed into silence, and even their host looking newly startled by the sheer size of his home.

Every few steps of her horse, Lilli tried to speak. But none of her usual flattering words seemed to fit.

Emily broke the silence as they reined in and began to dismount at the front entrance, a massive stone lion on either side of the steps. "Oh, George." Her eyes filled with tears. "Your mother will love it."

"Two hundred and fifty rooms, I read in the New York papers," Grant marveled, easing down from his horse. "Forty-three bathrooms. And what a display of innate talent and taste."

"I do apologize that I can't invite you to stay here at the house for your visit this time. The interior of the house, as you'll see, is far from finished, with carpentry crews everywhere. I only hope Battery Park is sufficient."

A man in full livery suddenly bolted from the house. "Right, and I'll be taking your horses back to the stables today, Mr. Vanderbilt, sir."

"Moncrief." Vanderbilt turned to the others. "This is one of Biltmore's fearless footmen, recently of Glasgow. Moncrief is temporarily filling the place of the butler I've engaged, Mr. Walter Harvey, until he arrives from London."

"It's in the bloody meantime, sir, that we've a problem. The stable's short on the hands, that it is." Darting forward so fast he spooked the horses, Moncrief lurched for the reins.

At the entrance, a matron in a black dress with chains of silver keys at her belt stood with arms crossed. Her skin against the black of the dress was the color of clotted cream.

"It won't do, I'm afraid," she observed. "Being so short of proper staff that we've left the butlering and the keeping of the stables to them that can't tie their own laces."

Vanderbilt mounted the steps to greet her. "A challenge, I realize, as we finish construction. But I promise you a full staff by the time Biltmore House actually opens." He turned to the others. "This is Mrs. Smythe, Biltmore's interim housekeeper until the new housekeeper we've contracted, Mrs. Emily King, can arrange passage after settling some family obligations. Mrs. Smythe comes to us from Liverpool, England."

"A scouser by birth," she admitted, her speech slowing as if she were ironing out vestiges of the north of England from her accent, "but more recently of London."

Vanderbilt shook her hand, pumping cheerfully with his whole arm.

"It won't do, sir." She glanced down at their employer-housekeeper handshake, then over at the footman—apparently including both in her critique. "He has more than a bit of the terrier pup about him, the lad does."

Vanderbilt smiled. "Surely, though, Mrs. Smythe . . ." He waited until Moncrief had trotted out of earshot, holding two horses' reins in each hand. Eight long legs jogged on either side of his own rather short ones. "Surely he can be taught by one as experienced with running a grand estate as yourself."

"The average man could be taught, that he could. But a Scotsman . . ." She let this hang ominously in the air.

"Ah. That is your primary objection?"

"Primary. But the list, sir, is long." Huffing, she shook her head at the far side of the esplanade, where Moncrief had been dragged off course by one of the horses, who'd spotted grass and taken the rest with him.

"Ah. I can see, Mrs. Smythe, this would not be the level of dignified comportment to which you'd be accustomed. The acting butler being led about by the equine."

"Not to be geggin' in, sir, but there's not much of the butler about him."

Moncrief was throwing his whole weight against the reins, finally persuading the horses to follow him through a porte cochere's opening toward a vast courtyard.

Lilli gaped, and her host followed her gaze.

"The stable complex. Several thoroughbreds will be arriving soon from my residence up in Bar Harbor." They watched Moncrief, jogging in jerky diagonals, disappear through the arched double doors that presumably led to the stalls. "Along with, I hope, more hands."

Emily turned to her friend. "Twelve thousand square feet, Lil, in the stables alone. And twenty carriages George will house there." She addressed her uncle again. "Lilli is quite the equestrian, you know, George. She will be fully swept away by the stables."

Lilli let her smile drift across the stable complex and her friend Emily, then land on their host. "I could not be more swept away than I already am."

It was, she could see, a direct hit. Cheeks flushing like a child, Vanderbilt gave an unsteady bow as he ushered his guests toward the front entrance.

Mrs. Smythe flung the double doors wide as the five of them passed through, four of them gasping and their host watching their faces.

Lilli rotated, gawking at the sweeping stone staircase seemingly unsupported as it rose inside a vast turret, the soaring ceilings—the sheer scale of it all.

In the main hall, four men jogged past, harried, each holding a hammer or screwdriver or saw.

"We'll view the upper floors later—if the foreman gives leave. I've had to hire more crews to have the house finished by Christmas Eve when the family arrives."

Emily squeezed her uncle's arm. "How thrilled we'll all be with it, George."

Madison Grant sauntered ahead. "I daresay, Cabot, there's room enough for you to play a full game indoors."

Emily cocked her head. "A *full game?*"

Grant nodded toward Cabot. "Football, Miss Sloane. As a Yalie, I was there for last year's Harvard-Yale matchup, later dubbed, I believe, 'the bloodbath of Hampden Park.' Mr. Cabot, as I recall, made quite a name for himself there."

Cabot turned only halfway. "Actually, my . . . life circumstances had just taken a sudden turn that very week. I confess I recall very little of it. And have no wish to."

Grant seemed not to hear this. "Cabot here knew how to obliterate a line. Quite the use of the lethal flying wedge."

Cabot's head jerked around at the word *lethal*, Lilli noted. A reaction that was hard to miss.

"Might I inquire," Emily asked, "about the role of the flying wedge—without unleashing an explanation of the whole horrid game?"

"There's nothing quite like it, is there, Cabot? Combatants meeting head-to-head. The occasional player ejected for *excessive brutality*."

Cabot's profile, rigid and dark, said he was thoroughly finished with the conversation.

Their host, meanwhile, appeared distracted, assessing the work yet to be completed. He clearly had no interest in this game football. Or in John Cabot's apparently violent role in it.

"I, for one," Lilli said, "would like to know what the room over there is—that wonder of sunlight and glass."

"The Winter Garden." Vanderbilt pronounced it reverently.

He led them to a sunken circular room at the front of the house. Its glass ceiling arched overhead. Around the marble fountain at its center stood palms and orchids and rattan furniture splashed in light.

"As if one had stumbled into the tropics," Lilli marveled.

"The crew will connect the fountain's water soon. Meanwhile . . ." George Vanderbilt's face suddenly grave, he tilted his head up toward the apex of glass. "Meanwhile, most people here in these mountains have no access to running water for their own cooking. Or hygiene."

Cabot joined him. "Honestly, I was just thinking the very same thing. Which . . . forgive me . . . which I mean in no way as a criticism of your Biltmore."

"My hope is to address just that sort of thing." Vanderbilt's gaze dropped from the domed ceiling to Cabot. "Remind me to tell you over dinner of a plan I'm hatching with All Souls, the new church we're building in the village. The needs of the mountain people I hope it can address. The schools, too, I'd like to fund. I'd also value your input on the Young Men's Institute for the black community here—you may have seen it in the village. The discrimination that community faces is substantial, so the shops and lecture hall and library . . ." He rattled on, eyes glowing.

Philanthropy. Lilli made a mental note. Mountains and art and philanthropy were all roads to their host's heart. Part of the challenge of attracting George Vanderbilt's attention: the forms of flirtation Lilli excelled at fell rather flat.

They swept next into a vast banquet hall. She gaped at the table that appeared capable of seating forty or so, the three-story ceiling, the organ whose pipes ran up one side of the hall, the tapestries that filled the entire facing wall and looked awfully old.

"Fourteenth century," their host offered before she could ask.

Emily clapped her hands together. "Your people have lit all three fireplaces for our visit today. And there's even a string quartet. George, how lovely."

The four musicians near the bank of fireplaces picked up their bows now, "Sheep May Safely Graze" floating through the hall.

Behind them came a small grunt. Mrs. Smythe stood with her arms crossed over her chest. "Housemaids had to be instructed on the proper way to lay a fire indoors. Bless my soul, the staff here that's not brought from England, they've grown up living outdoors as much as in. My job's a bit of the training chipmunks about it."

George Vanderbilt patted the housekeeper's arm. "Carry on, Mrs. Smythe."

Now he was gesturing for them to follow him past several other grand rooms and down a tapestry gallery.

Lilli nodded toward the tapestries. "They're lovely," she offered. Which sounded bland even to her.

John Cabot fell in beside her. "I understand you're from New Orleans."

"Yes." She should manage something more friendly than that. He was better looking than Grant, after all. But she'd no wish to speak of New Orleans. Especially not now.

Cabot must not have caught the chilliness in her tone. "When I was a freshman at Harvard four years ago, several of us on the *Crimson* staff . . ." He faltered there, as if reminded of something quite awful. But then went on. "We followed a story in New Orleans. It involved the death of your police chief and the violent aftermath."

Bristling, she drew a deep breath. And kept her tone airy. "My mother and I reside now in New York. We have little interest in being reminded of New Orleans."

"As I recall, the murder of the police chief was never solved. Hennessy, I think, was his name."

"It *was* most certainly solved." She shot this back before she could think.

Startled, Cabot stopped walking. "The group of Italians who were arrested . . ."

"Were the perpetrators," she said. "A mafia vendetta. The police chief named the Italians with his last breath."

As he opened his mouth to speak again, Lilli held up her hand. "Mr. Cabot, you had your reasons a moment ago—mysterious as they might appear to onlookers—for not wishing to discuss a game of football in which you apparently were ejected for . . . what was it? *Excessive brutality?*"

She watched him flinch. "Perhaps, then, you can abide by my wish to avoid the subject of New Orleans entirely."

Her voice had risen to a pitch she'd not intended, audible even over the strings. The others turned now and stared, as if they could see on her face the horror she'd so carefully tucked away out of sight when she'd dressed to come out this morning. The questions about her own father she carried inside her like internal wounds.

Cabot's face had grown hard again. "Consider it done," he said quietly. Then turned stiffly away.

In John Quincy Cabot, Lilli realized, she'd not made a friend.

Chapter 12

Lilli forced a smile—a charming nonchalance—in that center of stares.

Clasping his hands behind his back, Cabot was focusing on something else: the Sargent painting of Vanderbilt's mother.

In the next room, two stories of bookshelves still under construction covered all four walls. A balcony ran the perimeter, interrupted only by the fireplace that commanded one side of the room.

In the midst of the scaffolding, Moncrief suddenly appeared, holding a platter of hors d'oeuvres in one hand and a tray with flutes of champagne in the other. He looked like the lady holding the scales of justice—if the lady's face had been flushed and freckled, and without the blindfold. Lilli laughed aloud, and had to stifle it into a cough.

"Astrakhan caviar," the footman gushed. "With toast points. And Pommery Sec champagne. All the very best of the best, it is. Good gear comes in small bulk, we'd say back home."

At his elbow, Mrs. Smythe blanched, whispering acidly, "Without the commentary about the bevvies next time."

"More than ten thousand volumes," Emily was announcing. "That's what it will hold when it's finished—and thousands more elsewhere. Is that right, George? He's had most of them rebound to match in their literary series and groups. Things like that matter to George." Emily added this last comment as if there were something deeply peculiar about it. Though endearing.

He seemed to take no offense. And turned to touch the spine of several books—intimately, as if they were old friends.

Lilli tried on her best look of ecstatic and awed. But this much unmoving, unspeaking paper and ink was making her feel constricted. As if someone had hauled on the strings of her corset and blocked her exit to the outdoors.

"Emily has often mentioned," she managed, a little nauseous, "what a well-read man you are, with ex . . . with expansive tastes." She'd nearly said *expensive*. Which was also true. Just not something one said aloud. "How noble to create a monument to the books you cherish."

Their host tilted his head, considering. "Although *monument* would imply a static memorializing. Whereas books, once read, become fully a part of us."

Emily shot a sympathetic look at Lilli, whose arrow had clearly missed not just the bull's-eye but the whole target this time.

Lilli moved to inspect the carved black marble fireplace. The others pressed forward into the library's center to study the painting on the ceiling.

"*The Chariot of Aurora*," their host was saying, "by Pellegrini. It's actually thirteen separate canvases, although as you see here, only a few have been install—"

The library door burst open.

"Forgive me, Mr. Vanderbilt." The man at the threshold stood, breathing hard. His riding boots were covered in mud, leaves sticking to their sides.

Outside the door, the shadow of a second man shifted.

Vanderbilt addressed his guests. "Some of you met my estate manager, Mr. McNamee, yesterday." He turned back to the newcomer. "Come in, Charles."

McNamee hurried forward—oblivious to the mud he was tracking.

"I wouldn't ordinarily have barged in like this, but I've an issue with an intruder who came onto the estate looking for work."

"Much as I'd like to hire every last able-bodied man in the mountains . . ."

"Forgive me, but this one, a Marco Bergamini, carries with him . . ." McNamee reached into the pocket of his jacket and pulled out a small rectangular card, creased and badly stained. Lilli could spot an embellished *V* at its top.

She stepped to where she could peer back toward the tapestry gallery. A man stood there, broad shouldered, dark tumble of hair, square chin, not recently shaved. An olive cast to the skin. As the man glanced up, she realized with a start that she'd met him. The bandit from the forest who'd grabbed for her horse.

Behind her, McNamee was explaining, "I'd have had him hauled off except that he insisted you'd given him this yourself with an offer of a job. While you were in Italy, he insists."

"The name Marco Bergamini does not sound familiar."

"Then I will promptly—"

"But there's no denying my card." Vanderbilt peered down the tapestry gallery at the man, then smiled. "Or the story he tells. The Pensione DiGiacomo. The young Italian who added his own lines to a working sketch of the house, then chased down our cab to give us the drawing he'd thought we'd left by mistake. Extraordinary. That was years ago."

"Ah. Well. So then he was—"

"Telling the truth. Yes, indeed."

"I would caution, however, that we know little of him. He has a much younger brother with him. They've been in Pennsylvania cutting for stone."

Madison Grant stepped forward. "As the investigation proceeds into the recent murder at the train station, I would offer that this intruder would appear to be—"

"One of the suspects," Cabot finished for him. "Although there's been no more evidence to point this man's direction than there is for . . .

others of us." His gaze, pointed and hard, jabbed at Grant. "Who might do anything to preserve a reputation."

John Cabot surely didn't mean to imply Madison Grant ought to be considered a suspect.

One side of Grant's mouth lifted, but his eyes narrowed. "Innocent until proven guilty, of course. This sort of . . . *brutality* could come from most anywhere."

Cabot winced at the stress on that one word.

"Although," Grant continued, "let's not pretend that some categories of people aren't more prone to criminality than others."

McNamee cleared his throat. "As to the tragedy, I happen to know that the sheriff took Mr. Bergamini in for questioning early this morning. I can tell you he's either an excellent actor, which is quite possible, or he was genuinely shocked to learn there was a death at the station. Whether or not the authorities consider him a serious suspect at this point, I couldn't say."

The foreigner in the tapestry gallery shifted again.

Calling card or not, Lilli thought, *the bandit is about to be sent packing.*

Vanderbilt gazed up at the library's ceiling. "It was the summer I discovered the work of Pellegrini in Venice before making my way farther south. I believe I'd have stayed in Florence forever, surrounded only by art and the River Arno—had I not already found these mountains. My own canvas."

He remained in that position, hands behind his back, eyes straight overhead on the ceiling's half-hung masterpiece. "He contributed, you know. Hunt was nonplussed at first by his suggestions. But incorporated several of them in the end."

Nobody spoke as their host stared upward.

"Mr. McNamee, all of life is a risk."

"Yes . . . sir."

Vanderbilt strode into the tapestry gallery. "Welcome, Mr. Bergamini, to Biltmore. You've been in Pennsylvania since Florence?"

"My brother and I," said the man. A pause, as if he were calculating. "For the three years since leaving Italy."

"Ah. Well, then. Welcome also to the most beautiful mountains in the world. And how, if I may ask, do you think the actual Biltmore House compares with the sketch—that you, if memory serves, helped refine?"

"Spettacolare. Veramente."

Vanderbilt clapped the man on the shoulder. "Glad to hear you think so. Mr. McNamee here will be finding you a position on the estate, if you'd like. He'll also help you find housing with some of the other workers."

"Grazie. Grazie mille," the man said. From behind him, the dark-haired little boy hobbled forward.

"This is my brother. Carlo." More hurriedly, he added, "He is eight years. A good, quiet boy when I must leave for the work."

A pause. "Mr. McNamee, please see if there's a village school of some sort that would be suitable for Carlo to attend during the day. Mr. Bergamini, forgive me, but I have guests. I am glad, by the way, that you took me at my word all these years later and made your way to Biltmore."

The bandit shook George Vanderbilt's hand again, giving Lilli another look at his face. But as he and his brother retreated down the gallery, the scene was darkening before her eyes.

And suddenly, she felt as if she were falling. Back into time. Back into what she'd worked so hard to forget.

Now she was seeing a street lit with the flicker of gas lanterns—and with torches approaching. Iron balconies climbed on top of each other like they were escaping the burning below. Torches flooded the streets like so many rivers on fire.

And now she was seeing a child. Struggling to run after a man who was flailing and fighting and shouting a name as rioters dragged him away. A child and a man who might have been these very two in George Vanderbilt's tapestry gallery. But surely not. What were the chances?

"Come away from the window, Lilli," her father had begged that night four years ago.

Instead, she'd stood there and watched.

The child had sobbed as he sat alone on the street as Lilli peered down. Then he was being slung up on the shoulders of a broad, burly man who barked at him to be silent. But the boy sobbed and called out something foreign.

Lilli could still see the child's eyes—the terror in them—as he was hurled to the cobbles.

Chapter 13

It was Nico's eyes that haunted Sal in his dreams. Little Nico, exhausted and scared, as he scrambled on tenement stairs, past swirling balustrades of wrought iron in the hours of terror that night.

They'd crouched, Sal's arms tight around Nico, behind rows of shipping crates in an alley, only a sliver of light edging over the containers. But even in that splintered darkness Sal could see the trust in Nico's eyes.

"Mi fido di te," Nico had murmured, his words thick and soft. *I trust you.*

Nico had believed in his brother's power to maneuver them both through a mob calling for blood.

The mob swarmed so close to the column of crates where they crouched, Sal could smell the odor of sweat and bourbon. Alone, he might have risked skirting the crowd. Alone, he might have tried running.

But there was no one else to protect his brother.

Shouts now in the dark, the words lost at first in the stomping of feet, the hiss of the torches, the animal grunts of angry men. The crash of metal and glass: what must be the streetlight a few feet away pulled down, destroyed.

And now their stack of crates hurled to the ground. The crack of wood being smashed.

"Grab them!" a voice behind one of the torches ordered.

Sal sprang to his feet. *"Nico!"* Grasping to keep hold of his brother, he swung his right fist into the dark.

He could see himself clutching Nico as they dragged Sal toward the jail. Kicks to his gut, his groin, his chest. His brother ripped out of his arms.

But Nico's eyes, the trust still there as he reached for Sal . . .

Mi fido di te.

~

Sal jumped when a hand on his shoulder interrupted the rhythm of his shoveling, the memory spooling again in his head. He'd been too deep in his thoughts to hear the voice.

The hand on his shoulder belonged to one of the darker-skinned workers, a fellow named Bratchett. The man had just one fully functioning arm, the other useful only for steadying things. But he worked harder and lifted more with his one arm, Sal had noticed, than the other men did with two. He was gesturing now with his head to where the leader of the forestry crew, a German, was gathering the men near a just-planted birch. Swinging his shovel over his shoulder, Sal joined the group.

"Two newer members of our crew," Schenck announced in a thick accent. "They have both started this week, although you may not have met them yet. I had one working on the Approach Road and the other near the Bass Pond. To my right, this is Marco Bergamini."

Sal heard a murmur ripple through the crowd, some of the eyes on him hostile. There'd been no point in trying to pass as not Italian once he'd had to present Vanderbilt's card and the story from Florence. But he'd still have to go by the fake name. More than ever now that Berkowitz had been killed.

Who knew what someone had known about the story the reporter planned to expose? Enough, apparently, to be willing to kill to stop him. Whether or not that someone had learned also of Sal's involvement, that remained to be seen. Regardless, the sheriff had clearly believed nothing Sal tried to explain, eyeing him like a child claiming monsters had gathered under his bed.

"Dago," one of the forestry crew muttered.

But others only leaned on their shovels and nodded to him—the kind of men who reserve judgment until they've seen a coworker in action. *Their* respect, Sal knew, he could earn by pulling his end of the crosscut saw.

"And this to my left is Dearg Tate. He is new here, yes, but he knows these mountains well."

Vell, Schenck pronounced it, the man's accent nearly as hard for Sal to understand as the speech of these mountain men. But as part of the "old immigrant" crowd from Western Europe, Schenck's being fresh from Germany was acceptable, evidently. And his skin was the white of minced garlic.

Rubbing the back of his hand across a grizzled chin, Dearg Tate nodded to several men in the crowd.

"Well, hell, Dearg," an older man said. He stroked a bushy beard and spit tobacco to his left. "Thought you'd be the last damn man alive come work for Vanderbilt. You havin' plenty to say these last years about folks who—how was it you put it?—*sold the hell out.*"

Tate, already big, drew himself bigger. "Reckon I changed my damn mind."

"Reckon he got it changed for him," muttered a man in a felt hat, ragged on one side as if a dog had chewed on it.

The older man spit again. "Like the rest of us, you reckoned it was better to get paid regular-like than wonder what the weather and deer and beetles got in store for your measly crops. Only here's the thing:

didn't none of us but you call it spineless to come here looking for work."

Tate puffed out his chest.

Bratchett stepped in front of him. "So you got a bruise to your pride by deciding to come ask for a job. So what?"

"I didn't go *askin'* for nothin'."

"Steady now." Bratchett raised a palm to push Tate back a step.

Tate swatted it away and turned to Sal, then back to Bratchett. "You and Ella done me and mine a good turn here and there over the years. But don't go thinking that puts us in the circle of friendly."

Bratchett leaned on his shovel. "Won't catch me making that kind of wild-ass assumption." He winked sideways at Sal. "Our land might've been cheek to jowl with y'all's for years. Mighta come through plenty of starvin' seasons. But why would that make us some kind of friendly?"

Tate swung his pickax overhead and down into the mountain rock with such force the other men on the knoll spun around, the sound echoing through the forest. Schenck, a few yards away and conversing with another worker, turned in his saddle.

"With that sort of force there, we just might get us a forest planted." Winking at the men, Bratchett jerked his head toward Tate. "And with that kind of temper from him, we're all likely to end up prostrate in tree holes."

A tremor of laughter rumbled over the knoll. Most of the men kept their heads down, and their eyes away from Tate's as he stalked off.

Bratchett wiped sweat away with his sleeve. "Don't take it personal, Bergamini. Dearg, he'd be the next to youngest of twelve. Left here for a while to work for a cotton mill in Whitnel, east of the mountains. Hired on as recruiting agent. Come back just recent. Got a whole lot of bitter and bile left in the dregs."

Sal knew a thing or two about this. "He was a farmer, no?"

Bratchett lifted one shoulder. "Much as anyone deep in these mountains. Some tobacco. Some greens and wheat. Fair bit of corn.

Pigs. Shack for salting the meat. Tell you what, though. He never much cottoned to farming."

Sal plunged the shovel into a patch of loamy black soil that was free, for once, of rock. "Yes. The resentment I know."

"I reckon the gall for him now is having to work for outsiders he hates for getting richer every day. And maybe the gall of having to work alongside the likes of you and me. Not every place in this country puts whites together on work crews with people like us."

Bratchett hurled another shovelful. "Half the men in these mountains, maybe most by now, find the steady pay hard to turn down, especially after the Panic couple years back. Compared with worrying over the weather or the health of the livestock or if the soil's gone tired, at least here the pay comes regardless."

As he sliced his own shovel into the dirt, Sal pictured Sicily—the soil of the lemon grove behind their red-tile-shingled hut: desiccated. Gone gray and dry with too many years of citrus growing, and no more fertilizer from the landowner's horses they no longer tended.

A slight man, Schenck watched the tensions among his crew members, nervously twirling his mustache at one end. "Well, then. We do not allow belligerence on this crew."

Vell, then. Vee do not allow . . .

As Sal fell in beside Bratchett, Tate glowered in their direction.

But the darker-skinned man beside Sal was occupied pounding the head of his pickax back securely on its shaft. If he saw the glower, he ignored it.

∼

At midday, the sun filtering through the last of the birches that still held their leaves, the older man with the brindled beard plucked his lunch pail from the stream. After rummaging in his pail for what looked to

113

Sal like a ball of brown cornmeal, the man popped the whole thing in his mouth.

"Hushpuppy," he told Sal through a full mouth.

Sal had seen the poverty of the people here in these mountains— much like back in Palermo. He glanced wide-eyed at Bratchett. "Puppies? These are the . . . ?"

Bratchett chuckled. "Ingredients don't call for actual dog."

With no lunch and all his money gone to the boardinghouse in the village where Nico was now, Sal lay back to watch the hemlocks bob, green among red maples. Bratchett nudged him. "Can't eat the rest of my trout. My wife, Ella, batters a mean one."

With all the conviction he could muster, Sal shook his head. "I am not hungry." And then more honestly: "I could not take the food from you."

"Ella don't take kindly to me wasting her cooking."

Bratchett was acting out of pity—that much was clear. But Sal was ravenous.

"I thank you. *Grazie.*" He devoured the trout in four bites, embarrassed at how poorly he'd disguised his hunger. At least there'd be pay coming. And maybe ways to pay Bratchett back.

Sal scooped water out of the stream with cupped hands. The water, icy cold, tasted sweet, as if the buttercups of summer had leaked into it.

"Deeper still holes for each one," Schenck said as he rode past. His accent became more pronounced when he was on horseback, as if pronouncing his English and controlling a horse taxed the same part of his brain. "And remember: not in a line."

Jumping into the hole he was digging, Sal launched a pickax over his head to break up the stone. The soil of Sicily, too, had been full of rock—volcanic rock. The vintners who owned the tiered land rising in the hills above his mother's citrus groves claimed the porosity of the volcanic soil made for well-irrigated grapes, even in dry years, and incomparable wines.

But these were men who paid other men to till their acres. To Sal, the soil was only ever an enemy to be battled.

Bratchett spoke up suddenly: "Yesterday, Wolfe was stomping around town wanting to throw Ling Yong in jail, but not enough evidence. Which one of us you reckon they'll be hauling in next?"

Sal shoveled peat moss and cured cow manure into the hole. "My being Sicilian, this is not the help to me."

"Lord, you can say that again." But Bratchett's eyes were still kind.

"I was on the train," Sal added. "And at the station. This has put me on a list to be watched."

Bratchett straightened briefly from his shoveling. "Yep. You and me both."

"*You?* But you have lived here many years, yes?"

Bratchett rolled up his left sleeve with his right hand, then, with his maimed arm hanging loose, he pulled up the right sleeve using his teeth. He gestured with his head to his arms. "Don't take away from my color. Not to them that's got a problem with it."

Sal studied him. "We are alike, then."

Bratchett's mouth tipped up at one end. "Are we?"

"Men of suspicion."

Bratchett chuckled. "Men who are suspect. Yep. That'd be us." He flicked his hat back on his head. "And maybe also what you said: men of suspicion. I got my own theories on who's hiding what."

Sal lifted his voice toward Bratchett in the next hole. "This Tate, he does not like the newcomers? The owner of Biltmore?"

Dearg Tate himself loomed at the edge of his hole. "Heard my damn name."

Bratchett kept his tone cheerful as his shovel kept time. "Back to work, Tate."

Sal had kept his temper stoppered all morning. And now the stopper was edging loose. Looking up from the rock he'd just shattered, he tossed his shovel over his shoulder. "In Sicily, when a man—"

115

"Do I look," Tate demanded, "like I give a damn about Sicily?"

Bratchett was shaking his head.

For Bratchett's sake, Sal made himself go back to digging. "About this, you do not. And this is your loss."

Sal heard the crunch of rocky soil as Tate landed beside him in the hole. Spinning around, Sal saw Bratchett leaping to yank Tate backward by his collar.

"Slow down a spell, Tate. Think. Schenck'll fire you both, and you'll be back to weeding your turnips full-time."

Tate spat to one side. "Infestation."

Bratchett kept one hand on Tate's chest to hold him there. "Now that's a bigger word than I'd have wagered you knew. Four syllables, even."

As two other men hauled Tate back, Sal tipped an invisible cap. "A great country, this America is." And he meant it. But then he heard himself add, "Where the *infestation* becomes the American. Pretty soon, we are all of us the Americans together, yes? The mark of a great country."

Shaking off the men who'd gripped his elbows, Tate rounded on Sal. "Listen here, *dago*. You think nobody saw how you was talking to Kerry MacGregor at the train station? First thing I heard when I come back to town: how you was talking to her like you had some kind of right."

Sal shrugged good-naturedly. "She has the liking for the Sicilians, yes?"

Tate was in full flight, arms extended, reaching Sal's neck. Bratchett lowered his shoulders and caught Tate at his midsection, laying him flat.

At Tate's cry of fury and the thud as he landed, Schenck reined his horse in an about-face. "Vat is this?"

Bratchett reached his hand down toward Tate. "Edge of the hole's a bit slippery from yesterday's rain. No reason to worry, Mr. Schenck."

Red-faced, Tate was livid as he staggered up. He did not look at Sal. But it was clear who his words, low and menacing, were meant for.

"There's some that's suspected of *murder*. There's some got a hell of a reason to worry."

As Sal returned to his shovel, he could hear his mother's voice echo in his head, as clearly as when she'd stood the last time, sickled sideways in pain. The air had smelled of the market: the oregano, mint, and rosemary, the almonds and pistachios and pine nuts, the lemons and sun-dried tomatoes. She'd spoken as she'd sunk to the ground.

I beg you, my son, protect our little Nico. You are strong. Your heart is big and good. You must promise me this.

Sal shut his eyes at the memory.

Here was the chance for him and Nico to make another fresh start in this country together.

But even here, he was surrounded again by suspicion. On a list now for the murder at the train station in addition to Hennessy's in New Orleans.

And even here, Sal could be tracked down for that killing of the police chief four years ago.

The mist on his face, Sal lifted his eyes to the ring of shrouded blue mountains. Maybe this would be a refuge. A haven. The place where he could finally make good on his promise to keep Nico safe.

Or it could be the place Sal would finally be caught.

The death of the promise. The end of the line.

Chapter 14

As Kerry trudged up Patton Avenue to Asheville's center with Tully and Jursey, the riot of fall color that circled the town seemed to be mocking her, a spectacular party she could not join. Like the Cinderella of the twins' spine-splintered storybook, Kerry was not invited.

But Cinderella hadn't been worried about two younger siblings. She'd only needed to charm herself a prince.

The owner of the general store in Best—now Biltmore Junction— had shaken his head. *After the Panic a couple years back, times been hard. Hire you if I could.*

Shopkeepers all over Asheville told her similar things:

Since the recession in '93 . . .

Try down the street . . . Did you check . . . ?

Tully looked up with rounded eyes, her hair springing out of one braid. Carrying a large, lumpy burlap sack slung over one shoulder, she occasionally patted its side. But she didn't volunteer what it held. Tully was thirteen and responsible to a fault. She probably deserved to have a small secret or two.

Kerry smoothed her sister's hair. "You're hungry, Tuls. And you don't want to tell me."

Jursey, though, flopped against Kerry's side like he could no longer hold himself up. "I could eat a wild boar. Only just me."

Tully blinked at him. "You wouldn't share none with me?"

"Any," Kerry said. "Share *any*."

Jursey blew air through a rounded mouth. "Well, hell. Like a twin ever got a choice about sharing."

Kerry drew two hard biscuits from the pocket she'd sewn on the underside of her skirt. She handed them to her siblings.

Jursey tore into his. Then, guiltily, blinked. "What about you?"

Kerry waved this away. "I'm not hungry, sweet boy." Which was partially true, but only because her nausea had grown along with the rejections. "Maybe you two had better run on back to the farm. I could be a little bit longer here."

Tully, mulling something over, nibbled at her biscuit. "Aunt Rema's started her new job in the kitchens. Maybe there's more jobs at Bilt—"

Kerry held up her hand. "And they are lucky to have her."

"How come you don't like even hearing the name *Biltmore?*"

"I just hear it plenty these days." Kerry stopped there. The twins didn't need to be infected with her resentment. Because resentment, she knew, once under the skin, festers. And spreads. "Bushels of other places who'll hire me."

Jursey's face lit with bright expectation. "Where you headed to now?"

Tully, just two minutes older than her twin, could be years more skeptical. "Mighty seldom I've seen you look this discouraged."

Kerry had just been remembering her classes at Barnard. Miss Hopson's proud smile as she sometimes passed by in those high-ceilinged halls. The world of poetry opened to Kerry: Wordsworth and Spenser and Tennyson. Breaking down why a poem soared: its alliterations, its assonance, its rhythms, sometimes its rhymes. The pictures it painted.

Pictures, Kerry reminded herself now, *of fields and cliffs and copses and glades that so often caused me to ache for my mountains back home.*

Maybe, she thought, grown-up life was not so much finding your perfect place in the world, but aching for all the faraway places and people you loved—and learning to look at right where you are now, as Rema would say, through a long eyepiece of grateful.

Kerry tousled both heads. "You let me do the fretting if there's fretting to get done." From her skirt pocket, she plucked the two pennies she'd found last night in the cabin when she'd changed soiled bedding for her father again: all the cash money they had. "You all run and buy stick candy. I'll stop in real quick to this department store here. Meet you back on this spot in two shakes of a lamb's tail."

Jursey loped on ahead, penny in hand. But Tully hung back. "You still got the worry from the train station awful. And you got us to think of. You commenced to panicky yet?"

Kerry chucked her sister under the chin. "We're MacGregors, aren't we?"

Tully's face slid into a grin. Whistling, she strolled after her brother.

Which was a good thing. Since Kerry was nearly hurling up her breakfast with all that *panicky yet*. And she'd only had a handful of bleached apples and a bite of a half-rotted potato to start with.

Pausing at the threshold of Bon Marché, she scanned the mannequins in their ridiculous poses: The back of a hand to a forehead. Two arms overhead, both palms parallel with the sky. The mannequins' clothes gleamed with silk in long, flowing folds, the backs of the gowns studded with mother-of-pearl buttons.

That silk would shred down to a fringe with one good walk in the woods.

In one half of the store hung gowns with wingspans of puffed sleeves and not but a wisp of a waist, like it'd be a dragonfly wearing the dress. In the other half hung striped waistcoats for not-from-here men who cared more for fashion than for splitting a good cord of wood. One table held tortoiseshell combs and strings of pearls apparently meant to be woven through complex twists of the hair.

Each salesgirl looked to Kerry like the Gibson Girl model: tight, corseted waist and high, starched collar and swoops of coifed hair, little curls around the face. Kerry swept a hand back over her own mane, already falling out of her mother's half-rusted hairpins. The walk from the farm and then through Best was more than four miles—in addition to walking all over Asheville today. The mess of her hair was only a symbol of the far worse that actually mattered: of a falling-in roof and a sick father and only three hens left. Of winter's coming and the harvest of corn and turnips and potatoes counting up too short to be lasting.

Her skirt swung stiffly over the marble floors. She could feel the doorman drop his eyes to the dusty brown of her hemline. But she wasn't about to play the role of pathetic local girl. Beggar. Waif.

From across the department store, Kerry heard a male voice. Polished. Assured. And familiar. One of the gentlemen from the train station—Grant, the shorter one with the thick brown mustache.

"Building a palace here in a virtual backwater. George's grandfather, the Commodore, would have positively keeled over."

Whatever his taller, frowning companion Cabot said, Kerry could not hear. Nor did she care.

That they'd apparently chosen to come here or tagged along with the women in Vanderbilt's party was no surprise—Asheville was a small town, and Bon Marché was the only department store around that even hoped to meet a New Yorker's standards. Still, it was poor timing.

She'd intended to sweep well past the two men before they could recognize her. But in stepping out of her way, John Cabot backed against a rack of ladies' hats, feathered and bowed and bright colored. He sent it toppling, feathers catching the air on the way down as if the hats had taken flight.

Madison Grant reached to set the rack upright as he craned his head to address someone behind him. "Our friend Cabot, infamous for his brutality in other spheres, now turns his force on innocent, unarmed hats."

The remark may have been meant to be only teasing, but Cabot took Grant's measure a moment, then kept his voice low. "How ironic. For *you* to speak of the innocent and the unarmed."

Trapped between them, Kerry pretended to consider the hats.

"*C'est n'importe quoi.*" A young woman inspecting an evening gown tilted her head. "Really, Mr. Grant, if you're trying to convince us Mr. Cabot here is a man to be feared for bouts of violence, I'm not yet persuaded."

Another young woman, though, turning from a rack of white evening gloves, sounded enthralled. "But there've been several deaths, haven't there been? In the game of football, I mean. It sounds rather barbaric."

"Precisely its appeal." Grant winked at her. "Unless one happens to be on the receiving end of John Cabot's assaults."

Cabot's face hardened again to marble. He turned now, his eyes resting on Kerry.

An intensity behind those eyes that stopped her breath.

A salesman tumbled out from behind a green curtain and hurried to her. "Welcome to Bon Marché. And how may I . . ." His voice trailed off as he took in the whole of her. She watched his face register that she—of the falling hair and no hat and no gloves—couldn't possibly have come to purchase something. Clearing his throat, he straightened his cravat. "Help you." These last two words were only placeholders while he studied her.

Kerry kept her voice steady, but low. "I'm seeking employment."

His head jerking right and then left, the salesman appeared to be searching for the owner, Mr. Lipinsky, or anyone else to come to his aid. But no one stood nearby except the doorman, who was engrossed with the patterns of the tin ceiling. The clerk pursed and unpursed his lips, the early attempt at a mustache on his upper lip like a caterpillar crawling in place.

"We here at Bon Marché extend our concern, to be sure, miss. But we are not in the business of feeding the friendless."

"I'm no more *friendless*," Kerry shot back, "than you."

The salesman's eyes traveled over the not entirely clean cuffs of her dress. His tone became chillier still. "Much as Bon Marché appreciates its community, we are not a charitable organization for the . . . good people of the mountains."

Anger swelled in her throat. "I'd like to be clear. I inquired about employment. Not charity."

"Forgive me if I observe that you are slightly built—hardly suited for this work."

This from a man who, if his soft, doughy hands told any story, had never plowed a field in his life—much less without a mule. Or churned butter until his hands oozed red onto the plunger.

"You prefer your salesgirls burly?"

"Perhaps I've not made myself clear. It's more that you . . ."

Are too skinny and hungry looking was what he did not say—but she could see it there.

"Don't look quite the part," he finished.

Struggling to rein in her contempt, she strained for what Miss Hopson might say. One could never, after all, go wrong with squared shoulders and a good quote: "'So may the outward shows be least themselves. The world is still deceived with ornament.'"

The salesman looked dully back—no recognition sparking there in his eyes. "I see."

But he didn't see, of course. Didn't recognize the allusion at all.

"*The Merchant of Venice*," a voice said behind them.

Kerry and the salesman both turned to find John Cabot there. Eyes on her again. His expression unreadable.

The salesman turned back, squinting—apparently to reconsider the contradiction of Kerry: the clothes that looked as if they had been once rather fine but had since seen rougher wear. Kerry could feel him studying her features—pleasing enough, he probably thought, but with the eyes of an infantryman.

She turned her back to the cluster of Vanderbilt guests, all of them staring now. Kerry began counting to ten, just as Aunt Rema had taught her to do.

"The insides," Rema liked to muse, "is what the good Lord signifies by—the heart. Most other folks, though, calculate by the outsides. So if you're wanting to get on in this world, you got to smooth out the packaging some."

"Thank you," Kerry said, "for your time."

Without looking back, she kept her head high as she walked away. What she did catch, though, was the face of John Cabot, inscrutable as ever. His eyes still on her.

"I say," Grant was observing, "our Miss MacGregor from the train station appears to be having difficulty finding a job. First the inn and now here. I wonder how we might assist." He made no attempt to lower his voice, as if he wanted her to hear his concern.

Eyes straight ahead, she aimed for the exit, the doorman still studying the patterns of tin.

John Cabot must have thought she'd swept beyond earshot of the conversation. "The fact that you remembered her name, Grant . . ."

It was the last Kerry overheard.

And already far more than she cared to.

Just outside the department store doors, she stopped in her tracks. At the sight of Tully nearly in tears. Sheriff Wolfe standing there, fisted hands on his hips.

Jursey held his twin sister's hand, and with his other hand clenched at his side, he seemed ready to swing.

"Tully?" Kerry sprang forward. And stumbled over something in her path on the sidewalk.

"Exactly," Wolfe blustered. "Exactly why I told these two they couldn't sell a bunch of god-ugly roots outside the nicest store in town.

Folks'll trip over the things, sure enough. Ain't the kind of image the owner'd want to project."

In a semicircle near the front doors of Bon Marché, Tully and Jursey had arranged rows of ginseng root. The gnarled brown forms lay there like the bodies of so many malformed dolls. Ginseng root had a thousand uses, and the twins must have hunted and dug for hours for these over the course of days. But Kerry knew how it must look to city folk.

Throwing her arms around the twins, she wished she could cover their ears from what the officer was implying: that poor mountain folks trying their best to survive were unpleasant to look at.

Unless, Kerry thought angrily, you were like John Cabot and cataloguing all this—these humiliations and deprivations of her family, her people, her life—probably for some future book.

"We'll carry them some other place," she told Wolfe.

To the twins she added, "To sell them. For cash money you'll have earned to help out. How hard you two must have worked."

Kissing each twin fiercely on the top of the head, which she had to pull down to reach, Kerry glanced back toward Bon Marché.

Where John Cabot and Madison Grant stood on the other side of the window. Watching. Two ladies joining them now, each with a strand of pearls at their necks that glowed white and perfect and taunting through the glass.

I'm trapped, Kerry wanted to scream. *Trapped taking care of the twins that I love and a father I don't, trapped in this place with no job and not much left of the farm and no way out—no way at all I can see.*

And there you stand, staring.

Chapter 15

Uneasy all afternoon, since the police had stopped their group outside Bon Marché to ask questions about the murdered reporter, Lilli focused now on smiling. She reminded herself there was no going back. What was done was done.

If she could only move forward. Quit dragging the past behind her like an anchor. Quit letting her father's voice stalk her.

There's times a man's got to take things into his own hands, ma chère petite. *Otherwise, every damn Geppetto would have me paying a king's ransom so they can lay about on my wharves.*

Lilli shook the voice from her head.

Ever since the death at the station, she'd been plagued with nightmares. The reporter loomed over her bed in these dreams, his finger pointing at her. Sometimes, he was joined by the little Italian boy from New Orleans, that crippled leg as thick as a tree as he tried to pull it behind him. It was outlandish, really, that she would cross paths again here with the very child she'd seen from her balcony in New Orleans— at the moment, no less, that he'd been maimed. And now, as if that weren't disconcerting enough, she had to see him again in her dreams.

She'd not been sleeping well, despite all Battery Park's comforts. She'd even, Emily said, taken to pacing in the wee hours—which Lilli waved away each morning over breakfast at Battery Park.

"Sleep," she told Emily, "is for those with no imagination for what to do with moonlight."

Forcing a small laugh now, she strolled between Cabot and Grant through Biltmore's conservatory. "I find it intriguing that you both would be accusing each other of the crime of"—she paused for dramatic effect—*"remembering a name."*

She winced at her own use of the word *crime.*

With his crocodile's smile, Grant thrust both hands in his trousers. But Cabot only looked out toward the mountains that swaddled the estate.

The visitors followed their host past the last of the conservatory's orchids up through a walled garden. On his opposite side from Emily lumbered the Saint Bernard, Cedric—at his master's heels, as the great beast seemed to be always.

"*Pauvre petite bête.* The mountain woman, I mean. Poor little thing. She may even have overheard the two of you sparring. As if she needed more humiliation in a day."

Cabot stiffened.

But Grant waved this away. "Cabot fears, I believe, that I might tamper with the young woman's affections, given the chance. He implies, in fact, that I have rather the reputation of a rake, albeit an aristocratic one. Although I cannot help but ask: Why is this young mountain woman a particular concern of *his?*"

Lilli tried on the role of magnanimity. "It was broad-minded of you both to take an interest, however peculiar, in simple mountain folk. Imagine setting up a kind of roadside stand right outside Bon Marché with those two smudge-faced younger versions of her—those hideous roots they actually thought someone might buy? I suppose it captures your eye, Mr. Cabot, for the tragic."

He looked at her. But said nothing.

Lilli's gaze followed George's. She was thinking of him now in more familiar terms, by his given name—at least in her own thoughts. His eyes ranged over the gardens. Even here at the end of autumn, various shades of greens and browns and maroons swirled among the walkways.

She lengthened her strides under the blasted skirt. "What an artist your Mr. Olmsted is. To think of building a formal walled garden here in the midst of these mountains. And what a lovely view from down here of the house."

"We were hoping for just this effect, transitioning from the French Renaissance style of the house down to a formal garden, and from there, pathways through the woods that shift one still farther—to the forests of the New World. By spring, the roses should be well established. And well before that, the tulip bulbs we've imported from Holland and the azaleas just there up the bank should be well in bloom."

Lilli let her arm brush his. "Roses. And tulips! How I'd like to see that in spring." She looked up, the very picture of guilelessness, into George's face.

"Then indeed you shall see it, Miss Barthélemy. I very much want to share these mountains with those who appreciate their beauty."

She slowed her pace and he turned, brushing against her. "I hope," she said, "you count me in that number."

The fear that flickered over his face was probably a good sign, mixed as it was with pleasure. She stirred something in him that was not boredom.

"I wonder, Mr. Vanderbilt, if I might have your permission to explore the inside of your stables before dinner?"

His features relaxed into a genuine smile. "As the house isn't yet officially open, I suspect dinner will be rather a test. We've hired not only a chef whom Hunt recommended from Paris but also several locals from the mountains here. I expect a few shots to be fired."

She laughed with him. "Might we be safer, then, staying in the stables and missing this first battlefield dinner altogether?"

Nearing the front entrance of the house, he paused. "It is ridiculous I should have thirty-five bedrooms for my guests alone and currently be able to offer you only enough space to change for dinner. But with the construction . . ."

"I say." Grant was approaching. "Are you really living above the stables? We're all quite comfortable at Battery Park—lovely views from the verandas—but wasn't it rather preemptive for you to move out of the Brick Farm House and over here where the work is—if you don't mind my saying—far from complete?"

"The question is, now that I'm settled over the stables, whether or not I'll be convinced ever to move into my chambers once they're complete."

Lilli exchanged a glance with George that said she knew just how he felt. A nice moment of connection—that could be built upon.

The footman, Moncrief, burst from the front doors, balancing, just barely, a platter of flutes. "Champagne?" he asked in a low, dignified voice. But a grin cracked through his attempt at aloofness and calm. "It's Delbeck, the best that's grown, they say. Take you right off your head, that it will."

One side of Vanderbilt's neatly trimmed mustache twitched. He lifted a flute in a toast. "To good champagne, then, yes? And to enthusiasm."

They toasted with him, lifting their glasses high in the cool mountain air.

"And to your remarkable Biltmore," Lilli offered. "A place like none other."

To Biltmore!

Glasses clinked. Moncrief proffered more flutes. More tinkling glass. More toasting. And behind where they stood, the crunch of footsteps on the macadam drive. Murmured words, too. Lilli stepped away from the group to take in the house from near its front door, her head resting nearly on her back as she gazed up.

Near one of the stone lions, an older woman whose face was a homely web of wrinkles and whose hair was a striking, unlovely red striped with gray stood talking with the young mountain woman they'd encountered earlier.

Lilli Barthélemy wasn't the type of woman who intentionally overheard conversations—eavesdropping would've been far beneath her. If, however, others chose to bare their lives in her hearing, she refused to trouble herself and step discreetly away.

Kerry—was that the name Grant and Cabot had been squabbling over?—leaned in toward the old woman, who didn't appear to realize anyone else might overhear.

"Gone and changed up your mind then, have you, hon? Bless your sweet heart, you've had a time of it. You look rode hard and put up wet."

Her back to Lilli, this Kerry person was shaking her head. "Daddy won't be leaving the bed, ever. We're out of money. I'm out of choices."

"I know, hon. I'm sorry."

"I won't sell the farm. Ever. But the stable area here's bigger than every cabin left on our ridge, every farmhouse in the village, and the dry goods store, put together." She sighed. "Which tells me Vanderbilt and his people can wait until our hundred acres of overworked soil gives out not even one wagon of sheaves and a handful of twig-skinny carrots."

Lilli was startled to feel a frisson of compassion for the mountain girl.

The red-haired old woman patted the girl's hand with her wrinkled paw. "Hon, you'll be needing some in-betwixt care for your daddy. You're already purt nigh wore out, that'd be clear. You count on me to fill in some gaps, hear? Bet they'll let me slip off now and then for kin who's toeing up to the pearly gates."

"Since I need the twins to lay out of school to take care of him till I take back over at night, I asked if Miss Hopson could round up some books for us. I think they can be disciplined enough to . . ."

She trailed off there. Seemed to realize the Biltmore guests had fallen silent.

Life magazine couldn't have pictured the contrast better, Lilli thought. *The rough and ragged—but not wholly unattractive—mountain people standing outside the shimmering sprawl that was Biltmore. Surrounded by the mountains where these people had lived—isolated, no doubt—for so many scores of years.*

It made for a quaint image. And also, perhaps, a disturbing one.

The footman, Moncrief, having traded his platter of champagne for a small sterling tray, was approaching at a trot across the gravel, his already-red cheeks going brighter as he ran. Mrs. Smythe would not have approved.

Even as Lilli glanced at that too-eager face and the square of paper he held out to her, she felt her insides twist: some unforeseen crook in her plans to secure George's trust—and catapult herself beyond the threat of scandal and a tainted family name.

Resting on a sterling saucer, the soiled handmade envelope told her this was from no one she knew—nor was it from someone with whom she'd choose to correspond. Even as the footman stood there with his beagle's face waiting for her to thank him, she plucked up the letter. And felt the steps of Biltmore shift.

No return address. A postmark from Asheville. Her name, then *Care of George Vanderbilt*—no *Esquire*—*Biltmore Estate, North Carolina,* was scratched there. Its lines only crude, uneven attempts at the English alphabet.

Of course she should have waited to open the letter, especially given that curling of her insides. But curiosity and revulsion had seized her at the same moment—and neither sat well with patience for long. Ripping the envelope open, she found only a card, soiled, with only a handful of words scrawled in the same stiff, jerking hand:

We got to talk. Soon.

Lilli let out a gasp before she could stifle it.

That he would risk communicating with her like this. Linking her name . . . *Merde. The reckless fool.*

Emily turned toward her from a few feet away. "What on earth in that letter has made you go pale, Lil?"

"Letter?"

"The one Moncrief just gave you. In your hand." Emily swept to her side. "As if you wouldn't tell your closest friend of some marvelously sordid tryst. Who is it, Lil? I know: the Duke of Marlborough has come to the States to claim you as his wife instead of my poor cousin Consuelo."

"Consuelo," Lilli managed to echo.

"It's common knowledge, you know, about Consuelo's attempts at escape, her screaming pleas from a locked room. My aunt Alva, though, remains determined her daughter will marry the duke. Quite the family scandal."

Lilli flinched at that last word—and she rarely flinched.

Her mother had alluded to it, that word, just before Lilli had left for Biltmore. "You must be more open, Lillian, to offers of marriage. Particularly given our particular *unknowns.*"

Only the troubles four years ago had induced her mother to relocate from a city Mrs. Barthélemy adored—New Orleans—to *the snobbish squalor*, she called it, of New York.

And here Lilli was, far deeper in trouble than when she'd left New York.

Emily was dimpling now. "Whatever your secret, Lil, I'll have it out of you eventually."

She swept a hand toward the mountains beyond. "George needs to check in with his forestry crew, and I've suggested we all go along with him. I'm angling, of course, for your spending more time charming my perilously unmarried uncle."

Exactly what she needed, Lilli thought. A brisk ride outdoors. To clear her head. Time in the saddle to think about what this letter meant. What she ought to do.

She turned. To find the mountain woman Kerry's eyes locked on the note.

And then, evidently realizing it wasn't her place to be staring at a guest's private correspondence, she flushed and looked up. Lilli stared icily back.

Their gazes locked. Some sort of shock had sparked there in the girl's eyes. Something about the note—*its handwriting, perhaps?*—that she must have recognized.

Emily was just looping her arm through Lilli's. "Shall we then?"

The eyes of the mountain girl, the little tart, would not drop from Lilli's.

To their left, Moncrief was standing, that ridiculous doggy grin on his freckled face.

Emily lowered her voice. "I do believe his gloves are a finer-grade kid than mine. Democracy is all well and good, but when the footmen are the better dressed, where does that leave us? One shudders to think."

From the stables, George approached alongside a groom leading three horses between them, and just a few paces behind came Grant and Cabot, astride. Lilli made herself smile. She was becoming good at affecting ease—when what she was feeling was panic. She crumpled the letter inside her riding jacket.

But the girl Kerry was still staring at her. As if she were making some sort of connection between the sender and Lilli. As if this Kerry saw it for what it surely was.

A threat to Lilli Barthélemy of New Orleans, whom no one had ever dared threaten.

Chapter 16

Sal didn't mean to threaten Vanderbilt's guests with violence.

He didn't even mean to stray from the serpentine series of holes he'd been digging. But the bay mare at the crest of the hill was favoring her left front leg as the group approached, and Sal caught the stoical set of her head.

"Remember," the foreman called from the other side of the stream, "Mr. Olmsted's insisting it'll only look natural if nothing's in a straight line. Ferns and shrubs in the front, bigger trees to the back."

So focused was he on the horse, Sal paid no attention to anyone else—or their faces as he approached, a pickax gripped in his right hand.

It wasn't until the riders reined in their mounts and one of the men muttered, "Best always to be aware of potential anarchists" that Sal followed their eyes to the tool he held.

On horseback, Schenck shot in front of him. "Shouldn't you be working, Mr. Bergamini?" *Vorking*, he pronounced it.

"I have the concern," Sal explained.

"The concern of *mine* is that you return to your work, Bergamini." Sal did so, reluctantly, but studied the mare from a few feet away.

Seeming unconcerned by whatever threat Sal might pose, Vanderbilt addressed Grant. "If you'd like to join Cabot while he interviews some of the men, remember, please, that mountain people should be allowed their dignity."

Cabot dismounted and tethered his horse to a post oak. Then, with a nod to Sal, he walked toward where Tate and a cluster of others stood watching.

Grant began sliding less gracefully from the bay, who sidestepped on three legs as he struggled to release his left foot from the stirrup before flinging the reins over an oak branch and joining Cabot.

Waiting until Grant turned his back, Sal stepped to the mare's peripheral vision, where she could best evaluate him. He spoke softly to her.

"You no feel good, *cavallo*. I see that. *Non ti farò del male.* I no will hurt you."

Head sinking, the mare stared off into the distance—another bad sign. She stood stiffly as he ran a hand over her withers.

"You are well cared for, yes? I see your coat, *brilla*. It shines, *amica mia*."

From several yards away, Sal could see that Cabot had seated himself on a log with several of the forestry crew. Asking questions.

"My impression, Mr. Tate, is that some here in your mountains may have received a surprisingly sufficient education—to a certain point. I wonder if you could tell me a bit about that."

"Ain't a bunch of illiterates, if that's where you're headed."

"I didn't mean to imply . . ."

"Had a schoolteacher during my growing up who took her job serious."

"Could you tell me more of her?"

"Miss Annie Lizzie Hopson. Give her a hell of a lot of credit, even being a lady schoolteacher. She could learn an old shoat to read. Give out books."

"Books that . . . forgive me, but were these books she bought herself and brought here? As a kind of . . . ?"

Tate spit to one side. "If you're meaning charity . . ."

"No. I didn't mean that."

"She'd got people she knew in New York—college up there—took to sending down boxes of books. She took to spreading 'em out. Gave out pulled taffy candy to us kids for memorizing big ole hunks of poems. Plays, too."

"Like," Cabot said after several beats, "*The Merchant of Venice*, perhaps?"

"All that. Stayed a right smart while. Back when folks here still lived on their own land." He stopped there, voice tight. "Back before there was foreigners here. Back when things was safe."

As Sal watched, Dearg Tate shifted his gaze to the Grant fellow. Sal thought for a moment they exchanged nods, like men who knew each other. But he dismissed that; they were from two different worlds as much as Sal and Tate were. Maybe it was just the shared detachment in their eyes that joined the two of them for him. Sal knew all too well how full the world was of men who appeared aloof just like this, even as they molded that world to their own liking.

Turning back, Sal was only vaguely aware the conversation behind him had ceased. Gently, he ran a hand down the mare's left front leg. Leaning his own weight against her body, he lifted the hoof.

"Bergamini!"

Sal jumped, but hung on to the hoof. The last thing this horse needed was for him to drop her foot painfully to the ground.

Slowly, he ran a finger to where a stone had wedged its point between the wall of the hoof and the tender part of the foot's under-side, its frog. After prying the stone out bit by bit so as not to further the damage, he traced the laceration.

"Bergamini, may I ask why you have left your work to play black-smith?" Schenck's *w*'s had gone to harsh *v*'s again: *vork*.

But Vanderbilt turned to the forestry manager. "I wonder if I might ask Mr. Bergamini a few questions."

Schenck appeared to make himself pause before answering. "But of course."

Vanderbilt knelt next to Sal. "Mr. Grant thought he detected a slight limp up that last hill, I believe, but he was rather deep in conversation."

The scowl Sal delivered said there was no conversation so deep it warranted ignoring an animal's pain. Lowering the hoof along with Sal, Vanderbilt patted the mare's shoulder.

"Forgive me." Vanderbilt directed this last comment to the horse. He turned to Sal. "I assume we should lead her back and not ride?"

"*Si*. Yes. No ride. The Arab in her is her strength—but also her weakness. She will not show she is in the pain. Perhaps much in the pain."

"She does have Arabian in her, you're right. For endurance."

Sal ran a hand down the mare's nose. "And for the looks. The Arab is the most beautiful of the horses."

"You have experience with the breed, I take it?"

"In Sicily, we had much of the conquering. But it has given to us the architecture that is beautiful, and much varied. And a line of the horse descended from horses of the desert and the horses of the knights. The Middle Ages."

"You have a preference for the horses of the desert, then?"

"The lungs are strong. The hooves are sound. They drink less of the water. They need less of the food. The intelligence, it is superior. The heads"—he returned a hand to the mare's nose with its pronounced dip, its wide nostrils, its eyes large and deep set—"the most beautiful of all."

The others in Vanderbilt's party had drawn close, including the young woman whose horse had nearly trampled Nico and him in the forest that first night.

Cabot lowered his head toward Vanderbilt. "You may have found a new addition to the staff of your stables."

Despite the clang and shush of the digging behind them, the lady whose horse had reared in front of Sal appeared to be listening with particular interest.

Vanderbilt addressed Sal. "You are the young man I met in Florence."

"*Si.* I am."

"And yet you grew up far to the south, in Sicily?"

"There was no longer the work in Palermo. But when I was a boy, my father, he cared for the horses of a landlord and also the horses to rent."

"A livery stable?"

"Yes. For the tourists to Palermo who came off the ships. From him, I learned much."

"I remember now that you not only took care of the luggage but also cared for the horses at the Pensione DiGiacomo."

"*Si.* This is true."

"And I recall that they were beautifully tended."

Sal knew pride was a failing, but so was pretending not to know his own expertise. "Yes. The finest of the care."

Vanderbilt tapped his crop. "Your name, as you know, has been included among the suspects for the death at the train station. Many would advise me not to bring a man still under a cloud of suspicion closer in to my home."

A cloud of suspicion. As if this were new.

Sal could picture himself back in the darkened room near the Café du Monde, a few blocks from the wharves. The points of cigarette light and the hissed whisperings as he and Cernoia and the other dock workers argued.

Hennessy needs to be taught a lesson . . .

Insanity, all of this! The last thing Italians here need is to be suspected of murder . . .

"I will bring you no trouble," Sal said. The pronouncement was weak—even he could hear that. No protestations of innocence. No proof. No alibi.

Gathering the reins of his mare, Vanderbilt motioned with his head. "Mr. Schenck, I assume you can spare this man while I decide if he might not be better suited elsewhere on the estate?" Biltmore's owner waited for a nod—reluctant, but a drop of the head all the same—from his forester, then turned back to Sal. "Mr. Bergamini, if you'd please come with me."

Sal could feel the eyes of the two young women on him, but he knew better than to look either one full in the face. Especially not the one he'd met in the woods. The dangerous one.

"So," that one said softly as Sal passed, *"le bandit a trouvé une cachette."*

It was not difficult French to translate, even for a Sicilian whose language lessons came from hauling Parisians' luggage and laying out their Florentine picnics.

The bandit has a hideout.

Without thinking, he turned. To find her eyes on him.

From what he'd overhead on the train, one of these women must be the daughter of Maurice Barthélemy. And he knew now in a shattering flash, it must be this one.

Whipping back around, Sal jogged to catch up with George Vanderbilt and the limping mare.

God help him.

The daughter of Maurice Barthélemy.

Chapter 17

Kerry rose before dawn and groped through the hay in the henhouse for eggs, Goneril and Regan pecking at her hand. King Lear strutted about, unwilling to ruffle his feathers by engaging. Cordelia hunched in the corner, her little head low.

"You, Cordy," Kerry told her. "You *cannot* be sick. I got three people in there to feed. The math of your being sick won't work."

A scuffling by the door. "What don't work, Ker?"

Yawning, Jursey stood there with red hair poking straight up from his head.

"Doesn't." Eggs cupped in her left hand, Kerry turned from the shelves of nests to run her right hand over the ends of the strands. "I'd smooth it down, but you look so much like King Lear this morning, I think I'll let you two rooster about for a while."

"Daddy's moaning in there. Tully's got the water to boil and the feverwort you picked soaking. But he's saying he won't down a sip, not even to ease off the pain. Says he don't deserve it."

Because he doesn't.

But Kerry allowed her first thought, bitter as ginger root, to go where most first thoughts should go: unsaid. Skimmed off to leave something kinder beneath.

"I'll come see. And if you've still got any root stalks on those cattails . . ."

Jursey beamed. "Griddle cakes?"

Kerry kissed him on top of his rooster comb. "Not the season for eating the cattail pollen you like, but you and Tuls get the coals stirred up good, and I'll have the root stalks ground up in the batter and ready before I go."

Slipping back through the cabin door and stepping over the box that arrived from New York yesterday, Kerry glanced down. A note from Miss Hopson. She'd gathered a small library's worth of schoolbooks for the twins.

Tully had nearly fainted with excitement. She plunked down on the cabin floor with a McGuffey's Reader.

Jursey had only mumbled under his breath, "That much smarts in one place, it's like to make a man feel just real put out."

Kerry fried up two eggs for her father and four for the twins to share, which used up the entire haul from the henhouse, yesterday and today. Kerry added to their plates the dandelion leaves Tully had picked. They'd cook the roots later.

Keeping her eyes on the fork, she fed her father his breakfast. From under the bed, Romeo let out a moan, as if filling in for his master. Pulling two of yesterday's biscuits from her skirt pocket, she tossed them under the bed for the hound.

"Kerry," her father rasped.

But she pressed a steaming cup to his lips. "This one's mayapple root, snakeroot, and ratsbane."

He tried to form more words but couldn't.

"Good for the liver," she said, still not meeting his eye. *For people that drank other people into their graves,* she wanted to add, *and now are working on their own.*

Some days, and this was one, she felt as if bitterness were turning her insides to something like pine knots and sparks, just seconds away from exploding. She rose.

"Thank you." The words seemed to take all the strength he possessed.

She turned.

His eyes, pleading. He lifted the fingers of his left hand as if to touch hers.

"At the station," he managed. "The murder. Tell me."

From Rema's description of his condition, this was the most he'd managed in days. And there was more than just curiosity there. A kind of desperation, frantic and pained, to know more than whatever Jursey had already told him.

She heard the reporter's words in her head: *The secrets I'm referring to cost a whole bunch of lives and mountains of money . . .* But none of that could have anything to do with her broken, bedridden father.

And all Kerry could see was her momma in that very bed, face contorted, struggling for air. This man, years younger, with a glass jar in one hand, his fiddle bow in the other, cursing and kicking the butter churn clear across the cabin.

Kerry shut her eyes. "A reporter for the *New York Times* was here researching a story."

"Jew?" he asked, wheezing.

It was the last question she would've expected from her father. Except for Sol Lipinsky, who owned Bon Marché, had Johnny Mac ever even met anyone Jewish?

She rearranged his pillow, its batting the stale of sickness and sweat. "The victim was Jewish, yes. Nobody knows yet who did it or why: his being a reporter with stories that could uncover secrets or his just being a traveler with a wallet."

Her father's eyes grew suddenly round. *"Tate,"* he croaked out. After trying to rise, he fell back.

Easing him so that his breathing steadied, Kerry knelt by his head. "What about Dearg?"

"Not him." He shook his head.

But his eyes closed again, his body worn out. Whatever thought had dropped into his mind like a coin in a phonograph at the fair had vanished.

She waited a moment, shakily, to be sure that was all.

Silence from him.

"The twins are walking down to my work with me. If you need anything, they'll be back soon enough."

His next word came as not much more than a groan: "Where?" Or maybe it was only a groan—his or his old hound's.

Or maybe he was asking where she was working. And she knew she would not say the word *Biltmore* to him.

How ironic, she thought, *that I would be the one in this moment feeling ashamed.*

∾

Kerry tried to focus on her work and not where she was—or how the very size of the rooms upstairs dwarfed the people of Biltmore. The basement pantries and laundry and storerooms were a warren of servants' passageways, where hurrying feet echoed on stone. Just one corridor and a whole world away, the guests lolled, at ease, from the bowling alley to the swimming pool to the dressing rooms.

From the kitchen courtyard, Rema blew into the pastry kitchen along with a small cyclone of leaves and pine needles. "Well, I'll be pickled in whiskey."

She stopped to kiss Kerry roughly on one cheek. "Good to see you here, hon."

"I wish—"

Rema held up her hand. "Don't go thinking you're the first person to have to swallow her *nevers* and near choke. There's days for wings like eagles, but most of life's just the walking and trying not to faint facedown in the mud."

143

Kerry managed an almost-smile from where she stood at the cutting board. "Fresh peaches. In early November. Lord only knows how they get them here."

"Pineapples, too. Lord, you won't never guess who I saw coming in: our friend from the train give the twins that cap, that Mr. Bergamini, out there with the horses, sure's you're born."

From the next kitchen, two heads popped around the doorframe, Tully with her braids askew and Jursey clutching a whimmy diddle, its propeller still spinning, that their father had whittled years ago. "Is little Carlo with him?" Tully wanted to know.

Kerry's hands went to her hips. "How are you two still here? You said you'd walk with me to see Rema and skedaddle on back. Mrs. Smythe won't appreciate your being here. More to the point, you've got somebody who might be needing your help."

"We thought," Jursey explained, "Aunt Rema's pastry might need some tasting. Just to be sure it come out all right."

"Oui" came from the next room in a heavily accented male voice. "Just to be sure it isn't hard as the stone of Montmartre."

"I'd have thought," Rema called back, "most highfalutin chefs brung all the way from France would know how to make something simple as rhubarb tarts. Turns out, just because you seen a big ugly tower get built and shook hands with Mr. Eiffel hisself don't say a durn thing about how actual useful you're likely to be."

"From in here I can still hear you!" the chef called from the next room.

To the twins, who'd paused at the door to listen, Rema tossed a fried pie apiece, steam slipping from their slits on top where cinnamon gold oozed onto flaky brown. "Go on, now."

Jursey brightened. "We're fixing to see to Daddy, then go climbing for possum grapes and muscadines, if there's any left. Mess of cattails down by the pond here. Reckon folks'd miss a few shoots if'n I broke off a handful to boil?"

Tully wagged her finger at him. "We don't take a thing off Mr. Vanderbilt's land. Kerry can't be losing the last job she's ever like to get."

Rema winked at Kerry as the twins turned to leave.

"Don't stop for talking with Mr. Bergamini," Kerry called after them. "Go on now, fast."

Tully held up a hand like a flag to signal she'd heard as they thundered away.

"And also," Kerry said—mostly to the pastry crust, though partly to Rema—"our friend Mr. Bergamini's hiding from something. Going by a name that's not his. Rumors he may be an extortionist, a thief, and a killer. Oh, and an anarchist." She turned to the sink and began scrubbing baking pans stippled with grease and flakes of crust.

Rema poured a concoction that smelled of butter and thyme and chicken and cream into a pie shell. "I got me plenty of friends with lots of straight in their narrow. Time I had a few with swerve in their wide."

From the next kitchen, Pierre groused a rumble of sounds that only occasionally formed a sentence. "The pastry in there," he called at one point. "I can hear from all these yards away will be heavy."

Rema smiled serenely as she pinched together the upper and lower crusts in a crenellated circle. "Not the way I cut in the lard real good."

"Lard! Do not speak to me of the lard. I can see already that I will need a hatchet to cut these . . . pies in a pot, however you call them."

"Is there nary a chef in Paris with more sugarmouth in him? I'd a thought a place like Biltmore wouldn't settle for mean *and* liable to char the cheese both."

Mrs. Smythe bustled in, then blinked in surprise at the silence she found on entering, only the scraping and splash of Kerry's scrubbing and a soft, tuneless humming from Rema. "Ah. So on the culinary front, no one's got the cob on—no bad moods?"

Rema beamed up at her. "Nothing but fair weather between me and my friend Pierre."

"Splendid." Spotting Kerry, she sighed. "Miss MacGregor, I do appreciate your industriousness. Never sitting off, not even for a bit."

"I thought since I'll primarily be working the dumbwaiters once Mr. Vanderbilt has moved fully in, and since there are no diners just now except . . ."

"Indeed. So for now, do see to the loggia at the back of the house. Yesterday's storm dropped leaves everywhere, and it looks a poor show."

~

Kerry hadn't intended to cross paths with any of Mr. Vanderbilt's guests again so soon. She'd meant, in fact, to avoid them altogether.

She found the loggia unoccupied—a relief. For all Biltmore's splendor—its indoor commodes and hot water from faucets, its electric lights and a pool for swimming indoors, regardless of weather—her head ached with the vastness of it. She was beginning to feel like the creature years ago that her father caught in the stick-built trap set for whatever night prowler had broken into the smokehouse. The raccoon's eyes in their black mask were so mournful, so repentant, Kerry had thrown herself on her father and begged for mercy.

Straightening from the wicker chair she was drying with a towel, she turned to admire the view, the rolling deer park and pond with the mountains rising beyond that. The air still held the muskiness of autumn, but with the sharp tang of balsam and the bitter cold to come. In the distance, she was sure she could hear not just the splash of Biltmore's fountains, but beyond that the low roar of waterfalls.

The truth was she'd missed these smells, these sounds, these views so much it had hurt. For all she'd admired in New York, for all the ways it expanded her world, some bone-marrow depth of her had come back alive here in her mountains.

The November skies were a dark, menacing pewter. But she'd always loved November, the way the bare limbs of the trees opened up views that couldn't be seen in the warmer months. Opened up secrets.

"It's disconcerting, really," a man's voice said behind her.

Kerry jumped. Mrs. Smythe wouldn't have sent a servant to clean the loggia this time of day if she'd suspected a guest would've ventured out into the wind.

Kerry glanced both ways for someone else Madison Grant might be addressing. Briskly, she swept at the leaves. "Disconcerting?"

It probably wasn't the right thing to do, engaging in conversation with a guest. But also a direct address probably shouldn't be ignored by a servant.

Kerry flinched at that word, *servant*. The talons of regret it gripped into her.

Grant swept a hand toward the view. "Rather disconcerting that on a day like today, it's hard to distinguish the clouds from the mountains. Just range after range of the gray, all of it appearing to swell and move."

This seemed to require no response from her.

"Disconcerting, too, how the panorama is unbroken by any sign of human habitation. Or does that remoteness not bother you, Miss MacGregor?"

"It's one of the things I love most about our mountains, actually."

One of his eyebrows crooked upward. "'Our.'" He formed the word carefully.

She'd not meant to include him in the pronoun. "Those of us," she clarified, "who've always lived here."

Smiling, he turned back to the view. "I must admit that when I look at these mountains, I have the oddest, most unaccustomed sensation of feeling small. Almost insignificant, even, on some sort of grand metaphysical scale."

Kerry applied herself to drying the next chair.

"The light like this," he continued, "the color of sterling silver. Only with cracks of white in it. The immensity of it."

The new wicker glistened with beads of ice, its fresh black paint still unmarred. If Mrs. Smythe were to peek outside from the tapestry gallery, at least she would see Kerry working, not standing and chatting with a guest.

"The peculiar thing is I've a lifetime of looking at the ocean—summers in Newport, mostly. But I've never felt quite this way." He turned from the view. "Perhaps you've not seen the ocean?"

Rather than answer, Kerry bent to dry the next chair. Except for the past two years, she'd not left Buncombe County before. Madison Grant probably wouldn't include in "seen the ocean" having walked past the wharves and acres of tenement housing on Manhattan's Lower East Side and New York Harbor.

"But the ocean has never made me feel small. Dozens of times I've stood on the very precipice of the Cliff Walk in Newport." He motioned to the drop off the loggia. "Easily as steep as this. And a scene that ought to feel as immense. And yet . . ."

Kerry straightened. "It's part of the role mountains play in our lives. To make us feel small. Humbled." She offered this without looking at him.

"Ah." He drew alongside her. "Do pause a moment to look."

Kerry turned. Let her eyes scan the roll and crest of the mountains, an ocean of dark, swelling gray-blue. She felt her shoulders relax.

Madison Grant leaned in. Brushed the back of his hand down her arm. And stepped in closer, his chest nearly touching her back.

Chapter 18

For an instant, Kerry did not move. Couldn't.

Reaching with the broom for a rogue leaf, she stepped away. Did not look up. Pretended she hadn't felt his touch on her skin.

"You know, Kerry, I don't believe George would mind one of his staff taking a moment to stand in awe at this prospect, the very reason he built his house here." His voice was smooth as sweet milk.

"I don't believe, Mr. Grant, that Mr. Vanderbilt pays his staff to stare at the view."

"Then think of it as your helping to please one of his guests. With the others out in the deer park, the house is empty."

Because, she thought, *a small army of maids, cooks, and carpenters don't count.*

"Kerry, I want you to know that I empathize with you"—he stepped close again so she could see the concern in his eyes, the buckle of his brow—"in the abrupt change in your life. I know how you must feel."

"Do you, Mr. Grant?" She was aware, vaguely, of internal warnings—to stop talking. But the words were coming now, unfiltered. "I was raised in a one-room log cabin."

"That must have been horrific."

"It wasn't." She met his eye. "Our other rooms were the mountain hollows and peaks; our ceilings were the blue sky, the clouds and the fog—low one day, endless the next. I never owned more than two dresses at a time—with no burden of too much choice."

"That sounds . . ."

She didn't wait for him to grasp the right word. "Growing up, I'd never slept in an actual bed or been to the symphony, but the pallet I shared with my siblings smelled of pine straw, and when my father was home and sober, we fell asleep to the serenade of the crickets and the stream that cut through our clearing and my father's fiddle on 'Barbara Allen' and 'Nothing but the Blood of Jesus.'"

"That sounds . . ."

"Appealing, Mr. Grant? And it could also be miserable, cold, and exhausting."

As if a man like you, she stopped herself from adding aloud, *could possibly understand. You with your soft, small hands and tailored clothes. Your assumption that anything—and anyone—is yours for the grabbing.*

He stepped closer to her again, despite her hand on one hip, her fist around the broom handle. "It must be a wonderful relief for you, working here now."

She stared at him in disbelief.

Here, she wanted to say, *where envy stalks my every step? Where every electric bulb and vaulted ceiling reminds me some people live without fear of a falling roof?*

Madison Grant brushed two fingers—only two fingers—over the back of her hand, then slid them away. "I wonder if I might mention two things."

Tense, she waited.

"One is that I've noticed John Cabot's interactions with you. How unfriendly he may often seem. For no reason."

"Mr. Cabot has no reason to be friendly to me, Mr. Grant. Nor I to him." This sounded rude, she realized. But there it was, the muscadine jelly spilled out of the jar.

"Still, I feel I should offer this insight. I have good reason to believe that John Cabot and the poor late Mr. Berkowitz not only knew each other prior to this autumn but, even further, were in love with the same woman."

She let this wash over her.

In love with the same woman.

Meaning that John Cabot, who'd disappeared only moments before the attack, and whose wealth and connections with George Vanderbilt had apparently kept him above suspicion so far, would have had reason to kill Aaron Berkowitz.

The oldest reason of all.

"Mr. Grant, you've told this to the police, I hope."

"Be assured I've had to wrestle with my conscience in order to do just that. I trust they will indeed follow up."

In love with the same woman.

Kerry dragged her broom across the stone, but the words reverberated inside her head.

Brutality, someone had said in Bon Marché. Of John Cabot from, apparently, a few years ago. Could those same instincts have shown up again in a jealous rage at the train station?

"And regarding the second item: About your reasons for coming here. I want to offer my help. Truly."

Still clutching the broom, she crossed her arms over her chest.

"I'm aware how difficult it must be, a young woman in your position. Forgive me, but I took the liberty of asking Mrs. Smythe about your situation when I saw you seeking employment and then appearing here at Biltmore. If I may say so, I was startled that so well-spoken a young woman would—"

"Work as a kitchen maid?"

"Well, yes. After finding a life in New York. Suddenly dragged back. It speaks well for the stock you come from—the strength you've shown."

A tremor went through her. And perhaps he saw it—that his compassion had struck a chord.

"Thank you, Mr. Grant."

She felt his eyes on her. Heard the way the words came from her own lips just now. Sounding very much—too much—like some sort of *yes*.

Grant followed her gaze out to the rolling waves of gray and black. "I like to think, Kerry, I'm contributing something of significance to this world—in my law practice, my wildlife work, land preservation."

He paused as if she were meant to comment. She swept harder.

"But particularly in my work that will have lasting impacts on the future of humanity. It's within our power, you know, to annihilate inferior traits and breed desirable, superior ones."

Startled, Kerry paused in her sweeping. Surely she'd misheard. "I'm sorry. Did you say *annihilate*, Mr. Grant? And *breed*?"

"*If* one is willing to root out the laziness and criminality we see quite starkly in particular nationalities. While propagating the industriousness and intelligence in others."

Kerry stared at him. "Surely you don't mean . . . ," she began.

"One of our leading researchers has shown how the poorer classes of people, particularly in the slums of London, were also of a lower intellect—nationalities we know to be genetically inferior. Here in the Appalachians—"

Kerry held up a hand. "You're probably not accustomed to having your ideas challenged, particularly not by someone holding a broom. But surely you're not suggesting people are poor because they're genetically inferior."

He stepped toward her again, voice smooth. "Your intelligence and your industriousness, I must tell you, are tremendously appealing. And evidence of your Nordic stock." Before she could jerk away, he ran a hand down the line of her jaw. "As is your striking beauty."

"The porch," she said, momentarily paralyzed, "is finished."

He reached to lift a stray lock of her hair.

Her feet moved at last. She whipped toward the loggia's far door.

Grant's voice hung in the air, hazy and soft as a patch of poison ivy catching fire and turning to smoke—*and as lethal*, Kerry thought.

"Remember, Kerry, I'd like to help you."

Stay around to inhale that—she broke into a sprint toward the stairs—*and it'll blister your insides.*

Chapter 19

Dusting inside George Vanderbilt's office, which was tucked into the southwest corner of the library—its door nearly invisible in the woodwork—Kerry heard her name. And a scattershot round of bickering. She stepped closer to the door. If Mrs. Smythe had complaints about Kerry's work, she needed to know. Tully was right: this job of Kerry's might be their last chance.

"What bloody business of ours would it be, I ask you now? Away and bile your haid." That was Moncrief. Only the impenetrability of his Scottish brogue must be saving his life—Mrs. Smythe must not have made out what he'd said: *boil your head.*

"I'll thank a *footman* to keep his temper in my house."

"*Your* house, is it, now?"

"My house to run, it is. I wasn't brought across the Atlantic to sit idly by while the upstairs and down mix into proper gruel."

"By which you'd be meaning?"

"I'll not pretend to be blind when Biltmore guests are seduced by a maid."

Kerry felt the blood rush to her face.

Moncrief guffawed. "I'll not be an auld clipe—I'll not be a snitch—but I can tell you this much: it's not that direction the burn has been flowing."

"Meaning?"

"Meaning that not every lass as bonnie as her is a wee nyaff—"

"A *what* did you say?"

"A nuisance—by distracting the lads. The lads ken—they know—how to hunt on their own."

"Still, a young woman such as that can cause problems."

"Aye. And was there yet a young man who wasn't naught but a problem with a leg on each side?"

Mrs. Smythe's answer came clipped. "I'll thank you, lad, to watch your language." Then she sighed. "I confess I like the girl. Although it's a proper stew of motives even the nice ones can have. I shall speak to her myself of the dangers of moral turpitude. Even a bright young thing can be thick when it comes to the attentions of a rich man."

"So, the braw and bonnie Mrs. Smythe speaks from experience, does she?"

"Let's just say I had my share of opportunities offered."

Through the crack in the door, Kerry could see Moncrief dropping a theatrical bow. "And long may your lum reek, I say."

"I *beg* your pardon!"

"Long may your chimney smoke, that is. Long may you live and prosper."

Mrs. Smythe huffed as she turned to exit the library. "Moral," she called back to Moncrief, following not far behind, "*turpitude*."

"Aye." A chuckle rumbled below Moncrief's words. "Moral bloody turpitude."

~

Cheeks still flaming—from anger now more than embarrassment—Kerry slipped out of Vanderbilt's office as laughter and shouts broke just outside the library's glass-paned doors. Several figures—people and horses—appeared suddenly on the bowling green that bordered the south side of the house. To reach the bowling green, one had to take a stone staircase—that Lilli Barthélemy had evidently just ridden her horse up.

She dismounted, head thrown back, and gathered her reins to hand to someone. Marco Bergamini, Kerry saw now. Who must have come sprinting across the front of the house from the stables when he'd heard the commotion. As the other guests milled about Vanderbilt and his horse, Lilli Barthélemy paused for just an instant near the library's windows as the Italian reached her. Kerry could only see his face, but his eyes were all thunder and clouds.

Closer to Vanderbilt on the lawn, John Cabot suddenly turned. Unlike all the others, he stood unmoving. His eyes appeared to rest on Lilli Barthélemy. Tracking her.

Like a barn owl, Kerry thought, *stays perfectly still. While it watches a mouse.*

What was it Madison Grant had said? *In love with the same woman.*

"Ah, Kerry, there you are!"

Kerry snapped the drape and spun around.

Pursing her lips, Mrs. Smythe leaned toward the window as if she'd settled on what had drawn Kerry's interest. "Mr. Grant it was I saw. On the loggia with you."

Drawing herself up, Kerry reached to unload a stack of books from a crate. "The guests here can apparently move about as they please. Even places someone else has gone with the motive"—she met the house-keeper's eye squarely—"of sweeping."

"Sweeping, yes. It's the sweeping that was needed." Mrs. Smythe's voice was tight, nervous. And then seemed to change direction. "The vase here, did I tell you? Ming dynasty, that." She brushed the feather duster over its broad circular rim. "Which was . . . I've no bloomin' idea when. Very old." She lowered her voice. "And *Chinese.* There's your Exclusion Act here. To not let any more of them in, mind. The people, not the vases. A muddle, if you ask me."

Kerry looked up from the leather-bound copies of the *Atlantic Monthly* and the *American Architect* she was unpacking. "You had something in particular you'd like to say, Mrs. Smythe?"

The housekeeper frowned. "There is, yes. About what I observed—"

In a blur of brown-and-white fur, Cedric bounded up just as George Vanderbilt appeared at the doors opening to the bowling green. Nodding to both women, he approached the shelving where Kerry stood.

"Yes, marvelous. Thank you," he said. "Just onto the shelves, obviously, that have been properly finished. And has everything made the journey intact?"

Mrs. Smythe was first to respond. "All the books are arriving in brilliant shape, sir. Kerry here works like a ferry on the Channel, never sitting off for a rest."

Vanderbilt smiled down at her. "Glad to hear it."

But then his smile faded. Gesturing to the top of the stack of *American Architect* in Kerry's arms, he shook his head. "See the bookmark in that one?"

Glancing down, Kerry nodded.

"Open it, please."

She did, the pages falling open to an article with large photographs of wood-paneled rooms and marble floors and carved pillars. "*Royalty in Louisburg Square*," she read aloud from the title. Then looked up. "One of your homes?"

Mrs. Smythe's face behind him said that last comment must have sounded presumptuous.

But he merely shook his head. "My friend John Cabot's family, actually. We met in Maine just before the article ran, so I marked it. But then—"

Tail flapping, Cedric charged for the door.

"Ah. Speak of the devil. There you are, John. I was just mentioning . . ." But there he stopped, reconsidering. With one finger, he closed the volume. Handed it back to Kerry.

157

Cabot's gaze swung over the room. Then stopped on her. Unblinking, she returned his look.

If he'd been in love with the same woman as the *Times* reporter, could Cabot have been the attacker? Madison Grant might be a vile man with loathsome ideas, but John Cabot could still be the prime suspect for the reporter's murder, especially if he were as prone to violence as had been suggested.

By Grant, she reminded herself.

Aaron Berkowitz had tried to warn Marco Bergamini about at least one of the gentlemen: *Watch out.* The murdered reporter must have had information about one or the other or both of them. And that information, perhaps, had been enough to get him killed.

Vanderbilt clapped Cabot on the shoulder. "Let's take a ramble down to the Bass Pond, shall we?"

Allowing himself to be swept with Vanderbilt toward the door, Cabot glanced back just once. But Kerry turned away toward the bookshelves.

A man whose family home was so grand it was featured in a magazine about princely architecture. No wonder the police and the doctor and the city leaders of Asheville—no one seemed to harbor so much as a fleeting thought that the blue-blooded John Quincy Cabot might have been involved in the attack.

Kerry ripped open the next crate. "You had something you wanted to ask me, Mrs. Smythe? About the loggia."

"Some men," the housekeeper said at last, "have got to be taught to keep their kecks on. Their trousers, love." She leaned heavily against a red leather chair near the hearth. "Well, then, I'm glad we've had this talk."

The smile Kerry suppressed tipped up one side of her mouth. "Me too."

Mrs. Smythe's head jerked toward where Cedric had been sprawled by the fire. "Whenever you're able to clean where the drooling stuffed bear of a beast has been, do see to it." She lowered her voice. "No wonder Mr. Vanderbilt has not married yet, for all his excellent points. There's the head-to-toe fur of a Saint Bernard clinging to his clothes even when the beast isn't at the moment dribbling onto his shoes." She flung a hand toward a table across the room. "And there aren't many young women who can be wooed, more's the pity, over a chessboard."

She huffed her way back to the door of the library. "Yet even with all the chess and the books and this great sprawl of a house far past nowhere, there seems to be no shortage of women vying for Mr. Vanderbilt. He's a dear lad, that he is."

"Mrs. Smythe." Kerry caught the housekeeper just as she reached the threshold. "About my father. Who is ill."

Mrs. Smythe's face lost its detachment a moment. "What is it, love?"

"That's what Mr. Grant approached me about on the loggia. He offered . . . or wanted to make it seem as if he were offering sympathy. Because of my circumstances, which I believe you may have told him about."

The housekeeper knotted her lips to one side. "Perhaps it was a bit much I shared with the gentleman." She sighed. "From long years in service, let me leave you with this, love: a person's innocent until proven guilty, as they like to say here in the colonies."

"So then . . ."

Mrs. Smythe pivoted. "Innocent until proven guilty. With just one exception."

"Which is?"

"If that person's a man, the opposite should be assumed."

Chapter 20

Lilli was standing at the threshold of the library when she caught sight of the maid—the one who appeared to see and hear and remember too much, to take in everything around her like some sort of redheaded sponge.

She felt her pulse slow—a sure sign of risk up ahead.

Lilli was not like other young women of her set—catty and deceptively cruel. She was, however, ambitious. And a note like she'd received earlier could be the undoing of her future. As could a little maid who might have recognized the handwriting and assumed some sort of liaison between Lilli and the note's sender.

Or, far worse, a connection with the reporter's death.

Here was the maid now in George's library, which still smelled of new lumber and old books and whatever adhesive they must be using to hang all those cherubs and clouds on the ceiling.

Aurora, Lilli corrected herself. *Not random cherubs and clouds, but a masterpiece:* The Chariot of Aurora. If she expected to vie for George's attention—and distract from any stray whiffs of scandal—she'd need to think and sound like a woman who understood art. Assuming she could dredge up the terms she'd not heard since her last trip to Europe.

Chiaroscuro: Wasn't that one of the words Americans tossed about in the Louvre when they stood awkwardly before Rembrandts?

The juxtaposition of light in the Pellegrini, she might try out saying. Whatever it took to keep George's attention away from strange notes delivered to Lilli, or rumors of how Maurice Barthélemy had left Asheville in such a rush, or what the *Times* reporter had come here to ask.

Meanwhile, there was this maid to be dealt with. Lilli squared her shoulders.

She did not trust other women. Men could be managed in any number of ways. But women, who weren't supposed to be too publicly clever, could be slippery creatures whose intellect often sprang out— ambushed—in unpredictable ways.

This little maid from these mountains was savvy—that much was clear. But perhaps she could be persuaded to keep her mouth shut.

Now, though, the housekeeper, Mrs. Smythe, was charging into the room, pausing only for a "G'day, Miss Barthélemy" as she passed. "Kerry, you're needed in the kitchens, love. To peel potatoes. And to negotiate peace between Paris and Appalachia."

The maid stopped her unpacking and turned. Returned Lilli's look with one of her own. The maid's eyes never dropping as a maid's should have, she fell into step beside the housekeeper and hurried for the stairs leading down to the kitchens.

Lilli would have to watch for the next chance to catch her in private. *Soon.*

∾

Standing beside her in a clearing up a steep, brushy slope at the back of the house, George Vanderbilt was holding out his shotgun for her.

Several days into the visit now, this was their first hunting excursion. Grant and Cabot stood some respectful steps behind the pair with their own weapons over their arms as her lesson commenced. Emily, wearing a cunning little woolen jacket and a smirk, watched the scene from a few steps behind the armed members of the party.

Lilli made sure she reached for the shotgun tentatively. Like a woman who was frightened of firearms. Fumbling it a bit, she lifted the gun's stock to her cheek. Ran a gloved hand over the barrel.

"So well polished." An inane comment. But better one that made her look feather-headed than one showing what she felt: suffocated by a corset, the drag of her skirt through the clearing's tall grass, and this role she had to play.

This was the price of survival: feigning big-eyed incompetence when she was all but quivering with impatience like the panting spaniel holding his position at their feet. She ached to set the dog loose and follow him into the brush, to raise the double-barrel amid the sudden, desperate cacophony of birds driven to the wing and squeeze off two blazing rounds in such quick succession that the birds struck the earth as one.

Control yourself, Lilli.

"So *shiny*," she added. And cringed at her own voice.

"Regardless of the abundance or the paucity of a man's possessions, he should take painstaking care of all that he calls his."

Lilli turned to meet George's eye. Had he meant more by this than the proper maintenance of firearms?

"If you'd like me to demonstrate some tips about leading your target, Miss Barthélemy . . ."

She smiled up at him. "I'd be so very grateful."

Wrapping one arm around her shoulders, George repositioned her weapon. "When the quail are flushed, you'll want to take an instant to plant your feet, feel the wood of the stock against your cheek, and focus on a single bird, not the flock."

His breath near her ear, his cheek brushing hers, he nudged the gun down to the right. "You'll be swinging your firearm up and through from behind the bird, sweeping from tail feathers to body to beak and then, *bang*—pulling the trigger as the muzzle passes the beak. The key is to breathe deeply. To remain calm."

Yet she could hear his breath coming faster. His gloved hand covered hers on the trigger. "I'll be right here behind you." Did he really imagine she felt *nervous* about pulling a trigger?

Her own heart rate at a preternaturally slow thud, Lilli was scarcely aware of the others in their group standing in a clutch behind them. When at last the dog was released—"*Hunt*, Gurth," Vanderbilt all but whispered—and shot into the brush, she followed without hesitation, leaving all of them quickly behind. Her mistake, perhaps—the initiative that said she wasn't a novice at all. But hang it, there were birds to be shot.

Nose to the ground, the dog was visible only in flashes as he crashed through the brambles, quartering relentlessly toward the next open space. Seeing where Gurth must be headed, Lilli hurried to that clearing's edge and took her position. As the dog thrashed through the last of the brush—and the three men, huffing, caught up with her—a covey of bobwhite exploded into the air.

In a triumph of restraint, Lilli emptied only one barrel. The quail tumbled to the earth. Grant and Cabot shot, too, one of them missing, one of them dropping a quail. Gurth went happily about his business, collecting the birds.

George beamed. "Well done, Miss Barthélemy!"

"*Merci beaucoup.*" She cocked her head at George. "Beginner's luck."

Emily had by now joined them. Her tone was telling, a drawl that mimicked Lilli's own remnants of a New Orleans accent. "Why, however did you learn to shoot like that in only one lesson?"

Lilli shot her friend a look. Women never betrayed each other on these little deceits. Not women who wished to remain friends.

George's enthusiasm bounded over her silence. "Beginner's luck indeed! Marvelously done."

Joy Jordan-Lake

Leaning into him ever so slightly, she handed the gun back to him. "The credit is entirely due to my teacher."

He took this in. Blinked. And then smiled.

∼

After lunch, the group went for a ride, then after a time dismounted and, leading their horses, strolled over the fields, golden brown, and beside the French Broad River that wound through the estate. Above were the mansion and the blue mountains beyond.

George stopped, his hand scratching under his horse's mane but his eyes on the bottomland that rolled out on either side. "I hope, you know, for the estate to be entirely self-sustaining. The forest, the crops, the dairy, the nursery—all of it."

John Cabot drew up beside him. "I can see why anyone would feel so powerfully drawn here."

"Despite the destitution of the natives," Grant added, "and the harrowing depths of their ignorance."

Cabot's retort came with a vehemence that made everyone turn. "Poverty, I'll grant you. Grinding poverty, even. But we've witnessed examples of keen intelligence. Less access to formal education, of course. But a striking intelligence, nevertheless."

For a moment, no one spoke, the only sound the crunch of their footsteps and the horses' across the dried grass.

Emily splashed into the quiet. "Why do I think that Mr. Cabot is thinking of one intellect in particular, rather than the whole of the Appalachian populace?"

There was teasing in her voice—and a taut thread of jealousy, too. She dimpled in his direction.

Stuffing both hands in his pockets, Cabot pivoted back toward their host. "There's something mysterious, something magnetic even about these mountains of yours, George. It pulls one in. Powerfully."

"Could the magnetic draw," Emily asked, "have anything to do with the redheaded little maid?"

Cabot only turned his head away.

With a rare flash of sympathy for him—compassion was not Lilli's first instinct—she changed course by addressing their host. "I'm so glad you planned for us to walk the land with you."

"It reminds me," said Grant, "of my big-game hunting excursions out West. Where I first became passionate about conserving our land. And where I committed myself to the preservation of the American bison, who once roamed throughout our great country but whose numbers have dwindled now to the mere hundreds. An icon of our country's history, nearly lost to extinction."

"That," Cabot muttered, "seems a better use of your time than some other pursuits."

Emily, bless her, cocked her innocent head. "Forgive me if I'm not understanding, Mr. Grant, but were you hunting the very big game you're hoping to preserve from extinction?"

"Perhaps, Miss Sloane, it would help you to view the thing from the other end of the telescope. If we don't more assiduously preserve the wildlife and their habitats, there will be no more big game to hunt."

Emily appeared unconvinced. But Grant had already turned to George. "Another friend you and I share in common would be my fellow Boone and Crockett Club member Theodore Roosevelt."

"He is a friend of mine, yes. I wasn't aware the two of you knew each other."

"Not only know each other, but have hunted together and discovered we share so many important perspectives. Including the need to implement urgent measures to forestall the decline of certain species. Not only in the animal kingdom, but also . . ." He paused there, and seemed to be weighing whether to go on.

"Well then, I'm glad to know of yet another friend we share in common." Vanderbilt shot a smile at Lilli. That simple trust again, she could see.

She led her horse closer to his. "If I confide in you, Mr. Vanderbilt, in admitting that I prefer this"—she swept an arm across the vista—"to even Mrs. Astor's ballroom, would you promise not to report me to the keepers of New York society?"

"You have my word. I value my time outdoors, especially here in the Blue Ridge, as much as I expect to in my library."

"It is one of the great gifts this country has to offer, *oui*? The outdoors, I mean. Pristine. Unspoiled. Abundant."

"Forgive me, but I'd have to differ with you on the unspoiled nature of the land." He looked genuinely apologetic at having to disagree with her. Lilli marveled that this man could have come from the same family of men who'd dominated American business for decades now, devoured their competition whole. "Of the thousands of acres my agent, McNamee, has purchased thus far, much of it had been overtimbered and overfarmed to the point of depletion. It's been our challenge, restoring the forest and fields to something vital and fertile."

"Everything about your estate, Mr. Vanderbilt, suggests vitality." Lilli held his gaze. *"Tout le monde."*

She meant him to hear that she included the owner of Biltmore in this evaluation. She watched his eyes widen as the realization washed over him, a wave of affirmation: Of all he'd accomplished. Of what he'd dreamed for the future. Of who he was.

Lilli Barthélemy knew a thing or two about men, the first of which was that most of them possessed only a fraction of the confidence they tried to wear like a rack of sixteen-point antlers.

But here was the youngest child of eight, an artist and a scholar, grandson of a tyrant. With her affirmation, she'd just earned more of his trust. She liked George Washington Vanderbilt II, she was startled to realize. Genuinely so.

It was Cedric the Saint Bernard who disrupted the moment, the dog bounding around the horses and up to its master, then wiping a wet muzzle against his wool trousers.

Lilli concentrated on not wrinkling her nose in distaste.

George stopped walking to scratch the creature behind his ears. "Cedric's litter was from Bar Harbor, you know."

Shifting the reins to his left hand and kneeling to scratch the drooling beast under his collar, John Cabot's tone was low and affectionate. "You're a magnificent creature, Cedric. You know, you're the first Saint Bernard whose acquaintance I've been honored to make."

George was clearly basking in the praise of his dog. Which let Lilli know she would be making friends with the slobbering beast. And therefore changing clothes more than the usual seven times a day.

"About the murder," Madison Grant put in suddenly, apropos of nothing and jolting their calm. "Forgive me for bringing up a subject none of us wants to relive. But I feel we should keep abreast. Has there been progress in the investigation?"

Lilli's pulse dropped to a faint thrum.

Beside her, Cabot's hand stilled from scratching Cedric's oversized head.

As if, Lilli thought, *he's also uneasy with this subject.*

George frowned. "Wolfe rode over this very morning to update me. Apparently, something new has come to light."

Cabot straightened. "What was it?"

It struck Lilli how very guilty John Cabot might sound—to anyone not already assuming he was beyond suspicion.

"Wolfe has been interviewing everyone he can find who was there to learn what they saw. Apparently, several names continue to come up: Ling Yong's for one, Robert Bratchett's for another. And there's also, I'm sorry to say, my own stablehand still among the suspects."

"Not Mr. Bergamini, surely!" Emily said.

Grant tilted his head, considering. "Interesting." He glanced her way—or was it Cabot's? "Though hardly surprising."

Lilli's blood seemed to still in her veins. She had no sensation whatever of breathing. No one in this group except Emily and George would be aware Lilli's father had been here and left in a rush. And Emily's naive sweetness made her slow to suspect anyone of anything ever. No one here but John Cabot seemed to remember the New Orleans story.

As if he had his own reasons for disliking the topic, Cabot was looking straight ahead.

Grant smiled amiably. "From among the three current suspects, we have the common thread: genetic descendants of Africa, Asia, and Southern Europe—so far south it's nearly to Africa and the Middle East. They can't be expected to have the same moral fiber as you or I, George. Or Cabot. Or your excellent niece."

Lilli noted the flicker of hesitation before he included her in the next nod.

"Or our crack shot, the lovely Miss Barthélemy."

Cabot glanced wryly her way. "Apparently the French, too, will soon be asked not to breed."

Grant bristled.

Vanderbilt turned slowly, stiffly, as if his spine had been fused into a solid rod. "If I'm following what you're suggesting . . ."

"Merely that some races of humanity are simply beaten men of beaten nations, particularly those of darker hue—as it's been proved. With a proclivity toward theft. Toward rape. Toward murder."

"Good God," Cabot exploded. "That's Francis Walker you're quoting, that crowd and their pseudoscience. Let me suggest you let the president of MIT teach you what he can about numbers and gather your science elsewhere."

"Really, Cabot, your temper."

"My *temper* is hardly the threat here. And it tends to be triggered by *stupidity*."

Lilli braced for Grant's fury—and she could see George doing the same, poised as if he expected fists to fly next.

Instead, though, Grant only smoothed his mustache. Then smiled. "I hardly think this is behavior becoming a gentleman. *Scientific inquiry*"—he enunciated both words—"ought not precipitate raising one's voice."

"Scientific *quackery*," Cabot shot back. His face was a deep, dangerous red.

"It's biological determinism, plain and simple. We autochthonous Nordics evolved from *Homo europæus*, with the hard winters of the Northern European steppes and forests eliminating defective genes and producing a race of men renowned for virility, strength, industry, and intelligence."

"With you as the prime exemplar, Grant? Is that where all this leads—to your ego?"

"We are, quite simply, what our genes have destined we will be. No amount of education, social workers' sentimentality, or religious pity for the poor and weak changes that."

"No." It was George's voice this time, more harsh than Lilli had ever heard him—as much of a slap as it was a word. "You're wrong. And your ideas, undemocratic."

"Yet you yourself, Vanderbilt, are a shining exemplar: your Dutch ancestry, your grandfather's industry and savvy, the genetics that gave your family the capability of earning—and deserving—its wealth."

Lilli held her breath in the tension.

Picking up a stick, George hurled it with a force that startled them all to stillness for several moments—except for Cedric, who bounded after it. "Let me say this, Grant: I have no wish to banish a guest from Biltmore. Ever. Much less one of the nation's leaders in land and wildlife preservation. And a man with whom I share any number of friends."

A *but* hovered there in the mountain air.

"So perhaps we can agree on at least three things from today's conversation."

"And those would be?"

George ticked them off with his fingers. "One, that the attack on Mr. Berkowitz was a horrible thing. Two, that the assailant must be found."

"Indeed. And the other?"

"That perhaps the quite admirable wildlife and land preservation efforts you've led would be better topics for the future."

"My only goal in all my work," Grant said evenly, "is preserving what is good. Making room for that which is best to thrive."

Turning, Cabot sprang angrily up onto his horse. "No matter what, apparently—or *who*—that means rooting out." He urged his gelding into a run, stopping only at the far side of the field to wait for the group.

Grant cleared his throat, his tone smooth and unctuous. Lilli pictured oil dripping from the tips of his mustache. "I will of course adhere to any request of our gracious and generous host."

No one else spoke. And George, Lilli noticed, fixed his eyes angrily on the mountains ahead.

~

Lilli welcomed the clatter of their horses' iron shoes on the brick—a cover for the brittleness of their silence as they made their way back to the front of the house.

The stablehand, Marco Bergamini, reached for her horse's reins. She meant to avoid meeting his eyes. But dismounting, she landed with her face inches from his.

His eyes were crackling. Full of explosives.

As if, she thought suddenly, some sort of rage had made him unstable. As if all that anger were directed . . . at her.

Taking the reins from her, he stepped to the horse's left side close to Lilli. "You," he said, so low that no one else could have heard. "You are from New Orleans."

Now she was struggling to breathe. So her memory from that day George hired him had been right. This Italian and his little brother had been part of that night of torches and death. Had been, incredibly, under her very window.

So this Italian might know who she was. What her father might have arranged.

Might be looking soon for a chance to exact his revenge.

So then perhaps she would take the offensive.

Chapter 21

Sal was reaching for the currycomb as she entered, gliding toward him with some glittering, secretive purpose. Dropping it and picking up a cotton cloth, he buffed oil into the leather of an older saddle. Buffed it hard.

What the daughter of Maurice Barthélemy was really after in coming to visit him all alone, Sal could not imagine. And whether she recognized him as one of the Sicilians accused of killing Hennessy, and one of the few who'd escaped from the jail, the night of the lynchings and the riot, he had no idea. He watched her eyes.

She scanned the tack room in a leisurely way, as if she had all day to be here, watching him. Like some sort of long arm of her father. More beautiful—and maybe just as deadly.

From beside the saddle soap, she lifted a page from the shelf. He moved to take it from her.

Her eyebrow arched. "Is this your work, Marco? This drawing of a house?"

He hesitated, gauging if he could trust her. Probably not. But he could tell the truth on this much at least. "It is."

"I know proportion and design when I see it." She scrutinized him, the eyebrow arching still higher, as if he were a stray cat who'd learned to paint. "It's actually *very* good. Do you sketch these often?"

Hesitating again, he stepped to a lower shelf where he'd stacked others.

She flipped through them. "*Incroyable.* You wouldn't mind if I showed these to George." It was more statement than question.

Yes, he did mind. But Nico would be back at the boardinghouse even now, probably huddled in the kitchen with the landlady peeling potatoes, the boy's face crumpled with worry as it always was these days—and had been for years. Sal couldn't jeopardize his position here and risk losing Nico again.

Sal stared back at her without speaking. No need for an answer when there'd been no question.

She aligned the pages and tucked them under one arm. "Now. What I would really like to know"—her voice had dropped, breathless and low—"is what Sicily was like." Her tone said that wasn't all she'd like to know.

Her real interest could not possibly be the question she'd asked. Still, he could see Sicily as if he were there: parts of Palermo peering over cliffs to the sea, parts tumbling down terraced hills of vineyards to a turquoise bay.

Resuming his oiling and buffing of the saddle and keeping his eyes on its pommel and skirt, Sal began slowly, looking for signs of a trap. "From a distance, Palermo is much the pretty. The hillsides with the grapevines. Below, the blue—bright blue—of the sea. Up the hills are the churches, the mosques, the piazzas. Streets that wind."

"Churches *and* mosques?"

"Invaders, they come. They like the island for the good life. The weather. The domination—by sea. The invaders, they have been many: the Phoenicians, the Greeks, the Romans, barbarian tribes, the Arabs and Spaniards, the French."

"Intriguing. But if Sicily was conquered by so many others, your people could hardly be the marauding, extortionist villains that one always hears."

Ignoring what her comment implied, he continued buffing. He would keep his face as still as Michelangelo's marble. He would not let her see his fear that she knew who he was—what he knew of her father and had come here with the reporter to expose.

She leaned closer. She smelled of magnolias. Voice soft as petals. Her eyes watching him work. "Tell me more of your country."

A request that had nothing to do with New Orleans. Maybe she really did not know who he was. Maybe she had no idea he'd learned who *she* was, her father's daughter—and so, how reckless it was for her to have come to face him alone.

He looked up to meet her eyes as she shifted infinitesimally closer. "The buildings, they crumble. The new Italy that is unified, it has the center in the North, the—how do you say?—rebirth. The North with the wealth, it has little of the interest in Byzantine mosaics that chip or Gothic arches that collapse."

"Byzantine," she repeated, as if she enjoyed the buzz of the word in her mouth. Delicately, slowly, she licked her lips.

He could kiss them, he realized. Could pull her to him and kiss those lips. She wanted him to—he could see that—at least part of her did. His own body throbbing, he stared at her. Whatever dangerous game she was playing, he could not let himself play, too.

Focusing back on his saddle—by now it had a coppery gloss—he steadied himself. "For the North of my country, Sicily is the nuisance, the island of trouble that Italy's boot must kick away."

She ran a finger down a length of girth on its stretcher. "What of the women?"

"Most often, left all alone to survive."

"And you . . . ?"

Here it came. Her questions about Hennessy's death.

She tinkered with the curb chain of a bridle hanging from a brass hook. "Did you leave a woman alone back in Palermo?"

Sal straightened slowly. The scent of leather and grain and magnolias filling the air.

A woman alone.

Sometimes in their boardinghouse just before sleep, Nico still whispered "Mamá. Mamá died." Sal would kiss the child's cheek then and murmur, "*Buono.* You made the full sentence." Because there was too much else behind that to even begin.

"Our mother," Sal said now, not looking up. "My younger brother's and mine. She died. This was why Nic—Carlo needed to come with me to this country." He did not meet her eye to see if she'd noticed the slip of his brother's name.

"I'm . . . so sorry," said Maurice Barthélemy's daughter. "About your mother." As if she meant it. Several beats passed. Her voice softer still. "And you had no girl you left behind?"

Sal pictured Angelina at the market. The red awnings angled over the street. The purple and black and green of the grapes mounded at her waist up to her chest.

Come back to me, Salvatore.

For a moment, Sal did not speak. Or move.

"There was," Lilli Barthélemy whispered.

"Yes." He turned back to buffing the saddle. "But she has married my friend."

"Oh. How terribly . . . hard."

He made himself lift one shoulder. "Five years. It is too long for a beautiful woman to wait."

Five years.

She'd pulled that from him. Or he'd offered it, open palmed. Like a fool. She had proof now he'd been in the country the year Hennessy was killed. And proof he'd lied about the three years he'd told McNamee and Vanderbilt the day he'd been hired. Maybe this had been her purpose: to catch him in a lie. To ferret out who he was. What he knew.

After snatching up a currycomb and sliding the door of the nearest stall open, Sal entered. Each stall was surrounded by oak walls up to the horses' shoulders, then topped with wrought iron bars painted a glossy black. Directing all the energy that would have him move closer to Lilli Barthélemy and press her to him, he ran the currycomb in hard circles on the mare's neck.

"And your house?" she asked. "What was it like?"

Who could say what she was trying to draw from him now.

"It had the walls of stucco." *Flaking,* he could have added. "And the roof of red tile." As many tiles missing as were still on it—some blown off in storms and some pried off by thieves. But this he did not say out loud.

She glided to the edge of the stall, grabbing two of the wrought iron bars as she peered in. "Sounds enchanting."

"Yes," he agreed.

Because that was what she wanted to hear. But enchanting it was not.

He worked in silence for several moments, the only sounds the *munch, munch, munch* of the horses grinding grain between their teeth and the *shush, shush, shush* of the currycomb on the mare's neck. And sometimes a louder percussion, the stomp of the occasional hoof on the wood shavings that covered the brick.

Maurice Barthélemy's daughter ran the forefinger of a riding glove down the length of one of the bars. A kind of caress.

"I've been wondering, Marco."

His whole body gone tight, his circular swipes became stiff. The mare turned her head to ask what he was doing, and why with so much force. Stroking her nose in apology, he moved to her barrel and flank.

"I've been wondering about the murder."

He stopped brushing a moment. Frozen.

The one in New Orleans or the one here? he nearly asked.

"You know, Marco, there are people who think you did it."

His heart pounded in his throat. His palms gone so sweaty he could hardly hang on to the hard wooden oval. Both arms dropped to his sides as he faced her. He knew by the look on her face that his expression must've gone dark.

Her voice dropped to a whisper, sultry and slow. "Though not me."

Slowly, she let go of the iron bars. Stepped so close he could feel the warmth emanating from her body here in the chill of the stables. She tilted her face up to his. For a moment, she stood there, lips parting.

And him, looking down. Arms by his sides. Wanting to pull her to him.

He could not let himself move.

"Maybe I should tell you, Marco Bergamini, what I know for sure about you."

He waited. Throbbing.

"I know"—she leaned in so close now that her cheek pressed into his, then her lips brushed his ear—"that for all your strength, you could never hurt anyone. Ever."

Her right hand skimmed over his curls to the back of his neck. For an instant, she pulled his face closer to hers.

But now she leaned slowly back, eyes still on his. And swept out of the stables. In her wake, she left the scent of magnolias, here in the midst of leather and hay and the sweat that streamed down Sal's back.

Chapter 22

Uneasy about Dearg ever since their talk at Biltmore, Kerry had kept an eye out for his lurking: in the shadows of the smokehouse, in the chestnut grove near the falls, in the town's dark alleyways. Because something had changed him—the stabs at his pride from the millionaire outsiders, maybe, or her coming back from New York, but not returning the same.

Like a wild boar with a bowie knife lodged in his chest, Dearg Tate had been wounded by something deep in his core. And that hurt would likely come out less like a curling-up moan and more like a roar.

She knew this, too, about him: for all his size and strength, there was something childlike about him, something easily made afraid. And that's what made him most vulnerable: being used as someone else's bullhorn. Someone else's pawn.

He'd avoided Kerry so far. Had brawled all over town in taverns and on street corners. The stories found their way back to her.

Dearg Tate's gone to picking fights.

Says you and him is still likely to set up housekeeping one of these days.

But he'd given her a wide berth.

He'd not been in town when the attack occurred at the station. There was proof of that. But he'd been infected by some sort of fear and an anger that hadn't been there before.

On this particular morning of her day off, she'd gathered the eggs and changed her father's bedclothes. She fed him oatmeal with dried honeysuckle for sweetness—there was no more syrup from the ground cane. Despite his eyes looking unfocused today, his mind seeming to float in some other realm, she'd pressed a hot tea with dogwood bark down his throat for the pain. Halfway through changing his shirt to his one other, which Tully had brought in from the line, Kerry decided she had to confront Dearg. In person, she might be able to see in his face a shard of the truth.

"How come," Jursey wanted to know when she announced she'd be making the trek to the Tate farm, "you ain't marrying him? He used to be awful fixed on you 'fore you took off for New York."

Tully gave him a superior look. "You don't got to marry every man that goes fixed on you."

Kerry smiled. "My little sister is wise beyond her years."

∼

She left the twins back at the farm stretching the squirrel skins they'd tanned over the banjo hollows they'd made from gourds. The neck of the older banjo their father had made had cracked after years of hard use.

"Mr. Bratchett said it's got to be tighter'n that," Tully insisted.

"Tighter'n this, it'll split clean open."

"Not if you do it right. Like mine is."

They'd keep each other distracted, at least.

Kerry forced herself up the last climb of the path. Exhaustion from her work at Biltmore and caring for her father had been knocking her flat for the few hours of sleep she could steal. Today, her need for answers outweighed her need for rest.

A raccoon scuttled, then froze in place at the branch of the stream.

"What are you doing awake in the middle of the day?" Kerry asked him. The creature lifted both paws, then dropped to all fours and began following her. "Better go your own way, little guy. Where I'm headed, you don't want to be."

Out of old habit, she moved through the woods soundlessly, careful to step on the soft, spongy soil rather than dry leaves.

The Tate cabin sat just ahead in a clearing encircled by maples and a handful of small outbuildings: the smokehouse, the barn, the chicken house, and a privy. On all four posts of the cabin's porch, raccoon pelts were nailed to the logs, heads and tails and all, as if the creatures were climbing up to the roof: eight in all.

Like the stone lions, she thought, on either side of Biltmore's front entrance: a decoration with no function. A kind of welcome. And also the human urge to signal abundance and wealth. Whether or not it was true.

From the cabin's back door, a path wound down along a moss-bound creek. From somewhere down that way came a clang of metal on stone.

Quietly, she slipped down toward the sound and watched Dearg from behind a stand of mountain laurel. Making adjustments, he bent over the spiraled copper tubing, spigots, and barrels.

When she stepped into view, he glanced up. Gave the jerk upward of the head that was the mountain man's greeting.

"I need to know," she said. Because there was no point in not addressing this thing directly. "What's going on with you? Rumors all over about your brawling. Things you've said. None of it like the man I remember."

Jaw working side to side, he said nothing.

She could see in his face she'd been right: a flicker of fear passing over what he always was—the laconic mountain man. And now also a fair piece of defiant. She felt like she was being sighted down a gun barrel. Maybe not the only target of whatever it was he was feeling, but the one standing there.

She braced her feet wider apart. "You don't scare me, you know."

He let several beats pass as he glowered, then looked away. "Sure way to get yourself hurt, if you ask me: acting like there's nothing can hurt you."

They stared at each other. A threat, it might be. Or a warning.

Suddenly, voices sounded from up the path, and the clomping of hooves.

Dearg glared at her—a look of betrayal. "You brung people with you?"

Kerry shook her head. "Only the twins knew where I was headed."

A scattershot of voices she could make out over the rush and babble of stream: women and men both.

Snatching up his Winchester propped against a stump, Dearg jerked his head back toward the spirals and vats and barrels. Kerry nodded. These strangers, rich and Northern and from the outside, didn't need to see the still. Without speaking, Kerry and Dearg climbed together halfway up the path where they could hear more clearly, but still not be seen.

Now the squeak of leather as the group dismounted near the cabin.

Kerry peered through a feathering of hemlock. There stood horses whose coats glowed in the gold slant of late-afternoon sun. Biltmore horses, they had to be. And its people: George Vanderbilt and his four guests.

Here, of all places.

"Why is it again," the niece asked, "we're disturbing these people?"

The niece's friend swept a gloved hand at the cabin. "Perhaps they'll want to join us for the ride back down to admire the Rembrandts and Sargents."

John Cabot frowned. Maybe at that bit of snobbery. Or maybe at the smell of smoke and burnt sugar. Either way, his scowl deepened as Grant rapped at the cabin door.

"Whose cabin," the niece's friend asked, "did you say this was? Or do we know?"

But Vanderbilt, looking uneasy, didn't answer. Only a faint whistle of the wind through the pines, and the distant tumble of waterfalls.

Grant rapped again, this time using the end of his crop.

The cabin door creaked open. A crack of only a couple of inches, through which a gun's muzzle appeared.

A shot ripped just over Grant's head, zinging through the white oak just behind him.

"Good God!" Grant cried, staggering back. He looked as if he might faint.

Kerry could taste the sulfur of gunfire that hung in the air. An eerie, hollowed-out silence followed, as if the mountains were absorbing the blast.

"As I mentioned before," Vanderbilt said from behind him, "the mountain people need to be approached slowly. With consideration."

Grant turned back to the door. "For God's sake, hold your fire."

From behind the crack, one eye peered out, along with half a forehead.

Dearg watched, looking half-tense, half-amused. His right hand spun the Winchester up so that his finger rested on the trigger. He'd always been quick as a cougar, Kerry knew. The youngest but one of twelve, for years he'd probably felt he had to be something other than the biggest and strongest and best.

Shaking her head at Dearg, Kerry reached to point the Winchester's barrel down toward the ground.

"You'uns a government man?" came from behind the door.

"Most assuredly I can answer that in the negative, my good man."

"That mean *hell no?*"

"Yes. That is, no, I am decidedly not a government man."

The boy poked his entire head out now, the rest of his body still blocked by the rough pine door. "You talk funny as hell."

As Dearg gave a low, warbling whistle that drifted through the trees, the boy's head swung around. "Hold up, now."

Pulling what looked like a thick cigar case from his coat pocket, Cabot unlatched an accordion-pleated bellows with a lens on one end and snapped in a cylindrical cartridge Kerry assumed held film. Only tourists from up North owned portable Kodaks like this, and Kerry resented his using it here.

Emily shot a smile, winsome and sweet, his direction. "Goodness. Loading in daylight."

Cabot nodded but did not look up from threading black paper onto a reel with a brass fitting. Raising the Kodak to eye level, he aimed the lens at the raccoon pelts, advanced the film, then aimed at the other outbuildings.

Kerry drew a deep breath and held it to keep from speaking.

The boy put up a hand. "Let me check down yonder first, if you'uns can just hold on to your britches. Make sure it's all right."

"Britches," John Cabot murmured. To Vanderbilt, he said in a low voice, "It's fascinating—the connections of their speech with Elizabethan England, Scotland, and Ireland, as well as Africa, significantly. Their speech, the construction of their homes, their methods of farming, their musical instruments, all of it hardly evolved from earlier eras across oceans. Like a time capsule here in the hollows of the Blue Ridge."

Hardly evolved.

As if she and her people were only a newly discovered set of Charles Darwin's apes who'd not yet mastered the art of two-legged upright ambulation.

Kerry wanted to smack him—all of them—across their seven-course-meal faces.

The boy flung open the door and grinned. "Come to cogitate on it, Dearg told me to sit tight or he'd skin me alive. Let's just hope he don't think you'd be government folks come to smash up his work. Him being a hell of a shot."

"Indeed. Let us hope."

Kerry cringed at the strangers exchanging glances. What right did they have to assume they understood her world after only a few days in it? And even those they'd spent sequestered away in a fancy hotel and a castle.

"On the contrary, young Tate," Grant pronounced, "we have come here with the offer of help."

The door, which had been inching closed, now flew back open again. "We ain't lookin' for no help from outsiders."

"That ferocious independence you mentioned." Cabot lowered his voice again to address Vanderbilt. But Kerry could hear every word. "The Industrial Revolution has exploded all around them, yet even for those who understand there are places now where one can turn a tap for hot water or flick a switch for light, none of this is appealing. It's intriguing: that drive to remain separate from the civilized world."

Kerry bit down on her lip. The arrogance of the man to think he understood.

Grant gave the boy a tip of the top hat. "Farewell, then, young man."

"Like to get yer privates shot off," the boy said, brightening.

Grant paled.

Dearg emerged from behind the trees, the Winchester slung under one arm.

Vanderbilt stepped forward. "Mr. Tate, some of my guests expressed a desire to see more of the traditional culture around Biltmore. Please be assured, you're under no obligation at all to show us your place. If you'd rather we left . . ."

Grant, having left his horse standing beside Cabot's, strode toward the screen of pines to the right of the cabin.

"Grant." Vanderbilt's voice carried a sharp reprimand. "We've not been invited to walk Mr. Tate's property."

Dearg was stepping forward, raising his rifle, when Kerry laid a hand on his back. He paused. Seemed to consider. His gaze shifted to Vanderbilt. The gun dropped back to his side.

"Mr. Tate," Vanderbilt said. "Anything you show us or not is your choice. With"—a look passed between Dearg and him—*"no repercussions."*

Which Dearg must have understood referred to something specific. Because to Kerry's utter surprise, he turned on the heel of one mud-slathered boot. "What the hell. Don't matter now what you people see." He stomped away down the path. Then barked over his shoulder, "Follow me."

"I'm unaccustomed to being ordered about," Grant quipped to the women. "Particularly not by someone who couldn't spell *unaccustomed.*"

Stiff with fury, Kerry slipped into the path behind them. Only John Cabot, scribbling notes as he walked last in the line, heard the rustle of leaves behind that made him turn. Startled, he touched the brim of his hat.

Their eyes held.

"Ah," Grant pronounced as the group reached the clearing. "Moonshine. Also known as White Lightning. Income the government has long wanted to tax."

Releasing a valve at the end of one spiraled metal tube, Dearg held a tin cup underneath a dripping clear liquid. "No photographs here," he ordered as Cabot raised the Kodak.

Dearg held the cup up for Grant—like a dare.

Grant swiveled to address the others. "There is a reason, after all, that the government wishes to regulate the making of liquor in rusted metal pipes and pots. It can blind one, I've read."

He spoke as if Dearg Tate were deaf. Or too dense to make out the words. Kerry's chest burned.

Grant lifted the cup toward his mouth but then swept it out in a kind of toast. "No, thank you, my good man."

He'd already half turned back to the others as he thrust the tin cup back at Dearg. Spotting Kerry there at the back of the group, he opened his mouth in surprise. "Ah," Grant said. "A vision of loveliness here in the wilds."

Recoiling, Kerry said nothing.

John Cabot was looking from Grant to Kerry and back.

A few feet away, Lilli Barthélemy, the friend of the niece, was trying to slip past the still, her head turned away.

But Dearg thrust the cup in front of her, making her stop.

The niece's friend froze. Fixed a look on Dearg.

"I believe I'd like to taste it," Lilli Barthélemy announced, her voice cold. "This homegrown brew of which I've heard so much."

She snatched the cup from him and tipped it up to her mouth.

"C'est bon," she said, licking her lips, voice husky. "It is . . . very strong." She paused. Looked up into Dearg Tate's face, the air taut with those words. Her fingers slid away from the cup. *"Merci,"* she whispered.

Kerry's breath felt caught in her chest. Whatever she'd just witnessed meant something. Though just what, she'd no idea.

The group made its way back up the path to their horses. Numb, Kerry followed behind. That Dearg would allow these complete strangers to pound on his door, tromp on his land, even see his still—it made no sense at all.

Madison Grant walked beside Dearg. Chummily. As if they'd met before. Grant lifted his face to say something to Dearg that Kerry could not hear.

The others mounted and trotted ahead, while John Cabot lagged back with Vanderbilt. Kerry could feel Cabot's eyes on her. Could feel he was wanting to speak.

Leaning down from his saddle, Vanderbilt held out his hand to Dearg. "Do please forgive us for disturbing your privacy. I am well aware the land is still yours through the end of the year. I want you to know I respect that. I'm glad, Mr. Tate, that we were able at last to come to an agreement."

Jaw dropping open, Kerry stared at Dearg.

John Cabot was nudging his horse close to her. Leaning down as if to speak quietly.

But, fists curled, she was already marching past him toward Dearg.

"You sold?" She could barely make the shape of the words. "So that's why you didn't care what Vanderbilt and those people saw—'cause it's already as good as his. My *God*, Dearg. You said you and Bratchett and me, we were the last. Said you'd never sell. Not if he offered you *millions.*"

In one movement, Dearg raised his rifle and fired over their heads, the gun's report echoing over the trees.

That was his answer, she knew. The total of what he would tell her right now. Like that blast as the bullet left its chamber was the sound of his loss. A bullet shot into the blue sky but falling through the pines to the ground—powerless now. A man who'd soon have a wad of money in hand, exiling himself from his home.

Kerry stood alone outside the cabin as he mounted the porch and slammed the door so hard that chinks of clay fell out of the logs near the frame.

When exactly John Cabot gave up on speaking with her and left, she didn't know.

The sun beginning to sink behind the mountains, Kerry hugged her arms over her chest. She suddenly felt very cold. And very alone.

∼

Kerry told herself she was playing the fiddle that night to calm the twins, who'd been harried all day by a restive Johnny Mac; cantankerous, ungenerous hens; and Malvolio, who'd brayed for hours as they'd tried to tighten the tanned hides over their banjo gourds. But the truth was that she needed to play for herself.

She'd not picked up a bow for years. Her father had taught her the fiddle when she was hardly old enough to stand. She tuned the strings now with a kind of frantic need to hold her life together by wrapping the betrayal in strains of music.

Long and mournful they came, each song she played. Songs handed down through the decades—centuries, even. Songs of sorrow and longing and loss.

She played on as the twins fell asleep, their hands blistered but both their faces smoothed into peace for the first night since she'd come home. She played as her father lay staring up at the ceiling boards of their cabin as if scenes from his life were flickering there.

Or perhaps, Kerry thought with a stab of pity, *he's seeing its end.*

She was finally lifting the fiddle back to its place on the wall when a rustling stopped her. A soft rattle from inside the fiddle's body.

Turning it over, she shook it. A rectangular paper fell behind the strings, but was blocked by the size of the hole.

Shaking the fiddle and using her fingers like pincers, Kerry plucked the small paper out. Blank on one side. So maybe only a mistake that it had fallen inside.

On the other side, though, two men in a faded photo stared back at her. Their arms slung around each other's shoulders. Their military uniforms crumpled. Behind them, an American flag. Even with the blur of the black and white, Kerry knew their uniforms had to be blue.

Two soldiers. Two buddies.

Two neighbors.

The man beside the much younger version of her daddy was Robert Bratchett.

Turning toward the bed where her father lay, she held up the photo. His eyes latched onto the image, and even across the cabin's one room,

Kerry saw the spark of recognition in them. Silently, she crossed the floor to him.

"Daddy?" She asked it more gently than she'd addressed him since she'd come home.

He could lift one hand only an inch or so off the bed, but he reached for the old photo. He opened his mouth as if he would speak. But no words came out.

Instead, the tears flowed. And he turned his face to the wall.

Chapter 23

A week had passed since her visit to Dearg's cabin, and Kerry still felt betrayed and bitter, as if she and the Bratchetts stood alone, two little islands of independence surrounded by a rising ocean of wealth they couldn't possibly keep back forever. She'd taken her day off this week to spend at the farm, as always, but also to walk here to Riverside Cemetery with the twins.

Kerry spotted the Italians across the graveyard, the older one's walk stealthy and quiet, his eyes darting left and then right.

Like a fox sniffing for hounds, Kerry thought.

He held his brother's hand, the boy swinging his bad leg in arcs to keep up.

Guiding Tully and Jursey behind a fold of the hill, Kerry watched the Italians moving from gravestone to gravestone, heads ducked.

"It's an awful long walk from the farm to Momma's grave." Tully's voice wobbled on the edge of exhaustion.

Jursey placed a hand on each knee to help himself up the next incline. Riverside Cemetery was like a blanket of homespun that someone had lifted in the middle and set gently down, with its steep, stiff folds all around leading up to a peak. "Reckon Kerry's got to be more tuckered than us, taking her afternoon off to come here."

Tully scowled at being bested. Giving both their shoulders a friendly shove, Kerry heard her brother's comment for what it was:

tender-hearted compassion—and also positioning himself as the currently sweeter sibling.

Tully left her scowl intact to ask, "Kerry, you reckon he wishes he could go back in time—do things different?"

Kerry didn't have to ask who *he* was. She let a breath out through her mouth. "Reckon none of us live past thirteen without something we wish we'd lived better."

Tully frowned at this, evidently reviewing her young life.

"I reckon," Jursey charged ahead, "he's been trying to show he's changed."

Tully crossed her arms. "You always did defend him. Ever' last time."

"He always needed defending," Jursey returned simply.

The three of them pulled to a halt in front of a simple headstone with no dates, only a name: *Missy Murray MacGregor*. Even that had cost them a goat they couldn't afford to lose.

Jursey's forehead buckled. "How come she didn't want to be buried on the farm with Daddy's people?"

"Because . . ." Kerry hesitated. "Momma's people were more from Asheville itself." She pointed to other graves nearby with the name *Murray*.

And because the twins were only thirteen, only teetering on the ragged tin edge of adulthood, she didn't add the full bucket of truth: that their momma had had enough of the farm and a life of privation by the time she passed. Her final luxury—her first one in years—had been to be buried in town, with her maiden name an extra expense on the stone. In death, at least, she'd finally taken her stand.

Tully was still nursing her scowl. "He could've quit off the drinking before when he did. Kerry recollects better'n us how bad it was. How sad it made"—she nodded toward the headstone as her eyes filled—*"her."*

Kerry had no words to push back at this. She knelt to brush leaves off the gravestone.

As if reseeing scenes now that she'd not been old enough to understand at the time, Tully stood looking away. "I think Momma hated him sometimes for it. And then just her being swole up with sadness, all those babies she lost."

None of them said the word *stillborn*. But all three of them looked at the gravestone. A good half-dozen brothers and sisters born blue, not breathing. Their mother had wanted *And Children* added to her marker whenever she died, but when it came time, their father could only afford her name.

"And," he'd slurred, drunk for three days straight after her death, "how the hell'd it look, that *And Children*, with the damn three of you not very damn dead?"

Kerry's expression was rueful as she turned back to Tully. "She loved him enough to hate him for all the drinking. 'Cause when he drank, he wasn't himself."

Tully knelt to trace the letters of her mother's name. "And I think she hated herself a good piece, too, for acting like nothing much happened after he'd got to raging or shot through the roof. How 'bout you, Kerry—you forgive him yet?"

Kerry linked her arms through her sister's. *I'm trying,* she wanted to be able to say, if only for Jursey's sake. But even that wasn't much true.

She scanned the undulating green and brown of the cemetery—the rhododendrons with their waxy green foliage curled against the cold.

No more sign of the Italians, at least. She released a breath in relief. Quite possibly, they meant no harm. But whatever in their past brought them here, made them change their names, made the older one jump every time the door of the train opened, best to keep the twins clear of trouble.

"*Ciao.*"

The Italians appeared from behind a row of marble monuments. Little Carlo a shadow behind his brother.

"How long have you been there?" She asked it calmly. Not quite an accusation of spying. Still, she had Tully and Jursey to protect.

The twins both ran to little Carlo, Tully's whole body bouncing as her arm pumped up and down, shaking his small hand.

Marco Bergamini—or whatever his name really was—gestured back with his head. "I am looking for a man who perhaps is here. A man who"—he searched for the word—"carried my brother one night."

"Carried your brother?" the twins asked together.

"When it was thought I had died. In another place far from here." As if offering this next phrase up to Kerry's scrutinizing stare, he added, "New Orleans."

Jursey's head tilted. "I thought you come from Pennsylvania."

Bergamini shifted his weight. "Before Pennsylvania, before the cutting for stone in the quarries, we lived, my brother and I, in New Orleans." He smiled at them sadly. "And before that, Italy. Florence. And Palermo."

Kerry did not miss his shifting of weight. His uneasiness. But there was also something fractured in him that struck her as unable to hold in the spillage of lies very well. As if he might now be ready to offer up truth—or a piece of it.

"I ask all over town when I am . . . when I have the afternoon not to work. I ask about the man Cernoia. If he came here as we have heard. If he is still living here." He shook his head.

Tully's eyes saucered. "So your plan's to knock on every godlovin' door in the Blue Ridge?"

"*Sì.*"

Jursey swept a hand over the cemetery. "If you all'd be looking here, sounds like you ain't even sure this man Cernoia's still alive and kicking."

Tully smacked him. "You don't got to say what's strung up and salted right there in front of your face, Jurs."

193

Kerry had already seen those words, the weight of them in Marco Bergamini's eyes.

He shook his head. "*Non lo so*. He may be dead, yes. And also . . ." This part he seemed to consider whether to tell them or not. "There may have been the reason for the man to change what was his name."

"Like you?" Kerry asked—but more gently now than she did on the train.

Hesitating again, he lifted his head. Then lowered it just a notch. A nod. Almost imperceptible. But a confession, she realized.

Kerry gazed out over the hill, rumpled and studded with gravestones. Then ended on her mother's marker: *Missy Murray MacGregor*.

"Do you know any other names he might have been likely to use? His mother's maiden name, maybe? Or maybe there are names in Italian that had meaning for him."

"Like a profession, yes. In Sicily, we have many of these sorts of the names: Abate from the priest; Agricola from the farmer; Cavollo from the horseman . . ."

"And Bergamini?" Kerry asked.

"What?" He blinked.

"Your name." *The name you're using, at least.* "Is Bergamini from an occupation?"

"Oh. Our name. Carlo's and mine. Bergamini. That, too, yes. From *bergamino*, the cowherd, or here you might say the dairy farmer. *Grazie*. I will think. And I will write to Palermo to ask."

Without speaking again, Bergamini fell into step with them as they followed the river back toward town. At a bend in the river, Jursey picked up a piece of paper, crumpled and soiled, that the wind had blown to his feet.

Tully jerked her head. "What's got your face screwed up like a dried turnip?"

Jursey held up the paper.

KNOW YOUR RIGHTS!
DON'T LET YOUR JOB,
YOUR HOME
OR YOUR FAMILY
BE STOLEN BY THIEVING FOREIGNERS

Four caricatures illustrated the flyer, one in each corner. At the top left hunched a man, leering, with a shaved head and a long, thin black braid down his bare back. *Disease* had been scrawled across his forehead. In the top right was a man huddled with the Star of David emblazoned on one bare arm, a yarmulke on his head, the word *Lies* scribbled on it, and a fistful of cash in one hand.

And, Kerry thought, *a reporter's notepad stuck in one pocket. As if Aaron Berkowitz were somehow to blame for his own death.*

At the bottom left was a man whose skin had been inked in dark and whose muscles bulged, his right arm wielding a scythe, the word *Violence* lettered over its blade. At the bottom right was a man with a grizzled chin and a head of black curls. Dominating his face were wildly bushy black brows, an enormous black mustache, and a menacing smirk with *Anarchy* spelled out across the bared teeth.

At the bottom center, like a signature, were the letters *LNA*.

Where had she seen that before?

An image clicked into her head. The telegram whose message she'd crossed through to use as her letter to ask for schoolbooks for the twins.

A telegram sent to Madison Grant. Something about the LNA growing in influence, especially among educated people. And the odd part about a rooster, a Reichsadler, whatever that was, and a bald eagle. And then that last line that especially stuck in her mind.

CONTINUE TO SPREAD MESSAGE: THE RACE WILL BE LOST IF WE CONTINUE THIS WAY.

So Madison Grant must be connected somehow with these flyers.

"Are these," Jursey whispered, "supposed to be monkeys or real actual folks?"

Kerry lifted an arm over his shoulders. "I think that's the point. I'm sorry all of us had to see this."

Tugging at the paper to take it from him, Kerry risked a glance, just a shiver of one, at the faces of the two Italians. Only moments ago, she'd been shielding the twins from them herself.

She crumpled her end of the flyer. But Bergamini stopped her.

He ran a finger over the bottom right image. "My hair. It needs the cutting."

She laughed, relieved. Plucking the paper from him, she shredded it into confetti she tossed into the air.

Lifting both arms, little Carlo turned in a circle, his face thrown back to receive the flurry of white falling around him. *"Evviva!"* he cried, an eight-year-old's delight with pretend snow.

Jursey hoisted the child up onto his own skinny shoulders. "The bad paper's all gone."

Kerry smiled at Carlo, who was curling down over Jursey's head as they walked together. A clatter from the street they were passing made her glance left.

Dearg Tate in a gray hat and red homespun shirt was just slipping behind a corner, a hefty stack of white paper in one arm. There, at the corner of the street, one of the flyers hung tacked to a lamppost and fluttering blithely in the breeze.

"Not all gone," she murmured in little Carlo's direction as the child giggled on Jursey's shoulders. "Not all gone at all."

Chapter 24

Kerry had the distinct sensation of being watched. But each time she spun around, no one was there.

If she hadn't promised herself they'd try a kind of help for their father bought from the drugstore on Haywood, she'd have headed them all for home. But the image of her father's skeletal face, the pain in his eyes that he wouldn't speak, made her keep walking through town.

LNA, she mused. What might that stand for?

Jursey touched Kerry's arm. "My stomach's gone to hankering so loud I can't hardly hear nothing else."

Tully shot him a glance full of disdain. "Aunt Rema said mewling's only for barn cats."

Scowling, Jursey stopped. "You gonna let her talk to me that a way?"

Kerry waved him forward. "No skirmishing among our own troops, please."

Asheville's streets bucked up and down so that its shops seemed to be trying to hold tight, awnings braced and brick mortared thick against the pull, to keep from sliding to the bottomland of its valleys. A three-mile walk from Biltmore Junction's sprinkling of structures, Asheville was bigger and more established, but still small enough to feel like a village that kept tumbling over and down the next hill.

Up ahead on Spruce Street, a gentleman steered a black horse. A shock of dark-blond hair fell onto the man's forehead as he bent to adjust the bridle.

"Look!" Jursey pointed. "One of them rich men from the station."

Tully tilted her nose in the air. "Aunt Rema said it was him caused a ruction by calling our Kerry the village milkmaid. You won't catch me tradin' howdys."

The air smelled of maple wood burning in hearths and balsam from the nearby forest. Kerry could never think quite clearly with balsam nearby.

Reining in his horse directly in front of them, Cabot touched the brim of his top hat. "Good afternoon." For all his big-city polish, he seemed to flounder for what to say next. "I hope you each are well."

Jursey scraped his right toe on the street. "Could be a heap better."

Kerry shot Jursey a look. "We are well," she said evenly. "And we hope you are."

"I was out for a ride. Not . . . looking for anything, or anyone, in particular." The words came too rushed, then too slow. As if, she suspected, he most definitely was looking for something, or someone, in particular.

"How nice," she said, not helping him.

She remembered again his disappearing behind the train station. His never volunteering to the police that he'd met Aaron Berkowitz somewhere before. His having possibly been in love with the same woman as the murdered reporter.

Cabot cleared his throat. "So, then."

"No doubt, Mr. Cabot, your friends at Biltmore are waiting for you."

He only shifted in the saddle, though, as if he wanted to speak but didn't know where to begin.

"They say," Jursey blurted suddenly, "Mr. George Vanderbilt's got himself a whole field worth of carriages here. If our roof finishes out the falling sure enough, maybe the gentleman here'd put in a word for us to sleep the night in one of them setting empty."

Kerry tried to catch Jursey's eye to make him see the fire in hers. But he was chattering now to John Cabot directly.

"We could bring Daddy, too, 'course. Ride him down on Malvolio's back. Just the four of us curled up inside'd put nobody out."

Mortification rose through Kerry's chest into her neck, her face.

Glancing her way at last, Jursey dropped his voice. "Should I not a said that, Kerry? Don't be riled."

Cabot stared at her. "Your roof. Is it really in danger of collapse?"

Kerry's cheeks throbbed. "If you'll excuse us, we need to be getting back." Grabbing a hand on either side of her, even though the twins were too old to hold hands, Kerry bolted back into motion.

Hesitating, Cabot touched a gloved hand to the brim of his hat.

They'd climbed the next hill before Kerry turned on the twins—both clearly afraid to speak. Her hands went to her hips.

Jursey ventured something first. "Hadn't we oughta answered him about the roof?"

Tully spoke up—tentatively, as if she knew too much volume just now might trigger her sister again. "We don't want to end up all out of friends like the Little Match Girl from our storybook."

"We are *not* out of friends. Nor are we out of a home."

"But the roof—" Jursey attempted.

"Then we'll sleep in the barn if we have to. Malvolio won't mind sharing."

Both twins seemed to sense they shouldn't mention just now how the wind howled between the boards of the barn in winter. Kerry dropped a hand on each shoulder, partly to comfort—and also to say they needed to keep hushed for a while.

In silence, they walked beyond the busiest, most elegant of the shops on Patton Avenue. Haywood was a quieter contrast to Patton, the former's striped awnings muted, its storefronts less brilliantly lit. But the effect was pleasant, like the bookish child content in her corner of the schoolhouse.

The shop windows were filled with kettles and ironing boards, with red wagons and leather-bound volumes of Charles Dickens and Arthur Conan Doyle. But none of them had the more competitive gleam and glitter of the Patton Avenue shops like Bon Marché.

As if the shop owners here, Kerry thought, *would rather relax, read a few chapters of a good novel, and steal a sip of honeysuckle wine between customers before turning back to the cash register.*

They swung into the drugstore on the corner, Kerry pulling a few bills from the pocket she'd sewn into her skirt.

"Cash money," Tully admired, "that Biltmore gave you." Then, with a frightened glance up at her sister, she added hastily, "That you earned yourself."

At the counter, both twins picked out green penny candy with a white stripe.

"It's like you're one brain," Kerry muttered, amused. Then, to the druggist, she said, "Is that Chill Tonic an actual help, do you think?"

He turned with a brown bottle in hand. "Folks swear by it. For the heart palpitations. The dropsy. Liver complaints." Grove's Tasteless Chill Tonic had advertisements splashed everywhere, even in magazines up in New York.

"But does it actually cure anything?"

The druggist winked. "Even when it don't, it makes a body think it does, which is sometimes the same equal thing."

Kerry bought the tonic. Handing her the change from behind the soda fountain, the druggist pushed forward a frothing glass of brown liquid.

"Company's treat," he told the twins. "Free samplings."

"Co'Cola." Tully fixed the druggist with worshipful eyes. "Never yet tried it."

He smiled back at her. "Got a nice kick to it." They drained their cups.

"Enough kick," Kerry said to the twins, "to hurry us on back home."

They made their way faster now down the street. But something at this end felt wrong. Too quiet, like a landscape of downed trees right after a storm. Kerry slowed her steps. "That's Mr. Ling's shop, 55 Haywood. But . . ."

Tully let out a long whistle. "Glass all over the street."

Jursey ran ahead. In front of the shop, he squinted. "Lord. What's *Below Perl* mean?"

Kerry and Tully drew alongside him. The letters, painted in a sickly ochre, had been splashed across the jagged shards of what was left of the plate glass window.

Kerry struggled to make out the letters. "I think it's *Yellow*, not *Below*." She sucked in her breath.

"So what's special about a yellow pearl? And why'd they spell it *p-e-r-l?*"

Haywood Avenue seemed snapped still in time like a photograph, as if all the other streets continued their bustle while this one lay stunned.

Kerry lifted a finger to the ochre paint, still wet and dripping. "I'd say the person who did this couldn't think a lick better than he could spell."

"So what'd he go meaning to say?"

From inside the shop, something stirred. A man. His shirtsleeves rolled up, ochre paint blotting one arm. Whose face suddenly turned toward the shattered window.

"I think," Kerry said, rigid with fury, "he meant *Yellow Peril.*"

And she stared back at John Cabot.

Chapter 25

Kerry struggled for air. On either side of the shattered glass, neither she nor John Cabot moved.

"So what's a *peril* do?" Jursey wanted to know.

Behind Cabot, Kerry could make out shelving hurled on its side, the contents of tins and barrels and crates strewn across the floor. Potatoes and beets, brown sugar and bolts of calico lay trampled together.

She returned her gaze to Cabot's. "It's a term, an unkind one, that some people use."

"But what's it signify?"

"*Peril* means danger." That was all she could stomach to say.

Tully was pointing to a portion of the window still attached to its frame. In large, barely legible letters, another word was scrawled—and misspelled. "*Mur-dur-er*," she read slowly. Eyes wide, she turned. "Who is, Kerry? Is the murderer here?"

Glass crunched at the back of the shop.

Kicking at a hillock of flour, Ling Yong appeared. Then watched the cloud of white snow drift down onto his sparkling floor, little slivers of glass like so much ice. "Ruined. All of it."

Cabot dropped his gaze from Kerry to turn to the shop's owner. "I wish I knew what to say." He glanced back toward the shattered window, the painted smear of words. "To make it less reprehensible."

Through what was left of the window, Ling spotted the twins and Kerry. His eyes were so deep brown they appeared black—and bottomless. Kerry felt as if she were falling into a pit of despair.

Without speaking, Kerry stepped through the open door and held out her hand. Looking around the ransacked shop with wide eyes, the twins followed.

From behind a barrel, the one item still upright, a little girl of about three emerged. Clomping forward in too-large shoes over the rubble, she stopped beside her father and slipped her hand into his.

Tully stared. One of her hands lifted as if she might touch the black hair that silked down the little girl's back.

"Our shop," the girl said with a defiance far bigger than her small frame. "They came to our shop."

The child's words hung suspended in air that was still fogged with what must be flour and sugar. Kerry could taste it on her tongue.

"My daughter, Zhen," Ling Yong said, with a hand on the child's back. He gestured to hand-drawn pictures tacked to the wall. Several bore the letters of her name she'd apparently scrawled: *Z-H-E-N*.

Jursey cocked his head doubtfully. "It's got a *Z* here, but he pronounces it wrong—like it'd be nothing but *J*." Which was so like Jursey, to stand in the very center of chaos and find some kind of anchor in the distraction of how a word ought to be spelled.

Zhen looked from one to the other of them, her dark eyes already guarded, searching the strangers for signs of future betrayal.

Kerry scanned the shop. "How will you . . . ?" *Survive* was what she wanted to ask. *How will you feed your daughter? How will you reopen?*

All that hung in the air with the fog of flour and sugar.

"Just lately, I've delivered messages for the telegraph office—as you have seen. Only very early. And late. When we were closed. But that work only isn't enough."

Kerry followed Ling's gaze to the window. The word *Closed* seemed to rebound off the points of glass that no longer kept any boundaries between open or not. "They didn't even take any of it to use."

She heard her own words for what they were: partly compassionate. But also, God help her, she was thinking of Tully and Jursey, with little on their stomachs all day, and a floor here full of food. Oats and cinnamon and platters of round, white pastries like full moons—all frosted now with glass slivers and shards. All of it inedible.

John Cabot knelt to gather the larger shards of glass into a tin pail. For a moment, that was the only sound in the shop, the *plink, plink, plink* of the ruined window.

Crossing the floor, Kerry reached for a broom. Homemade, she noticed, as her people made brooms, a birch limb for its handle and a wide skirt of stiff straw and cornhusks tied off at a tight waist of twine. Kerry began sweeping.

The twins stood gawking at the ransacked shop. But when they met Kerry's eyes, her look sent them scurrying to find little pails and straw baskets to begin picking up trash and more of the larger chunks of broken glass.

Clomping her way again through the rubble, Zhen joined the twins in their work: a mashed pastry here with a footprint in its moon face, the cracked head of a doll there, her soft, velvet-clad body slashed open. Tully's eyes on the doll, she was biting her lip as she swept, Kerry saw. Biting it harder and sweeping more violently to keep back the tears.

Kerry lifted the pastry with the footprint and studied the indentation. Soft edges with the slightest suggestion of stitching. And a toe with a perfectly rounded symmetry, no right or left shoe. So a handmade boot. A local man. Or, at the very least, someone wearing a mountain man's shoes.

Kerry bent for a sheet of soiled, blank paper. Turned it over. But the other side was not blank.

Here was the flyer again, the one with the four caricatures and the warning. As Ling approached, she let go as suddenly as if Mr. Edison's electrical currents jolted through it.

With maddening slowness, the paper wafted to the floor.

And landed printed side up.

Ling gestured toward it with his head. "I've seen this already. Around town."

"LNA," Kerry murmured, not meaning to say it aloud.

Drops of blood appeared on the flyer at her feet. Cabot was crouching over it, reading its message.

His lips moved, forming the letters *LNA*. "I wonder . . . Ligue Nationale . . ." He hadn't seemed to have noticed that several fingers of his right hand were sliced open.

Reaching for the doll with the smashed porcelain face, Kerry whipped out the knife she kept in her boot and separated the doll's skirt from its lacerated body. Running the knife down the skirt's muslin, she knelt with the fabric next to Cabot.

Taking his right hand, she pressed the bleeding fingers so that they bled more.

After giving the muslin another shake to rid it of any slivers of porcelain or wood, she bandaged the hand. "It still needs a good cleaning when you get back, but this'll keep it from bleeding onto your shirt."

Cabot lifted his eyes to hers. "Thank you. You bandage well."

"Milkmaids," she returned, "have many gifts."

Cabot blinked, startled.

But before he could respond, Kerry pointed to the flyer. "You recognized the letters *LNA*?"

Cabot reached with his bandaged hand for the paper. "When I was in Paris several years ago, back before . . ." That expression flashed again over his face, the one Kerry had read as anger and arrogance—but maybe was closer to pain he was trying to cover. "Some friends and I were briefly the guests of the Rothschild family, who lived there."

Kerry had heard the name in New York. Something to do with banking. Or with social glamour. Or both.

"The Rothschilds—and the larger Jewish community in Paris— were being harassed in a number of ways by what I gathered was a fairly newly formed group. It was led by a nationalist named Édouard Drumont, who organized riots, pogroms, propaganda of all sorts. They called themselves the Ligue Nationale Antisémitique de France."

Kerry touched one finger to the flyer. "LNA."

"Yes. Although why we'd see this here . . ."

She hesitated, weighing how much she could trust him. "Perhaps you should know: a member of your own party at Biltmore received a telegram with those initials, *LNA*, on it."

"Grant."

She nodded, not missing how quickly he'd known which Biltmore guest it must be. "It mentioned gaining strength among the educated."

"That fits with the LNA. It's taken root in certain corners of the upper crust."

"But why would Grant be connected to a group in France?"

"Views like the LNA promotes have been showing up in similar ways here—at Harvard, Yale, Stanford, in private clubs. People push back at what they see changing. You must've seen it for yourself in New York: walking down the streets of our cities these days is like taking a trip around the world."

Kerry picked through glass for anything that could be saved. "The languages, the smells, the foods—the sounds of the prayers, even."

"And that frightens some people. Some people react like this." With his head he gestured toward the shattered window. Now he held up the flyer. "Or by trying to make others scared."

Kerry rose and began sweeping again with big, angry stabs.

Ling came to stand in front of her. Placed a hand on her broom's end to stop its movement. But gently. Like a man who disliked force of any kind, even just the stilling of a broom handle.

Kerry looked up.

Ling turned from her to Cabot to the twins, both picking up shards. "Zhen and I, we thank you."

Jursey straightened, puffing his chest. "We don't take kindly to bullies."

"Most especially," Tully added, tossing her head toward the ochre paint, "ones who can't spell."

One corner of John Cabot's mouth turned up in a sad smile. His eyes swung to meet Kerry's, and stayed there.

A shiver ran the length of her spine.

Chapter 26

Lilli Barthélemy's hands never trembled. But they shook now as she grasped the envelope.

Ducking into Biltmore's empty breakfast room and closing its doors, she drew a breath, long and deep, to steady her nerves. A platter of cheeses—Brie, Gorgonzola, Gruyère, and Roquefort, in a lovely crescent—had been set out with fruit on the sideboard alongside Madeira.

Her stomach knotted. Absurdly, she pictured her insides in the half hitches the stablehand, Bergamini, had used to secure the mare she'd been riding this morning. She'd stayed in the stables for a while again after her ride to chat with him as he'd worked. He'd talked with her, too—longer this time even than the last—but made a point of not standing still. And rarely meeting her eye. Except for one moment, one telling moment when she'd reached for his sketch, propped next to a finishing brush, at the same moment he did. He'd turned fully to face her.

She'd frightened herself at that moment. Because she'd meant only to flirt just enough to blur his thinking—take the sharp edge off whatever anger he might feel toward her because she came from New Orleans and her father was rich and the Italians from there might resent her sort of family.

But she was supposed to be in control of how all this went. Standing there facing him this morning and holding his sketch of a house, she did not feel in control.

Mon Dieu, she berated herself. *A Sicilian, for God's sake.* Threatening to turn the tables on her. The black curly hair and the dark eyes and the sweat that dampened the span of his chest. His sweet tenderness with his brother one moment, his gentleness with the horses, and then, moments later, something wild and unshackled as he looked at her. Her breath coming ragged and her plans blurred.

Merde. Stay focused, Lilli.

Nothing good could come from her thinking like this about the Sicilian. Hadn't she already taken too much of a risk by talking with him several times now in the stables? By standing too close?

Bon Dieu, Lilli. Stop it. The man was not part of her world. Could never be.

If the newspapers had had their way, her father's name would have been linked with the riots and lynchings, though he'd never left his offices on the wharves. Still, reporters had been waiting for him outside their home.

"Though clearly, *mon père,*" she'd said to him the next morning, the streets of New Orleans still wet with blood, "you're not to blame."

He'd patted her on the head as if she'd been a child, though she'd been fourteen at the time. "A strong man never lets the press push him around," he'd said.

Which hadn't exactly answered the question she'd never quite asked.

Nothing about the Barthélemy family in connection with the lynchings ever surfaced in print. Which her fourteen-year-old self had taken as proof her father could not be guilty.

And she'd kept believing that in the years since, even in the wake of the occasional nightmare when she relived that horrible night. She'd still believed it when he cabled to suggest she meet him a week early in Asheville—believed that he was traveling there just to see his daughter and breathe the fresh air. Until the telegram arrived at Battery Park from one of his underlings, apparently, letting him know the *New York Times* had dispatched a reporter not only to New Orleans but also, having learned where he was, to Asheville. Even then, when she'd learned he'd fled without saying goodbye, even when she'd made arrangements to defend their family name, she'd still believed in the innocence of her father—a man unfairly maligned.

She scowled at herself in the looking glass—and was startled to see how quickly her lovely features could look almost homely, contorted like that. Reason enough not to scowl.

Running a finger over the waving lines of the inked flag that cancelled the postage and the envelope's edge, Lilli squinted at where, in her hurry, she'd mutilated the paper in ripping it open.

Back home in New Orleans, her father would have reprimanded her for being so common, not using the sterling letter opener the butler would have brought her.

Brinkley, her father called their New Orleans butler. Though his name was Tom Brown, the son of enslaved people. But Lilli's father believed in the power of image and the power of name—and the power of power itself.

Their banker had advised that economizing, including releasing the butler, might be prudent in the wake of the crash of '93. And, he'd added delicately, also after the *unpleasantness*—the banker avoided the words *inquest* or *investigation* or *Barthélemy Shipping*—following all that *foreign unrest* in New Orleans in '91.

Lilli had heard her father fume: *Barthélemys always have butlers.* Regardless of financial teeterings and regardless of Lilli and her mother departing for New York, Brinkley, the butler, remained with Lilli's father at the New Orleans mansion. Probably not even a cook left by now.

Lilli eased out the paper folded inside the ragged envelope. She forced herself to read the barely legible hand again:

We got to talk. Soon.

Once more, with only that handful of words, Lilli could hardly breathe.

What if she'd made the thing worse by refusing even to acknowledge his note? She'd seen the rage building in him. Ready to blow.

Still, he'd been the one to botch the job. It was his fault she lay awake nights now and heard train whistles and a man's cries for help. *His* fault.

"Merde." Lilli crumpled the letter and hurled it across the room.

The door flung open before Lilli even heard footsteps, Emily sweeping into the room. She'd changed out of her walking dress and into a green watered silk gown with sequined butterflies taking flight as the skirt swished.

"The House of Worth," Lilli blurted. The first distraction she'd thought of. The designer in Paris where Emily had probably bought it, and always a safe subject. But one of Emily's feet landed next to the crushed note. Far too close for comfort.

"Who in heaven's name do you have hidden in here with you, Lil? I heard you say something before I came in."

Lilli swept her hand across the span of the room. "It's quite free of conspirators, as you see. Unless someone is hiding just there outside the glass." She gestured toward the windows with their sweeping view of the deer park.

If only Emily would cross the room now to look out at the view.

Instead, Emily made a show of checking both ways. "No handsome dukes? No renegade blackguards pining for your affections?" She turned, the letter crunching under the toe of her satin slipper.

Lilli forced herself to appear calm. Casually, she reached down for the letter.

Emily pounced on it. *"Voilà!* A note from a secret admirer!"

Now Lilli dove for it.

But Emily snatched it up before her friend could touch it. "Oh no. As your closest confidante, I have every right to know what kept you pacing at night last week. And to whom, just now, you were directing that French fury of yours."

Emily spun away, right hand overhead clutching the letter. Gazing up, she wrinkled her nose at the handwriting. "How very atrocious! Of all the men of our acquaintance, I can't say I know a single one with such an indecipherable hand."

Desperate, Lilli leaped upward. Sent her friend tumbling back against the wall.

Emily Vanderbilt Sloane sank against the hand-tooled leather wallpaper and all the way down to the floor, her expression its own complex design of bewilderment and surprise.

For a moment, the two friends stared at each other.

At this rate, I'll be not only at the center of a cyclone of scandal, I'll be fist fighting those who would get in my way.

Lilli held out her hand. "Forgive me. Please."

Ignoring the offer of help, Emily slapped the letter in Lilli's palm, then rose from the floor, brushing past to walk to the window. She spoke with a coldness Lilli had rarely heard from her. "I won't pry further into your private affairs."

Lilli shook her head. "I'm sorry. I never was comfortable in school days, either, with the other girls knowing my latest crush."

Better to have Emily assume she was being denied intimate details of Lilli's romantic interests than have her suspect Lilli's real connection with the writer of this letter.

Lilli forced her head to dip, a kind of embarrassed gesture that felt deeply unnatural. "The handwriting, as you say, is not that of an educated man."

Emily twisted the rest of the way around from where she stood, arms crossed. Already, her face was softening. "Am I to understand, then, that this secret admirer of yours is . . . not a gentleman of our set?"

Lilli allowed herself to blush. And as her thoughts flashed to the stables, her blush deepened.

"Why, Lils. I do believe you have an admirer of a more—what shall we call it?—*plebian* sort. But that sounds unromantic. My, how risky. And thrilling."

Apparently forgetting the letter, which Lilli crumpled behind her back, Emily swished across the room. "Let me guess, now. Had I not seen the penmanship for myself, I'd have presumed any clandestine messages coming to you these days would be from my uncle George. Although my dear uncle lacks the bravado with women, bless him, to send you a secret note this early in your acquaintance. Or Mr. Madison Grant—ah, a flicker of recognition here! Well, then, someone to keep an eye on, at least. Or from Mr. Cabot."

One finger tapping her lips, Emily circled her friend like a detective haranguing a suspect. "Still, we have the problem of the unschooled hand—the atrocious penmanship. Which could hardly belong to any of these gentlemen."

Lilli forced a girlish smile as her friend's inquisition went on.

"And now we see another flush on your cheeks. Really, Lils, the possibilities of liaisons are endless with you. I know: the desk clerk back at Battery Park. He makes eyes at you each time we pass, and finds every excuse to call you aside."

Holding her breath, Lilli batted her eyes the way she imagined other women did when they felt flustered. The heat of panic deep in her gut she let rise to her face.

"But, no. That won't do. He would write in a smoother hand, I feel sure. Any man who speaks English, French, and Italian as he does . . ." Emily stopped there. Whipped an about-face. "*Italian.* My uncle George's Italian? The new stablehand?"

Lilli turned away. This was bad—awful, even. But much better than having Emily stumble toward a far more dangerous truth.

Emily sat down heavily. "The Italian."

When Lilli turned, she found her friend no longer with the impish smile she'd worn only a moment ago. The expression she wore now was disbelieving. Confused.

And vaguely . . . what was it?

Lilli realized with a jolt what she was seeing on her friend's darkened face. And now it was too late to undo the lie she'd let cover the truth.

Disapproval. Thunderous and fierce.

Emily thought she'd uncovered Lilli's liaison with the Italian, a murder suspect, no less, and—still more disturbing than that—a *groom*.

Flirtations were one thing, but Lilli Barthélemy always took things almost too far.

And this time, Emily's face said for her, Lilli had driven the bounds of proper behavior right over the edge.

Chapter 27

Balancing a tray of biscuits and scones, Kerry stopped at the threshold of the breakfast room as George Vanderbilt's niece stalked away from her friend, the women clearly having argued bitterly over something. The door still only open a crack, Kerry hesitated, unsure whether to pretend she'd not seen.

It was the footman who saved her the trouble of deciding, Moncrief's brogue spiraling down the grand stairwell. From four stories up, he called, "Where's the wee American lass of the fells?"

Backtracking hurriedly down the servants' corridor, running behind the breakfast room and banquet hall, and dropping her tray on a hall table, Kerry raced to the foot of the grand stairwell before anyone might complain of the noise.

Mrs. Smythe appeared on the second-floor landing. "I'll not be having my staff yelling like a bevvied-up . . ." She deepened the ferocity of her glare upward.

Like a drunk clan of Scots, she was about to say, did ye see?"

Making way for three painters bumbling past, Mrs. Smythe shook a thick finger up at Moncrief. "As if it isn't enough, whole regiments of workmen tromping past us all day, the service stairs still a proper mess of sawdust, all these workers *and* the servants having to use the main staircase with Mr. Vanderbilt and the guests. Only in the colonies would this be allowed."

Kerry looked up with sympathy. "You're doing your best to retain standards, Mrs. Smythe."

"This, and the master's still being in want of a wife to take charge." Mrs. Smythe shook her head.

"Aye, but he won't be for long, God love him." Moncrief's Glasgow burr was amplified by the stone.

Mrs. Smythe threw up her hands, then drew a finger over her lips. "Be gone with you, before I ban your ruddy face from the house. And no more shouting!" Her mouth puckered with the effort of finding the right expletive for him. "*Scotsman*," she spit at last, and stormed off.

Three floors away, Kerry and the footman exchanged glances that said they both knew Mrs. Smythe's was the loudest voice of all echoing in the stairwell. Moncrief winked.

George Vanderbilt and Cedric came loping in from outside, the front doors slamming behind them with a force that echoed across the main hall.

John Cabot rose from where he'd apparently been reading in the Winter Garden. Madison Grant appeared at the door that led to the billiard room.

From the breakfast room, Lilli Barthélemy suddenly appeared, hurrying down into the Winter Garden from its far side. She thrust a scrap of paper into her skirt's waistband.

"Ah." George Vanderbilt strode toward Kerry, who'd just picked up her tray from the hall table. "Splendid idea to serve tea in the Winter Garden on a wet November day."

Stepping down into the glass-domed room, Kerry arranged the sterling pieces on a table near the fountain: the tea and cream and sugar beside mounded pastries on the left and buttermilk biscuits on the right—Pierre and Rema drawing their battle lines even on this platter.

Lilli Barthélemy lifted a chocolate croissant from her plate, its fragrance wafting toward Kerry, who, with effort, did not let her eyes drop ravenously to the platter. "Goodness, how I'll miss Biltmore."

Lifting his teacup in a kind of toast, Vanderbilt said, "Then you must return to Biltmore, all of you. In the New Year."

Lilli Barthélemy placed her hand on her chest. "How lovely."

She moved to admire an etching that hung at eye level. As Kerry swept past, the woman raised her tea almost to her lips and tipped it, tea splashing down her front. Without Kerry's having touched her.

"Comme c'est triste," she said, running a hand across the satin.

Vanderbilt was quick to turn. "I'm so sorry. Was there an accident?"

With an excess of graciousness, she smiled at Kerry. "Don't blame her, please. It could have happened to anyone—an unintentional jostle was all. We'll just step through here and repair the damage."

Before Kerry could protest she'd not touched Mr. Vanderbilt's guest, she was being pulled into the corridor, the door closing behind them.

≈

Lilli Barthélemy plucked the scrap of paper from her waistband. "I wonder if I might ask you about something."

Kerry took a breath, but didn't let it out yet. With the breath might come all sorts of words that could end this job, her way of supporting the twins. Her eyes dropped to the woman's skirts. "Your dress appears as if it will weather the damage I didn't do to it."

Lilli Barthélemy raised an eyebrow. "You're a cheeky one, aren't you?"

"If by cheeky you mean straightforward."

"Then I shall be straightforward in return. Perhaps you'd like to elucidate why you blanched the other day when you saw a letter delivered to me."

Kerry paused, sifting out what she could say like separating turnips from the weeds they were yanked up with. "It reminded me of the handwriting of an old friend."

Lilli Barthélemy took her measure. "And?"

"And it startled me."

"What I mean is, what did you make of it?"

Kerry returned the steadiness of her look. "You might imagine why I'd hesitate to say more."

Lilli Barthélemy crossed her arms and appeared to consider how to proceed. "*If* by chance the handwriting you saw was indeed that of an old friend of yours—which would be rather extraordinary, of course—I would ask you this: Can he be trusted?"

"There was a time I'd have said yes without hesitation."

"And now?"

"Now there are . . . things about him I don't recognize as the same man."

"I see. Let us be honest, then—as one woman to another who knows what it is to have men pursue them."

Kerry said nothing, waiting.

"I'm well aware our stations in life are different. But let me be blunt: your looks are striking. And you are surprisingly well spoken for a mountain . . . sort."

"Surprisingly?"

Lilli Barthélemy was plowing on. "You no doubt know what it is to receive unasked for—and often unwanted—attentions from men you hardly know. Come now."

Kerry only tipped her head.

"At any rate, I would ask that you say nothing to anyone of these letters." The woman stopped there, as if realizing too late she'd used the plural. She stepped closer. "I can assure you, the arrival of these has been loathsome to me."

"That I can see."

Lilli Barthélemy looked frustrated with their exchange. She frowned. "You may depart."

Instead of a curtsy, Kerry managed only a nod and strode down the servants' passageway.

~

With the Saint Bernard trotting close by her side, Kerry darted toward the library. She wouldn't have long before she'd be noticed missing. On top of a half-unpacked crate, she ran her fingers over the first editions— Dickens and Austen and Eliot.

But she had little time.

Before seeing Ling's shop, she might have convinced herself that Grant's mention in his telegram of a bald eagle and a certain sort of rooster—and whatever the German word meant—were simply allusions to birds in danger of extinction, or maybe species he meant to secure for his new project, the Bronx Zoo. All the servants who'd served a meal or afternoon tea or even collected coats for George Vanderbilt's visitors had overheard plenty about Grant's wildlife preservation. But the flyer covered in glass on the floor of Ling's ruined shop was related to or produced by the LNA, the group cited in Grant's cable. So the telegram must have been referencing something far more sinister than avian extinction.

Kerry pulled down a stack of bound *Atlantic Monthly* collections she'd cleaned and shelved. Miss Hopson had subscribed to the magazine. *A photograph in time,* she liked to say, *of American intellectual culture.* The fact that Vanderbilt viewed them as worthy of keeping and binding by year in fine leather underscored this.

Surely, then, if any periodical might hold a clue to the views Madison Grant and his sort were spreading . . .

Heart racing, she flipped through one at a time, scanning for mentions of the Ligue Nationale Antisémitique or anything else that even remotely might fit with the letters LNA. She could have asked John Cabot what he made of the mention of the bald eagle or the rooster in Grant's telegram, but somehow she wanted to trust herself first to find some sort of clue.

One after another, she scanned commentaries on Grover Cleveland. On the overcrowding of American cities—teeming sewers and filthy streets. On the poverty of tenement housing. On the robber barons and their opulent homes.

The Vanderbilt name came up often. The railroads they owned. The mansions in Newport and New York. A few mentions, even, of Biltmore.

One article addressed a growing distrust in Europe and the United States of Jews and immigrants. Kerry scanned it quickly, her eye caught by images of national pride in England (the Barbary lion, the rose, St. George's cross), Germany (a coat of arms with a black eagle), and also France (the fleur-de-lis, among others). None of the articles mentioned the Ligue Nationale Antisémitique in particular. Several, however, alluded to a nationalist fervor growing not just in the United States but around the world.

Kerry raced to finish flipping through the recent editions. Still nothing specifically about LNA. And now she could hear voices as several guests passed through the main hall toward the grand staircase. Which would mean they'd be changing for dinner. And that she'd be needed in the butler's pantry quite soon.

The bookmark was still jutting out of the edition of *American Architecture*. Kerry stepped quickly for the volume. Let it fall open to the article.

Though it was Grant who seemed most clearly linked to the flyers, and the person she most wanted to find connected somehow to the attack, it seemed only wise to learn what she could of John Cabot. Before she convinced herself he could not be involved just because her breath came tight and hitched when he was present.

She scanned down the lines, gathering quickly that the Louisburg Square townhouse on Beacon Hill had been owned by the Cabot family, a branch of John Quincy Adams's descendants. The article detailed the crown molding, brilliantly polished floors fixed with wooden pegs, the inlaid marble and mahogany paneling. One of the photographs showed a sterling tea set handcrafted by the silversmith Paul Revere, who'd become better known for a midnight ride through Lexington and Concord. Another showed a parlor, which had been painted, the caption gushed, a bright yellow-gold, the exact color chosen for them by family friend Henry Wadsworth Longfellow, whose clapboard home in Cambridge was the same shade.

John Quincy Cabot might as well have been from another planet entirely than the one where Kerry had begun life. A man like that must be accustomed to letting no one get in his way.

In love with the same woman as Berkowitz, Madison Grant had said.

Blue-blooded. Perhaps cold-blooded, too. Though Cabot's efforts in Ling Yong's ruined shop made that more complicated to believe now.

Kerry skimmed the pages again: a catalogue of riches and privilege. She slammed the volume with more vigor than she meant to and was just popping it back into place when a door shut on the library's upper floor. Spinning around, she found Vanderbilt, dressed in white tie for dinner, appearing from behind the chimney on the second-floor balcony.

"I . . . ," she began. *Shouldn't have been reading your books,* was the only way that sentence could end. *And had no idea there was a door behind the chimney.*

As if reading her mind, he gestured back with his head. "One of my favorite features of Hunt's. I can slip from my future bedroom and be in my favorite room in seconds without running into the staff." Blushing, he added, "That is, there are times I'd rather not discuss the evening's menu with the excellent Mrs. Smythe until I've read for a bit in the morning."

"I understand."

What an unimaginable luxury, she'd like to have added. *To read first thing in the morning—no bell ringing for you, no children hungry, no fires to lay.*

Hurrying down the staircase that spiraled from the balcony down to the first floor, he approached. "You were reading the article I mentioned. About Cabot's home."

Nothing to do but nod.

"I'm glad you did. But that article doesn't address what happened later, the compassion we should feel for him."

"Compassion?" It wasn't a word that came to mind after seeing the *American Architect* pictures.

"I actually met him in Maine that very summer—that this article appeared. He was working a good deal with Jacob Riis."

He must have seen no spark of recognition from her.

"He wrote the book *How the Other Half Lives*. Widely discussed."

"I'm afraid it's not so widely discussed in my world."

To his credit, he flushed. "It focuses on poverty in the tenements of New York."

"And now," Kerry offered, "Mr. Cabot is researching poverty in the Southern Appalachians. For his own book, perhaps."

George Vanderbilt gave her a slow smile. "You may not be surprised that I was drawn to Mr. Cabot, a man like myself: raised in wealth but pulled"—he glanced to the fire and back to her—"to see how we might address the problems of the poor."

The poor.

Kerry felt the slap of the label. Her people. Her world. But there it was.

Vanderbilt's face was pinched with concentration. However awkwardly, he was trying to speak from his heart—from across the chasm between them.

"So John Cabot and I had already connected over our mutual interests in philanthropy. Addressing poverty with action." He gestured toward the *American Architect* volume. "One can't help but admire the dignity with which Cabot conducts himself. Given . . . everything."

From what she'd seen in those pages, Kerry was having trouble imagining why John Quincy Cabot would have trouble conducting himself with dignity. He'd grown up a prince of Beacon Hill, Boston.

Vacationed with Vanderbilts. Probably never lost so much as a game of jacks in his life.

With a sudden glance at a clock above the mantel, Vanderbilt turned. "But I'm forgetting the time. I should rejoin my guests. A conversation for another time, then?" He disappeared out the doors to the bowling green, Cedric at his heels.

Alone in the library now, Kerry tipped her head back to stare at the ceiling. The Pellegrini painting had been mounted at its outer sections and several of the inner, the rest still to be affixed.

Maybe her initial impressions of John Cabot as cold and arrogant had been wrong. She could be impulsive that way with her judgments. Maybe she'd positioned the pieces she'd seen of him into something that perhaps wasn't the full picture.

Still, though, he was a man who knew nothing of life as she lived it: struggle and loss and long, grueling hours of work, all while looking for reasons to laugh with her siblings and not show the worry that gnawed every day at her insides.

Mrs. Smythe poked her head into the library. "Ah, Kerry, there you are—still unpacking the books, I see. We'll be at that for some time. Nip up to the observatory and over to the billiard room to collect the bevvies the guests have left about. It's been enough brandy flowing today to float an ark, it would. Then report to the butler's pantry."

Kerry wound her way up the grand staircase and then, farther, up a small spiral staircase to Vanderbilt's observatory at the very top of the house, where the owner of the house or a random guest could often be found alone. Thinking. Reading. Far above the hustle and hurry of the rest of the mansion still under construction.

The observatory was empty just now, only a cold mountain wind howling through a window someone had left open. Stepping to it, Kerry leaned out to peer down. And felt the ground four stories down spin.

Hauling it closed, Kerry staggered back away from her own vertigo. Such a long fall. She'd not be coming up here again if she could help it.

Without looking out at the view, Kerry spun through the room collecting glasses on a tray. Her footsteps shushing on the staircase as she ran, Kerry dropped back down to the main hall, across the Winter Garden to the billiard room. Glancing quickly around, she found it quiet and in good order except for two more glasses, which she added to the tray. Sumptuously paneled, the room was viciously cold despite a fire in the fireplace.

Just as footsteps approached from the hallway, Kerry spotted something glowing orange in the grate. Stepping quickly to the hearth, she plucked with her bare hand at the part of the cloth not already consumed. White cotton. A sleeve. Like a man's shirt.

As the whole shirt shifted toward her, the other sleeve fully on fire now, Kerry spotted a stripe of something down the sleeve. Something like paint—paint that was ochre in color.

The color of those words, sickly and still dripping, on the remains of Ling's shop windows.

Which meant that this was either John Cabot's shirt, or it belonged to someone else who'd been at the scene before. Someone, perhaps, like Madison Grant.

And now the doorknob was turning.

Chapter 28

Kerry might have tossed the flaming shirt back into the fire before Madison Grant had fully swung the door open, but she surely didn't smooth her expression in time.

His gaze flicked to the fireplace, then stayed on her. "Well. I'm a fortunate man to find you alone." He ambled toward her. Extended a hand as she stepped back.

With a jangle of the key ring at her waist, Mrs. Smythe bustled to the doorway. "Kerry, dear—" She stopped when she spotted Grant. Her voice tightened. "Excuse me, sir, but we're needing *the staff* downstairs."

The rebuke in her tone might have made another gentleman blush. But Grant only smiled cloyingly at the housekeeper. "Naturally."

Hurrying past him, Kerry did not meet his eye.

~

All throughout dinner, as the sterling clattered and the string quartet played, Grant squinted toward the doors of the butler's pantry at the far end of the banquet hall—watching for Kerry, it appeared. Unloading platters from the dumbwaiters to give the footmen, Kerry could see him repeatedly turning to stare each time the servants' entrance swung open, but she could mostly dodge out of his line of sight.

For once, she was grateful for her place at the bottom of the social hierarchy of Biltmore: it kept her walled off tonight, quite literally, from the advances and demands of these people who made as many outfit changes over a single day as they had courses at dinner. It kept her cordoned off, too, tonight from her own swirl of emotions, all the questions she'd not yet managed to answer about who could be trusted. And who couldn't.

As the pantry door swung open and closed, she caught glimpses of the diamonds winking, the starch of the men's winged collars, the women's long strands of pearls. The conversation rolled through the door's crack in snatches. Snippets of travel observations. Bits of flirtation. Shreds of questions about Biltmore's forest.

"It's the acoustics of our banquet hall at Biltmore," Mrs. Smythe had said while they'd set the table, as proudly as if she'd designed the house herself. "They allow for a person to whisper at one end of the table and be heard at the opposite end. Remarkable, that."

Which would explain all the diners stopping at several points through the long dinner to listen to Madison Grant.

"The pronghorn," he said at one point, "is actually an artiodactyl mammal, not an antelope, although it is often referred to as one colloquially. We at the Boone and Crockett Club have determined the pronghorn is facing annihilation. It falls to us to protect them and their habitat. Without intervention, they'll not only cease to thrive, they will cease to *be*."

Later, it was Grant's voice again audible over the others: "Their sort flooding in from Eastern Europe, from Russia. So restricting their immigration is key. The diseases alone they bring threaten the . . ."

The electric and manual dumbwaiters hummed and rattled as Kerry loaded the dishes of Rema's muscadine cobbler topped with Pierre's cream onto silver platters. But all evening she kept hearing Grant's words from that night at the station and that day on the loggia.

Another newspaper man who is a Jew. Extraordinary. Wouldn't you say?

Annihilation . . . Breeding . . .

The words from those moments and this provided the rhythm of her night as she scrubbed pots after dinner and walked home through the dark.

Extraordinary. Wouldn't you say? Invasion . . . Disease . . . Annihilation. Extraordinary.

As if by *extraordinary* Grant meant *disturbing.* As if Grant himself would have liked to see Berkowitz put in his place.

Or, perhaps, put out of the way entirely. Where Madison Grant's reputation would be safe from whatever the reporter might have known about him.

~

The next morning, Mrs. Smythe gestured for Kerry to join the other servants outdoors. "It's a poor show is the flimsy goodbye a guest is given in America, even from a great house. Back home, every servant of rank lines up proper. As it should be."

Kerry took her place outside the front doors facing the esplanade.

Dusting off his top hat, Madison Grant was walking backward. "One last view of your magnificent hall, Vanderbilt. I shall look forward"— bumping into Kerry, he turned and gave a slight bow—"to returning quite soon." He looked meaningfully into her eyes.

Emily Sloane smiled at Kerry as she and her friend passed, both elegant in dresses whose waists pulled in tight and plunged to a sharp *V.* The feathers of their hats brushed together as Emily tipped her head to say something, her eyes shooting toward where a stablehand was holding the team.

But Marco Bergamini's gaze had fixed upon Lilli Barthélemy. Even in this frigid November air, his shirtsleeves were rolled up to his elbows, his arms muscled and hairy—and strangely tensed. Like he was concentrating on not moving.

Lilli Barthélemy, though, appeared not to notice the stare focused on her. Kerry would not let herself look around for John Cabot.

Grant, his trunks from Battery Park already loaded, stood chatting with his host. "I do hope, George, there's more progress forthcoming on the attack."

Together, they walked to the carriage's far side.

"It's sad, this," Mrs. Smythe sighed, "all the guests leaving. The only excitement now will be keeping the footmen smoking outside rather than in."

All the guests, she'd said.

Inside the carriage, the ladies adjusted their satins and silks. No one else burst from the house as a last-minute addition.

So John Cabot was evidently leaving, too, without so much as a word of goodbye. Not that he owed Kerry a thing. They'd only shared a few hours of cleaning up a vandalized shop. That hardly made them intimate friends. And hardly answered all her questions about him.

Kerry kept her hands clasped in front of her waist. She would work her fingers to the bone in cleaning whatever Mrs. Smythe suggested. She would go home and be up much of the night taking back over for the twins in caring for her father.

By dawn, she would be done with all thoughts of John Cabot.

Marco Bergamini, his jaw set square, climbed onto the driver's box and snapped the reins to the team. A matched set of bays, they pulled out in perfectly synchronized steps. Coats gleaming in the early morning sun, they looked not even remotely kin to the horses that roamed free through the hollows and hills.

The carriage rolled away on the right side of the esplanade. Oddly, Vanderbilt was no longer standing at the far side of the carriage.

From behind Kerry came the scent of pine.

"George mentioned it's nearly time to cut wreaths for the doors. And to hang around the necks of the two marble lions here."

Kerry turned to find John Cabot standing there, a fir wreath slung over one arm.

"He insisted when he returns from seeing his guests off at the station, he and I will try our hands at the task."

Kerry made her eyes leave his and fix on the mountains. "I'd have thought you'd have left with the others."

"That had been my plan, yes. But I had nowhere to go for the holidays, and George was gracious enough to offer my staying on."

In love with the same woman as the reporter, a voice in her head warned her.

Maybe just words from an unreliable source. Still, there were too many things unanswered about John Cabot. And too great a divide between them. Every reason to keep her impulsive nature in check.

"I'm glad. For you, I mean. To stay on." Kerry turned quickly away and slipped through the front doors.

From the back stairs that led down to the kitchens, someone was shouting her name. At the top of his lungs. With a thick Scottish brogue.

Stumbling and crashing over the lumber stacked in the service stairwell, Moncrief burst up from it. "Kerry, lass. It's news. I'm so sorry, it's—"

"My father." Her head swam.

"No, I'm sorry, not that. I dinnae ken what I was thinking to scare you. It's your house, I'm meaning. Your brother's come with the news. Nobody's hurt, but the roof, it's fallen in."

Chapter 29

Kerry and the twins worked all the rest of the day and most of the night. The roof had collapsed between the woodstove and the one bed where their father lay. Unconscious, at least, through it all.

"Please," Kerry had asked Moncrief and Mrs. Smythe before she'd left, "don't mention to anyone about the roof." Because if John Cabot—or, for that matter, George Vanderbilt or the others—knew and wanted to help, she'd be mortified for them to see it, the collapsed roof and the cabin itself. Or if they knew and did nothing, she'd rather not know that, either.

And to the twins, she said, "None of us will tell the Bratchetts about this while we're still fixing it, hear? We're already so beholden to them."

The roof was far beyond patching or buttressing now, the weight of the snow and ice on its rotted shingles and beams too much at last. Snow lay in bright mounds on the churn, on the rocking chair her father had made for her mother before the twins' birth, on the foot of their father's bed.

They bundled the sick man in quilts and carried him on a wool blanket serving as stretcher out to the barn. Romeo lumbered beside his master and slid himself into a full-bodied sprawl, again at Johnny Mac's feet, in the barn. Kerry and Jursey hauled out the woodstove and cut a hole in a wall for its chimney pipe.

Not that all the cracks between boards won't let out the smoke. And let in all the winter cold.

They restuffed the tick with dry pine needles they dug out from under the ice and settled their father on it.

"The sweetest he's smelled for a long spell," Jursey pronounced.

They salvaged what they could: the schoolbooks first—blessedly unharmed in stacks along a far wall—and then the table and the three chairs and the cast-iron griddle. And last but not least, the fiddle, the singing bow, and the two newly crafted banjos from their hooks on the wall.

As they passed where the bed had stood in the cabin, Kerry bent for a square of paper, old and yellowed, one side a sketch of a woman. It must have fallen from somewhere between the bed slats and tick. Kerry's heart stopped.

She knew the face. With no photographs of her, this would be the one surviving likeness of Missy Murray MacGregor, a sketch her husband, Johnny Mac, must have done years ago. In the drawing she stood smiling, still young and unhurt by the world or her own marriage. She clutched a basket of eggs, wildflowers spilling out one side of it. Behind her on the ground scrabbled a couple of chickens and a rooster that must have predated King Lear.

Without speaking, Kerry waited until they were back in the barn with the stove stoked. Then she handed the sketch to the twins. They did not need to be told who it was.

The drawing between their two heads, the twins fell asleep on a quilt with no mattress or tick underneath.

"We'll scrape out more pine straw tomor—" Kerry was saying, but might have fallen asleep before completing the word. The twins were already snoring.

～

Rema arrived at dawn the next morning and insisted she'd be taking more turns with Johnny Mac's care.

"Mrs. Smythe's got a whole army of cooks now. They ain't near as good, so no chance of me losing my place." She winked. "But with Mr. Vanderbilt's family all descending on him like the plague from New York, they'll be eating nothing but highfalutin Frenchified food for the next week. Mr. Vanderbilt, he'd take my biscuits any day over croissants, but it gives me some time to help out around here."

She surveyed the barn as if it didn't smell of manure, didn't crunch with straw underneath. "Well, now. We'll hang some quilts in the stall here, keep out the worst wind. Be right snug and homey. Woodstove. Table. Chairs. Got all we need."

"And the fiddle Daddy loved, and the other instruments," Jursey pointed out.

Rema kissed him on top of his head. "Goes without saying you brung those."

She and Kerry exchanged glances. The weight Kerry felt—caring for her father, overseeing the twins, needing to work night and day, still missing the life that she'd left—had just gotten heavier still with the collapse of the roof and the move to the barn. She felt now like her own chest might cave in with the weight.

But Rema's eyes held her steady. Helped her breathe.

$\sim$

Letting the twins accompany her since Rema was there to watch Johnny Mac, Kerry and Jursey and Tully half slid, half slogged back to Biltmore—just in time for Kerry to change into the black dress and white apron she loathed. Still, the whole house smelled of pine and cinnamon and cloves. Every fireplace on the main level blazed.

Sleigh bells echoing from far down the Approach Road, a team of Clydesdales trotted through the front gates in perfect step, a fine spray of snow from each landing hoof. From the steps of Biltmore, Kerry could make out the sleigh's load: a magnificent Fraser fir.

Tully and Jursey and the children of other estate workers in the house and dairy and forestry crew had been pummeling each other with snowballs at the edge of the esplanade. Now they all stopped to gawk— the twins' heads, Kerry saw with a smile, pitching left at the same angle.

What a gift to be young, Kerry thought. *To not envy the glittering Biltmore and its acres of rooms. To not worry about how you'll be eating or where you'll be sleeping tomorrow. To just enjoy the moment, the snow, the beauty, the bells.*

Kerry tried to remember if she'd ever felt young.

To her surprise, though, she felt herself smile. Snow did that to her. So did the twins. And the scent of pine. Helped her forget for a few blessed minutes at once.

Charles McNamee gestured to Vanderbilt across a line of staff gathered to watch the tree's arrival. "From the Douglass farm. One of the larger single tracts purchased early on."

Standing near Vanderbilt, Kerry hadn't planned to speak out loud. "My neighbors."

But then both men were looking at her as she watched the approach of the sleigh and its tree.

This time she faced them. "The Douglasses were my neighbors."

Hesitating, McNamee edged closer. "She's right. I don't recall all the positions of all the farms without checking our records, naturally—not for tens of thousands of acres. But the earliest and the final ones are more vivid. I do recall the MacGregor land abutted the Douglass tract."

"Abuts," she corrected—smiling so it might not sound rude. "Forgive me, Mr. McNamee, but it's still present tense. Still my farm next to the old Douglass place."

The two men exchanged glances—*oddly troubled glances,* she thought.

Vanderbilt broke the silence, shifting his attention toward the sleigh gliding toward them down the long drive, the horses tossing their heads, the three men in the driver's seat all windblown and beaming. "Glad Cabot was able to stay longer."

"Poor fellow," McNamee added.

Picturing the palatial home on Louisburg Square in Boston that the *American Architect* had featured, Kerry's head lifted. But there was no time to ask why McNamee would call the owner of such a home a *poor fellow*.

The Clydesdales stomped to a halt in front of the stairs. Everyone talking and laughing, the sleigh bells still ringing as the horses shook their heads, the gathered crowd moved forward to help with untying the tree.

His cheeks flushed with the cold, John Cabot leaped from in between Marco Bergamini and Robert Bratchett on the driver's seat. In his arms were boughs of evergreen of all sorts—white pine and hemlock and fir. Fumbling, he thrust out a hand to Vanderbilt and then McNamee.

Turning to Kerry, he fastened the ends of a balsam bough into a wreath and held it out to her. "For the neck of a lion, perhaps?" Dropping to his knees in the snow, he circled another bough around the neck of the other marble lion. He leaned back. "What do we think, Mrs. Smythe?"

The housekeeper nodded approvingly. "I think, Mr. Cabot, that you, sir, have a proper good eye."

With his eyes brighter than Kerry had ever seen on him, he looked up at her. "The ridge up there—close to your farm, isn't it? Yours and Tully's and Jursey's?"

"Yes. And . . ."

"Yes?"

"You remembered their names."

"They're your family." He stood. Seemed about to say something more. But appeared to change his mind, sweeping his arm up toward the ridge. "It's spectacular in the snow. The views. The hemlocks and hardwoods. Not completely deforested like so many of the acres George bought."

Her heart squeezed as she pictured it. "Exactly why we could never sell. I'll work my hands clear to the gristle first."

She could see his eyes widen and fix on her—*almost,* she thought, *too fixed. As if determined not to exchange glances with anyone else.*

"I wonder," he ventured, "if you'd be willing to show me your farm one day soon. I know it's nearly the Christmas season and Mrs. Smythe has you working quite late in the evenings. But if you have a few hours off, would you and your brother and sister be willing to show me?"

He knew a surprising amount of her life. She yanked another long strand of twine loose from the Fraser fir where it was bound to the sleigh. Then raised an eyebrow at him. "So you can explore more of the oddities of hillbilly ways, Mr. Cabot?"

"Ah. Fair enough." The shock of hair flopped onto his forehead as he smiled. "I won't pretend to understand these mountains as you do. But I will tell you that I find myself drawn here. In ways I can hardly explain. As if I'd come home."

Kerry turned with the loosed strand of twine in one hand. And the smile she gave back was genuine. "Actually, Mr. Cabot, you did fine just now explaining."

~

Every available person on the estate, including several workers from the farm and the forestry crew—and the owner of Biltmore himself—bent a back to help drag the giant fir indoors and across the house to the banquet hall. The children of the estate workers bounced and milled

235

about, snatching up twigs of fir, then sticking them behind each other's ears and into frayed collars, all of them squealing.

"Proper gutted, far too crowded it is with all these," Mrs. Smythe groused—but quietly, out of range of the ebullient George Vanderbilt. "Doing my head in, that's what."

A man smelling of tobacco and burnt sugar shouldered in beside Kerry to grip part of the trunk.

"Dearg." She surprised herself at the stir of being both glad—the habit of years—and deeply uneasy. "It's been a while since we've seen each other."

"I seen you some. From a distance. When you didn't rightly see me."

"Actually, I saw you from a distance once, too. When I was walking through Asheville. There was the most awful broadside on a lamppost at the corner."

Even as they both sidestepped along with the Fraser fir, he gave her a look full of flint and powder.

Then, strangely, his gaze swung to Marco Bergamini. And back.

Had Dearg seen them walking together from Riverside Cemetery and made some sort of assumptions?

At the hall's end opposite the three fireplaces, Dearg and Robert Bratchett clambered up wooden ladders propped high against the far wall. From below, the Italian tossed them each one end of a long rope whose middle was looped around the top of the fir.

As a group of men below lifted and positioned its trunk into a tin bucket of water, the men on the ladders leveraged the tree's top until it stood straight. Forming a half circle below, the children clapped, their heads resting on their backs as they gaped up at the giant fir. It was Tully who began to sing, her voice clean and pure as the winter air, the others joining in:

O Christmas tree, O Christmas tree . . .

Close to where Kerry stood, Bratchett directed securing the tree. "Grown, spun, and twined it myself, this rope. Soaked that sapling for months before cutting the strips. Tie that one higher."

Dearg scowled. "Reckon I can judge my ownself what'll hold good," he barked from the ladder.

The children's singing faltered.

"A little higher." Bratchett pointed. "Good. Now at least three more. But not so many they show up from below. That's right. Tie the ends near the organ up there. That should hold."

"Buono." Marco Bergamini stepped back to survey their work. *"Sembra buono."*

Dearg dropped from a fourth of the way down the ladder to land beside him. "How 'bout you speak English, Geppetto."

Silence rippled over the room now until all was quiet. Dearg stood braced, head lowered slightly, like a bull ready to charge. "Had just about enough of your kind." Spittle spewed from his lips, and he wiped his mouth with his shirtsleeve.

Raising an eyebrow, the Italian said nothing.

"You people come here, getting paid more to cut stone than I do to break my back digging dirt."

"I have only just come," Bergamini put in. But Dearg wasn't listening.

It was as if, Kerry thought, some invisible hand were moving Dearg's mouth like a puppet's. Some other force slowing his movements, slurring his words.

"You come here with all your disease, and you sneak around scaring good law-abiding citizens. Don't think I don't know what you're after."

McNamee cleared his throat. "Mr. Tate, is it? Perhaps a short break . . ."

Kerry slipped forward to place a hand on Dearg's shoulder. "Hey. What's gotten into you?"

As if her hand were tongs just out of one of the fires at the opposite end of the room, he jerked away. "Don't be thinking people can't see what the hell's going on."

George Vanderbilt stepped into his path. "Mr. Tate, I believe it's time you left. *Now.*"

Scowling, Dearg stomped toward the main hall.

"Out through the kitchen courtyard with you, meff!" Mrs. Smythe called after him. "I won't be having the servants tracking more mud out where Mr. Vanderbilt's guests come and go."

Dearg whirled, fists clenched as the crowd huddled closer to the tree. A child whimpered, edging closer to his dairyman father.

Dearg's steps reverberated through the banquet hall as he stormed out through the back corner door toward the kitchens below. For several beats after the echoes of his footsteps faded, nobody spoke.

Tilting his head back to see to the tree's very top, Vanderbilt spoke pointedly in Italian. "*Buono. Sembra buono.* Not just good but excellent. And now, Mrs. Smythe, if you could bring some of that mulled cider for everyone as we decorate Biltmore's first tree."

Mrs. Smythe reappeared from the breakfast room, an enormous sterling tray in her arms, the air of the banquet hall filling with cinnamon and cloves, brown sugar and apple, on top of the scents of glowing maple wood in the three fireplaces and the Fraser fir.

From below came a crash, as if a whole line of copper pans had been knocked to the floor.

Dearg, Kerry knew. *Making his way out through the kitchen courtyard. With something vicious and raging inside him.*

Chapter 30

Christmas Eve 1895

Sliding from the long-legged chestnut Mrs. Smythe had insisted that Kerry use for this errand in town, Kerry led the horse by the reins toward the train station. She wasn't much of a horsewoman. Their mule, Malvolio, was fully as stubborn as the cliché about his sort would suggest, requiring maximum effort just to make him walk. But this gelding seemed willing enough to comply with whatever she asked, and glad just to be out in the winter air—as she was. She tied him to a white pine in a pool of full sun.

Being here at the station again made it all replay in her head. Like one of Mr. Edison's sprocketed movies, the pictures rolled in jerks and flashes, but she could see it all: the crushed boneset plant where the rail dog had landed, the reporter's too-still body, his phylacteries—small black boxes to aid with prayer—there in the mud . . . And before that, his turning around in his seat on the train to speak with her. His face, so alive with purpose and courage, when he spoke of newspapers and democracy.

Kicking snow in front of her, Kerry slowed as she approached the Western Union window. The telegrapher, Farnsworth, was probably more likely than anyone to know who was where in Best—Biltmore Junction—sitting as he did in the busiest part of the village and listening more than he talked. Today, in the few minutes she had before Mrs. Smythe's order was ready, Kerry needed to find Dearg. Word on the ridge was he and his brother had moved off their farm now for good.

As she kicked at the snow, she thought again of what she'd spotted that night on the ground. *The phylacteries. Symbols of the reporter's faith and background. Little black boxes that had gone . . . where? Did the police have them now?*

Kerry reached the window. "Mr. Farnsworth."

The metal arm of the machine on his desk was tapping out a message. Round glasses sliding low on his nose, he glanced up without raising his head, as if to remind her how busy he was.

"I wonder if you might know where I could find Dearg Tate."

Farnsworth kept his eyes on the metal arm. "Do I look like I'm paid enough to answer inane questions?"

"As part of your job, probably not. But I was asking you as a part of this village."

"Village is going to hell, if you ask me. That help?"

Beside Farnsworth was the framed crest on the desk Kerry had spotted earlier. Now, though, she looked more closely. In its swirl of embellishments was a fleur-de-lis and, inside its central shield, a silhouette that looked like her own King Lear posing above the hens at the break of dawn.

A rooster.

"A Gallic rooster?" It was only a guess, an impulse, a flash of recalling the fleur-de-lis in the issue of the *Atlantic Monthly* that depicted symbols of national pride, including of France. But she'd said it aloud before it occurred to her that caution might be in order in dealing with Farnsworth.

The telegrapher lifted his head. Narrowed his eyes.

"Edward Farnsworth," she continued. "Not exactly a French name."

Farnsworth's lips did not part, but one half of his mouth lifted in almost a smile. Like a chess master finally finding a worthy opponent.

"So the Ligue Nationale Antisémitique . . ."

An unlit cigarette dangled from his lips—just like on the night of the attack. "What the hell is it you're trying to ask?"

"On the night of the murder here, you'd disappeared, too, just before the reporter—the *Jewish* reporter—was killed."

Farnsworth lifted an eyebrow at her, as if daring her to go on.

Kerry's insides clenched.

From a few feet away, the stationmaster strode over and shook his head at the telegraph operator. "Farnsworth's been a real ass lately. More than usual, even."

The telegrapher pressed his thin lips into a line and held Kerry's gaze. She could see nothing there. Not guilt. Not an attempt at denial. Only . . . what was it? A kind of pride. A viciousness, maybe, too. And a challenge.

"As it happens, Kerry," the stationmaster offered, "I can answer your question. Hadn't seen Dearg myself since he got back from Whitnel—day after the attack it was that his train come in. But I heard the Tate brothers took up at a boardinghouse, 48 Spruce over to Asheville. Lived there myself when I first moved here, which is how I'd know. Keep up some with Mrs. Reynolds, lady that runs it."

"That's kind. Thank you." Kerry glanced at the sun. She'd have to ask the chestnut to run if she wanted to cover the three miles to Spruce Street from the village, talk briefly with Dearg—if she could find him—pick up the Biltmore order, then get back to the house in the span of time Mrs. Smythe would expect. And also before dark. The thought of the dark and Dearg together made Kerry queasy.

But, then, so did the thought of standing here with Edward Farnsworth and his crest.

Farnsworth. Now new images joined the others still jerking and flashing through her mind: The telegrapher circling behind the station. Wrenching the rail dog from its hooks. Hauling it high above his head. Bringing it down in one vicious arc on the newspaper reporter.

241

~

"He's here," Mrs. Reynolds pronounced. "Oddly enough. Because he rarely is." She sniffed, censorial and disapproving. She squinted at Kerry. "You may meet with him in the parlor just here." She gestured to the left, a room crowded with overstuffed chairs and fringed lamps. "Or you may go up to his rooms on the third floor. Depending."

On what type of woman you are went unsaid. But Kerry heard it clearly.

That was the wonderful thing about being from a class of people already suspect. You were free to do as you liked, since no one expected much from you.

"I'll just be a few moments. So I'll trot on up."

The landlady smirked. But Kerry was already mounting the stairs as fast as her skirts would allow.

Dearg opened at the first knock—apparently expecting someone else. At the sight of Kerry, his eyes rounded.

With a flicker of fear, Kerry thought, *before the defiance set in again.*

Even as he stepped back to let her inside, saying nothing in the way of greeting, his face had already shut down to defensive. Walled off.

He motioned to a chair. But remained standing himself. So Kerry did, too.

"I won't keep you long, Dearg."

He crossed his arms over the wide breadth of his chest.

"It's good to see you," she began. The truth was she'd have rather chewed rusty nails than come here to ask what she had to ask.

His voice came hoarse, more emotion behind it than he would let show. "Good to see you, too."

"Dearg, I'm not here to challenge your decision to sell your land. I know as well as anybody how hard it is to hang on. Especially now, with so few of us left."

His face relaxed a bit. Again he motioned her to a chair, and this time they both sat.

Kerry let her eyes roam over the room. Just a small, iron-framed bed and wooden dresser, and an army cot in one corner—no doubt for Jerome, who must be at school. Dearg had brought little with him from his homeplace, his mother's spinning wheel and churn and loom probably all left for the workmen who would surely dismantle the cabin now that the land was part of Biltmore. He'd brought three guns, though: his great-grandfather's old flintlock hung over the bed, the Winchester stood propped near the door, and a pistol sat on the small table. As if he needed to be ready for some sort of violence that could arrive at his door any moment.

Her eyes moved from the door and its rifle back to him.

"Ain't a safe world anymore," he said.

"Was it ever?"

His face, ruddy and handsome, contorted now—almost as if he wanted to cry. "Things was good before. Not easy. But good. Now look. At you and me, our land. We been shoved out. And by what? Some rich Yankees think they can hoard half the Blue Ridge. And a pack of foreigners coming here with all their damn crime."

"You mean the murder?"

He looked away. "Not just that."

"What else?"

"There's all kind of damage they come here to do." The amber of his eyes softened a moment. "You need protecting." He reached out a big, callused hand and touched her knee, but then looked quickly away.

"No, Dearg. I don't. I'm just fine."

He stared at her for a moment. Then clenched his jaw. His eyes that had been warm on her only a moment ago had gone cold. Defiant.

"Look as much doubtful as you want, Kerry MacGregor. You'll see. It's liable to not be our own damn country much longer. They're taking over."

"Who's *they*?"

"All them who shouldn't come in the first place—don't belong. The dagos. The Jews. The coloreds. All them."

Kerry thought of Aunt Rema's advice and counted to ten. "Isn't this really more about your feeling pushed out?"

"You wait. Whole damn race'll be lost if things keep on like this."

"What race are we running here?"

"Not running. It's the white race that's fixing to pass. Here. France. Germany. Everywhere. There's research—scientific—to prove it. Just a matter of time. Won't be nothing left of us. 'Less things get changed. Fast."

The white race. Kerry blinked, the image of that telegram Madison Grant received flashing into her mind: Gallic rooster. Part of the crest hanging in Farnsworth's office, and a symbol of French pride. *Reichsadler* must be a German word, though she'd no idea what it meant—some symbol of German pride, surely. So the bald eagle must stand for the United States, not some wildlife preservation effort of Grant's.

And the cable's last words: *the race will be lost if we continue this way.* So, then, the sender had used race with a double meaning: a competition about to be lost, but also a reference, fearful and frantic, to skin color and nationalism.

"My God, Dearg. How did Madison Grant and Farnsworth and their sort infect you?"

He pulled his pocket watch out and set it on his thigh. Kerry felt as if its second hand were throbbing inside the room. "Kerry MacGregor and her famous *noticings*, that it?"

"Dearg. I know you." His eyes met hers, and for a moment, she could see only the old schoolhouse slates, the forget-me-not flower chains, the bare feet in icy spring creeks. "You're parroting these things. What you're saying—it's not the boy or the young man I knew."

Her eyes swept over his room again, landing this time on the table to her left. She'd noticed only the pistol last time she'd looked, but now she saw the stack of paper beside it. Crudely printed with bold type and caricatures.

Kerry held up one of the flyers. "A man like Madison Grant seems so suave and polished and smart, but he can suck you down in a whole river of trouble. Cause a whole ocean of hurt."

The look Dearg leveled at her roiled with resentment. Anger that radiated from him.

And also confusion, Kerry thought, *at being left behind in a world changing so fast, so utterly—the ground shifting under his feet while he tries just to stand still.*

"Dearg, was it you who vandalized Ling Yong's shop?"

Rising, he walked to the door. Ran a hand over the muzzle of his Winchester. His way of saying he was done talking.

"Dearg, it's Christmas Eve. We've known each other our whole lives. We—"

"Been damn important to each other," he finished for her, his voice gone hoarse.

He opened the door for her. To leave.

"Merry Christmas, Kerry MacGregor," he said.

She waited, searching his eyes to see if he really meant her to go like this. Shoved out.

She squeezed shut her eyes against the sweet images of the past: the barn dances, the stolen kisses beside the falls.

When she opened them, he'd pressed his lips hard together in his square jaw, trapping in words he couldn't—or wouldn't—say. For an instant, his eyes softened again, his hand lifting as if he would touch her face. But the hand dropped. The eyes looked away.

"Merry Christmas, Dearg Tate," she whispered. And left.

Chapter 31

Leblanc glowered at the telegrapher, this scrawny little man with a mangy beard on the other side of the glass—*and splotchy teeth,* Leblanc saw, *like spots of a dog's urine in snow.* "You heard me. A cable to New Orleans. And I don't have all day."

Waiting by a sleigh near the platform, a groom in full livery was stomping his feet to keep warm. Full livery. Here. Miles past the middle of nowhere. What the hell was *that* about?

The telegrapher appeared not to take well to goading from an outsider. *Damn these provincial idiots—this whole sorry excuse for a town.* The man sat down with exaggerated slowness at his machine. "You want this telegram to go to . . . who'd you say in New Orleans?"

"Mr. Maurice Barthélemy."

"Spell that name."

Leblanc sounded out the letters.

"Sender's name?"

"L-E-B-L-A-N-C."

A beat of silence. "And you'd like to say . . . what?"

"Followed here from Penn quarry. Stop. Closing in on Catalfamo. Stop."

"That's it?"

"That's all the hell that's needed."

"Seeing as how it's Christmas Eve, most of my customers today have added a greeting of the damn season."

A snort: "So I can pay extra for the *Have a hell of a Merry Christmas*—that I'm having to spend in some godforsaken mountains hundreds of miles from any form of civilization?"

"I assume that is a *no* on the greetings of the season, then."

The groom or footman or whatever he was in that ridiculous livery, Leblanc noticed, looked like he'd walked out of a damn storybook. Hat pulled down over his eyes and collar up high. Gold embroidery on a red coat.

"Looks like a damn Buckingham Palace guard. Here in this backwater."

The telegrapher looked as if he might take offense but then shrugged. "George Vanderbilt's got his people all fancied up for tonight. Got a house here, just now getting finished. Whole pack of his family'll be arriving on the next train." He nodded toward a slim man with a neatly trimmed mustache who'd stopped to talk with the guy in livery. "Why Vanderbilt himself'd be here."

Leblanc huffed on the muddy edge of the street, his breath coming in puffs of steam. "So. Any hotels here fit for a man of taste? Looks to me like nothing but pine trees and snow."

"Should've gotten off one stop later for Asheville. 'Bout three miles up is Kenilworth. Battery Park Inn. Some others." He pointed to a road leading west.

"So now I'm supposed to walk three miles in the snow? Here to catch a dangerous criminal, and you're telling me I got to *walk* three miles to a decent hotel?"

On the other side of his window, which hadn't been cleaned for some time, Farnsworth glanced up indifferently from the metal arm. "Do I look like I'm paid enough to send messages for outsiders showing up here all rude *and* then solve their problems?"

Leblanc took stock of the man. "Fortunately for both of us, I'm paid well enough both to be rude *and* get the answers I want." Pulling a money clip from the breast pocket of his coat, he peeled off two bills, which he shoved through the opening where the glass ended and a narrow wooden shelf began.

The telegrapher slid the money into his pocket without comment. "Livery stable's a block that way"—he jerked his head east—"if anybody's still there this time of evening, night before Christmas. So what crime's he wanted for?"

The detective paused for dramatic effect. Then pronounced the word slowly, in two separate parts, as if he'd rolled both around in his mouth, tasting them: "Mur-der."

The telegrapher narrowed his eyes. "Who's he supposed to have killed?"

"Not *supposed to have*. The victim himself named his killers before he died."

"Said the man's very name, did he?"

"Identified the killers, let's just say. This was one of them that got away."

Farnsworth crossed his arms. "This was what year?"

"Ninety—when it happened. Ninety-one when the bastard slipped the grasp of justice."

"Hold on. You've been chasing this guy for four, five years?"

"'Bout the size of it, yeah."

"So this guy's kept you bumbling around for half a decade."

Leblanc clipped his words. "Pinkerton detectives do not *bumble around*."

"Just surprised you hadn't caught the fellow is all."

"Jackass," the detective muttered as he stalked away.

Farnsworth gave two taps to the metal arm of his machine. "Message received," he called.

But now the ground was shaking, the hemlocks shivering branches of snow to the ground. A train's whistle echoed off the mountains and drifted through the valley.

By the time Leblanc returned on a hurriedly rented horse, its saddle blanket rumpled under the pommel, a front hoof pawing at a snowdrift, the train had been unloaded. Through billows of steam he could make out what appeared to be several brown bears balanced up on two feet. The sallow light of a lamppost, though, showed them to be women in head-to-toe furs.

Out of curiosity—which was his damn job, after all—Leblanc kicked his nag forward to where he could both see and hear.

The oldest of the women was reaching for Vanderbilt's hand. "*George*, dear. We cannot wait to see your Biltmore in all its glory, son."

Vanderbilt kissed her on the cheek. "A bedroom has been designed specifically for you, Mother. How good to have you back."

The groom—or whatever he was—had been joined by others unloading trunks and hatboxes from the train into a second and third sleigh pulled now behind the first.

Bundled in their furs and clutching the servants' hands, the Vanderbilts piled into the first two sleighs, their towers of trunks being hauled into the third.

Another of the women, this one younger, perhaps in her forties, had been gazing in a full circle about her. "Oh. Heavens. How *remote* a spot, George. How do you bear the isolation from society?"

Leblanc couldn't make out what Vanderbilt murmured to the woman—something boringly bland and polite from the tone.

"Still, it's a relief to be out of New York," the woman said. "Really, George, three-fourths of the city now are foreigners. Good God, their goulashes and garlics, their pigs and chickens and hordes of children, half of them reeking of disease. And the *smells*. A complete dearth of simple hygiene."

Letting the servant in the ridiculous livery hand her up into the sleigh, she paused at its running board to address the others. "This mystery home of George's will be a lovely respite, I'm sure—if only for the pure, unpolluted air."

The servant's arm must have slipped then, nearly dropping the woman flat into the snow. But he recovered in time to catch her fall.

The sleighs loaded, the Vanderbilts and their furs and trunks went jingling off toward a break in the trees and a big, hulking arch of an entrance of some sort.

"Waste of my damn time watching all that," Leblanc muttered. He kicked his horse into a trot, snow winging out from each step, heading in the direction the idiot telegrapher had pointed.

Chapter 32

It took only the one sentence whispered to her from the doorway, and Kerry's hands went unsteady, which she realized not by a look down at them but by the sterling flashing in the firelight. Gold and red and green sparked from the edges of the platter that her hands gripped, wobbling.

Tully and Jursey had been invited to spend the night at Biltmore tonight in an empty servant's room with Kerry since she would be working late. Ella Bratchett had offered again to care for Johnny Mac in Kerry's absence.

Kerry had held her arm. "Please let me pay you for your time."

"If mountain folk can't take care of each other—especially with us about the only two farms in these parts not already bought up—and you all living here in this barn, then the world's gone clear to hell and took us with it."

"Please. It's the only way I'll feel comfortable staying over at Biltmore."

"We'll talk about it later. I'm just glad Rema finally let on to me about the roof collapsing so we'd know you could use some help. Y'all go on now."

Ignoring the issue of money, Robert Bratchett had shaken his head. "Johnny Mac and me, we got some things we need to get straight with each other. I'll stay with Ella, and we'll have us that talk."

Kerry had swallowed hard. Then lifted the photo of her father and Bratchett in their Union army uniforms from where it lay on their one table. "This was inside his fiddle."

Bratchett raised an eyebrow. "Was it, now?" He made no move to see it closer, as if the image were thoroughly preserved in his memory already. Ella stiffened her shoulders, like she was bracing against some strong emotion.

Silence followed, swollen and throbbing with things unsaid.

"Is there nothing either of you can tell me about this picture? Or why it stirs him up?" She studied her father, who'd not been conscious all day. "I mean, besides memories of the war."

Robert Bratchett's eyes were on her father's unmoving form. "Not everyone here in the mountains fought for that side, you know."

"We knew he'd been with the Union. But he's never talked much about it ever."

"No. He wouldn't."

"Is there anything about the photo that my father would associate with the attack at the station? The odd thing is he—"

She'd hit some sort of chord here, the visitors' eyes finding each other.

Ella Bratchett spoke at last. "Best let Robert talk with your daddy first if there's a chance in the coming days. See can they clear up some things. Then, later, you can ask all the questions you like."

～

Now the twins, their faces scrubbed and gleaming, stood peering out of the hall leading to the billiard room. Mrs. Smythe had commanded them to stay well out of the way as the flood of guests arrived.

This made Kerry jumpy enough, wondering what the twins might do or say. But it was Marco Bergamini's words to her a moment ago that had given her hands their shake, the tumblers of hot cocoa rattling on the silver.

The Clydesdales had been harnessed again tonight to the sleighs, their silver bells jangling through the falling snow as they returned, mounded with brown fur and top hats, blanketed passengers and luggage.

The footmen and grooms all occupied with the unloading of people and their towers of possessions, Kerry stood to the side with a platter of hot cocoa in one hand, Pierre's steaming croissants in the other. Rema had insisted on adding more cream to the hot cocoa at the last minute, igniting a battle downstairs.

"Because," Rema had triumphed in a final shot, "with all the jawing over Mr. Vanderbilt's prize dairy Jersey cows, the cream ought to get its own say."

Chuckling to herself, Kerry held out the platter to guests.

"There is trouble," Marco whispered as he'd staggered by with a trunk toward the freight elevator.

"Oh?" She'd turned, nearly sloshing hot cocoa onto George Vanderbilt, who'd leaped from the first sleigh as it jingled and shushed to a standstill.

On the next pass with a trunk, Marco added, "I have the confession to make."

Which was all they'd had time to exchange. But his eyes had gone tight and dark.

Kerry's heartbeat throbbed in her throat. If it was a confession of the reporter's murder, she'd rather roll buck naked in lye than hear it. For all that was murky about the two Italians and their past, she trusted them now and didn't want to have that changed for her.

A few feet away, John Cabot helped greet the guests. "I'll stay only to say hello," he told Vanderbilt.

"You're welcome as long as you'd like to stay. I won't have you cooped up all alone on Christmas at Battery Park."

"I'll give my greetings to your mother and briefly to the others. But this is a family gathering." He clapped Vanderbilt on the shoulder. "And I'll have a stunning view of the mountains in snow from my window."

"Come back, at least, then, in the afternoon tomorrow for the presentation of gifts to the children of the staff, won't you?" The bashfulness was back in Vanderbilt's eyes. "I expect it to be something you'd especially enjoy."

"All right, then. And thank you." Cabot's gaze slid to Kerry. Then away.

Having returned her tray of empty tumblers to the electric dumbwaiter and sent it below to the kitchens, Kerry pulled a tray of steaming wassail in the *V*-monogrammed cups from the manual version along the opposite wall. Tully and Jursey were darting like minnows, Mrs. Smythe sending them up and down stairs between the kitchens and butler's pantry like a third, far nosier food transport system.

"Did you see all them furs, Kerry, did you?" Tully demanded. "It's a wonder there's a fox left in the world."

"I don't think those were fox, Tuls."

"All I could do not to run up and pet 'em."

Kerry grimaced, laughing. "Let's be real sure you don't."

Jursey dodged out of her way as she turned with the tray of wassail. "The man Cabot—the one with the sad he wears in the eyes—how come he's still here when all the rest of the friends up and left a couple weeks back?"

"Not sure. Except that not everybody has family."

As if imagining such a thing, Jursey's eyes filled.

Maybe she'd done too good a job at stressing compassion to the twins: both their hearts were maybe more tender than was safe in this world.

As Kerry looked for a footman to take the tray from her, Mrs. Smythe swept by. "Mr. Vanderbilt assures me he cares not a whit if it's a footman or a maid who serves, but I can hardly bear it myself." She shook her head ruefully. "Still, we're two footmen short, and that mud monster downstairs broke out of the basement. It's back past the pantry we've got him caught, is our Cedric. Chaos, that's what Americans thrive on." She sighed. "I'll be sending you out, Kerry, where, God help us, there ought not be a kitchen maid."

Kerry stepped carefully down into the sunken level of the Winter Garden, its palms nodding in the currents created by milling guests. The air smelled of cloves and cinnamon and apples again—the wassail she carried—and also of the orchids that ringed the fountain.

The guests were gazing up and around, peppering Vanderbilt with questions.

Do show us where you chose to hang the John Singer Sargent of Mother.

A wonder, George, that you found skilled workers this far from civilization. You said not all were imported from England. So even to fill a competent staff . . .

The fact that all of them appear even to have recently bathed . . .

Kerry jolted to a halt there, the tray lurching sideways as she spun. But a hand slipped under her tray. Caught it just in time.

John Cabot was looking at her. Holding her gaze. "Steady on," he murmured.

Kerry pulled her spine straighter. "Thank you."

She dipped to her left to offer the wassail to Vanderbilt's eldest brother, whose face was upturned, assessing the glass dome overhead. "Hunt has outdone himself once again. I don't want to know how much of your inheritance you've spent, George. I'm still astonished that you chose a spot so remote that you had to construct a spur of railroad to it. And so close to a local populace who, let us just say—"

"Actually, Frederick," Vanderbilt interjected, "I've found the local populace refreshing. Their warmth and self-reliance. Their shape note singing in the chapels here. The banjos and fiddles they craft themselves. Their humor."

Cabot raised his cup of wassail. "Their keen intelligence, too."

All eyes turned to Cabot, and for a moment, he froze, hand in the air.

The right tip of Vanderbilt's mustache quirked up in a half smile. "Cabot has been researching the Southern Appalachians. The manager of the Battery Park Inn tells me he's pounded away at his Remington at such unseemly hours, the guests on either side and beneath his room have complained of the racket."

"I'm no kind of pleasant hotel guest," Cabot conceded. "Thank goodness Biltmore's guest rooms have been finished before I'm tossed out in the snow."

Emily Sloane, whose immediate family appeared to be flanking her now, spoke up. "Did George tell you about the murder we've had here? It's been quite the game solving it."

One of Vanderbilt's sisters crinkled her nose. "Heavens, I'd completely forgotten. We read about it in the papers—covered because of George and Biltmore, of course. That poor Berkowitz fellow. Even if he was a Jew, I'm not convinced that's a reason to be murdered."

"I'm fairly certain," Cabot murmured to his cup, "it is not."

"I understand," Frederick Vanderbilt offered, "that the fellow may have been sent by the *Times* to poke into some labor disputes."

Another Vanderbilt brother looked alarmed. "Good God, I thought we had our people on that—those labor disputes."

Frederick Vanderbilt shook his head. "Calm yourself, Willy. Not rail or steel. This was something to do with New Orleans. An old story the *Times* decided had never been fully told. Sent the Berkowitz fellow down to learn more. You know those newspaper types—their unnatural love for buried secrets and melodrama."

"But why on earth *here*?" Emily Sloane's mother asked. "Outside the realms of civilization?" She glanced about as if searching for knuckle-dragging men bearing clubs.

John Cabot's eyes flashed to Kerry's and quickly away.

Something, Kerry thought. *He knows—or suspects—something he's not told anyone.*

Frederick Vanderbilt raised his glass now. "The issue we've not broached yet, quite aside from the admitted beauty of the Blue Ridge, is what George has provided for the populace here. A rising tide raises all ships, and the very existence of Biltmore will open opportunities for the benighted locals in their pitiable hovels."

"Benighted?" Kerry blurted before she could clamp down on her own tongue. "Pitiable *hovels?*"

Arms froze in midlift of wassail to lips. All eyes turned to Kerry.

"Really, George," Emily's mother said, not bothering to lower her voice, "surely you're going to reprimand your maid for that outburst."

"Actually, I believe, Frederick," George Vanderbilt said without flinching, "if you were to find the time to stay at Biltmore longer, you'd see what I do: a landscape of beauty and a populace with great talent and skills, the latter often passed down for generations."

Frederick grunted rather than answered, his eyes passing over Kerry. "I'd love to hear, Cabot, what you've found of value in your research here."

John Cabot forced a laugh. "Be warned. I have a great deal to say on the ways these mountains and their people have surprised and . . . impressed me."

His eyes flicked to Kerry's.

She kept her chin high. And looked straight ahead.

"I for one," said one of the sisters as their host led them toward the banquet hall, "would like to hear more of this grisly, apparently unsolvable murder."

At those words, Kerry skirted a palm with her tray of empty cups to find Marco Bergamini huddled, nearly hidden, just behind the door of the billiard room.

Waiting, it appeared, for her.

To confess something, she guessed, that she'd rather not hear.

Dread clenching her stomach, Kerry gestured for him to follow as she hurried back toward the dumbwaiters.

With those words, *murder* and *confession*, still echoing in her head.

Chapter 33

Trying to breathe, trying not to be seen, Sal watched from the door of the pantry where Kerry MacGregor was unloading the dumbwaiters. A roast turkey, sprigged all over with rosemary, hulked there in the platter's butter and sage. But his need to tell someone the truth had taken any appetite he might've had.

At least Leblanc had not recognized him at the station. Sal had loathed the livery uniform when the new butler, Harvey, informed the stablehands they'd have to wear it while Mr. Vanderbilt's family was visiting. But the low-sitting hat and high collar and gloves—and work that kept him turned with his back to Leblanc—had been a gift.

Leblanc. The bastard. Only he could have shown up on Christmas Eve. Four years of searching for Sal had only made the man's jowls hang lower, the point of his beard sharper.

Kerry tipped her head back toward him. "I'm so sorry I can't stop to listen at the moment. Seven courses and cleanup from now, I can come find you. Or if you want to stick close by, there may be a minute here or there."

As the door swung open and closed from the servants' entrance at the back of the banquet hall, Sal glimpsed the family, these Vanderbilts and Sloanes and Shepards and Barkers and Kissams, all glittering and gilded in silks and jewels, all gathered around the banquet hall's table. Thirty or forty of them, it looked to be. Behind Sal, Nico huddled in the corner watching his brother with those big eyes and sipping the cocoa Mrs. Smythe had given him.

I trust you, the eyes said. *Mi fido di te.*

But that trust had not always served them well in the past.

Sal made himself breathe in and out. The butter and sage and rosemary. The fresh-cut greenery from the three giant mantles. The Fraser fir they'd hauled in on the sleigh. And the smell of wet, muddy dog from Cedric, poised hopefully, big furry head cocked, at a dog gate blocking off the next room.

Moncrief teetered by with compotes of apricot preserves. "It's me legs would be wailing like bagpipes if they could blow through the knees."

On the floor, Nico jumped as the dumbwaiter opened to show something red and white with great grasping claws.

"Lobster," Kerry told him. "It's more butter than meat, but rich people convince each other they love it."

In time with a string quartet at one end of the hall, Christmas Eve dinner passed course to course. Sal looked for his chance to catch Kerry alone. He could slip away without any confession. But he wanted someone to know.

The footmen serving had their own kind of dance, rhythmic and graceful, a floating walk with no bounce or jostle to it, the dip at the left shoulder of a guest, the three-quarter spin away. The musicians at one end of the hall slid from tune to tune—"Coventry Carol" and "I Saw Three Ships" and "The Holly and the Ivy"—with the clatter of silver on china providing percussion.

Sal's heart, though, thudded heavily in his chest. He and Nico wouldn't have long to get a jump on Leblanc. Since he'd only just come to town and all would be quiet tonight and on Christmas Day, they'd surely have at least a day and a half to plan and then disappear. But they also needed help knowing where they could go in these mountains.

Which was part of telling Kerry MacGregor the truth. Hearing what she had to say.

Like the trained poodles in black vests that Sal had once seen in a street show in Florence, the footmen bent at the same moment to refill the wine—a different one for each course, it looked like—then straightened and circled in a synchronized line.

Sal found himself mesmerized by the light, the platters' filigreed edges catching the glow of the candelabras, of the three chandeliers and the three roaring fires, of the diamonds and emeralds and sapphires on necks and earlobes and waists. He'd seen rich tourists from all over the world come and go from the *pensione* in Florence, but nothing like this.

The branches of the Christmas tree had been weighted with garlands and hothouse flowers, velvet bows and gilt packages. At its base, more packages mounded, hundreds of them, together with a painted wooden rocking horse and a white wicker doll carriage, an army of toy soldiers and a doll whose curls spilled from a green bonnet, gloved hands clutching a parasol.

Sal tried not to think of his mother's face, silver strands of hair spilling back on a ragged green pallet, the stuccoed wall behind her crumbling onto the floor. Shaking his head to rid himself of the image, Sal turned. Perhaps he and Nico should leave, even before the confession. Before hearing where a native like Kerry MacGregor might recommend hiding for outsiders who knew nothing about this valley or the blue range that cradled it. Assuming she was willing to help.

The footmen swirled through the butler's pantry as Kerry loaded their platters again. Sal's mind spun over a host of possible hiding places in the village, none of them good.

"Our name," he said casually from a few yards away. Kerry and the footman waiting for a porcelain tureen of soup both looked up. "Bergamini. Our name. I hope that you will remember our name. If a question is ever asked of yourself—if you ever must wonder."

Kerry's head cocked. It made no sense, this strange comment of his, Sal could see. But Kerry MacGregor recalled things. Mulled over them later.

Sal would wait for a chance to say more. But meanwhile, he'd drop a hand on Nico's shoulder to let his brother know everything was all right.

Which it wasn't. All too soon Nico would have to know they were hiding again.

"Terrapin soup," Kerry said over her shoulder. "And then after that, or maybe after the salmon course or the saddle of mutton or the chaud-froid or the quail course, or maybe after the coffee and mocha biscuits and cognac—*dear Jesus*—maybe then I'll have thirty seconds to listen. I do want to."

He could tell she did not. That she dreaded what she might hear. But she'd said it, which was kind. And that kindness was why he'd risked their coming tonight, Nico and him. That kindness might be all that stood against his being separated from Nico again.

With the back of one arm, she pushed hair from her face. "I'm sorry it's so—"

Suddenly, a racket in the main hall brought the cello and violins to a faltering halt. A man was charging through the front door past a frantic Mrs. Smythe.

His black topcoat dusted in snow, he'd turned up its collar to cover the lower half of his face. His eyebrows worked furiously as he glowered over his shoulder to the housekeeper chasing him. Both hands raised to her shoulders, her mouth was an *O* of horror at the disturbance.

For a moment, Sal was fixed to his spot behind the crack in the door. His breath stopped.

"I won't keep Mr. Vanderbilt but a few minutes is all." Stepping around Mrs. Smythe, who'd thrown herself in his path, Leblanc raised his elbows like spikes on chariot wheels to keep her at a distance.

"But on Christmas Eve, of all the things!"

"Exactly. I've spent enough damn time following leads that came to nothing. This time, I'll not wait for anyone else's convenience. I'll have my man."

From his place in the middle of guests at the banquet table, sitting indignantly quiet, George Vanderbilt rose. "This is rather irregular, surely."

Mrs. Smythe's cheeks blazed. "I'd have sent the divvy down the banks, like, but he wouldn't be stopped."

The man in the topcoat flashed a badge. "Pinkerton Detective Agency. Perhaps you've heard of us."

The smirk on the intruder's face said he knew the answer to this: that the Pinkertons were the stuff of legend now. Detectives who'd tracked assassins and bank robbers, who'd quelled strikes and intimidated workers. Investigators who *always* found what their clients were searching for. "Name's Leblanc. Hired by a prominent family from New Orleans. To track down a killer."

Sal did not stay to see Kerry MacGregor half turn at the words *New Orleans* toward where he stood. But she seemed to miss little. He had no doubt she remembered his mention that day at the cemetery of where he'd once lived. She would already be piecing together his changing his name and his words to her tonight, *I have the confession to make,* along with more of a picture.

A picture that now included, he knew, the word *killer.* Coupled with his own face.

Chapter 34

Kerry saw the crack in the door behind her close shut just as the string quartet at the far end of the banquet hall slid into "Silent Night." She knew without fully turning her head that little Nico would no longer be in the corner. That the Italians had run. Head cocking toward the departing footsteps, Cedric whined and lifted one muddy paw as if to ask a question.

Pinkerton. The word buzzed over the table. *The nerve of the man.*

You know the Pinkertons stopped Jesse James.

Yes, and we've used them ourselves. Sniff out the source of a strike better than any bloodhound.

"Why on earth," George Vanderbilt asked, "would a Pinkerton man be hunting someone here at Biltmore?"

Kerry did not miss the faces of at least two of the men at Vanderbilt's table, the flicker of fear, the defensive pushing back from the table. Perhaps that was the nature of the business world these men lived in: Vicious. Omnivorous. A stab that could come from behind any cloak.

Kerry forced herself to stare directly ahead.

The intruder, whose face looked like one of the snarling giants from the twins' fairy-tale book, stalked forward. "I'll keep it short, seeing as how you got family here."

"Another thought would be," Vanderbilt suggested mildly, "that you come back in two days, after Christmas, and tell me everything at your leisure."

The Pinkerton man ignored this. "I got my orders to bring in a man I've been tracking for years. Got reason to think he's not only here in these mountains somewhere, but more specifically"—he reared back to deliver this last—"*here.*"

Ferociously, the man swung his head first left and then right, as if demonstrating the kind of predator's search he was capable of. Another rumble of comments from the guests rolled over the table.

As Kerry watched from the crack in the door, most of the family appeared more amused than concerned, as if he were providing some needed entertainment in the midst of their meal. Only the two men who'd looked so alarmed at the flash of his badge continued to pull at their collars as if breathing had become suddenly a chore.

Behind her, Cedric leaned harder against his gate. Another whine. Another muddy paw lifted. A plea.

"Be patient," Kerry whispered. "There'll be scraps."

"Leblanc," the housekeeper supplied for her employer. "The bloke's name is Tom Leblanc. That much I heard before he barreled quite by me. Bothering a family on Christmas Eve. I said to myself, says I, *What's bloomin' next?*"

Vanderbilt held up his hand. "We do not blame you, Mrs. Smythe. Mr. Leblanc, I believe I understand your sense of urgency to be done and return home to . . ."

"New Orleans," Leblanc thundered. "High time I got back. But first, I got me a slippery dago to catch. Name of Sal Catalfamo."

Checking behind her and hoping the twins hadn't heard, Kerry glimpsed Tully's expression at the far door of the butler's pantry, Jursey's right below that: two identical slivers of wide-eyed confusion at the demand—and the unfamiliar name.

Turning back, Kerry saw on George Vanderbilt's face a flash of something—the twitch of a brow, a flint strike of the eye—but then it was gone.

Vanderbilt lifted his glass of wine as the string quartet swept into "God Rest You Merry, Gentlemen." "And the hunt for this man really needs to be conducted on Christmas Eve? Surely, Mr. Leblanc—"

"Christmas Eve and four damn years up till now!" the man bellowed.

The string quartet stuttered to a stop, the viola's bow screeching on its strings.

"The ladies, Mr. Leblanc. Your language. What merited four years?"

Leblanc paused, letting the moment build. In the silence, only the crackle and sigh of the three fires sounded.

Leblanc lowered his voice so that the long table of diners had to lean toward him. "I'll tell you, then, shall I?"

The hiss and spit of the logs. The guests with their jewels winking, their eyes wide on the detective.

"Right, then. I'm tracking the dago for the murder in 1890 of the police chief of New Orleans. There's been sightings around here of a man who sounds a hell of a lot like Catalfamo. I'll be searching your house and your stables." He swept a burly arm. "I've also had a report from a reliable source with knowledge of this estate that there's reason to connect Catalfamo with your murder here back in October."

Afterward, Kerry was not sure if she met George Vanderbilt's eye or just imagined she did. She did know, in that sliver of second, that she'd made a decision.

"Cedric," she whispered as she lifted the gate. "It's dinner."

A scream from George's sisters brought everyone to their feet as the Saint Bernard bounded into the room, mud flying as he paused to shake his thick coat. Wineglasses pitched forward and sterling clanked as the big dog spun to find his master. Ecstatic, Cedric leaped to his master's side and lifted two filthy front paws to the table.

It might have been the result of the jolt of the dog's body or the footman who'd bent with the tureen being suddenly flustered, but terrapin soup flew over the guests at George Vanderbilt's left: soaking the bodice of one, spattering the diamond tiara of another, and sloshing the tuxedo front of Frederick Vanderbilt, turning his torso a deep, gelatinous green.

The man, Kerry thought with satisfaction, who'd made the *pitiable hovels* comment.

George's mother was calling for everyone to sit down. Stipples if not entire swaths of green had found their way onto at least a half-dozen diners.

Leblanc, disgusted, yanked out a watch from his waistcoat pocket and scowled at its face.

Vanderbilt surveyed the chaos of his family wiping at jeweled stomachers and tailed jackets, several of them stalking away from the table. "I will, of course, have everything thoroughly cleaned. And what cannot be cleaned, replaced."

Apoplectic, Mrs. Smythe appeared in the butler's pantry. "They said below it was that beast of a creature who's . . . dear Lord, it's worse than disaster, is this." She waved to the nearest footman. "Go 'ed, lad, *now*. Get the four-legged fur bag downstairs and locked up. All that clobber he's ruined."

Stepping into the banquet hall, Kerry cleared her throat. As always, she'd acted on impulse—in this case to give Bergamini more time. But what if that meant the twins would go hungry now because she'd be fired? "I'm so sorry, Mr. Vanderbilt. It's my—"

But Vanderbilt held up his hand. "It's *my* fault, actually. For not properly training my dog." In the glance that snapped between them, Kerry caught the hint of a smile.

He faced Leblanc. "And you, sir. I can tell you we employed literally hundreds of men from Italy up until a few months ago. They laid the limestone for Biltmore, scored and carved it. I did not, needless to say, know all their names. Since then, most or all of them have returned to their own country. What I can assure you is that there is no one currently employed on my estate by that name."

Leblanc let his scowl singe the length of the table. "Murder. In New Orleans. And maybe also the one here. So I'll just be searching your house and stables."

The guests looked up from their dripping jewels, their ruined gowns and tails.

From the far end of the table, a hesitant voice—hardly more than a whimper. "Uncle George? About the Italian . . ."

Emily Sloane was swaying slightly, her face a ghastly white.

"Yes?"

"That one Italian stablehand of yours. Is that who Mr. Leblanc might mean?"

Kerry watched in horror. Emily Vanderbilt Sloane, who'd been here in the autumn when Marco Bergamini was hired. Who would have known not only that he was here, but also that he'd been connected at least in some minds with the death at the station.

And now, Emily Vanderbilt Sloane, standing straight in her diamonds and turtle-soup-spattered silk, was about to confirm for Leblanc that he'd come to the right place.

Chapter 35

With Nico on his back, Sal bolted through the stable courtyard, lit only by a single lantern on either side of the main doors and the glow of a fresh dusting of snow. He'd counted on the bricks still being clear after he'd shoveled and swept late this afternoon. But now every step marked their path from the main house.

Sal's feet fought for traction over the slick of the bricks. Nico wrapped both arms around his brother's neck as if their lives depended on his holding fast—which they did.

No time now to fret over the tracks. No time to ask the best place to hide. No time to tell anyone why they had every reason to run.

He'd thought confessing to Kerry MacGregor could be protection if he and Nico got caught again in a maelstrom of blame. One person, at least, who would stick by them. But now he was cursing himself for not guessing that Leblanc would ram his way into a private estate. Without permission. On Christmas Eve.

Stupido. Cosi dannatamente stupido. How could he have been so damn stupid?

Slipping and sliding and cursing himself as he ran, Sal carried Nico through the stables and out the far double doors toward the woods. With no clear idea where they were going, Sal wanted only right now to put distance between himself and Leblanc. Nico's survival depended on Sal's.

Crashing through the thickest parts of the forest, Sal was banking on Leblanc trying to track him on horseback. The more mountain laurel to wind through, the more frozen streams, the more blackberry brambles, the better.

Snow dropped from pine branches as they ran. Nico clung tighter to Sal's neck, impeding his breath.

Sal would have to think quickly of a place they could hide that wasn't too far away. Running through ice and snow alone would have been taxing, but with an eight-year-old boy on his back, Sal was already winded, and they were still within sight of Biltmore's spires.

Nico pressed a frigid cheek against Sal's neck, and the message was clear: Trust. That Sal would keep them safe and unhurt. That in this next place they'd no longer have to use phony names and fear strangers and wonder who might want the foreigners gone and do whatever it took to drive them away.

Trust, Sal thought with anguish, *that had not been earned.*

Lungs burning, Sal gripped his little brother's legs harder at both sides and ran on.

Chapter 36

Kerry stared at Emily Sloane. Prayed she would suddenly lose her voice. Or keel over with a sudden palsy. Anything to keep her from speaking.

The girl stood before the detective. "The one Italian in my uncle George's employ was in the stables, Mr. Leblanc. But he left yesterday. I saw him myself. Headed, I heard him say, for the train station. To leave town. Though I *obviously* didn't follow the man to see him safely on."

She laughed then, as easily as if she'd been raised on the stage. Her laugh let the detective see how much her word could be trusted, a young heiress who could not possibly have any motive to lie.

Kerry turned to find the twins creeping forward. She put a hand out to each of them, which they took.

～

Now, a couple of hours later, icy pellets of snow plinked on the stable roof as Kerry stood at the opening to the courtyard listening for snapping twigs, running footfalls, a voice from the shadows—anything. Though the fugitives would surely be long gone by now.

From inside the stable, a horse whinnied. Then silence again, except for the patter of sleet.

Footsteps now behind her: a man's.

Kerry spun around, reached for a shovel propped against a wall.

Cabot stepped quietly through the doors leading to the porte cochere. "I should have been back at Battery Park by now, as I'd planned."

Slowly, Kerry lowered her shovel.

"I confess I was slow leaving the estate—maybe not wanting to go be alone at Battery Park. And then when I saw Bergamini bolting out of the kitchen exit with his brother on his shoulders . . ."

Kerry was grateful for the silence. If he had questions for her, she had no real answers for him. It had been only instinct that made her side against Leblanc. And instinct could sometimes be wrong.

From the Approach Road came the clatter of steel on stone, a horse galloping. Which might have been Leblanc leaving. Or merely venturing deeper into the estate.

Head down, Kerry traced the perimeter of the courtyard, its eastern wall rounding toward the north where the arched barn doors opened to the stable. Without speaking, Cabot followed, his gaze tracking hers on the snow-dusted pavers.

"Only one set. He's still carrying Carlo here," Cabot said, looking at her.

"He'd have to. If he wants to make any time."

Cabot looked away. "The owner of Bon Marché told George he's been worried about a mob deciding who was guilty for the death of the reporter at the station. This detective on the hunt for Bergamini won't help."

Kerry twitched at the word *mob*, a distant memory flickering in her head—her father's face in a crowd, men shouting, fists raised, axes held up overhead like weapons. Closing her eyes, she tried to recall more, but couldn't.

Inside the stable, the outlines of footprints in snow disappeared. But it wasn't hard to guess which direction they'd gone at this point. Staying anywhere connected to Biltmore's main house would not be safe. And the far double doors were cracked open to the forest beyond.

It occurred to Kerry again that John Cabot might not be worthy of trust. But with the twins inside the house and Rema taking a shift back at the cabin, Kerry had no other allies. Except, perhaps, George Vanderbilt, who'd seemed oddly unconcerned, and possibly even approving of her letting Cedric barrel into the banquet hall and distract from the search for a killer.

Pulling her eyes from Cabot's, Kerry stepped to the north doors of the barn that led into a clearing and then the woods. The small icy pellets of snow were turning into larger flakes, the sky gone the color of the inside of a summer cattail, a dazzling white. Temperature dropping, the wind whistled through the cracked door of the stable.

And there, disappearing now under the snow, were the tracks. Walking into the forest. Into the storm.

"If we hurry . . . ," Kerry began.

But even as they watched in the dim spill of lantern light, the footprints were fast being covered in white.

Chapter 37

Taking one of the lanterns from its hook on the stable wall, Kerry steeled herself against the cold and followed what little she could still make out of broken sticks or crushed leaves or the edge of a shoe print on the path. Cabot followed closely behind.

Looking up into the falling snow, she shook her head. "I can't track them in this. The last of their trail will be covered in another few minutes."

Cabot fell in beside her as they retraced their path.

Kerry took a step toward the basement room she and the twins had been assigned for the holidays. She'd seen them safely asleep hours ago. She was exhausted. Yet in a few hours, at first light, she and the twins would trudge through the snow to spend Christmas morning with their father—in whatever state they might find him.

"Thank you," she said, turning partly back. "For searching with me."

But John Cabot touched her fingers. "It's past midnight, so . . . it's Christmas Day."

She blinked. Tipping her face up toward his. "So it is. Yes."

"Perhaps not the happiest Christmas we've ever known." That sorrow that slipped over his face had fallen back. "But I do wish you good tidings. And peace."

She stood there a moment, her fingers still just touching his. A current flowing between them—a jolt. And something else, something steadier that ran underneath. A shared sadness and loss and raw pain that somehow, instead of seeming out of place on Christmas, felt strangely fitting. As if sadness and loss and raw pain had a place inside joy—part of what made it real.

$$\sim$$

The whole staff and the entire Vanderbilt clan gathered to watch the owner of Biltmore disperse gifts.

Kerry's thoughts kept winging off toward the Italians somewhere out there in the snow, and toward her father, who'd never come to consciousness this Christmas morning as she and Tully and Jursey cleaned his bedclothes. They'd tromped through the woods gathering more firewood for the stove and stoked it full, though only beside their father's bed, pushed so close to the woodstove that the quilts could nearly catch fire, was it not miserably cold in the barn. Kerry repositioned the quilts they'd hung on the walls in order to block more of the north wind. They'd sung old Appalachian carols softly and tried to pour warm pine needle tea between his lips.

"For inflammation," Kerry told the twins. "And he needs more liquid."

Because the fiddle on the wall looked as if it ought to be picked up on Christmas, she'd leaned in to every haunting verse of "Greensleeves," with Jursey on one of the squirrel-skin-and-gourd banjos and Tully on the singing bow. Jursey kept his head down so no one could see a young mountain man's tears. Tully knew the words of the carol that had been set to the old English folk tune, and the notes of her soft soprano floated in the silence of the barn.

What child is this who lays to rest . . .

Their father's eyelids fluttered at the words, but he had not otherwise stirred.

Now Tully and Jursey sat among the other children of estate workers, each opening a hand-selected gift. But it was the owner of the estate, eyes shining as he distributed packages, that Kerry watched most closely.

"I don't think," said a man's voice behind her, "I've seen George even remotely this happy before." John Cabot stood there against the doorframe.

Kerry watched the owner of Biltmore presenting the next child with her gift, a doll in green velvet with a green velvet parasol. The child blinked, speechless, in wonder at the porcelain face, then up at the owner of Biltmore, whose eyes glowed.

"Even more," Kerry agreed, "than he is with his books and his art. And equally as much as he is with his mountains."

She exchanged a smile with Cabot. And was grateful there was sorrow in his face along with the smile, just as she knew there was in hers.

She'd admired framed Currier & Ives prints at a Barnard friend's home. Part of her, though, had suspected the people in those lithographed sleighs and those glowing homes were also weighed down with secrets and worry and illness.

Which, perhaps, made the insistently giddy jingle of those sleigh bells hard to bear some days. Other days, maybe, the sleigh bells got to drown everything out.

～

From the refrigeration rooms where Kerry had just finished her work, she padded up the back stairs. As the string quartet migrated from the banquet hall to the Winter Garden, she could slip through shadows at the back of the house undetected.

Surely no one else would think to come to the library tonight. The last hint of smoke tendrilled from the maple logs in the fireplace.

Pulling *Nicholas Nickleby* and *Middlemarch* from one of the unpacked boxes, Kerry dragged an armchair close to the embers. Not even opening the books, she held them close to her nose. Smelled their leather, felt the supple spines. She'd read both during her time in New York, and now it felt like she was gathering their characters around her like friends.

Feet aching, she closed her eyes. From the Winter Garden, the string quartet's performance of a Handel composition drifted through the house, amplified by limestone walls and marble floors.

A single footstep a few yards away.

Kerry bolted upright in the armchair.

John Cabot stood in the shadows to the right of the fireplace. Might have been there all along, in fact, and her too exhausted to notice.

"Forgive me. I've startled you."

She stood. "I can go."

"No. That is, please don't." He stood at an angle to the fire, his profile toward her. "George mentioned he'd given you full access to his library. For what little spare time you might have."

"Still, I should go." She was turning when she realized what he was holding: a volume of the *American Architect*. With a maroon bookmark.

"Someone left this sitting out." As if he were suddenly not conscious of her being there, he laid two fingers of his right hand on his left lapel. The same sign she'd seen him make at the depot in New York.

"The article about your family's home on Beacon Hill."

"Former home."

She waited for him to go on.

John Cabot put the book down and thrust his hands into his pockets as he stared into the fire. "I wonder if you'd allow me to tell you the story behind that article—that is, the story that came after it."

"Of course." Kerry could see the pain that tightened the corners of his eyes.

"I don't speak easily of my life to those I don't know well—those I don't have ample reason to trust. I hope it's not too presumptuous if . . . forgive me if I say that you strike me as utterly trustworthy."

"I think," she said softly, "I can forgive you for that."

"It seems somehow deceitful *not* to tell you." He paused. Then nodded to the issue of *American Architect*. "It happened shortly after that article came out. Both my parents and my sister, Adelaide, drowned late that summer in a sailing accident off Nantucket. I'd just gone back to Harvard for my final year."

"That . . ." She struggled for words, her throat tight. "That must have been horrific."

His eyes drifted to the fire. "I went on in a bit of a daze, I think, as if I were handling it well. I was not, I'm sorry to say. When the lawyers settled the estate, it also became clear my father had been in debt. For years. I became the sole heir overnight—and the sole debtor. The house was actually sold just a few months"—he nodded toward the volume Kerry held open—"after the article's publication."

Kerry's own gaze dropped to the fire. Suddenly cold, even there near the hearth, she shuddered. "I'm so very sorry."

"I erect walls in my life. Not so much to keep others away, but to keep myself standing up. But then, you've no doubt already perceived that."

Cedric, who must have found his way here whenever Cabot came in, rose from the hearth to position himself directly under Kerry's left hand. Moving her fingers across the silky ears, Kerry did not raise her eyes from the coals. "I sometimes notice bits and pieces that others don't. But it would appear I also sometimes puzzle the pieces together all wrong."

She met his gaze and held it, the grief on his face so raw she could hardly keep from looking away. "To lose your entire family at once . . ."

He stepped to the hearth and reached for a poker to stir the embers. "You strike me as a person of great compassion. I suspect you've seen your own share of loss. All people of real compassion have, I believe."

He turned. They looked at each other across the flickering dark. "Losses change us. I've become a much less jovial man. Less . . . fun, I'm afraid, to be around." One end of his mouth attempted a smile. "But I hope I've become a kinder, more compassionate man without fortune than I was with."

She waited a moment before speaking again. "I wonder if I could ask: that sign you make . . ." She placed two fingers of her right hand to the left side of her chest.

"My mother. Like an unspoken *I love you* in settings where we couldn't speak. Or when words weren't enough. She tucked us into bed with it when we were little. Sent us off to school with it." He met her eye. "We made the sign to each other before anyone left on a trip. Including that one, to Nantucket. When she boarded the ferry from Cape Cod."

Kerry's eyes filled at the image: a mother smiling on the deck of a ferry, two fingers of her right hand over her heart as she waved goodbye with the left to her son, headed back to his college. Her disappearing days later, along with her husband and daughter, into the sea.

When he spoke again, it was quietly. "And you? Your life can't have been easy, I suspect."

She gazed longer into the fire. "Every day up until two years ago, my whole life was wondering how the next meal could be trapped or baited or skinned or pulled from the ground. I'd no idea a person could go day after day through winter and never feel the cold right down to the bone, never lie awake feeling the wind cut through the walls, the damp deep in the quilts and the straw."

She raised her eyes to his. "I spent the past two years at Barnard—on scholarship—at the arrangement of a former schoolteacher who once taught here. I only returned this fall when my father became ill and my aunt, who'd cared for my brother and sister, came to work here at Biltmore." *At least,* she thought wryly, *I can say the word without choking now.*

She shook her head. "Honestly, I don't think I knew until coming back how desperately poor we were. I wish I could say, like you, that I'm the better for it."

"Surely the additional education you received . . ." He spoke gently, nodding at the two novels she still clutched to her chest.

"Was a great gift. And also a curse. It taught me envy like I'd never known before. Knowing about what's out there in this big world. What I might have become. It haunts me. Not all the time. But envy pokes its ugly head into my days."

"To have to return under your circumstances . . . I don't doubt that was hard." His eyes swept toward the tall windows, where a bright winter moon lit the outlines of hemlocks. "And yet . . . forgive me if I'm romanticizing these mountains, but there's something here that draws one in—and surely must draw one back. Almost whether or not you want to be drawn."

"That's right," she said softly. "That's it exactly."

His eyes swung back to hers. "If I may be incredibly intrusive . . ."

In the charged silence between them, he waited. She looked back warily.

"I wonder if I might ask you about your . . . friendship . . . with Madison Grant."

Kerry would've been less astounded if he'd asked her the recipe for lye soap. "My *friendship* with Madison Grant?"

"His . . . interest in you."

Kerry saw again Grant's face as he offered his help at the train station and Battery Park, as he stepped close to her on the loggia, ran his hand down her arm. But Kerry had assumed no one noticed but her. And Mrs. Smythe.

Cabot looked away and then back. "It has worried me."

Kerry recalled what she'd perceived as John Cabot's rudeness: his curtness at the station, his scolding Grant for flirting with the village milkmaid, for remembering her name.

"That he'd targeted you as an innocent young thing he could . . ."

"Seduce?"

"Well. Forgive me. Yes."

"Mountain women, you may have noticed, are ferociously stubborn." She studied Cabot's face. "There is something Mr. Grant suggested, though. That Aaron Berkowitz and his attacker were both in love with the same woman: Miss Barthélemy, I think. Who might somehow have known them both prior to coming here."

"But the attacker . . . ? Good God. You mean me." He looked away. "There are a number of reasons I should be a suspect. But my being in love with Lillian Barthélemy is not one of them."

The strains of the quartet, now playing Strauss in the gallery, rose and swirled, the crackle of the embers underneath. Gently, John Cabot lifted the books from her hands and placed them on the chess table that sat near the fire.

Then he opened his arms. "I wonder . . . might I ask you to dance?"

She saw awkwardness pass into his face as soon as the words were out. "That is . . . the waltz. I'm not sure if you know . . ."

She smiled up at him. "I did learn, yes. In New York. Part of my friends' educating the backward hillbilly." Just about to put her hands in his outstretched ones, she hesitated. "But if someone were to come . . ."

"Then they must grab a partner and join us." He stepped closer, his evening coat smelling of wood smoke and leather book bindings and the outdoors. And a whiff, too, of Cedric.

Holding one of her hands, he opened the windowed doors from the library leading to the terrace outside. The moon lit the snowflakes like glitter sifting to earth.

With the distant strains of the quartet swelling, they stepped outside, faces upturned toward the bright flakes. Waltzing, they twirled through the falling snow.

Lifting her face as they slowly spun to a stop, Kerry stepped in still closer to John Cabot's tall frame. Let herself sink into the kiss.

Sounds and sensations swirled around her, the deep stir of his kiss, the soft sifting of the snow on the pergola rafters and its withered wisteria vine. The far-off undulations of the violins. And from across the valley, the low bellow of a cow. She felt as if she had jumped from one of the mountain cliffs but found herself able to glide on currents of air. She moved still closer into the kiss, her arms twining tightly around his neck.

Slowly, slowly, she pulled her head back—but only to see his face. To see that his expression was inexpressibly tender, his eyes bright and intense on hers.

Standing there hearing her heart pound, Kerry suddenly went rigid.

"Marco Bergamini," she whispered. Hardly the time to whisper another man's name. But there it was, the words already out. "From *bergamino*."

Cabot stepped back, his face quizzical—but not angry. He waited for her to speak.

"It's a long shot. And Leblanc surely . . . But if they stayed in the woods while he searched it . . ."

"I'm afraid I'm not following you."

"I think I know the place we ought to look for them next."

Chapter 38

Leblanc glowered up at the night sky. Only moments ago, snowflakes had been fluttering softly down on his horse and him as they trudged through the estate. But now the flakes were landing with an icier, meaner plink, as if adjusting themselves to his mood. At least there was this: Catalfamo and that cripple of a brother of his could not travel far—unless they'd taken the train out of town like that chit of a girl, Vanderbilt's niece, had said. If they were still here in this cold, they could hardly sleep outside without freezing to death from exposure.

That last possibility, he cheered himself, would at least expedite his mission. If he couldn't drag Catalfamo back to New Orleans, he could at least deliver a copy of a coroner's certificate.

Leblanc had no reason to distrust George Vanderbilt, who'd have nothing to gain by involving himself. And yet he did distrust him. Something about the man—a softness, maybe, around the eyes—made the owner of Biltmore look like someone who might just harbor a fugitive with some pathetic story and a cripple for a sidekick.

This estate of Vanderbilt's was far too vast to ride over—something like a hundred thousand acres, maybe more—looking for a criminal. But the cold and now the sleet cut the scope of Leblanc's search down immensely. If the two dagos were here on the estate, they'd have to take shelter somewhere indoors. For now, he'd done only a cursory search of the damn house, which was the size of a castle, and the stable, which was the size of a large house, since Catalfamo, like every criminal Leblanc had tracked, would have bolted as far away as he could from the one on his trail.

Only because Vanderbilt's niece looked so stupidly sweet and innocent did Leblanc bother with checking the train station where she claimed to have seen the Italian on his way out of town. But the station-master and the telegrapher had both looked at him blankly, said they'd not seen the pair of guineas come or go lately.

The telegrapher, Farnsworth, had more to say when Leblanc slid another bill to him, but that only amounted to seeing too many guineas in these parts over the past several years, since Vanderbilt started building his house. And, yeah, one of those types, along with a limping boy, had been at the station the night of the murder that still hadn't been solved.

"Good rooting out's what they'd be needing," the telegrapher had said, taking a long pull on his cigarette, then blowing smoke on the other side of his telegraph office window. "Sure as hell can't let any more of them in. Whole country's going to hell. It's the good genes that's imperiled."

Leblanc had turned back at this last word with a smirk. *"Imperiled?"* Fancy words for a hillbilly cable operator in a backwater spill of a town. Where the hell had he picked *that* up?

After returning to the estate to search the conservatory and Vanderbilt's piggery, which left Leblanc's shoes stinking, he'd aimed his horse to his best target yet. Leblanc rousted a Biltmore nurseryman named Beadle out of bed to ask him about other outbuildings on the estate, and the man, at the sight of the Pinkerton badge, had groggily complied, then stumbled back to sleep.

The dairy barn. That made perfect sense. It would be warmer than most other buildings. It was more remote from the house than the stable or conservatory. And Italians would feel right at home in the conditions: primitive, fit for animals.

Now Leblanc, clutching a lantern, sat his horse in the sleet that speared down on them and surveyed the dairy barn from a hill above it. A clock tower rising over its main door was just visible in the faint glow of the moon reflecting off a snow-covered roof and the pastures below.

He spat to one side. Who had so much money to burn they built a clock tower for *cows*? Rich people like this funded his work, made the thriving of his professional life possible—but sometimes he could not stand them.

Leblanc guided his nag in a circle of the barn, quiet here well past midnight. Gripping the lantern in one hand, he held it out from his body to search for footprints. Even being unfamiliar with snow, he was certain a man and a crippled child walking all the way from the main house or stables would surely have inadvertently left some indentations, if not actual tracks, if they'd come this way. In fact, he calculated now, the chill in his bones growing to a positive ache, a man and a badly crippled child probably couldn't have made it this far at all through the cold.

Still, he would search. Quickly. Before his feet froze into solid blocks.

Dismounting at the entrance to the barn, Leblanc tied the nag to a post just under the tower and eased open the big barn door. Inside, he tried not to breathe in the smell of hay—he despised barns of all sorts, and his having to actually enter a stinking *dairy* barn on Christmas Day felt like an especial affront.

He stood still to listen: silent but for the shifting and breathing of cattle and scuffling of mice. Leblanc's sense of hearing was, if anything, sharper than his eyesight. No person, much less two, was hiding here in the barn.

Ignoring the nag, whose head lifted slightly at his approach, as if this might be a sign they could leave, Leblanc circled the barn's exterior again. Covered delivery wagons with the name *Biltmore* painted on the side stood in a row. Growing colder, angrier, and more exhausted by the moment, Leblanc checked each one: nothing but silver metal canisters. And no footprints anywhere.

Only a hay wagon at the barn's northwestern corner sat alone. He approached, but now he could no longer feel his own feet. He and the nag still had to make it back to Asheville to get a few hours of sleep before dawn.

For good measure, though, and because he was a thorough man, he snatched up two pitchforks leaning against the side of the barn. He hurled the first with such force that its prongs sliced deep into the hay. The second he threw even harder, its whole handle disappearing. Just as he thought: no sound. Nothing at all.

So, then, Catalfamo and his little brother, wherever they were tonight, had better plan to die of exposure. Because by tomorrow when Leblanc finally found them—and he damn well *would* find them—he'd make them sorry they'd cost him not only four years but now, here at the end—Leblanc knew he'd closed in—nearly a whole night of sleep and, in a few moments more, the use of his toes.

Leblanc retraced his steps to the entrance. In jerks that tried to put feeling back into his hands, he untied the nag, mounted, and aimed its nose toward the delivery road. With only the circle of light his lantern threw and the pale fuzz of moon, he couldn't see the mountains, but he knew they were there, and they made him nervous, pressing in and crushing like mountains did.

Passing under the clock tower, he scowled up at it—a clock tower on a damn barn. As much as he loathed the criminal lowlifes he spent his days chasing, and as much as he detested dagos and mountains and barns, he decided he might just hate rich people worst of all.

Chapter 39

Sal heard the rumble and jangle and crunch of a wagon approaching. But it was the wrong time of day.

The dairy barn at Biltmore had come alive this morning before dawn, a platoon of local men arriving while it was still dark to light the lanterns and arrange the stools and gather the tin pails. He and Nico had burrowed themselves into the loft above the barn, which lay down the hill and across the lagoon from the main house, in the estate's bottomland near the French Broad River.

At first when they'd run from the stables, they'd hidden in the conservatory behind mounds of orchids and palms, but only for a few hours that night before Christmas. Sal knew Leblanc would search there before long, so they'd left sometime in the dark—well after midnight, Sal guessed—and trudged through the woods to a far pasture, stopping again for warmth in a run-in shed, open on one side but blocking the wind on three others. They burrowed underneath mounded hay and kept each other if not warm then at least alive. Down the hill from the shed was the sprawling dairy barn.

"Off past the barn is a hay wagon," Sal said to Nico. "We'll hide there just in case he comes to search the—"

In the quiet, they both heard the crunch of Leblanc's horse over the icy crust of snow before they could see his lantern round the bend in the delivery road. They stayed where they were while Leblanc searched the barn then reemerged with the lantern and glared around him at the barnyard. They exchanged wide-eyed looks as he hurled two pitchforks into the wagon's load of hay.

Once Leblanc remounted his horse, standing up to its fetlocks in snow, and rode out of sight, Sal and Nico hobbled inside. Sal was limping now, too, his feet numb from having crouched, unmoving, there in the woods for so long—and he carried Nico, who was nodding asleep from the cold. It was the cows and the blessed heat they threw off that warmed them. That and burrowing themselves together deep in the hay of the loft.

～

Just after dawn, when it appeared a worker would be climbing up to the loft, Sal had shinnied out through the upper window near the barn's clock tower and down a nearby maple, Nico clinging to his neck. They'd slipped back into the barn after the workers, finished with the morning milking, dispersed. On Christmas Day and again today, the day after, the cows still had to be milked and fed and the deliveries completed, but most of the other work in the barn seemed to be suspended, on partial holiday, as if waiting quietly for the evening milking.

It was afternoon now, all the wagons long since gone to deliver the Jersey cows' milk to the main house and the workers' families, and the surplus milk on its way to the hospital, a gift from Biltmore. From his time in the stables, Sal knew at least that much of the dairy barn's schedule.

No wagon should be rolling and racketing into the barnyard this time of day.

With no weapon, Sal reached for a pitchfork. It would be no match for Leblanc's pistol, but it gave him something to grip against a swell of helplessness. Edging from behind a mound of hay, Sal peered down to the barnyard, where he could see only the top of a Clydesdale's head.

They'd not really eaten since the evening before last, Nico and him—except for a small cheese rind and a heel of bread a worker had left. And plenty of milk.

At least, though, the two of them had managed to disappear.

"Mr. Bergamini!" came a child's voice—or, no, a voice that was almost a man's. Sal edged closer. Jursey MacGregor's already large hands circled around a boy's mouth. "Mr. Bergamini! You there? Kerry says you all are."

"We got to hurry!" his sister, Tully, bellowed—a large sound from such a *piccola ragazza*, such a small girl.

From the driver's seat, Kerry shaded her eyes as she scanned the dairy barn's upper level—like she could make them out through the cracks in the boards.

Nico reached out, letting Sal know they should go down.

"Mi fido di te," Sal said quietly, echoing Nico. *I trust you.*

Sal tucked his hand under Nico's elbow, and the two of them tromped down the stairs from the loft and presented themselves, hay still clinging to their clothes and hair, in front of the wagon.

Tully held out her hand in greeting. "Reckon you ain't got much choice, but we're real glad it's us you'll come out for."

"Mr. Vanderbilt hisself give us the wagon to take," Jursey whispered, as if speaking too loudly might jinx their mission.

Kerry leaped from the bench. "Mr. Bergamini of the cow-herding and dairy-farming Bergaminis, I'm glad you and Carlo are safe."

"I am grateful you thought of"—he gestured to the dairy barn—"this." He shook her hand warmly. "The name is Sal. Salvatore Catalfamo. This is my brother, Nico."

Rounding to the rear of the wagon, she flipped back a horse blanket to reveal what they'd brought. "I'm fairly sure Mr. Vanderbilt knew why I was asking to borrow a wagon. He didn't ask where I was taking it—so he can answer anyone's questions by saying he doesn't know."

"I would like to tell to you the truth. Of New Orleans." He could see from the stiffening of her shoulders that she wasn't sure she wanted the truth. That she'd chosen to help on instinct alone.

"Thank you. And soon. Right now we have to hurry, like Tully said." She slipped chicken baked with butter and thyme inside biscuits and handed one first to Nico and then to Sal. "We brought plenty more. Left in a hurry as soon as I could slip away without Mrs. Smythe's seeing, and while Rema had time to help us pack something up." She winked at them both. "Rema wouldn't let us out the door of the kitchens without this." She peeled back cheesecloth to reveal a blackberry cobbler, still steaming.

Sal asked no questions, numb with hopes he was afraid to form into words.

Jursey stepped forward shyly, red hair in his eyes. "Reckon we ought to say our howdys again. Glad to make your acquaintance, Mr. Salvatore Catalfamo." He grinned at the bounce of the name on his tongue. "You too, Nico."

Before Sal had a chance to respond, Nico looked up from a big bite of cobbler, blackberry smeared across his mouth. *"Grazie,"* he whispered, eyes filling. *"Grazie mille."*

Glancing at Sal, Nico added to the MacGregors, so low the twins had to lean forward to hear, "We trust you."

Chapter 40

Quietly, Kerry slipped out the front door of Biltmore into a world of white. Mrs. Smythe would have turned a deep Liverpool purple at a servant using the front entrance, but Kerry was past caring.

It had been several days since Christmas, Kerry having snuck twice more to the dairy barn with food, both times after dark once the last worker had left. Today, since it was Sunday, she'd have the day off—from Biltmore, at least. She'd spend it caring for her father as she did every early morning and night the rest of the week. She'd been testing the limits of how little sleep a person could get and still function. But there had to be a point, coming soon, when the tide of exhaustion always lapping at her would one day crash over her head and carry her off.

Today, she'd be with Tully and Jursey. That lightened her mood as she turned to admire Biltmore's copper roof caps and spires glinting above the snow.

Two gardeners bent into the task of shoveling paths straightened to wave to her. With no guests awake and George Vanderbilt likely ensconced in his observatory at the highest point of the house, and with the servants tiptoeing about, Biltmore sat serenely quiet but for the *shush, shush* of the shovels against the snow.

Kerry felt strangely warm as she walked, despite having left her father's coat for the twins. It was as if those moments shared with

John Cabot on Christmas night were still sending the blood coursing through her.

Which was why, she told herself sternly here in the clear light of day, she had to be wary.

Despite the deep, swirling pull of that night, and despite what she'd learned of his story, there were still reasons for caution. Like the cliché of the servant girl falling for the handsome gentleman on the grand estate, convinced that he loved her only to find she'd been just an amusement. John Cabot seemed nothing if not authentic, but wasn't that what every abandoned young woman said, looking back? And he'd somehow known Aaron Berkowitz before that night on the train platform, yet he'd volunteered nothing to Wolfe that evening. For a man who claimed to value transparency of the heart so highly, there was something unsettling about his not divulging that he'd known the murder victim before.

She didn't have to let his rumpled good looks or her sympathy for him pull her feet out from under her like the French Broad in a flood. She'd have to exercise caution.

Kerry veered into the woods, the snow thick. The beeswax she'd rubbed into her shoes helped only so much with moisture, her stockings wet through now.

At the barn, Tully and Jursey were up and dressed, Tully's hair neatly braided, Jursey's in its rooster comb. The three of them changed their father's bedclothes, the air once they were done smelling of the pine needle tick.

Kerry kissed each twin on the top of the head. "So. Has he said anything?"

The twins exchanged glances.

"Okay, you two. What's that about?"

Jursey frowned at Tully, then at their father, just beginning to stir. "He said not to tell."

"I don't care, Jurs. I'm not keeping secrets from Kerry."

Kerry's hands went to her hips. "Whatever it is, I'm guessing I need to know."

Jursey sighed but said nothing, crossing his arms.

Kerry focused in on her sister, who strapped on every responsibility like a soldier with his pack. Tully had no capacity for shrugging off duty.

"Spoke just enough yesterday to ask Jursey to take a message," she blurted.

"A message?"

"Jurs took a kind of letter thing. Delivered to Biltmore."

"To Biltmore." Kerry stared at her brother. "And you didn't tell me?"

Jursey sulked. "Said I's to deliver it straight to Mr. George Vanderbilt. Said I most of all wasn't to tell you."

Kerry took a breath to steady her anger. "And what exactly did the letter say?"

"No idea. Had it folded up tight. Said I wasn't to open it."

"Where'd he even get the paper or pen?"

"No idea about that, either. Looked to me like it was maybe some kind of fancy paper somebody must've give him somehow. All's I know was he told me I was to take it down there."

Kerry turned back to her father, his eyes open now, his breathing shallow, uneven. "Well, then. Would you like to tell me about that letter you had Jursey deliver?"

If he heard, nothing in his face moved.

"Or maybe you want to tell me about that photograph with you and Robert Bratchett? What it's got to do with your looking riled up when he comes around?"

Still no movement at all. His eyes closed again.

Tully tugged on Kerry's sleeve. "He's slipped on off back to sleep. Aunt Rema's coming to take a watch-over so the three of us can slip off to the chapel."

~

Uneasy, Kerry kissed Rema's cheek when she arrived and let the twins pull her away. Carrying two cane fishing poles and a spear, they slipped unseen around the edge of the clearing and into the back of the chapel, their Methodist church down by the branch that flowed so close to the corner of the square little structure that in spring, when it swelled, it splashed up on the foundation and clapboard. The itinerant preacher would be coming later from Black Mountain, but they stayed only for the hymns, mournful and joyful at once. No instruments today. Just the ragged little congregation standing wet from slogging through snow, the potbellied stove hissing, their singing rising to the hand-hewn rafters. Here were the pained and hopeful voices of people who knew despair was life and life was despair—and grace was there for the taking.

> *Come thou fount of every blessing,*
> *Tune my heart to sing thy praise,*
> *Streams of mercy, never ceasing . . .*

Kerry stopped singing to listen to the babble of the branch instead, barely audible beneath the music. That branch, at least, she'd never seen dry. The mercies of the divine, on the other hand, seemed a whole lot less sure—at least from where she was standing with four hours of sleep from serving a castle of American royalty by day and a dying father by night.

Slipping out the back while the music still throbbed and thrummed from inside, Kerry and the twins walked upstream along the bank. Decades ago, the Cherokees had built weirs throughout the mountains, including here, a *V* of stones piled in the river with its wide mouth facing upstream to guide the trout toward a narrower, easier catch. Unwinding their lines of twined horsehair slicked with beeswax, Tully and Jursey began digging under the snow in the stream bank's soft soil for worms. Tully retied the bullet she'd melted and punched a hole in for a sinker.

Kerry watched them a moment. Then waded to the tip of the weir.

Jursey grinned, watching. "It's chancy, if'n you ask me. Water's ice-cold if you slip in. And you used to could gig a trout in the gills without blinking. But two years layin' out . . ."

Cocking back her arm, Kerry aimed her spear, a knife blade strapped with squirrel-hide strips to a hoe handle, and let it fly.

~

Back at the barn, the three of them cleaned and filleted their trout, then rolled the fillets in cornmeal and cracked pepper to cook on the griddle outside.

Tully stomped back from the henhouse with all the outrage of thirteen years old, thwarted. "Only Goneril laid this morning. King Lear, he just struts around like everything's just fine and it's all thanks to him."

Kerry gave her sister's braid a tug. "So we'll make cornpone—doesn't need eggs. All the hens'll lay tomorrow."

Tully's lips pulled to one side. "Your face has got some fret to it—says you're afeared they won't."

Kerry attempted a laugh. "Then how 'bout you don't look at my face and we'll both just pretend we believe they'll lay tomorrow."

~

They washed their dirty clothes in the big iron pot outside over a fire—poking and turning with the long paddle, and making several trips each to the branch for more water. Kerry's hands were raw from the heat and the lye, her hair frizzed from the steam.

Bending over the pot, she mulled over the people of Biltmore.

Lilli Barthélemy's going pale each time the Italian stablehand had walked near. The letter she'd gotten with Dearg's handwriting—that made her hands shake.

Madison Grant with all his veneer of wealth and polish—but also his leering. The hateful things he spewed about immigrants and Jews and who knew what else.

Dearg's resentful reactions to the newcomers, his fit at the Christmas tree raising. His seething under someone's influence—apparently Grant's. Or Farnsworth's. Or both. Someone who stoked his fears.

Sal's initial attempt to disguise whatever his connection might be with New Orleans, then his fleeing from the Pinkerton man.

Even John Cabot: part of his story making sense now—the tragedy of his family, his anger in the face of Grant's flirtation with Kerry. But his having withheld the truth—his somehow knowing the murdered reporter.

She was still bending over the steaming lye when rattling bridles and creaking saddles and a low rumble of voices sounded above the trickle of the half-frozen falls. Three men on horseback appeared at the edge of the clearing.

George Vanderbilt rode first, closely followed by his agent, Charles McNamee. Who'd been trying for years—even well before Kerry left for New York—to purchase the MacGregor land. His presence alone was enough to make her want to run and grab the breechloader.

She barely heard McNamee's words. Because behind him rode John Cabot. Looking ashamed of being there with them.

Yet here he was: part of this unasked-for visit. This intrusion.

"So if we might speak with your father on business," McNamee was finishing.

Through Kerry's blur of confusion and rising rage, she could see the agent was smiling, that his easy manner assumed he'd be welcomed. He was already shifting his weight, about to dismount.

She batted curls back from her face. "Our father is unable to accept visitors today. And I cannot imagine any reason he'd have to speak with you about any matters of business."

Vanderbilt looked confused. McNamee looked unflappably confident.

And Cabot . . . looked pained. "Kerry," he began.

She ignored him. By being here with these men, he'd made himself their ally.

Charles McNamee drew from his pocket a folded letter. "I do apologize if it's an inconvenient time. We can certainly come back."

"I cannot imagine," Kerry heard herself say, her voice hoarse and unfamiliar to her own ears, "there'd be a reason to do so."

McNamee held up the paper, a Vanderbilt crest embossed at its top and several lines of neatly flowing script down its page. This design, with its central *V* and twining leaves, she saw now, was considerably different from the one in the telegrapher's office with its fleur-de-lis and silhouette of a Gallic rooster, the crest she'd first assumed was Vanderbilt's doing.

Where McNamee was pointing now, though, was under the flowing script. Where five crudely formed words had been scrawled in what appeared to be charcoal.

Kerry knew before she deciphered the blurred lines what the message would amount to. The twins watching her face, her stomach churned as she read aloud: *"Ready to talk selling farm."*

Chapter 41

Late winter 1896

In a daze since leaving New York in a late-winter freezing rain, Lilli did not know the names of the hamlets they passed as the train climbed into the mountains, nor did she care—not with all she had on her mind. She smoothed the brown satin of her traveling dress, tight over the waist and flaring like a bronze bell just past the hips. But how well she looked in the dress wasn't first on her mind, either.

The only part of this trip she'd dreaded was arriving at Biltmore Junction's station, where the reporter had died.

She refused to think the word *killed*. And, *certainement*, not *murder*.

"You know," said a man's voice from behind her, "you've seemed distracted and quiet this entire trip. Not much like you, Miss Barthélemy, if I may say so."

Madison Grant. How she loathed the man. That was the one other thing she'd dreaded about coming: having to share the travel with him.

She smiled at him wanly and wondered if he could see contempt on her face. "Indeed, Mr. Grant? No doubt a few weeks at Biltmore will cure that. This landscape. How lovely." She could feel Grant watching her from his upholstered chair as she gazed out the window. The crystal chandelier at the car's center swayed as they rounded the next curve.

The wheels beneath them clacked out the time—all these minutes wasted with Grant staring at her. Because what she wanted to do was open the letter.

And the truth was, the landscape was only lovely this time of year if you liked bare, silver limbs and pines that grew straight out of cliffs. Lillian Barthélemy had been born and bred in New Orleans, and she thought none of these things were lovely.

Although she ought to try harder to see the beauty in them. Her being invited back to Biltmore meant George wanted her here. For all his interest in art and farming and philanthropy, he must have felt enough attraction for her that he'd renewed his invitation just after New Year's to join a small party of friends back in the Blue Ridge.

Madison Grant, she'd heard through society grapevines, had not been invited back explicitly. Rather, he'd made it clear he wanted to learn more of Biltmore's strides in forestry, and had essentially invited himself as a leader in American land preservation. Grant was well enough connected in the same social and intellectual circles as George that bluntly banning the man from Biltmore would have been a central topic of society gossip—which, as Lilli knew well, George avoided at all costs. Look how far from New York he'd come to build his home.

"I say."

Grant sounded like every American who wished he were English: pretentious. She cut him off with a quick lean toward the window. "Perfectly *lovely*." She said it loudly, trying for George's sake to mean it this time.

"Indeed. Although given my own work, I should point out the ravaging of the natural resources. These people chose to desecrate their land."

Lilli was no social reformer, but it did strike her that they might have had less *choice* in the matter than a man like Madison Grant, who'd never once in his life needed to cut down a tree or plant a crop for his next meal. Keeping her face to the window, she began easing open the envelope with her finger.

Grant was droning on. "George's purchase of the land will rectify this depletion with intentional, sustainable forestry, and furthermore . . ."

She'd plucked the letter from its sleeve now. Her fingers ran over the page as if they could read its message for her.

Grant seemed to have switched topics from his precious conifers to a costume ball at Mrs. Astor's. Would he never hush? It was one thing to tolerate the posturing of men who might benefit her in some way. But a man who could do her no personal good . . .

"A Yale man like you, Mr. Grant, with a multitude of connections— not to mention your work saving the American bison and the noble pronghorn—must stay terribly busy." Like a bone tossed to a yapping dog, the flattery was meant to pacify him into silence a while.

"I believe, Miss Barthélemy, that I saw you at the Met a number of times over the winter. Though never, to my surprise, with our friend Vanderbilt."

Lilli leveled a gaze at him. And did not answer the question implied.

"Although," he went on, "he's done us both the honor of having us back to Biltmore."

She refused to betray to Madison Grant her own disappointment that George, known to attend the opera sometimes four times in a week, had not asked to escort her there a single time during the season. Still, she was on his private train car, his niece Emily asleep in an arm-chair in the far corner, and they would be staying at the house itself this time, now that Biltmore had officially opened.

"Which," Emily had commented just this morning at the station, "is far more than any other young woman of our set has achieved so far." She'd squeezed Lilli's arm.

Grant lifted a magazine from the mahogany table to his left. "I do so like the opera."

"Yes," she agreed so she could ignore him.

She despised opera. It was indoors, for one thing. It attracted the types who cared about social rules, for another. The only risks she faced there were leaning too far out over a box seat or having her name not listed in the "Some Happenings in Good Society" feature of the *New York Times* as one of the glittering people present.

Also, on the high notes, Lilli always wanted to scream.

Madison Grant flipped open the *Harper's* magazine. Facing the train window, Lilli glanced down. But she got no further than recognizing the same, nearly indecipherable hand as the letters before. Grant—*impossible man*—popped from his armchair to walk toward her, the open *Harper's* held out.

"You might well be intrigued by this article on the cotton mills of the Appalachian Piedmont."

She gave him the most wan of smiles, the more polished version of her standing at the back of his chair and shrieking into his ear, *Why the hell would I be interested in that?* He appeared to be one of those men who could not read smiles.

He held the magazine so close to her face she had to push it away a few inches to focus. Pictures of little children in front of giant spools appeared. Rather than skim the article itself, Lilli scanned the captions—even as she flipped her letter facedown.

"How striking." The pictures piqued her interest in spite of herself. "How young these workers are. Just little children."

"Although one wonders if they derive from genetic stock that could perform at higher levels. Probably not. The mills may actually be a beneficent alternative to slums."

Lilli intended to push the vile thing away. But more of its rather distressing pictures—little girls in pigtails clambering up on machines that dwarfed them—drew her in. And then the byline.

"By John Cabot!"

"An early peek, one would assume, into the book he's been researching."

"I'd be delighted to borrow the *Harper's* from you, Mr. Grant. Just as soon as I've had the opportunity to catch up on my correspondence."

"Of course." He dropped the *Harper's* on the table in front of her. "No hurry in returning it to me, as I've had the chance to peruse it."

Waiting until he'd settled himself back into his claret-colored chair, she scanned the letter. The messages like this had stopped when she'd left Biltmore before the holidays. But just as she was leaving her mother's on Park Avenue, about to climb into the Sloane carriage headed for Grand Central Depot, the butler had presented this one. As if the horrid thing might disintegrate into the clouds and steam of the station if she pretended it wasn't there in her handbag, she'd not so much as looked at it until now.

But now . . . Lilli scanned the letter. Again, only a handful of words:

Police come knocking. Stuck to my side of the story.

Found out why it was you wanted B- stopped. Reckon you'd wish I hadn't.

The threat he meant to imply—the blackmail to come—was perfectly clear.

Lilli laid a hand at her own throat.

Chapter 42

At the far end by the fireplaces, all blazing tonight, three musicians played classical pieces. The cellist and flutist bobbed their heads in time with the strains of Strauss, one of the composers Kerry had learned to recognize during her time in New York. A fiddler who'd once owned a farm near the MacGregors' gripped his bow sternly, as if he feared any minute it might break from his carefully executed violin part into a riff of "Come All You Fair and Tender Ladies."

As Kerry unloaded the dumbwaiters to fill the footmen's sterling trays, Moncrief kept up a running commentary peppered with Scots Gaelic. "They're up to high doh—keyed up, if you're asking me. And the one's got an angry streak as long as me arm."

She settled the charlotte russe onto his tray. "Which one?"

"The lawyer preservationist blether. I dinnae ken his name. It's a peely walley face he has, pale as a poisoned ghost."

Kerry laughed. "I got very little idea what you said. But I know who you mean: Mr. Grant."

"It's pale, his face is. Makes a sport of the *trioblaid*—of stirring up trouble."

For her part, Kerry noticed Grant fingering the outline of something, a slight bulge, in his jacket pocket. *Stirring up trouble* seemed about right.

～

After dinner, Mrs. Smythe summoned her.

"They've decided to retire to the . . . bowling alley." She said this last part as she might have discussed London's sewer system—a part of the city best not mentioned. "As that divvy Scots of a footman is needed to reset the ninepins, I'm told, and all the rest of the staff occupied in the Oak Room just now, I'd like you to take the port to the guests who've chosen to"—she sniffed—"bowl."

～

Moncrief was bounding about setting up the pins that had been left splayed all over the two parallel lanes. Kerry stood near the threshold until he could set up a table for the port—which gave her time to observe the group.

Lillian Barthélemy and Mr. Vanderbilt's niece, Emily, had both returned. They stood in dresses more casual than their evening gowns, the jewels they'd worn to dinner stored away.

John Cabot turned as she walked in with the wine, and he held her eyes. When, after a few beats, Kerry looked away, Lilli Barthélemy tilted her head. At an angle that said she'd taken note.

Cabot studied his ball. Then, shoving three fingers awkwardly into its slots, he slammed it toward the pins, sending them flying.

Leaping horizontally several feet, Moncrief caught one pin in midair before he and it hit the wood floor. "*Air leth, math dha-riridh!* Excellently done, sir!"

Madison Grant lifted a glass of port from Kerry's tray. "As brutal with the pins as he once was with bodies on the gridiron."

"*Mon Dieu,*" Lilli Barthélemy said. "*Enough* with the football." Marching to the left lane, she sent a ball slicing through pins, leaving only one standing.

Grant lifted his glass in a mock toast. "A sport for the making of men. By which I mean not only football but also bowling, when Miss Barthélemy takes the lane."

She ignored him.

"Football," Emily Sloane pronounced, "will not catch on outside a handful of places. Not permanently. Mark my words."

Grant shook his head. "I will say only this: to see a player like Cabot here leap with the grace of a gazelle over piles of fallen men, *that* was a thing of beauty. Although I'd forgotten—how clumsy of me." He turned to the others. "Cabot prefers we not discuss that particular Harvard-Yale game. Issues, as I recall, of the extraordinary brutality of several players."

Lilli Barthélemy waved this away. "Nothing that the introduction of the forward pass shouldn't address."

In the stunned silence that followed, she held a hand to her chest, delicately. "That is, I believe I read as much. Obviously, I've not followed the sport myself."

Mrs. Smythe appeared sputtering at the entrance to Biltmore's bowling alley. "Mr. Leblanc to see you again, sir." She lowered her voice, the sophistication chipped off her accent when she was under stress and the Liverpool showing through. "I told the meff he'd not been invited, I did. But he pushed himself in, that one. As if!"

Kerry braced herself against the cold stone of the alley's wall as Leblanc's form hulked past Mrs. Smythe. He wasted no time with preamble.

"Against my own better judgment, I followed a lead out of town, a trail that went a whole hell of a lot of nowhere." He leveled a glower at Emily Sloane. "Now I'm more convinced than ever there's damn well got to be a connection between a killer escaping justice in New Orleans and what happened here—Catalfamo as the common factor. So, since the local police are incompetent rubes, who here wants to give me the official Biltmore version of the train station murder?"

Kerry kept her eyes focused directly ahead on the opposite wall. To her right, though, she sensed Lilli Barthélemy drawing herself up. Stiff. Defensive.

Vanderbilt began by meeting Leblanc's eyes coolly. Then handed him a glass of port from Kerry's tray. "Let's agree, Leblanc, that this will be the *last* time you barge into my home uninvited, shall we?"

Leblanc's upper lip lifted in the beginning of a sneer. But his gaze darted around the bowling alley and, as if suddenly reminded of Biltmore's sheer size—and its owner's influence—his mouth flattened. "Agreed."

Briefly, George Vanderbilt recounted what happened.

When he finished, Madison Grant sauntered forward. "Mr. Leblanc, you have a point about the Italian."

"My God," Cabot muttered. "Here we go again."

Grant's hand brushed the lines of the square bulge in his coat pocket again. Perspiration dotting his forehead, he'd not shed his jacket like the other gentlemen, who were bowling in shirtsleeves. "The man slipped away out of sight, as I understand it, moments before the attack occurred."

Cabot stepped to the right lane. "If that's the criterion, they'd better suspect me, as well."

Emily Sloane clutched a ball close to her chest but did not approach a lane. "No one, Mr. Cabot, suspects you."

Cabot's gaze shifted toward Kerry as she stepped to refill Vanderbilt's port.

Grant sent a ball down the right lane—so badly aimed that Moncrief had to jump to keep his legs from being knocked out from under him. "I assume," he said, turning, "we all see what the actual suspects have in common, yes?"

The thunder and crash of the balls and pins stilled. Even Moncrief quit moving.

"I'll spell it out, then," said Grant, "if no one else will."

Emily Sloane drummed her heels on the wood floor. "Not this again, surely."

"Let us be honest: we all know the tendency of certain races toward criminality."

Vanderbilt reached for another port but only swirled it. "*Do* we all know that?"

"Our top universities, all the best minds in eugenics agree. And America is currently leading the efforts to encourage superior genetic strains."

Cabot lifted a ball, and for a moment, Kerry thought he would hurl it at Grant. Instead, he thrust it at him. "I confess I must amend my earlier assessment of you. You're not just a silly, self-important, ignorant man. You're a lethally ignorant one."

Leblanc stomped several paces. "Look, I got a case here to solve."

As if he'd not heard, Grant took the ball. "We don't allow religion or false sentimentality to cloud our findings on race and social progress."

"Such as," Cabot suggested bitingly, "caring for the hungry, the outcast, the stranger in the land?"

Grant's shoulders hunched. Brittleness, Kerry thought, behind the smooth finish. Like mountain clay that, without a kiln, would hold no more than shadows. "I would refer you, Cabot, to our colleagues in Germany, assisting in our cutting-edge work."

"Frankly," Leblanc cut in, "I don't give a damn about any of this. I got me a killer to catch."

Grant straightened, stroking the square lines of something inside his coat pocket again.

"I still wonder . . ." Kerry heard her own words before she realized she'd said them.

All eyes turned to her as if one of the bowling pins had begun to speak.

"If Miss MacGregor," Cabot put in, "has something to say . . ."

"Sure." Leblanc snorted. "Why the hell not waste more of my time? Let the damn maid blather now."

But Vanderbilt turned to her. "By all means, if you have something to add . . ."

Kerry squared her shoulders. "I know comparatively little of the new science of fingerprinting. However . . ." Their blinks of disbelief—so preposterous that a maid would insert what was supposedly her knowledge of science—rattled her only a moment. "We did touch on it in one class at Barnard—how it will become a significant tool for police. It's a shame the science isn't further along, since the phylacteries—the black boxes used to accompany prayer—found at the scene might give some sort of clue."

Leblanc frowned. "Yeah. So make your point."

Vanderbilt spoke more kindly. "But since those boxes belonged to the victim himself, I'm not sure that would be of much help."

John Cabot inclined his head. "I suspect she means something more."

Kerry's gaze shot to Grant, his hand brushing the square bulges in his pocket again. It was a guess on her part, based only on the square outlines his fingers repeatedly traced and his pointed mentions of the reporter's being Jewish—but maybe the guess was worth the risk.

She addressed Vanderbilt. "You're right that Mr. Berkowitz's prints would of course be there. But so would those of the person who took the items from the scene. Those prints would not necessarily point to the killer, but it's an interesting question: why, exactly, someone would have taken items related to the victim's religion and background."

In a silence that felt dangerous—*flammable even,* Kerry thought— none of the guests looked at one another.

Kerry shifted her gaze now to Madison Grant, though she continued to address Vanderbilt. "Since one of your guests was clever enough to have brought the phylacteries with him tonight, perhaps he could answer that himself."

As one, all eyes shifted to Madison Grant. He stood frozen, a bowling ball held poised to aim. His face fast draining of color, he looked as though he might drop the ball now on his own feet.

Slowly, he lowered it. Kerry could see the calculations in the sparking of his narrowed eyes. The whole group was staring at his left pocket.

Now an easy smile slid over his face. "Apparently, Leblanc, we have a potential addition to the Pinkerton force right here on the kitchen staff of Biltmore. She is precisely right that I brought these very items here tonight to show Vanderbilt. Although I'd quite forgotten I had them with me—until this moment." He turned toward Kerry, the dazzling smile on his lips at odds with the cut and slice of his glare. "Allow me to thank you for that reminder."

From his coat pocket, he drew out the two phylacteries.

Cracked, Kerry noticed. *As if someone took a cudgel to them. As if Grant relished doing violence to them.*

Just like someone took a rail dog to the reporter's head.

Grant relinquished them to Vanderbilt, who turned them over in his hands. "Good Lord, Grant. It's as if you'd smashed them on purpose."

Leblanc elbowed his way closer. "Worse for the damn wear, I'd say. Maid here's actually right: there's work in some parts of the world—Argentina, for one—where fingerprints have solved a crime. Change the whole game if they can perfect it. Match fingerprints to that rail dog, for instance—and *presto*, murder solved."

"Interesting," Madison Grant observed, "that you would associate the Italian word *presto* with murder. How fitting."

Leblanc turned his heft on Grant. "My feelings exactly. Although I got to say: it's odd as hell you'd have these. Anybody tell you that you can't take souvenirs from a crime scene?"

John Cabot sent a searching gaze toward Kerry—as if he was trying to guess how she'd known. Leblanc spun to him.

"And you, Mr. John Quincy Cabot. Did a little background research on you. You and this Berkowitz, you were students at Harvard at the same damn time."

The bowling alley stilled again.

"Yes," Cabot said quietly.

"Yet," Leblanc demanded, "you didn't manage to speak up when that idiot sheriff here was asking if anyone knew the deceased or had information—anything?" He blew air out of his mouth. "It's not even necessarily my case, this thing at the train station, but I can tell you right now there've been plenty of lies. Plenty of people not speaking up with what they know."

Kerry watched John Cabot's eyes grow hard again, and look away.

Grant lifted a ball casually. "Ridiculous to think it might be Cabot. But certainly, whoever the killer was, he would have to be athletic to wield a thing like that rail dog."

Leblanc shot both hands in his coat pockets as his gaze swept the room, stopping on each one of the guests. "The thing about detective work . . ." No one else moved. "You think you're getting nowhere, and then . . . *presto.*" He fixed Grant with a look. "Suddenly something falls into place."

Grant seemed to coil back into himself, eyes narrowed. *Like a rattler,* Kerry thought, *before it strikes.*

Leblanc's gaze swung over the guests again now.

Skipping, Kerry noticed, only Lilli Barthélemy, who stood haughty and distant.

The lady raised her chin. "That will be all now, Leblanc." She spoke icily—but also as if she had some sort of connection with—or power over—the man.

She drew a breath as if to steady herself and glanced toward Vanderbilt—as if she'd just realized she'd let her irritation with Leblanc slice away her caution in not revealing a link before.

George Vanderbilt had indeed turned to look at her quizzically. But said nothing.

Leblanc, running a hand once down his black triangle of beard, opened his mouth as if he would speak. Then, closing it, he spun away on one heel and stalked out.

Chapter 43

"Lils?" Emily asked, bewildered. "Surely you couldn't have known this Mr. Leblanc?"

Lilli felt their eyes like weights on her. She'd shown too much of her hand.

"Forgive me," she said. "I seem to have a bit of a headache."

~

They'd assume she'd gone to her room, the Chippendale, with its two separate Renoirs. She'd gushed about them this morning to George. But truly, all she saw was a dull girl with an orange.

Like a sea creature drawn to water, she ducked into the swimming pool's vaulted room down the corridor and shredded the silk of her stockings as she yanked them off. Hiking up her skirts, she lowered herself to the pool's edge, bare toes skimming the water. Which, *bon Dieu*, was actually warm. Strangely sensual.

Which made her think of the Italian. The strength of his arms as he'd carried saddles from the tack room. The way, when she'd been near, he kept his hands frenetically busy—brushing and oiling and stretching and buckling, often repeating work he'd just done. The smolder and fire in his eyes when he looked at her. Stepped close to her, arms tensed by his side.

She arched her feet in the water.

Extraordinary, really, how Biltmore catered to its guests' every whim and need. Except peace of mind.

Lilli sighed. If she looked scandalous with her skirt hiked up like this and her calves bare . . . well, so be it. She had good calves. Now if she could just slash through her corset strings, that would be progress.

Alone for some time, she felt her spine relax. Then, from across the corridor at the pool's far end, sounds echoed off the stone walls. From the gymnasium.

Rising, Lilli padded to the door to peer across: the climbing rope, the weights neatly lined on one wall, the parallel bars. But only the male guests could use it.

Not seeing her, Madison Grant, in a sleeveless shirt, turned, his arms oyster-white and without definition, his gut rounding out like a puff of uncooked beignet. He leveraged up from the floor a bar with weighted plates.

"Simple physics," he murmured to himself as he strained to press it over his head. "Angles more than mere muscular power."

Here came the maid, Kerry, scurrying past the broad entrance to the gymnasium.

"Ah!" Grant called. "Kerry!"

Ducking into the pool's room, Kerry flattened her back against the wall.

The maid and Lilli regarded each other in silence for a long moment. Lilli studied her: the red hair pulled back into a maid's cap, with rogue wisps curling around the face. The sunburned cheeks, even here in winter. The chapped hands, their knuckles cracked, nearly bleeding as she clutched a bottle of port in one hand, a glass in the other.

Without a word, the maid stepped forward, filled the glass, and handed it to Lilli.

"Well. How timely that you appeared to refill my glass." They continued eyeing each other. "You caused quite the stir, you know. *The help* participating in a conversation. Is that the way things are done here in Appalachia?"

The girl kept her face still. Unafraid. Lilli had to give her that.

Lilli leaned closer. "The truth is, I enjoyed seeing Grant caught with his hands in the phylacteries, so to speak."

"Kerry!" Grant's voice echoed off the gymnasium's stone walls.

With a tilt of her head, Lilli acknowledged the look in the maid's eyes. Strode to the door of the pool and called across the corridor to the gym. "Why, Mr. Grant. Were you looking for someone?"

"Ah." He stopped, flustered, as he approached the door of the pool room. "Miss Barthélemy. What a surprise."

"I'll bet."

Grant's eyes traveled from Lilli to the maid he'd spotted now, her back still against the wall.

The maid was blushing a fuchsia that clashed with her hair. But her eyes were striking. Defiant. Perhaps Lilli had given her too little credit before.

"So, then. Mr. Grant." Lilli arched an eyebrow. The arch of that very brow had yanked men far more powerful than this pathetic New York attorney back into line.

She was from New Orleans, and she was French. Two very good reasons not to be much startled by a man flirting with a pretty house-maid at a friend's vacation estate. Still. She was unaccustomed to stumbling directly upon it herself. Perhaps because the men in her orbit typically orbited her.

Grant offered a smile gleaming with polish and calm—and money. "Miss Barthélemy, I must tell you how refreshing it is in an era of mannish cycling clothing and walking skirts to see a lady dress so elegantly for dinner—and then even for bowling."

Reflexively, though she saw his game, she smoothed her skirt. To breakfast, she'd worn a wonder of tiered lace, a gown designed to turn heads—though with a modest neckline. Tonight's gown, by contrast, had not had a modest neckline. She meant to make the most of her time with George Vanderbilt.

"Our host," Grant added, "is a more complex man than most, is he not?"

In answer, Lilli steepled the other brow.

"He'll require a wife who'd rather read by the fire in a remote corner of the Blue Ridge than waltz until dawn to 'The Blue Danube.' Wouldn't you say?"

The maid took a silent step toward the door. But Grant's hand shot out for her arm.

"*Monsieur*," Lilli said, "one may not always grab what one wants."

Straightening one lapel, Grant cleared his throat. Then plucked a telegram from his jacket pocket, which he held out to the maid. "The man Ling delivered it earlier. Though I'd forgotten about it, I confess, until this moment."

The maid lifted her head. "Rather like the phylacteries?"

Lilli laughed.

Taking the telegram from him, the maid's curiosity—or, from her expression, her dread—appeared to get the better of her. She tore the telegram open.

Casually, Lilli glanced over her shoulder to read.

YOUR SCHOLARSHIP ABOUT TO BE REASSIGNED.
CAN YOU ASSURE TRUSTEES OF YOUR RETURN TO NY?

Crunching the telegram in one fist, she fled down the hall still clutching the bottle of port.

Madison Grant's eyes followed her.

Lilli waited until he'd turned. "One petite memory from my childhood, Mr. Grant. As a girl, I once stood on my father's wharf in New Orleans and watched a shark circle a wounded fish just thrown back into the sea. I recall, Mr. Grant, wanting to jump off the wharf to save the poor fish, small as it was."

For a full moment, neither one of them spoke, or moved.

"Interesting," he finally observed, "that the police have not yet suspected your connection with Aaron Berkowitz."

Lilli's pulse dropped to the faintest thrum.

Grant knew. She could see the dare in his eyes. The triumph. Lilli could not breathe.

"I've no idea, Mr. Grant, what you mean."

"Really, Miss Barthélemy? Because a friend of mine in New York who does legal work for the *Times* responded to a letter of mine. He tells me reporters had been sent to New Orleans and Asheville both to talk with a certain Louisiana businessman about whom they had new and quite interesting information. If *I* know this, I suspect someone among the police does, too, by now. Don't you?"

Chapter 44

Lilli watched Emily smile at John Cabot from beneath her lashes—frosted prettily with ice pellets on this misty late-winter day. Biltmore's deer park, gone a honeyed brown, crunched under their horses' hooves.

But the profile of his face that Cabot turned away from poor Emily was less warm than one of the men in the friezes over the banquet hall fireplaces. Lilli nudged her own mount closer.

"Cheer up, *chérie*. He has a fine face, I'll grant you. But with no suitable income attached."

Emily sighed. "If only I could make myself flirt with a suitable income attached to a pudding face. Oh, well." She patted the gelding she rode. "At least the grooms matched me with a sweetheart of a horse today."

Lilli grimaced. "Rather a plodder, though."

"Only to those who do not plod well."

"Ah. *C'est vrai.* Fair enough."

"I did notice that the stablehand who's disappeared"—she cut her eyes toward Lilli—"had learned a great deal about your . . . particular preferences."

Lilli waited, her face giving away nothing. Emily could not possibly know how many times Lilli had lingered in the stables last fall to talk with the Italian. Unless the servants had talked.

"What sort of horse, I mean, to saddle for you." But Emily's face said more.

Lilli glanced away. "He did tend to saddle the most high-strung of George's hunters for me."

"Yes. He must have sensed that in you. That you relished a good risk."

Lilli gave a laugh that sounded false even to her. "That, or he was trying to help me break my own neck." She shielded her eyes from the sun with her hand. "Where's that uncle of yours, I wonder?"

"Lils."

Lilli turned in her sidesaddle, her right knee raised nearly to the mare's neck now.

"Lils, surely it's a good thing the Italian has disappeared—for your sake, I mean. No, you needn't respond. Just answer me this: Do you find my uncle intriguing? Honestly."

"I . . ." Lilli slowed to choose her words carefully. "Your uncle George possesses something I've rarely found in men of our class."

"Yes?"

"An overarching kindness."

Emily beamed. "Why, yes. That's so true."

The other truth was, Lilli thought, it bewildered her. And all that kindness bored her a little, too. The complete consistency, the utter predictability of it.

But surely kindness in a man was the sort of thing one could learn to live with.

"You know, don't you, Lils, what people are saying?"

Lilli stiffened. "About . . . New Orleans?"

"I meant about George's inviting you back to Biltmore. The society pages are crackling with anticipation over a forthcoming announcement."

Lilli lowered her eyes. Sweet, loyal Emily: she deserved a humble reply. Kind, trusting George: he deserved gratitude.

Lilli looked up and managed a smile for her friend. "The society pages would appear to know more about my life than I do."

Trotting up to join them, Cabot swung down from his mount. "Remarkably fine horses Vanderbilt keeps."

"Doesn't he, though." Lilli squinted toward the base of the next hill. "I suppose that's the forestry crew gathered there by the river."

Cabot gestured with a bob of his head. "Black and white men together. Working side by side as one crew. You don't see that too often down here."

"Or in New York, ever," Emily pointed out.

A chill ran down Lilli's arms. The burly Dearg Tate, off to one side in the farthest cluster of white men, sat staring at her. She'd heard somewhere that he no longer worked for Biltmore and had finally sold George his farm. Yet here he was on the estate.

Leading his horse up to the three of them, Grant ran a hand across his jaw. "That man appears to be looking at you, Miss Barthélemy. Rather intently."

Given what she'd seen near the gym of Grant pursuing the maid, he wouldn't dare expose Lilli in front of the others. She tilted her head at him. "Is a man staring at me so very hard to understand?"

"Ah. You make a splendid point."

She was desperate to change the subject. "Mr. Cabot, you are awfully quiet today. I wonder if your in-depth study of the mountain people has you distracted."

"No doubt," he said. And looked back at her impassively.

"Kerry MacGregor in particular must prove a challenging case. Part refined lady. Part tanner of hides and slopper of hogs. Part scullery maid. Part wildcat."

Emily sucked a breath in. "Really, Lils."

"I agree," Cabot said at last. "She is indeed a young woman of many gifts."

George Vanderbilt was cantering now up the hill.

"Perhaps," Lilli murmured to Emily, "I might entice George away from the group. Temporarily only, of course."

"And risk his feeling pursued?" Emily looked skeptical.

"The real art of the thing, of course, is convincing the fox that he's really the hound."

Lilli urged her mare into a gallop. Reaching George, she reined in her horse. "You'll be glad to know we delayed all scintillating conversation till your arrival."

He smiled—those good, friendly brown eyes. Much like his Saint Bernard's, really. "Forgive my delay in coming. I was attending to business at the stables. We're a bit shorthanded."

She'd not meant to broach the subject, but then, she'd not expected him to mention the stables. The question shot out of her mouth: "I wonder about where that Italian, your stablehand, has gone."

"Of course . . . Bergamini."

Lilli heard the hesitation. As if George knew for certain that wasn't his name.

Salvatore, Lilli thought, hearing the name in her head that he'd confided to her. Confided, and then looked the next instant—for only a flash, but she'd seen it, nevertheless—as if he wondered if he could trust her fully. She could feel the rough of his cheek against hers as she'd whispered his name the last time she'd been alone with him. His hand at the small of her back. That last time they were together was the first time he'd not kept his arms full of tack and hay bales. Even that had only been moments.

George's brow furrowed, a screen of apprehension dropping over his face. "Being from New Orleans, you would naturally be concerned about him."

She could see he mostly believed that was true, that her motives were pure as the frost that tipped the fields that morning. That even if he'd caught a glance exchanged between her and Sal, he would've already convinced himself he'd been only imagining things. Mostly.

"I am, yes. We are a loyal lot, from New Orleans." With pressure from her left leg, she turned her mare so George could no longer see her face. She'd overstepped. Time now to change course. "I wonder which of these two hunters we're riding is more fleet of foot."

"Well . . . ," he began.

"And I wonder how we might prove it." Snapping back her head to smile at him, she shifted her weight forward in the sidesaddle and gripped the upper pommel with her right leg. She and the mare shot away from him.

Glancing back, she saw George posting in a half circle, unsure. Another glance, and he was urging his own horse to full speed in pursuit.

Lilli bent low over her horse and aimed the mare's head toward a split rail fence she hoped—but was not entirely sure—they both could clear.

It was George Vanderbilt who was chasing *her* now. Quite literally.

Her pulse dropped as she neared the fence, its crisscrossed rails like big wooden stitches across the field. Lilli felt the mare gather her body, the power centralized in her back legs as she launched. Up. And up. That moment when they were no longer tethered to earth. No longer subject to its laws and constraints.

That moment when it remained to be seen how they would land.

Which, if John Cabot and his Kodak had been poised to photograph this moment, would be the perfect image for her life right now. Impeccably dressed and well strategized. Graceful and soaring.

And, depending on what secrets came to light, perhaps about to land in a shattered heap.

Absorbing the jolt of the mare's front legs as they made contact again with the ground, Lilli glanced back only once more—and found George Vanderbilt close at her heels.

How odd, though, that it wasn't George's kind face she saw as she rode. Instead, it was the Italian's. Her thoughts churned with each stride of her mare, a storm of self-interest and compassion. And, God help her, desire.

◇

Keeping her skirts clear of the sizzling pots and mounded pastries in the kitchens, Lilli kept her strides light and carefree. But not without authority. "Hello, Mrs. Smythe."

"Why, Miss Barthélemy!"

The housekeeper's voice betrayed what Lilli knew full well: it wasn't her place to be here downstairs. She was not mistress of Biltmore—not yet.

Still, a guest of George's couldn't be corrected by the housekeeper. Especially since the servants probably knew better than anyone else that their employer was quite possibly smitten with the heiress from New Orleans.

Heiress. That sounded a great deal better than what also might be whispered belowstairs. How, for instance, she'd been seen talking animatedly and at length on several occasions with the Italian inside the stables.

Or how, the servants might have caught wind, she came from some sort of bloody past in New Orleans.

Or how, the servants might whisper, she was connected somehow with the death at the station.

Lilli gave herself a hard shake. She was growing suspicious and fearful, neither of which was like her.

"I was just popping downstairs to see if I might find that maid . . . what was her name? Kerry, I believe."

Mrs. Smythe cocked her head. "She's only in the next room scouring pans, is our Kerry. But I do hate to see you have that lovely silk ruined down here."

From the pastry area came the rumbles of a man's voice with a heavy French accent and a woman's with a thick mountain twang. "*Zut!* I tell you once, I tell you a thousand times, the meringue it must be whipped until it stands up stiff as the tower."

"I hadn't got issue with your meringue till I saw it slump down and roll to its back like a possum trying to hide hisself from the hunt."

Mrs. Smythe cringed. "Beg forgiveness for our kitchen staff. There've been a few differences we've yet to smooth out."

"Of course." Lilli took this as her chance to sweep past the housekeeper. "I wouldn't dream of mentioning the unrest belowstairs to Mr. Vanderbilt. Particularly as you have the rest of the house so beautifully in hand, Mrs. Smythe."

The pacified Mrs. Smythe, Lilli was relieved to see, did not follow her into the next kitchen, but rather withdrew to the pastry area where the two battling voices grew hotter.

The maid, Kerry, straightened at the sink, her red hair corkscrewing at her temples. Lilli could see that, from the set of the maid's jaw, she already guessed what had brought a houseguest down here—diamonds glinting incongruously, no doubt, in this fog of boiling water and steam.

"The Italian." Lilli blurted it out before she had time to arrange her words like playing cards in a game of whist. She regretted her haste, but there it was. "Mr. Bergamini and his brother. I'm wondering if they are safe."

The maid turned from the sink, wiping those chapped hands on her skirt. She appeared to be studying Lilli's face. Waiting.

Lilli recoiled at the thought of what her face might be revealing. It could make her vulnerable to the maid. Even more than she already was, since this Kerry MacGregor had seen handwriting she recognized in the letter from Tate.

Despite the set of Lilli's shoulders, always regal, and the arch of her eyebrow that gave warning, Lilli suspected the maid could see she was nervous.

The maid, Kerry, gave a slow blink that seemed to say she was choosing not to say what she was thinking.

Lilli met the maid's eye. The knowing there. The things this maid might be suspecting.

Lilli's trill of a laugh came an instant too late, and an octave too forced. "It's ridiculous, of course, my even bothering. But I was concerned when they so suddenly disappeared."

Silence. The maid taking her measure, Lilli thought with growing unease.

Then, finally: "They are, for the moment, safe. How long that will be true, I couldn't say."

Lilli had more she wanted to ask. Though it might show more of her hand.

A squawk came from the pastry area, where the two voices had battled over meringue.

"He ain't never!" the mountain woman was shouting. "I won't believe it was him gone and done it. I won't. And that poor little brother of his. What's become . . ."

Footsteps clattered across the tile floors.

Lilli and the maid both turned as the older redheaded woman, the cook with the face the color of escargot, burst over the threshold and, ignoring Lilli entirely, demanded of the maid, "Kerry, you got to find out if it's true. That footman Moncrief just come from upstairs saying that awful man with the look of a bloodhound to him, all jowly . . ."

The maid's eyes went round. "Leblanc?"

"He's back again, Moncrief said. Not at the house. Somewheres on the estate."

Chapter 45

Kerry moved through that evening in a haze, the dinner at Biltmore passing in what felt like time slowed to nearly a stop. Walking past the clock in the servants' dining room, she was surprised to see its pendulum swinging—like some sort of prank someone was playing. Time was still moving on.

Just this very evening, as a cello sang back in the tapestry gallery and sterling tapped against sterling, she'd let herself think that life at Biltmore had become almost steady. It was still foreign to her, too walled in with marble and glass, but with its own rhythms now—the swishing of silk, the clinking of crystal, the scuffling of maids in the back halls.

"Blimey," Mrs. Smythe said when Kerry bumped again into a wall. "Don't tell me *you're* bevvied up, now."

"Not drunk," Kerry assured her. "Just clumsy." Kerry could not tell her the truth: that her mind was with the Italians in the dairy barn. And her not even able to warn them for fear Leblanc, watching everyone's moves, would only follow her there.

Just after serving the cognac and coffee, Kerry slipped out the porte cochere doors just to breathe, the night air full of the scent of melting snow and thawing earth.

Like everyone else at the estate—everyone else in these mountains—she'd been haunted by questions since autumn, the wondering whose laugh could be trusted, whose smile was only a cover, a rattler in its old skin.

Maybe Leblanc coming onto the estate had been nothing but hearsay.

Maybe, just like the Pellegrini, completed at last on the library's ceiling, they were finally free of the dark and moving toward light—toward the truth of what happened last fall.

She'd felt it this morning, that brighter tone: the chuckling from the men at one end of the hall, the crackle of the hearth logs, the low babble of voices like a brook over rocks.

She felt it on the staircase earlier, that brighter mood: the women's heels tapping out time on the steps, the cantilevered stone seeming to float four stories up.

"Kerry," John Cabot whispered as she'd swept past, "we need to talk. It's . . . urgent."

His voice—tight as a singing bow's thread—backed this up.

Pausing, she'd let her head shift just a notch. And given the hint of a nod. Enough that he would have seen it.

Enough that others might have, as well. That was a risk she might regret.

Lilli Barthélemy had brushed past. Watching pointedly.

Raising her chin, Kerry had met her gaze.

But now, if only for these few stolen moments, Kerry was alone—where she could gather herself and brace for whatever it was John Cabot considered urgent. Just her and her mountains. The earth smelled of unfurling fiddlehead ferns and bloodroot and all manner of mosses.

A mist had settled like a fine silk over the front esplanade, wound up the house's main turret, and snagged on its spires. In the electric light blazing through Biltmore's windows, the world shimmered.

Her attention swung to the dark outline of the gazebo high on the hill rising at the far end of the lawn. Had it only been a few months ago when she'd stood up there at its edge on a day much like this—the fog and the riffling blue of the ridge all around?

Just a few months and a lifetime ago.

From inside came more strains of the string quartet brought down this week from New York. The cello led the way through another slow, swirling waltz.

Suddenly, the towering doors behind her swung open. Footsteps across the stone: sharp and loud, because he was tall and the heel taps of his shoes weren't softened by years moving over wet ground like hers were. A pause punctuated each step, like he was asking permission to join her.

Turning, she met Cabot's gaze.

He had followed her out, waiting just long enough so it might not be clear to the others what he was doing.

Even so, there would be those who would guess.

He took one more step from behind.

She crossed her arms still tighter over her chest. "I need to know who I can trust."

"We all do." His voice came low, barely audible over the string quartet and a chorus of wood frogs, fervent and loud, who'd made their home in the garden pools just below.

"They thaw themselves out from a deep freeze, those wood frogs do," she said. "And they start sometimes when there's still snow in the groves and up on the peaks, just calling like that."

"Calling . . . for what?"

She didn't answer. Surely even in Boston, creatures called that desperately to each other for only one reason.

"Kerry, there's some news." He stepped to where he could see her face. "And before I tell you, I need you to know." He reached out as if he would touch the line of her jaw, but held back. "I'm on your side."

She heard the loyalty there in his voice—quiet, but fierce.

But she could not meet his eyes—not yet. Because he would not understand the turmoil in her they raised.

Your side.

Living in two worlds as she did now, she'd become like the rag doll she'd made for Tully, the one left by the hearth. Her father's two hounds—including Mercutio, who died years ago—had discovered the doll at the same time, one cloth hand in each set of teeth. These days, that's what she'd become, seams ripping.

My side? she wanted to ask. *What side would that be?*

Instead, she kept her arms crossed but lifted her face.

Here all around were the mountains, life about to burst out again in a wet, giddy green. And here he was: Part of the throb and the thrum and the new. Part of the questions. Part of the seam-ripping pull.

"Kerry, I need you to know also . . ." He seemed to be waiting for her. She turned.

"I knew Aaron Berkowitz. Before that day at the station."

"Yes," she said. To say *I saw it on your faces that day* was no help now. "Although you didn't volunteer that at the time." *Which has made me wonder if you could be trusted.*

"Call it cowardice. Call it being ashamed of the past. Both would be fair." He drew a breath. "While we were at Harvard, our interests aligned not only on the classics and political affairs, but also . . ."

"You were in love"—her voice had gone husky—"with the same woman."

"*He* was in love, I believe. With a girl from an old family on Brattle Street in Cambridge. But it was nothing so noble as that on my part." He waited to go on until Kerry raised her eyes again to his. "I've told you I was reckless and angry in the months after my family was killed. I pursued her, this woman he loved, only because, perhaps, I liked the feeling of power, being able to shift her attention to myself. I had no real interest in her. Which was . . ."

"Cruel."

"Yes. To her and to him. I was numb, I think, during that time. Prone to smashing things up just to see if I could make myself feel—something. Anything. I probably did the young lady no permanent harm. After I quit calling on her, she recovered, married another classmate of ours. But I destroyed Berkowitz's trust in her and in me—whatever future they might have had."

He sighed. "I should have offered this to the police right away. But I've been ashamed by the whole affair—my own handling of it. Then, after I waited so long to speak up, I was afraid I might seem . . ."

"Untrustworthy. Yes. You did."

"I didn't think that one omission mattered much at the time. But now . . . I'm headed to the jail. To point out other suspects the police have overlooked, including me."

The call of the tree frogs thrumming in her head, Kerry pictured the brothers huddled under the hay. She turned in the direction of the dairy barn, as if she could see past Biltmore House itself and the acres of deer park and pastures and woods.

"Kerry, there's something else urgent I need to say. Leblanc seems to have gotten a tip on where the Bergaminis were hiding."

She spun back toward him. "No. Did they . . . ?"

"They were found, Kerry. They've been arrested."

Chapter 46

Sal gripped the bars of his cell, one hand around his brother's shoulders, which were trembling. Nico pressed closer, as if the strength he felt in his brother could be passed through damp skin and dripping clothes. Sal reached for the thin blanket flopped on the cot. Wrapped it snugly around Nico.

"We must keep you warm."

His mother's words echoed in the silence of concrete and cold: *I beg you, my son, protect our little Nico.*

"I'm trying," Sal said into the quiet. "I won't give up trying."

In a driving rain, Leblanc had arrived at the dairy barn with Wolfe. Through the cracks in the planks, Sal had seen Leblanc turn up the collar of his black coat.

"Best come on out," Wolfe had called. "Can't say I'd relish hurting a kid."

Leblanc had made a show of aiming his revolver up toward the dairy barn's loft. "Nothing but a dago. Not much of a loss."

The steady thrum of his fear for Nico that always lived in his chest had swelled to a roar.

Now, at the jail, Sal was no longer seeing Wolfe a few feet away but a much older man. Steely eyes. Hunched behind a mahogany desk, as if its bulk reflected his personal strength.

"How do I know," Maurice Barthélemy had demanded of him that day four years ago, "that *you're* not Hennessy's murderer? How do I know it wasn't *you* our valiant chief saw in that alley where he was shot? How do I know you weren't the dago he mentioned with his final breath?"

Sal could have told him it had, in fact, been his own face—and Frank Cernoia's—that Hennessy saw there in the alley. But Sal had skipped to what mattered most.

"My brother, he is lost. Last night. The riot."

The man lit a cigar. "You dagos can't even trust each other."

All these years later, Sal could still feel the seething that made his whole body throb. "My brother is very young."

And afraid.

The man chewed on the end of his cigar. "*Comme c'est triste*, as we say in my family. How very sad." The man's tone dripped in sarcasm.

From behind Sal, the office door slammed then, the heavy tread of one of the man's thugs approaching.

"Mr. Barthélemy, I was told this guy here needed removing."

"Indeed, Leblanc. This guinea here appears to be under the impression that *I*, of all people, might somehow be responsible for the regrettable unrest last night in our fair city." He swigged from his Scotch. "Can you imagine?" Barthélemy laughed hoarsely, as if the Scotch or his own words had shriveled his throat.

Sal had said no such thing. And until that moment had not even thought it. He'd only come here to a man who owned much of the wharves because he'd hoped for his help finding Nico.

And now, suddenly, here in this jail cell, blocks of thought moved in Sal's mind, arranging themselves into a picture like the sections of the painting being pieced together at Biltmore on the library ceiling. Only instead of a bare arm extending to share the lamp of knowledge, here before Sal was the image of this man's arm in its glossy white shirtsleeve, its cufflinks of pearl, as he motioned to his thug Leblanc.

"Catalfamo here was just leaving."

Jerking away, Sal had stalked to the door and turned. "This country does not have the kings."

Barthélemy's upper lip had buckled into a sneer. "You guinea trash don't know when you're beat."

Sal had planted his feet. "My brother, Nico. I will not leave without finding him."

"*Comme c'est triste.* A shame. Mobs have a way of being no respecter of persons, including little dagos. I can't answer for the mood of the mob this morning. I'd lay money, though, since you've been one of the ones on trial, Catalfamo, that they'll recognize your face."

Rage lit Sal from the inside as more pieces shifted into place now.

Through Sal's mind flashed the memory of the alley: Cernoia and him sent there as envoys to talk with Hennessy. Not to threaten, exactly. And certainly not to kill. Sal had not even been armed, and Cernoia carried only a knife in case they were jumped. They'd come to remind Hennessy that the Italians of New Orleans would not allow themselves to be divided into warring families. That they demanded fair treatment.

And then the shot from behind all three of them just as Sal and Cernoia approached the chief, his back toward them. Hennessy whirling to see two Italians standing there gaping. Horrified.

Sal had bent over the chief. Seen where the shot had entered, and known the chief would not live but moments longer. Heard running footsteps out on the street. Someone calling the chief's name. Conveniently, searching for him seconds after he'd been shot. Someone who would serve as witness to what wasn't the truth.

Sal and Cernoia had fled toward the opposite end of the alley. But they'd been spotted as they clambered over the brick wall. And even without that, Sal had realized, the Italians of New Orleans would be blamed.

A frenzied rounding up of suspects had followed, the shouted repetition of Hennessy's supposed final word: *Dagos.*

Hatred swelled in the city toward its Sicilians. Nineteen Italian men rounded up. The court trial. The lack of hard evidence. The dismissal of charges. The mob gathering to bring justice itself. The breaking into the jail. The cries: *We want the dagos!* Italians riddled with bullets and strung up like so many sides of beef in the market.

Eight men escaped.

And now, here in this dank Carolina cell with its icy stone floor, the story finally made sense.

"It was Barthélemy," Sal said to Nico, though his brother was curled in a fitful sleep. "He ordered Hennessy's murder. He knew who would be blamed. And that would give to him control of the wharves."

Barthélemy must have seen in Sal's face that understanding was dawning even then. Barthélemy's eyes had become slits.

"This garlic eater," he'd told Leblanc evenly, "has taken enough of our time."

And breathed enough air was never voiced, but crackled there in the room.

Leblanc's hand resting on the hilt of a pistol punctuated his boss's command. Bursting out of Barthélemy's office, Sal dropped down the steps four at a time, bullets whizzing over his head.

As his feet hit the boards of the wharves, he dodged shadow to shadow. The bodyguard fired again, the bullet grazing one ear.

Sal lost him at last near the Café du Monde, where he hid until nightfall in a storeroom bursting with chicory and coffee and pulverized sugar.

After dusk, as the café brightened to gold and laughter hung in the air with clouds of suspended sugar, Sal slipped through the crowd back to what they called Little Palermo. He ran up staircases, ducked into alleyways, asking anyone he could find: *A little boy caught in the riots—my brother, Nico, is lost. Have you seen him?*

But doors were locked, people huddled inside hiding from the mobs that still roamed the streets like rabid dogs.

Finally an old woman, hunched like a shepherd's crook, opened her tenement door just a crack—then more fully at Sal's description.

"An old woman, she is the most fragile in any crowd, and the most brave. What can a mob do to me? End my life when I'm already so close? Make me afraid when I've already seen hunger and death? I hoped I could stop them, that mob."

She shook her head. "It was John Parker who got the mob shouting, lifting their fists, dragging our men—innocent men—through the streets. I was knocked down. They stampeded, this mob."

"*Sì*, yes, and the boy?"

"I saw a boy crying, calling out, *mio fratello*. Trampled. His leg badly hurt. Another man—one of us—picked up the child and ran. Toward the rail yards."

The old woman pulled Sal's face down toward her so close their foreheads touched. "*Dio ti benedica.* God bless you in your search."

Covered in coal ash, Sal searched car to car for hours. He finally found his brother huddled behind crates of rum and Madeira with Cernoia, who would stow away the next day in search of stonecutting work. Much later, Sal would hear through another Sicilian in the quarries with him that Cernoia had gone to an estate in North Carolina that was hiring Italians for its limestone exterior. An estate with a vast house that Sal had not realized until then really existed beyond memory and dreams and an espresso-stained page.

Sal's own Pellegrini had formed—the full picture: why a man of power and wealth had never given up on his search for the nobody Salvatore Catalfamo. Because Sal had pieced together just who was behind the killing of Chief Hennessy. Whether or not anyone would believe a penniless Sicilian was a question Barthélemy apparently had never been willing to leave to chance. More powerful men than the Napoleon of New Orleans, after all, had been toppled by less.

Even as Sal and Nico had stowed away in a train car headed north, Sal had seen the face behind the lynchings: not so much John Parker, the mouthpiece of the riots who'd riled and rallied the mob, as Maurice Barthélemy himself, overseer of the tide of imports and exports that enriched the seaport's salty lifeblood.

Barthélemy, whose greatest competitors there were the two powerful Italian families, the Provenzanos and the Matrangas, who battled for their own control of the wharves.

A man who stood to benefit more than any other if suddenly New Orleans despised and distrusted its Italian population.

Barthélemy, who would now dominate the waterfront, if no one suspected him. If Salvatore Catalfamo and anyone else who might point a finger at him could be found and silenced.

Maurice Barthélemy, whose daughter Sal could have taken revenge on. He'd lain awake thinking of this when she'd been only a name, only the idea of a daughter of the man behind so much death. He'd wanted to hate her as he did her father.

The daughter's flirtations had probably been only a wild and dangerous gambit meant to distract and manipulate Sal—at first. But they'd quickly become something else for them both—a deadly pull, a kind of quicksand.

A key clanged in the lock of the cell. Nico pressed hard into his side, and Sal's arm went more tightly around his brother as Wolfe shambled into the small space. His face, twitching and tense, was at odds with the casual way he was trying to walk.

Wolfe jerked his head down toward Nico. "Group of townspeople out there fussing how it ain't right to hold a kid in jail. So I'll be taking the boy now."

"No." Sal wrapped both arms around Nico. The boy buried his face in Sal's chest.

"Relax. We'll get him housed. Somewhere."

"We will not let you do this."

From outside the cell door, Leblanc appeared, smirking. "Good thing I hadn't left town yet. Always like to be of service, even after I snag my man." He leveled his revolver at Sal's nose. "It's not some eight-year-old kid I'll be hauling back to New Orleans for a trial—assuming they don't want you here for murder charges at the same time. It's you, Catalfamo. Just you."

Ignoring Leblanc, Sal appealed to Wolfe. "I beg you. My brother will not feel safe. Nico is used to me only."

Wolfe reached to cinch Nico around the waist. And pulled.

Sal's arms stronger than Wolfe's, he held tight to Nico. "Please listen, *please*. My brother, he cannot walk right. He needs the help. *Do not separate us!*"

Nico reached for Sal's face. *"Ti amo."*

Leblanc sprang forward, punching Sal in the jaw.

Hunched sideways in pain, Sal clung to his brother. "Without me, he will not eat. *Please*—"

Leblanc raised his revolver again. Aimed this time at Nico's head.

Sal saw Nico's face turn toward the gun's muzzle, his body suddenly gone still. His eyes held steady on Sal's.

"Mi fido di te," he whispered. *I trust you.*

"Best let go of the kid," Leblanc spat, "or my next bullet'll be to his head."

Chapter 47

Anguished, Kerry stood over her father's bed.

From the other side of the tick, Tully and Jursey watched her to gauge how they should feel. But Kerry herself could feel nothing. Except the sharp, torn edges around the hole where she ought to feel grief.

She should be in town at the jail to help the Catalfamos. She could picture little Nico, shivering, his frame already more bones than flesh, curled up on the cold floor.

Or she should be up at Barnard, her English lit professor expounding on the Romantic poets and their excess of emotion, Kerry writing down every word. Thinking how she came from people who let loose their sorrow and rage and desire only in lyrics and the keening draw of a bow over strings.

But here she stood instead, keeping watch over this man as he lay unconscious, a small moan every few moments. The father who'd wrung her mother dry. The turmoil he'd wreaked.

Kerry lifted her gaze from his face, gray and drawn, to the twins. Their eyes were a mirrored reflection, two sets of rounded blue pain.

"You said when you came to get me that you saw a change in him?"

"He'd got better," Tully said. "Sitting up. Even spoke enough to wheeze out, 'Get your sister.'"

"Tossing," Jursey echoed. "Liked to stand up all by hisself."

Kerry reached a hand to both of them across the bed. "I believe you. The final—" She stopped herself there. After all, she couldn't be sure. "The stages of a sickness can be odd. You were right to come get me."

The snap of twigs and a low rumble of voices from somewhere outside made them all spin toward the door.

With no windows in the barn, Kerry hurried to its entrance to see who was approaching. From behind her, Romeo growled, brown hackles raised.

Kerry slipped a hand to her right boot. There: the knife.

Jursey joined her at the door, his legs already spread out in the best mountain man stance a thirteen-year-old could manage. He glanced down at her hand. "You always could gig a trout in the gills from a good dozen foot back."

It was an exaggeration, but they both took a moment's comfort in it.

More snapping of twigs from just below the ridge where the path dropped straight down toward the falls. The low nicker of a horse.

And then, the muffled sobbing of a child.

Kerry exchanged looks with her brother. Tully joined them, wide-eyed and braced, at the barn door.

At the crest of the path, Robert Bratchett appeared on his ancient horse. And huddled on the same horse just in front of him, little Nico. The hand of Bratchett's immobilized left arm rested tenderly on the child's shoulder as Nico curled in tighter and cried.

But most astounding of all was Bratchett swinging down from the horse, easing the child off after him, carrying him on his shoulders and steadied with his one good arm through the barn doors. Nodding to the three younger MacGregors, he didn't stop until he reached their father's makeshift bed.

Johnny MacGregor's eyes blinked open.

He lay conscious for the first time since Kerry arrived, breathless, from Biltmore, as if the sheer force of Bratchett's presence now and whatever past they had shared had ripped the clouds from the dying man's mind. And not gently.

"Johnny Mac," Bratchett said. The voice seemed to open some sort of secret door. Kerry watched, astonished, as her father's eyes filled with tears and he lifted his right hand an inch or two above the tick.

"Bobby Bratch," he rasped.

Little Nico set gently on the floor, Bratchett dropped his good arm to grasp the hand lifted, just barely, to him. "We need a place to hide this boy, Johnny. Ella and me, we can bring food, but you know better'n anyone, we're no kind of safe place."

Something passed between the two men, Kerry saw. Johnny Mac squeezed shut his eyes as if there were something he'd rather not see. "I do know," he said.

"I figure," Bratchett went on, "you owe not only me but also the world in general a favor."

"Yes," was all Johnny Mac said, voice crumbling to nothing but dust. And yet he managed the same word again. "Yes."

Chapter 48

Kerry spent several hours getting Nico set with the twins, who made him a pallet beside their own near Malvolio's stall and showed him where to pet the mule on the soft of his muzzle so that he'd flicker his eyes. She spooned wild peppermint tea and creamed corn down her father's throat.

Kerry held up the photograph for him. And gently—more gently than she had since she'd come home—cradled his head to let him see better.

He smiled—a strange, distant smile. "Bobby Bratch," he whispered. Then gave in to the weight of his head falling back.

~

Exhausted, Kerry slipped through the woods back to Biltmore the next morning. All she could see as she walked was Madison Grant, his suits perfectly pressed, hair perfectly smoothed. Somehow, surely, he was behind all this: the attack at the station, the blaming of innocent men, the child ripped from his brother and huddled now in her barn.

Not sure what she'd do or how, Kerry checked in first with the cooks. Rema stood in front of row upon row of glass Mason jars filled with spears of green. "I declare I can like a man who grows a good okra."

Kerry didn't point out that Vanderbilt didn't weed his own fields or preserve his own produce, but only nodded absently. And slipped upstairs. Tracked the sound of Grant's voice to the billiard room, the clack of the balls, the scent of cigar smoke emanating into the hall.

Which meant she had at least a few moments to slip upstairs to his guest room.

Kerry had no evidence of Grant's part in the train station attack, only a sense deep in her gut. Maybe if she'd been able to track him like she'd hunted wild boar, or been allowed to pummel him with questions as the police should have. But that wasn't an option for a kitchen maid supposed to be roasting potatoes right now.

Swiftly, she walked—never breaking into a run, which would attract attention—back toward the servants' staircase, finished at last. Climbing to the second story of the bachelors' wing, she looked both ways down the corridor. A kitchen maid shouldn't have been there for any number of reasons, but she would hurry. She would not be found.

Every Biltmore guest room had a brass fitting on its door for the current occupant's calling card, so the room Kerry was searching for took only moments to find. Grant had left his coat strewn over a chair near the fireplace. A patterned tweed. Heart pounding, Kerry checked its pockets one by one. Nothing but an old train ticket to Best, a receipt from Bon Marché, and a scrap of paper scrawled with words she couldn't make out.

Kerry scanned the room. Nothing else out of place. A stack of letterhead stationery left on a small table. Approaching, Kerry flipped through: all the pages embossed with the Vanderbilt crest, but otherwise blank.

Except.

The top one bore the imprint of what someone had penned on the page above it. Kerry held it up to the light filtering in from the far window.

The letter *F*, she could make out. No salutation, just a word beginning with *F* . . .

Footsteps echoed outside on the marble. Heart hammering, she squinted at the imprinted lines.

F . . . Family . . . no. Farm . . . work?

The footsteps stopped in front of the guest room door. The metal click of a hand turning the knob.

Or a name, perhaps. Like . . . Farnsworth . . .

Someone else here Grant is influencing. Another of the pieces in the LNA puzzle.

Kerry crumpled the page. Thrust it deep in her apron pocket just as the door swung open.

Madison Grant smoothed his face into a flat, mirthless smile. "Kerry. How . . . interesting to find you here. In the bachelors' wing. I was under the distinct impression only valets and footmen assist the male guests. Perhaps the rules have changed to my advantage."

They stood sizing each other up. Then one of his hands shot back to flip a lever on the door's knob. Locking it. He kicked it shut behind him. Strode forward.

She felt the breath leave her.

As she stood her ground, he stepped in close.

Stealing a glance at the stack of stationery, his features relaxed. Reassured, perhaps, that he'd not left the letter there.

Stepping back, Kerry could feel the fireplace mantel against her shoulder blades. Nowhere to run.

He wasn't a muscular man. But he was a man with much to lose. And desperate men, like cornered boars, were ferocious.

She gripped the back of the chair with his tweed coat strewn across it, the coat he'd worn the day she'd applied at the Battery Park Inn for work. An image flashed across her mind: Grant in the tweed coat in the inn, the clerk calling across the lobby: *So good to have you back again this season, Mr. Grant!*

"You were here before last fall," she said. "Last fall wasn't your first visit to Asheville. You've been here before, spreading your putrid, hateful ideas. A place where the rich have been coming since the railroad arrived, so no one thought a thing of your being here, doing your work among people you knew to be angry and scared with all the change, just looking for someone to blame."

The smile did not wane. Even as he pushed her against the wall next to the fireplace. Now he pressed his groin against her so hard her spine crushed against the wall.

"I've no idea," he said in her ear, "what you mean."

Churning inside, she eased her right leg up as she reached down toward her calf. His hands moved on her. But she couldn't fight him. Not yet.

He kissed her neck as if he would bite down on her throat, feral, going in for the kill, then shake his head so hard her spine snapped.

Kerry had slipped her hand under her skirt's hem. Her fingers could just brush the knife's handle now. Just another inch . . . If he could just be distracted, even for an instant, she could reach farther down and get to it.

Her voice came strained from her crushed chest. "You're behind all of it: the flyers promoting hate, the group in France and the people here you've been in contact with, the fear you've tried to fan."

He eased back an inch, eyes sparkling with triumph. A hunter with a deer in the crosshairs.

Slowly, taking advantage of his leaning slightly back, she managed to lift her leg enough to slide the knife up out of the top of her boot with two fingers. "So," she managed, "did you kill Berkowitz yourself or hire Farnsworth to do it?"

His lips stretched into a sneer. "So, you've landed on me as the killer, have you?"

She wasn't at all sure she'd hit on the answer—Grant killing the man out of sheer loathing or a fear of what the reporter might've known that could've sullied Grant's public reputation. For all his superiority and polish, Madison Grant seemed capable of attacking someone he loathed just like he'd smashed the phylacteries—and she had to see his reaction. Her hand wrapped fully around the knife now.

"Did he have particularly damning information on you and the LNA—something, perhaps, that could have hurt your public persona if the public knew what an utter scoundrel you are?" She began easing her right hand up.

One of his eyebrows lifted. "And what, pray tell, does a little kitchen maid know of the LNA?"

Her right hand was nearly in position for a clear strike.

But then he pinioned both arms to her sides. "*No one*, you understand, will believe a pretty little servant, dirt poor, over an Ivy League man from a prominent family of New York. Try it and I promise, I *will* ruin you." He thrust himself hard up against her again, and her spine slammed into the wall once more.

The impact loosened her grip on the knife, and it slipped soundlessly to the room's carpet.

Oblivious of what she'd just dropped, Grant yanked upward on her skirts and grabbed under them. Kerry ducked away from him even as she strained toward the knife he'd not seen.

But Grant wrenched her back. "You little slut."

Just as he'd bragged in the bowling alley, Grant did know his angles. Clamping down at her wrist, he twisted one hand behind her back so hard she was sure it would snap and lowered his mouth to her ear. "You realize, of course, if you scream for help, you expose yourself as having snuck up to the bachelors' wing—of your own volition. Driven, it would appear, by ambition and lust to the bedroom of a guest. A sullied end to a poor mountain girl's employment."

Kerry groped with the fingers of the hand he'd pinioned behind her, digging her nails into the soft of his wrist. Grant's grip on her loosened only long enough for her to leap a few feet away and dive headlong for the knife, even as Grant dove to block the door. Snatching up the knife, she leaped for the far side of the room and flashed the blade now so that he could see.

"Ah, I suppose it should be no surprise that hillbilly trash would know how to put up a fight." He looked entertained—not in the least wary of her or her weapon.

From the opposite side of the room, she braced for what she knew would be her one chance as he lunged at her. One sliver of a second to let fly the knife at a moving target.

Then all at once he was coming for her, and she was drawing back her arm.

Now came a pounding on the door that stopped them both in their tracks and turned them toward it.

"Everythin's all right in there, is it?" came a voice from the other side.

Kerry spun back first and let the knife fly.

A bloodcurdling scream from Madison Grant.

Jursey had been right: sometimes, at least, she *could* gig a trout in the gills.

Her eyes not leaving him, Kerry stepped swiftly to unlock the door. Moncrief, the footman, swung the door wide.

"Bloody 'ell."

Kerry, her hair pulled wild and loose from the maid's cap that dangled by one hairpin, marched to the opposite side of the room. She yanked her knife from the wainscoting just a hair to the right of Madison Grant's thigh. He stood frozen in place, face drained of all color.

"You have Moncrief here to thank," Kerry told Grant over her shoulder as she drew even with the footman. "It's only because he showed up when he did that I aimed"—she glanced back one final time—"to miss."

Chapter 49

In the hours after they dragged his brother away, Sal faced what had to be done. Robert and Ella Bratchett had stepped forward from the crowd to volunteer to care for Nico for the night. Sal trusted them.

But he'd also seen his brother's face: worse than an expression of horror.

Instead, Nico's eyes had gone blank, insensible, just as he'd looked when Sal found him after the night of lynchings. Nico's mind had clearly moved to a place where he could not feel, could not hurt, could not panic. But also, Sal knew, he would not eat or speak. For Nico to survive, Sal would need to break out.

Leblanc caught him staring at the bars. "Plan to gnaw through those with your sharp little teeth, guinea?" He turned to Wolfe. "I'd watch that one if I were you."

Wolfe scowled. "Like I ain't never learned my own job."

"Apparently, you haven't. A murder months ago at your train station and the killer still at large—unless it's Catalfamo, in which case I did your job for you. In fact, I can't trust a fumbling backwater piker like you not to muff up a simple thing like keeping a watch on the Italian for the night. I'm staying here myself, Wolfe, overnight. Then transporting Catalfamo tomorrow back to New Orleans for trial."

"Thought you said he and the others already stood trial four years ago and got off."

Leblanc looked Sal up and down. Then shrugged. "Bringing him in's what I was hired to do. That's what I'm doing. 'Cause some of us know how to do our jobs. What happens to him once I get him there isn't my concern."

Wolfe met the prisoner's eye but addressed the detective over his shoulder. "No. I don't reckon it would be."

There would be no second trial, Sal knew. From the expression on the local lawman's face, Sal gathered Wolfe knew it, too.

Leblanc made a show of moving one of the jail's army cots near Sal's cell. Sullenly, Wolfe served Leblanc and himself slabs of salted venison and a clear liquid Wolfe referred to only as "home brew" before shoving a tin cup at Leblanc.

"So, little man," Leblanc said to Wolfe as they ate, "time to show you how to do your job."

Ramming a metal dinner tray under the metal flap at the foot of Sal's cell door, Wolfe said nothing. But he stood there unmoving at the cell as Sal picked up the tray.

Wolfe's eyes dropped to the tray. Sal's followed. A tin cup of water sat there. A tin plate of venison, mostly gristle by the look of it. One metal spoon. No fork. No knife. Both of those, presumably, could be used as weapons.

But under the upturned lip of the tin plate, two long, thin nails, one bent slightly at its point.

Sal's eyes flew up to Wolfe's, but met his only for an instant, Wolfe already turning.

"Go the hell to sleep, Catalfamo," Wolfe said. "God knows you'll need it with the journey you've got ahead."

Sal did not eat. But he made himself choke down the water. And made himself lie down on his cot and pull the rough wool blanket up to his chin. And lie there. For hours.

The nails might have been a trick, the setup for Wolfe's plan to showcase a local lawman's savvy in catching a prisoner attempting escape. But it was Sal's only chance—so a chance worth taking, even if it earned him a bullet through the back.

He waited until after moonlight flooded his cell. Leblanc's snore rose and fell.

Sal knew little of locks, though he'd picked one once years ago on a steamer trunk belonging to an Oxford don staying at the *pensione* in Florence. Sal had been quietly coached by the *pensione*'s old cook, who'd apparently led quite another life as a young woman. She'd murmured tips in his ear: where to hold the ice pick and the small paring knife she offered him from the kitchen. The professor, who'd lost his spectacles and his trunk keys on the first day, had tipped them both a half crown.

Now Sal worked the nails gently. He couldn't afford to clank them inside the lock. A half hour passed as he prodded and poked with them, using the straight one as the tensioner, then gently pulling with the bent one. His back and shoulders tightened to the point of pain. Sweat poured from his face despite the chill of the brick floor and walls. Try after try after try. Nothing.

Then, finally, a lever sprang up. Tumblers shifted.

Pocketing the nails, Sal slipped through the cell door, crept past the snoring Leblanc. Glancing back toward where Wolfe sat hunched, head down in his desk chair against a wall, Sal thought he saw the sheriff's head raise just an inch. But Sal didn't stay to be sure.

He had no idea what direction to go to find Nico. Only that Kerry MacGregor once mentioned that the Bratchetts, the nearest neighbors to her own farm, helped care for her father. But Sal had only a general idea what direction Kerry walked in the evenings when she went home: north from the stables and up farther onto the ridge.

Outside on the street, he dodged away from the streetlamp's pool of gold light and into the shadows. Biltmore Estate would be where they'd look for him first. But also where he'd need to start to find the way to Nico.

Chapter 50

In the vaulted room with the horse stalls, Lilli stood still, listening, just inside the door that led to the stable's corridor near the tack room. Her voice echoed across the polished brick. "Were you looking for someone?"

More footsteps sounded from the other side of the door—slow and deliberate. The door swung open, the man stepping inside.

"Name's Leblanc. But then, you know very well who I am." A pause. "With the Pinkerton Detective Agency now."

"*Bien sûr*. Yet you work also still for my father, *non*?"

A pause. "Only he prefers going through Pinkerton now. Calls less attention."

"Since when, Mr. Leblanc, has my father wanted to call *less* attention to himself? It is a family failing. Your purpose here today, Mr. Leblanc?" She'd play dumb if need be.

"The dago your daddy sent me to find—and I damn well *caught*— broke out last night of the tin can these people here call a jail."

Lilli felt her heart rate drop—alarmingly.

"A breakout, did you say? *Mon Dieu*. How very unfortunate for you. I know you'd so hoped to appear at least marginally competent."

Having just turned away, Leblanc rounded on her. In the red of his face and the bulge of his eyes were the words, vulgar and raging, that he could not let himself say to the daughter of Maurice Barthélemy.

"You know," she said, "my friend Emily—Mr. Vanderbilt's niece— told me of your visit at Christmas."

"Dago bastard. But I'll get him the hell back. And make him pay for the trouble."

Stepping to her right, Lilli bumped a girth stretcher and sent it clattering to the floor. "Why, how clumsy of me. Is it in there with the stalls that you're wanting to go?"

She fumbled with righting the stretcher. "Goodness, it's surprisingly heavy." She could hardly get the words of helplessness across her lips, but desperate times called for desperate measures. Even if that meant feigning a weakness she'd never felt in her life. "Why, Mr. Leblanc, I wonder if you could assist me."

Leblanc's voice softened slightly. "Glad to. Only where are the damn grooms who ought to be helping a lady?"

"I'm sure there are some about, perhaps in the carriage house at the other end or cleaning the courtyard. But, of course, as you point out, Mr. Vanderbilt has lost one of his stablehands to your hunt."

She extended her hand to the detective's coat lapel and pulled him in closer. Laid the palm of her free hand on his chest. Saw his eyes go hungry on her. Felt the swell of her own power.

"Mr. Leblanc, as one New Orleans native to another, let us be perfectly frank with each other. I have something to tell you."

Chapter 51

Lilli's pulse had dropped to only a distant flick, it felt like. No thud at all.

Somewhere out there in the woods or fields, or in the alleyways of the village, was the man her father had evidently paid a detective to track for four years. But he couldn't have gotten far yet. Leblanc would have looked here first once the escape was discovered.

This much was clear: the longer Leblanc stayed here, the farther away Sal could run. If she'd learned anything from the example of the Napoleon of New Orleans, it was that some men could be made to do things they'd no intention of doing.

Lilli was sure her face had gone the pale of abalone. But this Leblanc would not be able to see fear in her—or hear it.

Lilli leaned in toward the detective. *"Comme c'est triste."* Her voice came out soft. Seductive. Steady. "Mr. Leblanc, I have a confession to make." She lifted his hand to her waist, just under one breast.

"I am telling you this only because I believe I can trust you. Because I sense you know what it is to be swept away by passion." She looked deep into the man's bloodhound of a face—small, droopy eyes with jowls dropping well below his jawline. No man ever looked less likely to have been swept away by passion.

His palm had gone clammy against her waist.

"Lillian!" came a shout from the carriage house at the other end of the complex. "Lilli, are you here?"

Emily. Who could easily ruin the scene and Sal's chance of escape.

Putting a finger to her lips, Lilli sniffed dramatically. Averted her eyes. "Before I am found, I will confess to you, Mr. Leblanc, what no one else knows."

Emily's footsteps approached from just a few feet away on the other side of the door, left slightly ajar. Another step more and she would be in earshot.

Lilli's back to the door, Emily would not know that Lilli heard her approach.

"Mr. Leblanc, I will confess to you my distress. Have compassion, I beg you, on the Italian, who is even now hiding inside the house. If you've ever yourself been madly, disastrously in love, Mr. Leblanc, have mercy on him, my lover."

Emily's gasp from the other side of the door said that she'd heard.

The moment of stunned disbelief. Now Emily threw open the door and stalked forward. "Lilli, good God, how *could* you? And to blather it like this to a stranger!"

First confused, Leblanc reared back. Yanked at his collar as if he were having trouble catching his breath. Then smirked from one young woman to the next as Emily railed.

Sweet and guileless as she was, Lilli mused, Emily would never have caused this sort of scene if she'd known Lilli was acting. Lilli listened with a bowed head—a posture she'd never tried on before. When at last she looked up, it was at Leblanc.

"I beg you, sir, to leave the basements of the house unsearch—" Her hand flew to her open mouth. "*Mon Dieu!* I should have said nothing!"

Leblanc snorted. "I can promise this much: I won't report this back to your daddy. But as to slowing me down on trapping Catalfamo again and hauling his ass back to justice . . ." He tipped his hat to her. "It's my damn job. I do wish you *bonjour*, Miss Barthélemy."

Lilli counted out retreating footsteps. She knew that in a moment she would need to turn, face Emily, and insist that she'd lied. And a very convincing choice of a lie it was, too. Because no young woman of their social class would have put her own reputation on the guillotine for something untrue. Which was why Leblanc had not hesitated in stomping to the vast basement to search.

Lilli felt a little lightheaded. She'd used the specter of scandal about herself to save someone else. If she was going to be a whore in some minds, then she might as well be one who had guts enough to stick her neck out.

"Walk with me," Lilli said to her friend, who'd gone speechless. "While we talk."

But before they'd crossed the courtyard, the maid, Kerry, burst from the porte cochere door, face horribly flushed. Her skirt ripped.

And, holy mother of God, her maid's cap at the left side of her head, her apron horribly wrinkled, and her red hair as mussed as if she'd been brawling like some sort of street tramp.

The maid, panting hard, met Lilli's eyes.

Emily, kind heart that she was, moved toward her first. "Are you quite all right, Kerry?"

The maid's eyes stayed on Lilli's. As if Lilli Barthélemy might be trusted to hear what was not spoken.

Lilli muttered a single word and did not make it a question. *"Grant."* Then she added two more, because they had to be said. *"Le bâtard."*

But before they had time to move, Mrs. Smythe burst up through the courtyard doors that led to the kitchen's delivery entrance below. The housekeeper, so concerned with propriety, so distraught over Americans' loose grip on culture . . . was running. And beside her was that smaller replica of Kerry.

"It's Daddy!" the girl called. "Kerry, it's Daddy! Rema and Jursey's up with him now, but Rema says it's the death throes, sure enough. And he's asking for you."

Chapter 52

Holding the last of the warm honey and whiskey to his lips, Kerry rose. Whiskey had done this man a world of harm most of his life, and her stomach roiled at the memories the thickly sweet smell brought flooding back. But maybe now whiskey could help him leave this life with less pain.

Rema laid a hand on her back. "You give your daddy all you could. And now what he'd be needing, we got no kind of power to give."

Tentatively, as if afraid of disturbing the silence, Tully reached for her singing bow. Then handed her brother the fiddle. Jursey had gotten better on the instrument than Kerry herself ever was, she thought as she listened. Like their father's, Jursey's playing pulled all the shields away from your heart—left it exposed and raw to the sorrow of his notes.

In the corner of the stall near the woodstove, Nico huddled under a quilt. Rema knelt to offer the child a biscuit. Kerry could smell the ham and baked apples Rema must have carried here with her and slathered inside the biscuit.

"*Grazie,*" the boy whispered. "*Grazie mille.*"

"Lord willing and the creek don't rise, we'll find your big brother, sugar," Rema told him, stroking his hair. "Don't you fret none."

Nico blinked back at her. Then seemed to decide this was meant to be a comfort. Biting down on the biscuit, he gave a weak smile.

Then leaned forward to kiss Rema on the cheek. Which made the old woman's eyes fill.

Softly at first, the twins' voices rose like they were one, the very same timbre, then split into two, harmonized. Haunting.

Come home, come home,
Ye who are weary, come home . . .

Kerry leaned against the half wall of the stall and closed her eyes to listen. From behind her, footsteps she knew. Approaching slowly. Cautiously. Robert Bratchett. Ella just behind.

Thank you, Kerry mouthed, startled by the tears that welled in her eyes just for the gift of their coming. Just for their standing alongside the raw and ugly.

She waited through several more stanzas of the song. But then she had to ask. She leaned in toward Robert Bratchett. "Please tell me. About the photo."

He turned, startled, to her. Several lines of the old song went by.

Oh for the wonderful love he has promised,
Promised for you and for me . . .

He raised an eyebrow.

Stepping toward the barn doors, Bratchett ran the back of his right arm across his forehead. Then dipped his head close to hers. "We both volunteered for the army, the Union army."

Though we have sinned he has mercy and pardon . . .

"Plenty of mountain boys didn't—for either side. Didn't feel much connected to the federal government up North or to a bunch of slaveholders hadn't ever so much as gotten a fingernail dirty. But your

355

daddy and me, we volunteered. Got assigned to the same unit. Made it through, both of us, to come on back home."

Kerry braced herself against a barn door for support.

"It was after the War things got stirred up. Packs of men, mostly come back from the Confederate Army, went riding at night. Terrorizing."

Kerry gripped the door's rope handle, the music from behind them swelling, Bratchett's words floating somewhere on top. "And my daddy?"

"Your daddy wasn't of them that went out night riding, no. Him and me were still friends. Our wives, too."

Holding her breath, she waited for whatever was coming.

"But one night the riders come to him first, trying to bring him along to my place. He wouldn't go."

Bratchett's good arm passed over his forehead and eyes again. Kerry could see he wanted to stop. Let the old song have the final say. But she would not let him look away.

"Your daddy didn't ride with them, but he didn't try and stop them, either. Told me later the bunch was drunk and bored, bruising for some-body to bully. Long and short of it, he was scared. They left your farm, come to my place. I fought them back, best as I could. Just me, maybe seven of them."

Kerry's eyes dropped to his arm.

"Only good news was Ella'd stayed overnight with a cousin in Black Mountain. No idea what they'd done to her if she'd been there. I'd have had to kill one or two, and they'd have strung me up, sure. As it was, they set the cabin on fire. Left me for dead."

"On fire," Kerry repeated.

"Clear to the ground. Your daddy felt bad. Bad enough to help me rebuild—a good three arms between us." He smiled sadly. "Thought he maybe could have stopped them."

Robert Bratchett looked her in the eye. "He was probably right. They might've been worked up enough to throw some punches his way, but they likely would've listened to him. People respected your daddy back then."

Kerry heard the *back then* and knew it wasn't a barb. Just simply true. For most of her life, he'd been known all through this hollow as just a drunk. Who could fiddle the stars into falling.

"The crime your daddy laid at his own doorstop was maybe he could've said something. Maybe could've stopped Tate."

Kerry's mouth opened. But she was slow pulling out sound. *"Tate?"*

"Dearg's daddy. Their ringleader back then. That pack always looking for who to hate next. Seemed like the poorer they got, the more land or jobs or women they lost, the more they went looking for trouble."

"Tate," she repeated, seeing Johnny Mac's eyes again, round with terror back in the cabin when he'd asked about the attack at the train station. But no Tate could be connected with that—Dearg's father long dead and Dearg not even in town.

"Kerry, your daddy had his demons, I know—and a temper like hell. But I've wondered if part of what made him rage so loud was the guilt—of back when he'd kept too quiet."

A hemlock shuddered, its limbs slapping the barn, as the wind blew. Side by side, the two of them stood in silence.

Then Bratchett walked back toward the stall and the man lying there, his breaths just a faint rattle now. As Kerry watched, Robert Bratchett reached down and held Johnny Mac's hand. From under the bed, Romeo moaned.

She followed Bratchett back into the barn, letting the strains from the fiddle and the singing bow and the twins' voices flow past her like the brook past the corner of the old chapel.

Ye who are weary, come home . . .

It wasn't that she believed just now the words they were singing. But there was comfort in standing nearby to listen. To feel the music swirl around her and hold her. While the fissures inside her widened and her tears came streaming at last. And the part that had been hardened against her father for years broke fully open now—not in forgiveness, not yet, but in raw, unguarded sorrow.

Chapter 53

Nico was all that mattered now.

Sal tensed, listening to the rhythm of hoof beats on the Approach Road's macadam. Peering from behind the screen of rhododendrons, he watched a rider approach. But this was a slim man and well dressed, on a horse that held its tail high and its neck arched: Arab blood, Sal could tell even from this distance. Definitely not Leblanc and his rented dun.

George Vanderbilt cantered past. His head shifted right and then left as if searching for something.

Avoiding the shafts of morning sunlight, Sal moved swiftly through the forest. He would come only close enough to Biltmore House to get his bearings for the direction Kerry MacGregor headed when she walked back to her farm. That might at least put Sal in the general vicinity of the Bratchett farm—where Nico would still be staring blankly out at the world.

Sal felt the strength of his chest, his arms. He was ready to stop Leblanc however it had to be done.

He listened for the sounds of Vanderbilt's horse receding. But now there were more coming. Galloping from just the other side of the bend in the Approach Road, nearest Sal.

As they burst into his line of sight, Sal crouched lower. But the first rider, his hat pulled low on his face, glanced right as if spotting a movement behind the rhododendrons. Leaning forward and right, he'd plunged with his horse off the road and into the woods before Sal could run more than a few strides.

With all the fury of years of running from a crime he'd not committed, all the anguish of knowing he'd been branded a vicious animal in this country he'd adopted, Sal swept a branch from the ground and spun, arm raised, to face the horseman.

As the horse shied violently left, the rider kept his seat, barely.

"Cabot! *Mi dispiace*. I thought—"

"You thought I was Leblanc. In which case I can only be grateful my head is still fully attached to my shoulders."

A second horse—the Arab—broke through hemlocks to join them, George Vanderbilt breathing hard, and behind the Arab this time, another horse, riderless, had been tethered. "Thank God, Catalfamo. We were hoping we'd find you trying to make your way to Bratchett's place. But Leblanc will look for you there at some point, probably soon. So Nico's not there. We're here to take you to him."

∽

Third in line behind Vanderbilt and Cabot on their horses, Sal leaned forward on the horse they'd brought for him as if he could by sheer force of will leap over the others to reach Nico first. But not knowing the way, he could only remain pitched forward, the gelding turning his head as if to ask why his rider's body gave signals for speed when the rocky, root-webbed trail and the two horses ahead all demanded nothing above a fast walk.

They rose to a break in the trees. Sal's eyes adjusted to the blaze of sun as they emerged from the thickly forested trail.

In the clearing stood a scattering of wooden structures. The one straight ahead, a small log cabin with no windows and its door left ajar, stood defeated, its roof collapsed.

Behind the cabin stood another, even smaller structure with some of its boards pulled loose, as if they'd been needed for another purpose. A chicken house sat to the left, its hens and rooster flapping and scuffling to announce the presence of the strangers. From the largest structure, a barn, came a deep bray.

At the barn door, two identical heads appeared, the red of the hair flaming in the clearing's blast of sun.

"It's all right," Jursey MacGregor announced. "It's not who we thought."

Tully stood squinting at them down the barrel of an old flintlock.

"I can see that for my ownself," she said. But did not set the gun down, as if, seeing what she'd seen of the world lately, she'd rather greet these visitors with a weapon already leveled.

"Where is—" Sal began. But no need to finish.

A third head appeared at the barn door—lowered, just a dark swath of hair. And a scuffle of hay as one leg dragged across the ground.

Sal slung himself off his horse, not even bothering to tether the gelding. *"Nico!"*

Clutching hard to the slight little body, convulsing now, Sal felt his own tears falling into his brother's hair. "Nico. My Nico. You are safe."

Words were being exchanged behind them. But Sal held his chin over Nico's head, kept both arms tight around the slight frame. Let his brother feel safety on every side.

"May we speak with your older sister?" Cabot was asking the twins.

Even holding his brother to him, even flooded with relief to find Nico safe, Sal realized now the tension in the air he'd missed before.

The twins exchanged looks.

Tully gestured for them to follow. "She's back in here. With our daddy. And some neighbors who've come to . . . say their . . ." She looked to her brother.

"Goodbyes." He reached for his sister's hand, like he could talk better if he felt his other half. "They come to say their goodbyes."

~

Holding fast to each other, Sal and Nico followed the others to the back of the barn into what had been a cow stall, swept clean, its door broken off its hinges. In its middle was a pallet covered in patterned quilts, a man with gray skin unmoving at its center. To one side stood Rema and Kerry. And at the other, Robert Bratchett.

The man on the pallet was trying to speak, lifting his hand toward Kerry. It was his lips more than his crackle of a voice that made the words: "I'm . . . so . . . sorry."

Then, to Sal's surprise, the dying man turned his head toward Bratchett. And formed the same words: "I'm . . . so . . . sorry."

Bratchett's good arm went to his bad one. He nodded.

For long moments they all stood that way, MacGregor's older daughter holding his right hand and his neighbor holding his left, Rema with an arm around each twin, and nobody speaking.

Kerry MacGregor bent over her father. "Daddy," she said, then stopped and looked up to Rema and to Robert Bratchett, like they might know how to finish for her. The two gentlemen who'd ridden with Sal up from Biltmore she didn't even seem to see as they stood silently behind their circle.

She looked back at the dying man. Tenderness was there in her face, but also anger. A strange mix that had her face pinched. "Daddy. I have so many questions."

The man turned his face back to her. Tears rolled down both gray cheekbones.

The whole barn stilled. Even the mule in the next stall quit swishing his tail.

"So . . . very . . . sorry," he whispered.

But that was all.

Tears ran down Kerry's face, too. "It's not enough," she whispered. The tears coming faster now. "It's not enough." A sob escaped her throat.

"God help me, I can't just say it's okay—that all the past is okay. I *do not want* to forgive you." Tears streaming down her cheeks now, she sank to her knees. "I don't want to. *I don't.*"

"I know," he managed. "I know."

Dropping her face into her hands, her shoulders shook. "I love you."

The man's own tears coursed down gray, sunken cheeks, his eyes on her deep wells of pain—with a tenderness and regret that looked harder to bear than his body's hurting.

After a moment, Kerry touched his hand. Then reached for something beside the man's pallet. And rose, a bow in one hand, and a violin, Sal saw, in the other. Only here, maybe, it was a fiddle.

Kerry MacGregor began playing while her brother and sister and aunt—and also their neighbor—took turns bending over the man on the pallet and kissing his cheek.

She played one song after another as her father lay there—slow, keening songs, like the bow was raking right over the heart. Her head cocked over the instrument's body, her tears splashed onto its weathered wood. Her hands, trembling as they played, made the notes deepen and sing, like they'd rise up through the roof of the barn, through the canopy of the forest, and through the mist that hung today over the mountains.

Sinking to hold Nico tighter, Sal let his brother turn and bury his small head in his chest. Nico, whom he'd not been able to protect as he should have. Whose shattered leg would never be right, never be without pain. Sal's fault. If he'd only fought harder. If he'd only held on.

And yet here they were. Safe, at least for another few hours.

Sal squeezed shut his eyes.

The words spoken here seemed to twine through the keening notes, and they felt like the whole of what it was to be broken and hurting and human: *I'm sorry, so very sorry, it's not enough, I love you.*

Chapter 54

The minister was speaking of a land where joys never end.

But Kerry was picturing the cabin when she was a child. There was her mother at the fire, stirring rabbit in a thick stew with mushrooms and wild onions picked that day from the woods. On the pine board table, a sorghum-sweetened cake in thin layers with cooked apples and cinnamon holding the stack together. The twins were toddling near the flames, but her father was placing one foot on the ladder-back chair he'd put in their path. He lifted his fiddle to his chin, his bow hand sweeping across the strings in wide, mournful arcs that drew heartbreak from the instrument's hollow body.

Holding hands with each other and with two cornhusk dolls, the twins swayed as their father sang:

> *I'm just a poor wayfarin' stranger*
> *Travelin' through this world of woe*
> *Yet there's no sickness, toil, or danger*
> *In that bright world to which I go*
> *I'm going there to see my father . . .*

Kerry's father had left school in third grade to work his own daddy's farm. But he could finger the neck off a fiddle, the tunes like thread on a whirring spindle, pulling them close.

Kerry was vaguely aware of the people on the pew beside her: the twins on either side and Rema to her right; to her left, Robert and Ella Bratchett; and, just behind, Miss Hopson, who'd evidently left out of Grand Central Depot within hours of receiving Kerry's telegram. The presence of all these steadied Kerry. Yet she still felt in danger of toppling.

Behind them were several people from Best—Kerry was in no mood to think of it as Biltmore Junction today—and from Asheville. There sat Ling Yong, his arm around Zhen, her eyes wide and curious on the crowd. Behind Ling, Moncrief and Mrs. Smythe and several others from the Biltmore staff.

Sal and Nico would be huddled up safe—*please, God*—in the dormant brickworks in the village where Biltmore's bricks had been made. Though Leblanc would have no reason to connect Kerry with the Italians, he might've soon ferreted Sal out looking on the farm next to the Bratchetts'—especially now with the MacGregor farm about to be sold. Kerry felt the stab of that again in her gut.

John Cabot was there in the chapel, too. He was watching, waiting to meet her eye. Which she did—for one, jolting moment. But it was too much, the storm of emotions she felt around him.

As she was pulling her eyes away, he mouthed something to her: *I'm sorry. I'm so sorry.* His face did look heavy—battered even—with pain.

Sorry for the death of her father, for her and the twins' loss? Sorry for being with Vanderbilt and McNamee when they'd arrived with the contract on the farm? Sorry for kissing her in the falling snow weeks ago and then keeping his distance?

Their eyes held a long moment. And before hers dropped, he lifted two fingers of his right hand to the left side of his chest.

For the first time today, she felt her heart lift just a bit from the weight that threatened to crush it.

Beside him stood Charles McNamee and George Vanderbilt.

Here out of kindness and community ties, Kerry thought. *And perhaps also to be sure the sale of the land goes through.*

Which maybe wasn't quite fair. But maybe she was allowed a thunderhead of emotions today.

Kerry refused to meet their eyes.

At least Madison Grant didn't try to show his face here. The knife from her boot had at least had that much effect.

Far in the back corner of the little chapel stood Dearg Tate. Head down.

Kerry took a long breath. Tried to focus up there on the pulpit again.

"Because Johnny MacGregor," the minister was saying, "was a man whose conduct might not have been perfect every day of his life."

Rema lowered her voice only slightly to mutter, "Well, if that ain't a clatterment of understatement."

"But whose path, thanks be to God, finally brought him the wisdom to ask forgiveness. The courage to change. The grace to come home."

Kerry tried to swallow down the shout that rose in her throat, the protest that this man had changed too late to calm all the chaos he'd caused. Too late to bring her momma back from the broken-down dead.

Kerry knew she'd be able to recall the funeral's words later, be able to replay it like a wax phonograph recording. But right now she was only numb.

Her head swung back toward the pews of singing congregants. Some of them openly weeping. Not for Johnny Mac, Kerry suspected, so much as the strange and disturbing injustice of grace.

The minister stepped aside as the harmonies branched and the notes swelled.

> *There's a land that is fairer than day,*
> *And by faith we can see it afar . . .*

The service easing to a close, the people rose, stiff, from their pews to belt out the final lines.

And our spirits shall sorrow no more . . .
We shall meet on that beautiful shore.

Then it was over. The Bratchetts both hugged her and moved on to let the other mourners press forward.

Kerry and Rema and the twins stood near the pine casket to shake hands. On top of the casket, they'd propped the photograph of her father and Robert Bratchett, their young faces beaming at the camera, their Union uniforms pressed and spotless, buttons gleaming. Beside that sat the one surviving likeness of Missy Murray MacGregor, the sketch that Johnny Mac must have done, her trusting and hopeful and smiling with her eggs and her chickens and rooster.

"A real fine likeness," Rema pronounced it. "She always was a pretty thing."

"A rooster," said Kerry.

Rema looked at her like she'd gone stark raving mad, driven by grief. "What?" She looked at the sketch again. "Well now, I reckon there would sure enough be a rooster there." She looked back at Kerry and patted her hand. "A real fine likeness of the bird, too, honey."

But Kerry's mind had shot to another rooster, this one on the crest in Farnsworth's telegraph office—not just any fowl with a comb but a Gallic rooster, a symbol of France—and, in this case, the kind of France that Ligue Nationale and others envisioned: one without Jews or immigrants or anyone who wasn't white.

It had been Farnsworth's name imprinted on Madison Grant's stack of stationery—him that Grant had been writing. Farnsworth was one of the many in town, no doubt, infected by Grant's views.

What if it was Farnsworth, after all?

Not as the killer, as she'd thought at one point, but as the one who'd provided the cover. It was Farnsworth whose receipt of Dearg's telegram to her from Whitnel, and whose testimony to the police that he, along with Jackson and others, had seen him come in on the train the day after the attack, stood as proof that Dearg couldn't have been behind the killing. But Dearg could have walked miles back down the line to Black Mountain or Round Top to catch a train there and make a public appearance the next day at Biltmore Junction. Only Farnsworth, though, could have transcribed a cable from Whitnel that had never been sent. And Sheriff Wolfe, distracted by so many other suspects and thrown off the scent, might never have checked with the other ticket offices.

What if Dearg had been driven for some reason by someone to attack the reporter, then handed his alibi by Farnsworth in the form of a fabricated telegram. And a testimonial that was a lie.

Kerry grabbed for her father's casket to steady herself.

"Tate," her father had rasped with a kind of panic. Maybe just a reliving of an old memory—or maybe, in his few moments of conscious thought, an instinct that the frustrated, despairing son of the older night-riding Tate might have also given vent to resentment.

Kerry stood gripping the casket and did not want to look for his face.

A few of the mourners nodded to her, a way of saying they were trying to shoulder the sorrow alongside her.

But one set of eyes far at the back met hers, then shot quickly away.

One set of eyes told her they were afraid of what she might see there.

"I don't," she said aloud.

"What, honey?" asked Rema.

"I don't want to know," Kerry said, speaking to Dearg at the back of the room.

But it was too late. It had all snapped together, as if the memory pictures she'd seen before had been only dots of paint on a larger canvas, like Miss Hopson's favorite painter, Seurat. With one final, pained look back at her, Dearg Tate ducked out the back of the chapel.

Her father's casket open at the front of the little chapel, the music flowing around and over and under her, Kerry felt the scene finally take shape. And she could not breathe.

In another few minutes—or longer, given this state she'd fallen into—the chapel had all but emptied. Except for Ling and Moncrief, chatting while Zhen went skipping outside, only Kerry and Rema and the twins remained, along with one last mourner. John Cabot was approaching, tentatively—eyes soft, face grave. "Kerry—"

"Thank you for coming," she told him, the edge of her voice beginning to fray. "Truly." Part of her wanted to step into his arms—a comfort, a buttress to help hold her up. But she felt as if leaning into anyone right now might mean collapsing entirely.

"Kerry," he began again.

Voices outside the chapel were rising, though. And now a man was shouting. Raging.

Kerry and Rema exchanged glances. And ran ahead of John Cabot and the rest to the door of the church.

Chapter 55

"Make a move for me, and I shoot. Hear me?"

Dearg Tate's voice from the other side of the clearing in front of the chapel. And there was the man himself beneath the pines not but thirty feet away. Holding a pistol, he aimed unsteadily at the crowd that formed a crescent to the left of the chapel door.

Kerry froze in the doorway.

With his own gun trained on Dearg and his eyes darting to the cowering crowd, Sheriff Wolfe made the third point of a triangle, several yards from his target.

Beside Wolfe, Madison Grant leaned against a post oak, his top hat on, collar in perfect, starched wings. He appeared entirely unfazed by the crisis—almost enjoying it. "Come now, Tate," he said. "Just because Wolfe has discovered the evidence all points your way doesn't mean you'll be locked up for the entirety of your life. Necessarily. He's come to arrest you. Let the man do his job."

"Not a step closer!" Dearg glanced Wolfe's way, even as he kept his aim on the crowd.

Wolfe took a step back. "Easy now, Tate. Just lower that gun. You don't want to hurt anybody."

"Certainly not," Grant said. "At least not again."

As if struck physically by that last comment, Dearg wobbled a step, but steadied his aim.

"*Damn* it, Grant," Wolfe hissed. "Shut the hell up." To Dearg, Wolfe spoke more soothingly, "Easy now. Just lower that gun. All we got to do is talk. Just talk."

Little Zhen, her father peering over Kerry's shoulder in the chapel doorway, meandered into view from the crowd's far margin, and just that quickly was free of it. Starting across the fifteen or so feet *toward* Dearg Tate and his crazed, contorted features—and his weapon.

It was the awful, shiny thing in his hand she wanted. The girl's dark eyes appeared utterly transfixed by the muzzle of the pistol, glinting bright in the spring sun.

Ling made a choking sound behind Kerry and pushed past her. Dearg, though, swept his pistol arm to aim at Ling, then at the stunned crowd, then back to Ling, who froze in place, his eyes flitting in horror from his daughter to Dearg.

"Dearg." The word came from Kerry strangled and dry. But she had to get him to hear—to really listen.

Head cocked, little Zhen kept on across the chapel's clearing toward Dearg and his pistol, reached toward the flashing silver as if it were a toy.

Dearg's hands shook, making the gun's barrel quiver. "You," he growled at the child. "Stay back."

"Dearg. She's just a little girl." Kerry's voice had returned to her. She took a step toward him, then another. Tried to keep her voice steady. "Put the gun down. Please. Listen to me."

"I didn't mean no harm to that Jew. You hear me? No real harm."

"I know you didn't, Dearg. Easy now. Put the gun down."

"All I meant," he cried, "was to rough him up just a little. Lady paid me to scare him back to New York was all. Just scare him off the story was all, some New Orleans story she said he'd gotten all wrong but wouldn't let it go."

Lilli Barthélemy. It must have been.

"Nothing but scare was what I was aiming to do. But then there he was, and I was thinking how it was folks like him that's been pushing us out, all them coming and *coming*, infesting all the good here." His voice had become plaintive. Almost childlike.

Kerry walked slowly on toward him. Step by gentle step. "Dearg. Please. Lower your gun."

After landing on Grant for an instant, his eyes swung back and he pled with her. "He's right, Kerry. Every last thing he's been saying, it'd be right. It's people like you and me, like all us around here, getting replaced, and by what? Not by people like us."

"Dearg, no." Kerry could hear the panic edging her voice. It was as if she and the little girl were locked in a dreamlike race toward the man and the terrible thing in his hand. She took another step closer, another. "Dearg, listen to me."

Zhen's eyes flitted once to Kerry, but then back, mesmerized by the pistol's flickering silver.

"Dearg—"

His voice broke. "I didn't, Kerry. I didn't mean to."

Kerry eased another three steps closer. Three more, and she'd almost have the girl. "All that fear," she whispered to Dearg. "All that hate he wants you to feel."

Shoulders slumped, Dearg shook his head.

"Dearg, listen to me. Just set your pistol down easy now. Right on the ground by your feet. Behind you, though. Don't let that little one get to it. Then you tell me about it."

Inch by inch, Dearg turned. Lowered the pistol. Inch by inch, Kerry eased closer.

But the girl's slow progress continued, too—until, suddenly, she could bear it no longer. Stretching her arms out, Zhen leaped toward that peculiar, gleaming silver stick.

Startled, Dearg turned toward her, raising the pistol . . .

The shot rang out at the same instant that Kerry screamed. The same instant that Dearg's mouth rounded into an *O* of eternal regret.

Zhen sprang back, crumpling, the dark gloss of her black hair splayed on the grass. Dearg Tate took a step toward the child but, seeing her lying still, stopped. Sank to his knees.

Behind Kerry, Ling Yong cried out. She heard him running toward his child, but Kerry reached the little girl first. Scooped the limp body up into her arms.

Zhen's breath came soft on Kerry's cheek. No blood anywhere on the child's frame. Zhen was unhurt, knocked flat, no doubt, by the sound of the blast and by fear. With a sob of relief, Kerry held the child out to her father. Zhen in his arms, Ling dropped to the ground.

From behind them, Dearg moaned, an unearthly sound, as if pulled from his marrow. He knelt there, face contorted in misery, and turned the muzzle of the gun to his own head. *"Look,"* he cried. "Look at what all I done."

Almost within arm's length now, Kerry called out his name, the boy she'd known since childhood, who'd grown up to be the man so full of fear and of rage and now, suddenly here, of regret.

"Dearg, *no! Dearg—!"*

Kerry was still calling his name when the pistol fired again, and his body, destroyed, slumped to the grass.

Chapter 56

Breathless as she mounted four flights of stairs, Kerry reached the observatory.

Numb with horror, she'd stayed beside Dearg's ruined body until Dr. Randall arrived. Randall wasn't needed to pronounce Dearg dead: that was only too clear from the damage his gun had done to his head.

But somehow only with Randall's arrival could Kerry stop being the stoic in charge of sending the twins away with Aunt Rema, the guardian of the corpse, the commander sending someone to break the news to Dearg's younger brother, Jerome. Now, stepping away with a choking sob, Kerry could begin feeling the event for herself.

John Cabot had stepped forward. "Kerry. My God. Tell me how I can help."

But this process of beginning to feel was sending her reeling, a white-hot rage, blinding and desperate.

"Could you tell me where Grant went?" Her voice sounded foreign: Deeper. Monotone. Some other person's voice.

"Back to Biltmore, I assume. George had already left before . . . what happened with Tate. Please, let me take you back to your farm."

But Kerry had swung up on Malvolio. The twins had asked to ride him down to the funeral, and it seemed a day to say yes, even to the presence of an old mule. Now she urged the mule into a slow trot up the Approach Road, faster than he'd gone in years. Not once did she feel the jolt of his gait. Not once did she stop to consider the danger of tracking down Grant *now*. Not later, when she'd had time to think how he might react, but *now*, while her blood burned in her veins.

It took only one question to only one servant at Biltmore.

"I dinnae ken what's wrong with the man," Moncrief swore. "It's off his head for certain, I'd say. I took him the Scotch he asked for—a whole bloody carafe, mind you, not a wee glass—all the way up to the observatory. Up to high doh, that one, I've said."

As she burst into the lower floor of the observatory, footsteps echoed directly above her on the uppermost level. She stormed up the staircase, a tight, iron spiral opening to a three-hundred-and-sixty-degree view.

There he was, his back to her despite the racket she'd made climbing the stairs. Slowly, he turned, Scotch in hand. "I presumed it would be you." As suave, as polished as ever. As if all his money, all his connections formed some sort of armor around him that let him leer at her now, triumphant, untouched, after all this.

Incredibly, he raised a glass in a toast. "Join me, Kerry. I'm celebrating a political victory of sorts. Messy as that can sometimes be. Approve of my methods or not, the general populace deserves to be informed of what's coming if we continue to be overrun. The white race, every last one of our researchers will tell you, must be protected."

The words shot from her, scorching: "Like the bison."

"Why, yes, as a matter of fact. Much like the bison. Endangered as it is without . . . intervention."

"You're a monster. And a madman. It was *your* mind, *your* influence behind the murder." Kerry saw it all over again: the kind, idealistic reporter sprawled in the mud. "Aaron Berkowitz knew something about you through his work at the *Times*. Something, I'd imagine, that suggested you were the sort of man who would kill to protect your reputation as a preserver of wildlife and a cultured"—she spat the next word—"gentleman."

"And yet, as we've seen, it was not I after all who culled the herd, so to speak."

"You are truly despicable."

"Apparently you thought me well worth pursuing up here—for who knows what lusty reasons of your own. Followed me here despite your knowing the little Jewish reporter thought I'd kill if necessary to protect my reputation." He took a step toward her as if to demonstrate his willingness to do just that.

She stood her ground. "All the theories the killer was the Italian or Robert Bratchett or Ling . . . you helped spread those, too."

Grant smirked. "Any of them *could* have done it, or worse—predisposed toward violence as their sorts always are. Who knows what any of them might already have done? But in any event: yes, it all fit our purposes perfectly. Merely a matter of fanning the flames."

Fear as a tactic with the people here—the rich tourists and the natives alike. Whoever would swallow what Grant and his kind were spooning out.

Stretching as if his small confession was a relief, he leaned into the wall away from the top of the staircase.

"The Gallic rooster," she said. "The crest. The LNA."

"And Farnsworth's uncle, Édouard Drumont . . . Ah, I perceive this is still murky to you, of course. The pretty little kitchen maid, for all her cleverness and her noticing the framed crest in the telegraph office, did not deduce a familial connection—second cousins or something, it seems—between the not-so-mild-mannered telegrapher Edward *Drumont* Farnsworth—his initials *EDS* on telegrams, you may recall— and the Édouard Drumont who is well known in France these days."

"Infamous, some people might say."

He ignored this. "Our leaders are partnering with those of like mind in Germany and France, nations worth protecting from infestation from outsiders, much like—"

"This country, you and Farnsworth believe," she finished for him.

Trying to keep her own mind steady as the blood pounded inside her head, Kerry saw the images fan out like a display: Lilli Barthélemy, having arranged for what she thought was scaring someone into silence; Grant, who'd not instigated the attack but saw a chance to spread suspicion.

And Dearg Tate, who'd perhaps not meant to kill, but had become first a pawn, then a killer. And then a corpse.

Grant's eyes narrowed on her, then dropped to her right boot.

He'd not forgotten, she could see, where she kept her knife.

He lifted his eyes to her, his smile still in place. "You know, Kerry, I can't help but wonder at the wisdom of your coming up here all alone, with the intent, I presume, of finding me here."

She should be wondering at it, too, she knew. She'd acted without thinking, driven by the horror of Dearg's death and the reporter's death that he'd caused, all that wasted life, all that blood spilled at the train station and in the chapel clearing—and by the fire in her veins after realizing the truth. It burned in her still. However this turned out, this was where she had to be.

"A shame, Kerry, because I only came up here for one last view of the landscape before leaving on the last train tonight. I've no reason to run away, of course, having committed no crime, but I've little taste left for staying. A shame that you would think so lowly of me. What was it you said? A monster? And a *madman?*" Grant's mouth twisted beneath the thick of his mustache. "I'm known as a man of intellect and organization. A man whose name will be remembered in history for the creation of national parks, the saving of entire species from extinction—including, of course, the master race. Political leaders will heed my writings, the research I've done and yet will do, and they will thank me. I can't have my reputation publicly slandered. I'm sure you understand."

He hadn't yet moved for her, but Kerry knew he was coming. She leaped to the right, ducking past him toward the stairs. But Grant was just as quick. As if his arm had suddenly lengthened like wet cord, he snagged her by the waist and yanked her to him.

"You're a little too smart for your own good, aren't you?" His body blocking the only exit, the stairs, he released her, his eyes glinting.

Backing away, Kerry gripped the sill of the open window behind her. Her eyes darted out and down: the ground, four stories below.

"It will be a sad story, Kerry, that they'll tell about you: a charming but quite replaceable kitchen maid with an unfortunate urge to end her life—brought on by grief after her father's funeral. And the loss of her land, poor thing. Tragic, really."

He finished his thought with a grab for her.

This time, though, he lowered his shoulder as if he were making a tackle and caught her in her middle, sending her tumbling backward, flailing for balance. One minute she was perched at the edge of the window, her hands on its frame, and the next she was plummeting backward onto the narrow balcony with its low stone balustrade.

And over.

Chapter 57

As she flailed backward, one of Kerry's hands caught the edge of the stone railing. She clung to it, hanging precariously from it. Instinctively, she swung to grip it with her other hand as well. Her whole body extended, feet dangling free over a four-story fall, she tried to scream, but the air came from her in only a choking rasp.

As she looked up, Grant stepped to the edge, eyes narrowed in concentration, with the same expression—analytical, calculating, detached, almost amused—he'd worn watching the farmer in the buckboard hurtling with his mules toward the train tracks all those months ago.

She turned her head to look down. Somewhere off in the distance—the walled garden maybe—the tulips of early spring stretched out in yellows and reds and pinks that pinwheeled in her dizzied head.

Kerry could not afford to look down again.

Far below came shouts for help. Estate workers who'd spied her swaying there, she assumed. She could not look down to see them.

Now Grant, surveying the landscape below, leaned over the railing. "Help!" he cried. "Help! She's jumped, and I'm not sure I can reach her! I tried to reason with her, to calm her, but she's jumped!"

Kerry could see Grant bending forward, the look in his eyes not concerned, not panicked, but steely. Assured. His hands reached for hers—not, she knew, to pull her to safety, but to pry loose her grip on the ledge. If she stayed like this, desperately holding on to this stone railing, he would make sure she fell even as he appeared to help her.

Without first formulating anything resembling a plan, she let go with her right hand and grasped at a stone baluster to the right, frantically gripping it as she swung her body so that her left could grip the baluster beside it. Reaching again with her right, hands clawing for a better grip, arms and back aching, she swung herself to the end of the line of balusters.

But Grant followed, still shouting for help. Eyes piercing on her, he bent to reach where her hands had moved.

"Almost got her!" he called to the people below. Even as he made a show of leaning to reach for her hands.

The instant before he touched her, Kerry let go her right hand, her left barely keeping its grip, and strained for the copper gutter at the edge of the slate along the north side of the tower. With her left hand, she did the same, just as Grant's arm shot toward it.

She hung there, dangling, hearing the groan of the nails that held the copper gutter—nails that might decide not to hold this new burden of weight. Inching her way as fast as she could, she slid her hands, bleeding, down the gutter. She was past where Grant could reach her now, but her fingers were giving out.

She was almost, *almost* at a different section of roof. If she could just . . .

With a rasping screech, several nails pulled loose, the gutter peeling away from the slate. No time to think now. She swung both legs toward the slope of the front-facing roof and launched herself toward it.

Slamming into the top of a fourth-floor dormer, she clawed at it, seizing the sculptured finial at its peak and holding on with both hands. But almost immediately the finial, only ever meant for ornamentation and never to bear the dead weight of a person, was pulling up from its nails, about to give way.

Shouting came below her, and still from above: Grant calling for help for the poor, grieving kitchen maid who, he'd say, tragically took her own life—though in that so-common last-minute regret, she'd tried to reverse her decision, too late.

He was counting, she knew, on the triumph of gravity and of angles.

The finial pulled free and then slate was sliding under her body with nothing, now, to grip as she slid. Three stories beneath her, she knew, were the limestone slabs of the front terrace.

Then her feet found the next edging of copper gutter. For the moment, it arrested her descent.

From below came voices shouting to her to hang on, to slide down, to hold fast.

Slowly, Kerry found her balance, as she had so many times as a girl on a mountain cliff. Slowly, she stepped her way carefully, so carefully, along the gutter, leaning hard into the still sharply pitched roof.

She was almost to another dormer, this one positioned so that she could hold on a moment and straighten.

Inching along the roofline, she reached the dormer's edge. And now risked another look down. Still three stories below to the limestone slabs, but now the glass dome of the Winter Garden rose to meet her.

The portion of gutter where she teetered was now giving way. Crouching with the dormer to help her balance, she leaped for the copper edgings of the glass roof, hitting its edges with a painful thud. She let her body slide down the panes of copper and glass to the edge of the domed roof. Her whole body hurt, bruised and scratched and aching. But now she was perched at the lower edge of the dome, the flagstones only a story below. And a crowd of people whose faces she couldn't make out, her vision swimming, were running toward her. Were reaching out arms to help ease her final climb down.

Just before she swung herself down from the edge of the dome of the Winter Garden, Kerry paused to look up. Madison Grant was leaning out over the stone railing, his eyes narrowed to slits on her.

"Thank heavens!" he called. And he waved a kind of thanks to the crowd.

Kerry knew in that moment how it would be. His version of the story that he would tell: himself as the would-be rescuer of the poor kitchen maid who leaped that fateful day from the very top of Biltmore House in despair, who changed her mind at the last and struggled to save herself. Who, thankfully, did not drop all those scores of yards below to her death, but whose memory, poor thing, of the events became understandably rattled.

It would be his word against hers, and his would be the story most people heard and believed. But she lifted her head, let him see her face, bruised and bleeding as it had to be now. Let him see that she knew. No matter how many people he seduced with his wealth and connections and sheen, no matter how many he convinced to see the world as he did, *she knew* what he was.

Chapter 58

Lilli turned as George took her hand to help her down the stairs of the front entrance, and for a moment she nearly held on. Nearly tilted back her lovely face and told him it was all a mistake, her arranging to go back to New York.

Biltmore Estate was in full bloom now—dogwoods and tulips and azaleas, George had listed for her, along with who knew what else. Lilli cared little for landscaping, but she did like a bold palette in life. And Biltmore was that in the spring.

The house towered above her. Like a call. Reminding her it wasn't too late. That maybe, after all, she didn't have to leave . . . that this still could be hers.

The footman with the hideous brogue might have caught her indecision as she slowed and glanced back toward the house. He raised an eyebrow at her.

George—bless him—squeezed her hand. "I am sorry that you can't stay."

Leaning into him because, even now, she could not quite give up the chase entirely, she squeezed his back. "I only wish that I could."

His expression grew softer still. "I do understand family concerns that demand one's attention."

"Yes," she said. Because he did. Bless him. A man loyal to his family.

She looked deep into his brown eyes, poetic and almost sad. And she saw there a man who, with a bit more managing—more long walks with Cedric, more of her earnest questions about his Sargents and Renoirs on the walls, more long rides into his precious mountains—might well have been convinced he was in love.

He's been swimming about in the net for weeks now, she'd chided herself. *All that's left, the final hauling in.* Yet she found, to her horror, that she could not do it. That she liked George Vanderbilt far too well to marry him.

Because for all his worldly travels, George Vanderbilt still had the heart of a boy—one who expected to love and be loved. Expected to trust and be trusted.

Honesty, Lilli found, had become her undoing.

The more she'd grown to like him, the more she'd discovered she couldn't deceive him about who she was and the lengths to which her drives and instincts as a person of action might take her. Nor, she found, could she deceive George about her own feelings. Which, to her mortification, ran in another direction entirely. One she could never act on.

In fact, he was coming right now. The Italian groom, tailed by his little brother a few yards back, was approaching.

Her heart seized.

But hearts could be ignored.

"Mr. Salvatore Catalfamo," she said.

He stopped beside his employer. "Miss Bar . . ." He did not finish her name, as if it had caught in his throat. He looked away. And then back. The black of his eyes, as always, intense. And now also sad. So terribly, ineffably sad.

"Mr. Catalfamo," Lilli said, rescuing him, "I wanted to mention to you and to your employer that I've learned Leblanc was hired by my father, and that he will be leaving Asheville altogether. I've telegrammed my father to call off the search for the men who"—she would not use the word *murdered*—"were accused of Chief Hennessy's death."

She and Sal exchanged a look, raw and painful on both sides.

Sal Catalfamo might have every right to expose her father as a possible instigator of the riots and lynchings, and as someone who profited from the Italian community's losing control of the waterfront. And perhaps he would do so. Though for Sal's sake, she hoped not—desperately so. Her father and his kind had a way of pulverizing all who crossed them.

Lilli's eyes dropped to the child Nico. She felt an unaccustomed twist of guilt as he hobbled forward to rest his head on his brother's side. The leg a result of the riots she'd witnessed beneath her window that night in New Orleans—and those riots incited by who knew what forces her father had sparked.

Later—tomorrow or next week or next year—she might think more about this. Might even confront her father about it.

For now, she knew only that she was making a sacrifice in walking away. More than one, and both of them painful. Saying no to position and riches and George, before he could ask her to stay as his wife. And saying no, also, to a passion that would come with a poverty, a social plunge she knew she could not possibly bear.

Suddenly, her hands went to her purse, jerking the silk drawstring open. She drew out a folded stack of pages, crumpled for the wear. Unfolding them, she handed the stack to George. "I should have given these to you long ago."

He flipped through the drawings, his eyes going wide. Then lifting to her. "These are superb. Surely you didn't . . ."

She laughed. "I surely did not. These were done by your stablehand here. Perhaps Richard Hunt's son, if he's still working with you, would be interested in taking on an apprentice."

Nodding only once, briskly, to Sal Catalfamo so that no one, particularly not George, would see the bright wet of her eyes, she twisted away.

"I have dearly loved your Biltmore," she whispered.

George brought her hand to his cheek and held it there for a moment. In a gesture, she thought, of a genuine friend. She wondered for a moment, wistfully, what it might have been like to be good friends with one's husband.

"*Au revoir*, George," she whispered.

With that, the footman, Moncrief, handed her into the carriage.

Because it was good manners, Lilli Barthélemy lifted a gloved hand in a wave to her host and also to the man she'd liked to have let herself love in some far distant world where income and background and rank did not matter.

And because Lilli Barthélemy had never looked back in her life, she turned her face toward the walled garden and the mountains beyond. And tried to breathe through the iron bands cinching in on her heart.

Chapter 59

Kerry twitched Malvolio's reins, but the mule was already stopping. For so homely a creature, he had a way of pausing in a patch of sunlight, with dogwoods and redbuds framing his bony gray form, then looking over one shoulder as if he sensed a camera waiting. Just now, he'd chosen to stop on the hill sloping down to Biltmore near the statue of Diana, as if he and the goddess were two of a kind.

Kerry slid from his back. "I still say one of you should be riding him."

Jursey shook his head. "It's you got near up to killed."

"A harrowing," Rema pronounced, giving Kerry's shoulders a quick hug. "That's what you been through."

"I'm fine. Truly."

Although, truly, she wasn't. Her whole body was bruised and sore. But that wasn't the worst of it. She'd seen death before, but not in this way. And not so close together, going back to Aaron Berkowitz, who'd believed in the goodness of exposing the bad, if it was the truth.

Her father's death had, in fact, become now an actual loss—the grief for the gentle, laughing fiddler of his sober days in her childhood and also grief for the penitent, physically broken but finally whole man at the end.

She grieved, too, for the man he might have been, the family they might have had, the calm that might have cocooned them instead of the turmoil that cycloned.

Adding to the weight of that grief was the loss of the land her father's family had farmed for generations.

"It's like," Kerry leaned in to say to Rema, "somehow watching them shovel earth onto Daddy's casket, and his signing that deed there toward the last without consulting a soul, it was like a burial of our whole family. Our pride."

Rema shook her head. "Can't nobody bury your pride but you. You just recollect that, hear? I reckon they handled it all respectful enough?"

"Yes. With apologies for the timing."

"And a price more'n they agreed with your daddy."

Kerry frowned. True, it was more money than any MacGregors had seen in their lives. But it was also just money. Not the land where for a hundred years her family had hauled the rock and plowed the fields. Made love in the groves. Watched the sun rise over the hemlocks. Birthed babies whose cries rang over the hollows. Then finally been laid to rest back in its soil.

"It was inaudible, selling the farm was," Jursey offered now, poking his head between them.

"Inevitable," Kerry corrected. "And you're right, Jurs. It was. Also, it's good you can go back to school."

Miss Hopson, just joining them from her climb up the hill, smiled at Kerry. "How was your contract meeting with Mr. Vanderbilt? Not full of sound and fury, I hope?"

"We finished just now, in the Winter Garden. It was so"—she let the simplicity of her next word, a tiny one, carry the full weight of the day's cargo—"sad."

"But with a payment, I hope, that makes all sorts of opportunities possible for you and the twins."

"And for Rema. I'm insisting she share it with us. Though she says she'll stay in the kitchens of Biltmore a while longer. I think she likes a good spat over pastry."

"You'll not be coming back to New York, then?"

Kerry shook her head. "Not while the twins need me. And maybe not at all. It's strange, devastated as I was to have to leave. But now I have so many ideas brewing of what I'd like to do here." She reached a hand to her old teacher. "Thank you for all you've done for me. I won't let all you've taught me go to waste, I promise."

Crossing Biltmore's lawn and strolling toward them came the Bratchetts, Ling Yong and Zhen, and the Catalfamos, invited here by Kerry—with George Vanderbilt's welcome—to help give Miss Hopson a send-off before she returned to New York. Tully stood on her tiptoes to wave as the group approached.

Jursey stroked what wasn't yet even fuzz on his chin. "I've been cogitating. We got plenty of cash money to buy something else. Not far from here's a farm up for sale, Rema says. On Sunset Mountain near in to Asheville. One hell of a view. Or we could build us a small inn."

Miss Hopson's gaze swept over the house and the mountains. "Spectacular."

Tully leaned into Malvolio's shoulder and crossed her arms. "I was sure enough expecting to hate it leaving the farm. But I'm not feeling so much in the way of that now—even trying."

Jursey leaned into Kerry. "You reckon all the pack of houseguests left Biltmore by now?"

"I suppose they have."

Rema tried to meet her eye. "You said that peckerwood Grant snuck off back to New York?"

"He did."

"Slithered off," Tully suggested. No one disagreed. She snapped off a twig of redbud and slid it behind Kerry's ear. "Will he get faced up to justice, you think?"

Kerry sighed. "I wouldn't be surprised if they can't attach anything criminal to him. It was ideas that he was helping spread. That's harder to prosecute."

Rema laid a hand on her shoulder. "A man like that, whopper-jawed jackass, good people see through in time."

Kerry squeezed her hand but gazed out at the mountains. "Maybe you'll turn out to be right, Rema."

They stood in a line shielding their eyes against the dazzle of the early spring sun and the glimmer of all the new green.

Jursey stroked one of Malvolio's ears. "So about all the last guests and their leaving . . ." Kerry's brother had never excelled at subtlety. "That Cabot fellow that come to the funeral . . . Awful nice of him to come."

"As did quite a number of other people," Kerry pointed out.

"You reckon," he persisted, "you'll ever hear from Mr. Cabot again?"

Kerry made herself shrug. "It wouldn't look likely. I imagine he already left." *Without saying goodbye.* "Which is just as well as far as I'm concerned." She pulled the twins to her. "We've got lots of plans to make. Whether the three of us will be building an inn. Or a shop. Or a farm just for us—with a farmhouse to sleep in, I'm thinking, instead of a barn."

Tully's arm reached up to encircle Malvolio's head and bring it down closer to her. Absently, she stroked his muzzle, the mule tilting his head in a self-conscious new pose. "So if Cabot showed up somewhere out of the blue, you'd just up and ignore him straight out?"

Kerry followed where Tully was staring down the long slope of grass.

George Vanderbilt, smiling, had slowed his steps, as if happy enough only to witness this scene from a distance.

But John Cabot was closer, striding up the hill toward them. He held his top hat by its brim in his right hand, but as he raised the hand in greeting, a spring breeze blew it from his hand. Not seeming to notice, he walked steadily on as the hat somersaulted across the new grass. He arrived at the gazebo at the same time as the Bratchetts and Lings and Catalfamos, handshakes all around.

"I am glad," Sal Catalfamo said, "for the chance to meet the most famous of teachers, Miss Hopson."

Without speaking, John Cabot came to stand near Kerry. He met her gaze, and held it. Then stared out at the mountains with her, the wave after wave of blue. He brought the back of his hand to brush hers. Kerry uncurled her fingers to let the whole back of her hand press up against his. And something inside her—something anxious and resentful and bitter—began to uncurl, as well.

When he spoke at last, he kept his eyes on the rolling blue out ahead. "I can imagine no better fortune than to get to live out one's days in these mountains."

They all stood there in an uneven line and watched the sun play over the hollows and peaks. The early rhododendrons were in bud, nearly blooming, and the air smelled of clover and roses and violets and moss.

There would be hard work ahead, as soon as tomorrow. There would be struggle and laughter and passion and death. There would be ugliness in this world that spread like rot from men who traded in fear.

But right now, in this moment, these mountains made her feel small. Humbled. And awed. Reminded her she was connected to these people beside her—and to the people connected to them, in endless waves. Like the mountains themselves. On and on, far beyond where the eye could see.

And then farther still.

Historical Notes

Although *Under a Gilded Moon* is, of course, a work of fiction, many of its characters either represent or were inspired by historical figures, many of whom would now be considered obscure but who influenced the course of history—Madison Grant, for example. Below is a bit of background readers may find intriguing. The author will also be adding historical photos and background regularly to the Behind the Scenes section of her website, www.joyjordanlake.com.

George Washington Vanderbilt II was the first owner and, along with Richard Morris Hunt and Frederick Law Olmsted, one of the visionaries of Biltmore. The character Emily Vanderbilt Sloane is based on one of his nieces who, like her uncle, became an ardent philanthropist.

Though he's little known now, Madison Grant was a prominent name in the late nineteenth- and early twentieth-century eugenics movement, as well as in land and wildlife conservation. While there's no evidence that he ever visited Biltmore, he knew the Vanderbilt family, some of whom contributed to his Bronx Zoo project, and was close to George Vanderbilt's age. They shared a common interest in the natural world, as well as prominent friends in New York, including Theodore Roosevelt. While Grant's conservation efforts did, as the novel suggests, contribute to national parks and to saving the American bison, his other legacy was an incredibly toxic view of racial superiority that would later help fuel the Holocaust. During the years of this novel's setting, 1895–96, Grant was apparently known at least in some circles for his carousing, while publicly he was praised for his nature preservation leadership. He was also just beginning to formulate the white supremacist ideology that he would later pour into his 1916 book, *The Passing of the Great Race*, which was translated into German and became a kind of model for the race-hygiene arguments that would be embraced by the Third Reich. Prior to World War II, Adolf Hitler wrote Grant a fan letter referring to *The Passing of the Great Race* as "my bible."

A number of the household staff characters are based on actual people. The head of stables in Biltmore's early days was Italian, and while Salvatore Catalfamo and his contribution to Richard Morris Hunt's architectural drawings are fictional, the surname comes from the author's husband's family. The violence against Italians in New Orleans in 1890–91 is, sadly, historical, although Maurice Barthélemy as the instigator of it is a product of the author's imagination (fueled by the fact that some merchants did apparently benefit from the Italian community's being blamed for the police chief's death). As in this novel, the head chef at Biltmore was French, and other members of the staff included the forestry expert Carl Schenck and Vanderbilt's manager, Charles McNamee. Biltmore's first head housekeeper of note—and long tenure—was an Englishwoman named Emily King, but since Mrs. King didn't arrive until 1897, the author invented a fictional Mrs. Smythe.

The character Lilli Barthélemy was inspired, as fans of Edith Wharton will no doubt have guessed, by the protagonist Lily Bart in Wharton's *The House of Mirth*. Mentioned as Lilli's aunt in this novel, Wharton was a close friend of George Vanderbilt and a visitor to Biltmore.

Sol Lipinsky, briefly mentioned, was an early Jewish resident of Asheville whose Patton Avenue department store, Bon Marché, was an elegant addition to the town, which began its boom with the arrival of the railroad and visitors arriving from the North.

Annie Lizzie Hopson is named after and loosely based on the author's great-grandmother, who arrived in the Southern Appalachian Mountains as a young woman to teach in a one-room schoolhouse.

Ling Yong (listed also as Ling Gunn, which the author surmised was a mishearing of the Chinese name) is based on an actual man who lived in Asheville in 1895–96. Clippings referring to his existence and apparently brutal death after this novel's time period were deep in the city archives.

Robert Bratchett is based on an African American man who lived in the region at the time. His life ended tragically at Biltmore Junction in 1897, the year after this story stops, in racial violence. He is also commemorated at the National Memorial for Peace and Justice in Montgomery, Alabama, founded by Bryan Stevenson.

Other historically based groups and events mentioned in the novel include the Ligue Nationale Antisémitique de France, as well as the Chinese Exclusion Act of the 1880s and the lynchings of Italians in New Orleans in 1891. The Center for Peace and Justice has documented that the 1890s saw more lynchings of African Americans and all groups in the United States than any other single decade.

The Biltmore Estate, still owned by George Vanderbilt's descendants, remains the largest private residence in the United States and has become one of the largest employers and tourist destinations in the Asheville, North Carolina, area.

Just for fun, as a kind of shared wink with the savvy reader, I included some addresses with historical and literary significance. The boarding-house where Kerry visits Dearg Tate at 48 Spruce Street, for example, was indeed owned at the time by Mrs. Alice Reynolds but was later where the writer Thomas Wolfe lived as a boy, and is the boardinghouse at the center of his novel *Look Homeward, Angel*. Ling's fictional shop at 55 Haywood Street is the address of what is now the much-loved Malaprop's Bookstore/Café.

Dog-loving readers will be pleased to learn that the four-legged char-acter Cedric, the faithful, drooling Saint Bernard, is based on the his-torical canine, and was beloved by George Vanderbilt. A pub in Antler Village on Biltmore Estate is named in Cedric's honor.

Acknowledgments

I always come to the task of listing those to whom I'm indebted with an overwhelming sense of gratitude—like being reminded that, while I've been doggedly swimming along, I've been held up less by my own strokes than by wave upon wave of friends, family, and incredibly talented fellow writers and publishing professionals.

I've often listed friends and family individually in the past, but part of the richness of living and writing for increasing years is having a longer and longer list of folks who deserve naming—which also makes it more treacherous if you can't stand the thought of leaving someone out. Please know I'm so grateful for you friends who make life rich and challenging and good—and that I'm thinking of your faces and names as I type. Enormous thanks as always to my family: my husband, Todd Lake; my kids, Jasmine, Justin, and Julia Jordan-Lake; my mother, Diane Jordan; my brother, David Jordan; my sister-in-law, Beth Jackson-Jordan; their kids, Olivia, Catherine, and Chris Jackson-Jordan; my mother-in-law, Gina Lake; my brother-in-law, Steven Lake; my kids' godparents, Ginger and Milton Brasher-Cunningham, also a writer; and a host of treasured cousins and cousins-by-marriage all over the United States.

As with every book, I'm so grateful to my agent, Elisabeth Weed of The Book Group, for being wise, encouraging, savvy, and generally fabulous. At Lake Union, I continue to be grateful for editorial director

Danielle Marshall's being willing to take a risk on my last novel, *A Tangled Mercy*, and for being intrigued by the idea behind this one, even in the roughest of early forms. Danielle, I am so thankful for your support, your insights, your strength, and the way you ferociously champion the books you care about. On the editing front, I've never yet had an editor on any book whom I didn't like and appreciate for the ways in which he or she was helping my writing be better than I knew how to do alone, but developmental editor David Downing is among the very best out there, from giving an insider's view of quail hunting and shotgun handling to helping judge whether a particular character was too saintly, too sinister, or just plain dull. Erin Calligan Mooney provided invaluable insights on the manuscript, as did Blake Leyers. In copyediting and proofreading, Emma Reh, Lindsey Alexander, and Carrie Urbanic kept me honest on all sorts of details I'd have missed. Graphic designer Rex Bonomelli designed a cover that somehow beautifully suggests the tension between Gilded Age wealth and Appalachia culture, as well as the mystery I was hoping for. From author relations manager Gabriella Dumpit to PR gurus Dennelle Catlett and Maggie Sivon and so many others, the entire Lake Union/Amazon Publishing team has been such a pleasure to work with.

I feel fortunate to get to learn from, laugh with, and vent alongside a multitude of writer friends, including those in the fabulous Dutch Lunch writer tribe, the NINC 4Ever group, Lake Union Authors, the SCBWI Mid-South group, the Historical Novel Society of the Midsouth, and individual writer-colleague buddies, including Suzanne Robertson, Susan Bahner Lancaster, and early reader and giver-of-feedback Elizabeth Rogers. Novelist Bob Dugoni and the multitalented Cristina Dugoni became encouragers and friends of Todd's and mine at a time when my writing life badly needed an extra shove. It's a privilege to ride the crazy writing life roller coaster with all of you writer friends. Thank you for the times you've been vulnerable about your disappointments and struggles, as well as for letting me celebrate your triumphs with you.

Sometimes as an author, you look back—way back—and realize you were doing research on a book long before that novel ever came to be plotted or pitched. In my early twenties—quite some time ago now—I was able to spend several summers working for two different and equally beautiful summer camps in western North Carolina, Camp Rockmont in Black Mountain and Camp Gwynn Valley in Brevard. Those long, lovely summers helped solidify my enthusiasm for the Blue Ridge Mountains and my respect for the culture that has grown and evolved there.

One of the summers I worked for Camp Rockmont, some of us on camp staff—all of us sunburned and sweaty—were invited to a home on the grounds of Biltmore Estate belonging to a young woman my age, Dini Cecil (later Pickering), who was connected to Rockmont through a young man she was dating and would eventually marry. Dini, whom I remember as gracious, down-to-earth, and unassuming, turned out to be the person, along with her brother Bill, who would later inherit Biltmore. This seemed a fitting place to thank her again after all these years for the hospitality and pizza that night, and to thank the current staff of Biltmore Estate, who've unfailingly responded to all my questions with patience and interest.

I should admit that I began research on George Vanderbilt fully prepared to depict him as merely a background, one-dimensional character, nothing more than the privileged benefactor of his robber baron relatives. But the more I read, the more intrigued I became by the actual man's complexity: his love for art and the outdoors, his voracious reading, his desire early in life to become an Episcopal priest, his ongoing interest in matters of faith, his contributions to forestry and sustainability, his hospitality, his generosity, and his commitment to bring hundreds of new jobs, as well as training and schools, to western North Carolina.

Thank you to the owners and staff of Parnassus Books, my local independent bookstore, so committed to writers and readers alike.

Thank you to Bryan Stevenson and the National Memorial for Peace and Justice. It was through your work that I discovered the historical Robert Bratchett of North Carolina and created the character in his honor.

Thank you to the keepers of the Asheville Public Library Archives, where, close to closing time one night, I found Ling Yong (or Gunn) in one of the thick stacks of newspaper clipping folders an uncomplaining archivist brought, even though I looked like just the sort of scatter-brained researcher who loses all track of time and stays up till the last nanoseconds of closing.

Like all historical novels, a significant amount of research went into the writing of this book. I'd particularly like to thank the following authors for their books, which were among the most helpful: Denise Kiernan for *The Last Castle: The Epic Story of Love, Loss, and American Royalty in the Nation's Largest Home*; Ellen Erwin Rickman for *Biltmore Estate* (Images of America); Emma Bell Miles for *The Spirit of the Mountains*; Drema Hall Berkheimer for *Running on Red Dog Road and Other Perils of an Appalachian Childhood*; Jerry E. Patterson for *The Vanderbilts*; Witold Rybczynski for *A Clearing in the Distance: Frederick Law Olmsted and America in the Nineteenth Century*; John Alexander Williams for *Appalachia: A History*; Arthur T. Vanderbilt II for *Fortune's Children: The Fall of the House of Vanderbilt*; Sean Dennis Cashman for *America in the Gilded Age*; and last, but decidedly not least, the Foxfire series on Southern Appalachian life. Jonathan Peter Spiro's biography *Defending the Master Race: Conservation, Eugenics, and the Legacy of Madison Grant* was enormously helpful in sparking my imagination about the complex and appalling Grant. (More on him in Historical Notes.)

Throughout this book, I tried to keep historical details accurate, since that's part of the fun, of course, of reading historical novels. In a few instances, though, such as with the express train from New York to Washington, I took small artistic licenses: the elegant Royal Blue actually left from another station in New York besides Grand Central Depot, but I chose the Depot for its location and because, as the precursor to Grand Central Station, it would have more resonance with readers.

Finally, thank you so much to the book clubs and individual readers who've brought your own stories and insights to thinking about my earlier books and this one. It's always one of my favorite parts of the often-isolated writing life when I get to visit with readers in person or over social media. A thousand thank-yous always.

Book Club Discussion Questions

1. Have you ever visited Biltmore Estate? If so, what elements of its history stuck with you? Did you see some of those reflected in this story? Were there particular parts of the story you connected with in a different way for having been there in person?

2. A number of the characters in this novel are based on actual people. (Please see the section of this book entitled Historical Notes for more information.) Which characters from this novel did you wonder about and possibly look up? How do you reconcile the good and evil in some of these characters?

3. The author embeds a number of allusions to other novels and plays, which seemed especially fitting since George Vanderbilt was quite the bibliophile and scholar and was personal friends with a number of authors, including Edith Wharton and Henry James, both of whom later would stay at Biltmore. Did you catch the connection of the character Lilli Barthélemy with Edith Wharton's *House of Mirth*? What allusions to Shakespeare and other literary works did you notice? Here's an obscure one, for

example: the hunting dog Gurth, while fictional, was named for a character in Sir Walter Scott's *Ivanhoe* to fit alongside the historical canine Cedric, whom George Vanderbilt named for a character in the same novel.

4. What did you think of Lilli's final decision regarding Sal and George Vanderbilt?

5. The Ligue Nationale Antisémitique de France mentioned in the novel was an actual anti-Semitic group operating at the time and was influential in the Dreyfus Affair. Are you familiar with the group or their influence?

6. Did you find yourself more attracted to the Gilded Age characters or the Appalachian characters and why? Which aspects of their lives did you find most appealing or, perhaps, off-putting?

7. How did the American version of Gilded Age wealth as depicted in this novel differ from, say, the British version you may have read about or seen in such television shows and movies as *Downton Abbey*?

8. Did you find yourself angry along with Kerry and the other mountain people that their land was changing so quickly, or did you take a more practical stance that things simply change? Have you faced cultural changes in your lifetime that have initially made you bitter or resentful but to which you have eventually adjusted? When is it important to push back against change and when is it wise to adapt or be willing to think differently?

9. Did it surprise you to learn or be reminded that people of Southern Italian and Chinese descent were among the groups discriminated against in the 1890s? Were you familiar with the lynchings of 1891 in New Orleans or the Chinese Exclusion Act from this era? Did any of the characters' challenges from this novel connect directly with you and your own family background?

10. Were there aspects of cultural debates from the novel's setting in the 1890s that struck you as similar to cultural debates of our time, including wealth inequality? What can we learn from this particular decade in history and its aftermath?

11. Kerry struggles to forgive her father. Her mother, brother, sister, and aunt all respond differently to Johnny MacGregor. Does the family's journey toward forgiveness connect in any way with friends or family in your life?

About the Author

Joy Jordan-Lake is the author of eight books, including *A Tangled Mercy*, a #1 Amazon bestseller and also an Editors' Choice recipient from the Historical Novel Society; *Blue Hole Back Home*, which won the Christy Award for First Novel; and the children's book *A Crazy-Much Love*. Raised in the foothills of the Appalachians, she spent several summers in and around Asheville, North Carolina, where the Biltmore Estate is located. She continues to love the Blue Ridge Mountains and drags friends and family there with her whenever possible. Jordan-Lake holds two master's degrees and a PhD in English and has taught literature and writing at several universities. Now living outside Nashville, she and her husband have two daughters, a son, and a ferocious ten-pound rescue pup. To learn more about the author and her work, visit www.joyjordanlake.com.